DR(

Book 3 of '

Help save hedgehogs!

You've caught a travelling book! Enter the
BCID below at **www.bookcrossing.com** to see
where it's been, then follow where it goes
after you **READ & RELEASE** it!

For Eve Phillips

And for John and Ben,
with love always

DROGOYA

Book 3 of "Circles of Light"

—————

E M Sinclair

Drogoya – Book 3 of *Circles of Light*
First published 2007

Typeset by John Owen Smith

Published by Murrell Press

© E M Sinclair 2006

E M Sinclair can be contacted via the **Circles of Light** Facebook page.

ISBN 978-09554135-2-0

Printed by CreateSpace

Chapter One

Farn had overheard Gan speaking with Kija. Gan referred to Tika and Elyssa as "the two girls" during the conversation. Farn was greatly taken with the phrase, much to everyone else's irritation, especially the two girls themselves. He let no opportunity pass where mention of "my two girls" might be made. Kija grew so disgusted that she announced she was flying north to the Sun Mountains to visit the Elder Seela. At least she would enjoy some intelligent conversation there, she pointed out icily. She instructed Brin to keep a careful eye on Farn, Tika and Elyssa, and most definitely not to encourage Farn in any nonsense. With that, the golden Dragon flew north in a cloud of annoyance.

When Emla, Shan and their three Vagrantian companions appeared in the circle to the north of Tagria, they learnt that Rhaki was gone from his tower. Emla held council with the Lords of Far, Tagria and Andla in the comfort of Raben of Tagria's manor. The Lords were at first cautious and sceptical of this Golden Lady of Gaharn, but were won over by Emla's transparent openness. As Zalom of Andla pointed out privately, she had not needed to admit that the dreadful Rhaki was in fact her brother.

Her distress was genuine when she heard of the death of Lord Hargon of Return's eldest son and the disappearance of both his younger son and his daughter. A long day was spent in talks with these Lords and their advisors which lasted into the early hours. It was agreed that Raben and Zalom would escort the Golden Lady to Return to meet Hargon but their departure was delayed by the arrival of a Merig. He insisted on speaking to Emla alone and gave her the news of the Drogoyans presence in the Stronghold. He also told her of the mutilated remains appearing in the circle in the Asataria, of Rhaki using Serim's body, and of Bartos, Hargon's younger son.

Emla decided to disclose the latter news for now only to Kemti and the Sapphrean Lords. She asked how she should tell Hargon of this new bereavement. Both Tika and Elyssa became unaccountably distressed and it was with some relief to Emla that Seboth of Far suggested some of her party might like to rest at his town for a few days. So they divided. Gan, Sket and Riff remained with Tika, Elyssa and Maressa. The two other Guards would accompany Emla, Shan, Bagri and Kemti to Return.

Hard on the heels of that message, came another. Emla heard that Discipline Senior Fayet had staged some kind of revolt and barricaded himself within the Asataria buildings. Emla's head ached as well as her body, jogging along on the konina she was expected to ride with ease. Kemti grinned at her discomfort.

'Will you tell Hargon of his son's death?' he asked.

'I will have to,' she replied, wincing as her konina did a silly side stepping hop and nearly unseated her. 'Stars forfend that he asks after his daughter. Kija was much disturbed at the child's disappearance with Kadi. I think part of her reason for going to visit Seela is to see if she can glean any hint of their whereabouts.'

'And what was Vagrantia like?' Kemti's face was innocent. 'I believe you had intended to travel to the Stronghold – it must have been quite a surprise to find yourself and poor Shan so far across the Wilderness?'

Emla sniffed. 'Using the circles is a little more complicated than I had believed. But to answer your question: Vagrantia is quite extraordinary. I only saw Parima Circle of course, in the short time I was there, but I look forward to many more visits. And hopefully, things will not be so fraught – the High Speaker Thryssa was devastated over the affliction her people suffered. The death of her councillor affected her badly.'

After a night at a way station, Navan, Armschief of Return, met their party half a league from the town. The escort he brought formed up around Emla and the Lords of Tagria and Andla, riding on towards Return's western gate. Navan eased his konina alongside Emla.

'Lady, Hargon is beset with worry,' he said quietly.

Emla looked at him searchingly. 'I have heard Gan speak highly of you Navan, so I beg your advice. Hargon's second son is dead in Gaharn. How best may I tell your lord of this unfortunate news?' She told him briefly and bluntly what she knew of the circumstances.

Navan's breath hissed through his teeth. He rode in silent thought for a few paces.

'Let me ride on and inform him Lady. I may not tell him all the details you have given me.'

Emla nodded gratefully and Navan spurred his konina forward, barking an order to one of his men. The armsman took up Navan's position and the company of riders drew nearer Return. The seneschal Traff greeted them formally in the inner courtyard and conducted them to guest rooms.

'My Lord is engaged at present, but he will join you shortly for the midday meal.'

'Not a very big place, is it?' Shan commented, poking into cupboards in the room Emla had been given.

'It is large by the general standards of Sapphrea, Shan. Do try to be a little tactful.' Emla stared out of the window. 'What must it be like to lose two sons within days of each other?' she thought aloud.

'People in Gaharn lost all their children when that fever came four cold seasons past,' Shan reminded her.

'Yes I know. You might come to terms with deaths by a rampant fever, but Hargon's boys did not die so simply.'

'My Lady? Why are Tika's eyes changed? There has been no sign here of that dreadful affliction we saw in Vagrantia. And do you see how she and Elyssa could almost be sisters? Oh I know Tika is so dark and Elyssa so fair, but you know what I mean Lady – alike in their heads.'

Emla laughed. 'No, I have no idea why Tika's eyes have silvered, and yes, I have seen the strange closeness of the two. What it all means, my dear Shan, who knows yet?'

There was a light rap at the door and Kemti came in with Bagri. As Kemti was about to speak another knock sounded and a young serving boy announced that he was to take them to the dining hall.

'We will talk here later,' Emla murmured, following the boy to the meeting with Lord Hargon.

Hargon advanced to greet the Golden Lady, bowing politely and mouthing the ritual words of welcome. Emla's heart smote her, seeing the pallor under the man's tanned face, the emptiness in his blue eyes.

Conversation languished, helped only by the efforts of Lord Raben, Lord Zalom and Emla, their host sitting silent and leaving his food untouched. An awkward silence fell as servants cleared away the last dishes, broken at last by Hargon. He roused and looked round the table as if surprised to find himself in company.

'Forgive me my Lords, Lady Emla. I am a poor host of late.' His eyes met Emla's. 'I have to tell you honestly Lady, I am glad to hear of Rhaki's death. I do not understand how my son should come to die with him, but I choose to believe he may have helped to achieve the end of that evil being.'

Emla's expression remained sympathetic. Now was not the time to inform Hargon that Rhaki was not dead, that somehow his spirit, if not his body, lived on in this world.

'I will take another wife and, stars willing, there will be other sons,' Hargon said with a determined effort.

'Your daughter...' Zalom began inadvisedly.

'I have no children left,' Hargon declared. 'The girl is dead to me. I would not have her here to remind me of my lost sons.'

Emla thanked the stars that Tika had not come on this visit to Hargon: she could imagine the angry response Hargon would have faced had Tika heard that comment. She caught Navan's eye and read the mingled relief and worry he felt.

'How long might you guest with us Lady Emla? We can provide entertainments for you should you wish.'

'No. No thank you Lord Hargon. I have – erm – matters to attend to in Gaharn of some urgency, but I must go to this tower which Rhaki constructed before I leave.'

Hargon's face hardened. 'As you will. You will excuse me if I do not join you. Navan will escort you of course, but I have no wish to go there.'

The next morning, Navan led them out of the town's southern gate. They rode through fields where men and women worked steadily, hoeing along the rows of plants. Rhaki's tower came into view when they had passed the last fields, and a short while later they saw armsmen posted at a hundred paces from the tower itself. The smell hit them as they rode within the ring of sentries, the koninas tossing their heads and snorting.

'I did not realise it was this bad Lady,' Navan apologised.

8

Emla dismounted and glimpsed several green faces. 'I will go on alone. There is nothing to fear, but I have to go inside. You may all wait for me here.'

Shan obstinately moved to Emla's shoulder at the same moment Navan stepped forward. They began to walk to the unfinished and now abandoned building that adjoined the tower. To distract herself from the stench, Emla studied the way the blocks of the tower fitted seamlessly together and admitted how far Rhaki's skill and strength in using power must have grown.

Shan bolted aside and bent double, violently sick.

'Go back Shan. That is an order child.'

Navan stepped through the half built doorway and glanced about. A narrow stairway protruded from the blocks of the tower which he indicated to Emla. Nodding, she moved ahead of him and began to climb.

The Golden Lady stared down at the remains of her brother's body. A quilt partially covered him but even through the decomposition, the gaping ulcers were still visible. His eyes were open, red scaled but for the black pupils, and his face was contorted in what may have been final agony or a laugh. She tore her gaze from the hideous corpse, seeing the room was empty of anything except a few pots and jars on the floor near the body.

'Enough Navan, let us go.'

Neither spoke as they retraced their steps to where their escort waited. Shan sat on the ground white faced, Kemti crouched beside her. Emla smiled at the girl but spoke to Kemti.

'Can you join with me, to call fire? That must be destroyed at once.'

'What of the circle that must be close by?' Kemti came and stood at her side.

Emla lifted her chin towards a low rise of hills.

'Thryssa showed me how to feel the presence of a circle, and Bagri can too. It is over there. We must find it once this is no more.' Emla touched Navan's sleeve. 'Move your men back Navan. Kemti and I will fire this monstrosity.'

Navan stared for a moment, realising she meant to use the power. He nodded and ordered his men back, past the ring of sentries.

Kemti and Emla faced the tower, letting their minds expand

into the web of power which embraced the world.

'Now,' Kemti said softly.

Flames flowered through the tower roof, blooming down the walls and smothering the annex with creepers of fire. Sharp cracks ripped through the air as stone cracked and split in a heat far too intense to be natural. The sun moved across the sky, and still the two tall thin figures stood facing the conflagration until it was a tumbled, smouldering shell.

Their shoulders slumped and Emla swayed against Kemti for a moment. Without speaking, they turned back to their silently watching escort. Emla was grateful for Shan's shoulder to lean on as Bagri hurried to support Kemti. She drew herself up to face Navan.

'Now we must search over there to find the circle. Then your men must guard it Navan, but it will not be as unpleasant for them as this duty has been.'

Tika was astonished by the turmoil in her emotions when she first saw Elyssa. It was similar to the instant bonding she had experienced with Farn, but not quite the same. She somehow felt that Elyssa was a mirror image, the other half that made her a whole person. She wept when she saw Elyssa, and Elyssa had come straight to her, holding her until the tears ceased. From that moment they were inseparable and Farn had accepted Elyssa as immediately and fully as had Tika.

Tika scarcely paid any attention to why Emla had arrived in Sapphrea, although the air mage Maressa intrigued her. Farn appreciated Maressa's compliments on the beautiful colour of his scales and his eyes. When Tika told the two Vagrantians of the battle with Rhaki's creatures, the Cansharsi, and they saw the long scar snaking down Farn's neck, tears flowed down both faces. Tika cried too at the remembering and Farn proudly folded all three in his wings to offer comfort. Kija had been outraged at hearing Farn's account of his bravery and had taken Tika severely to task for encouraging such boastfulness in her son.

When Emla told them of the bodies found in the circle inside the Asataria, Tika and Elyssa sensed a great tearing apart of something inexplicable, and both became agitated and distressed. Maressa was the only one who seemed able to calm them and had offered to stay behind when Kemti expressed doubts about making the two travel to Return.

Tika found it strange to be in Seboth of Far's manor. She was amazed to find that Seboth did not spend most of his time in his great hall with his armsmen, drinking and shouting. On the contrary, Seboth had apartments above his hall where his womenfolk moved freely and without fear of reprimand. She was struck speechless to find that Seboth's wife, Lallia, could both read and write.

'Most of us can, my dear,' Lallia confided. 'Seboth doesn't mind in the least, as long as we do not let too many outsiders know.' She laughed at Tika's expression. 'Seboth loves people to think he is a little bit stupid, a little bit slow, but indeed he is neither. Lord Hargon spoke of the old legends and Seboth made light of it. In truth, he has many of the oldest texts still existing in his library here. He has sought them out all over the land, and buys them wherever he finds one for sale. He does not regard the legends as Lord Hargon does. Seboth sees them as a history, a true history of this land, not tales to frighten children.'

Maressa was much taken with Lallia's latest infant, but gently laid a now sleeping baby on a pile of pillows and stretched.

'I too would learn the history of this land, Lady Lallia.'

Seboth's wife studied the air mage thoughtfully, then glanced at Elyssa. 'I think you have not yet told exactly who you are. You say you came from the north with Lady Emla, but that is not your home I think?'

Elyssa's eyes locked with Maressa's and Maressa gave a tiny shrug, turning her attention back to the baby. Elyssa drew a breath.

'You are correct Lady Lallia. Maressa and I come from a place we call Vagrantia, many leagues across the Wilderness, far east of Gaharn.'

Lallia frowned in thought and repeated the name: 'Vagrantia.'

Elyssa waited while Lallia's mind juggled with the word. The frown vanished.

'Vagrantia!' she exclaimed, excitement in her voice. 'Vagrants. You are one of the Vagrants?'

Elyssa smiled. 'A descendant of one of the Vagrants, yes. Our ancestors wandered all over this land until they found safe

11

haven inside five craters left from long dead volcanoes. I suppose it was a sort of stubbornness that made those survivors call the place Vagrantia. Taking the word that most people used to curse us and making it a name to be proud of – as we are.'

'Vagrants.' Lallia breathed the word. 'May I tell Seboth? I swear I will not if you so desire him not to know, but he would be enchanted.'

Elyssa laughed aloud. 'I hope he will not decide to chase us away.'

'Farn would not permit that,' Tika said quietly.

Maressa chuckled. 'I have yet to see one of these Great Dragons annoyed.'

A disturbance at the door proved to be Lord Seboth and his Armschief – who was also, they had learnt, Seboth's brother. Seboth waved a scroll case and joined the group of women by the hearth.

'Raben's man brought this – it is named for Maressa.' He pointed to a tag on the seal.

Maressa took it with some surprise. 'It is from the High Speaker of Vagrantia,' she told them, reading the upper seal. She flattened the roll of paper and read silently. 'I have to go to the circle tomorrow Lord Seboth. Two will arrive from the Stronghold at mid morning.'

Seboth settled on a large pillow and poked a stubby finger into the baby's midriff.

'Leave that child alone Seboth, he has only just decided to sleep at last,' Lallia told him sharply. She arched her brows at him. 'Have you connected the name of Vagrantia with anything yet?'

Seboth sat up straighter. 'I have, but it seems a rather wild connection,' he admitted, looking at his wife then at the three visitors.

Elyssa repeated to the Lord of Far and his brother what she had told Lallia and watched their rising excitement.

'All these cycles you have been hidden safely away,' he exclaimed. 'I suspected as much.' He gave them a shrewd look. 'And do you now intend to lay claim to your old lands? They were once called Valsheba, but the local leader of those left after the catastrophe was named Sapper and the lands were thus called Sapphrea in honour of his slaughter of the greatest number of your people.'

Maressa paled. 'I had not known that. We have had no contact beyond Vagrantia's walls for near two thousand cycles Lord Seboth.'

'So you know nothing of the Ganger Wars, or the appearance of the tall ones in Gaharn?' Olam asked with interest.

Maressa shook her head. 'Nothing of the world at all since the catastrophe. But we have had to learn rather a lot, rather quickly in the past days,' she added ruefully.

'And who are the two who will travel your magic circle tomorrow?' Olam questioned.

Maressa glanced at the paper in her lap. 'Lashek. He is the Speaker for Segra Circle. He is an earth mage as I am an air mage.'

'One of your leaders?' Seboth sounded surprised.

'He is also filled with more curiosity than anyone else I know,' Maressa smiled. 'I have no doubt he has wheedled and cajoled the High Speaker until she permitted him to travel out of sheer exasperation!'

Elyssa nodded. She had always found Lashek the kindest of men, and remembered especially how gentle he had been when her eyes first became silvered.

'Who else?' she now asked.

Maressa frowned. 'Someone called Ren.' She looked at Seboth, Olam and Lallia and sighed. 'We have just learnt that there is another land, on the other side of this world, called Drogoya. Ren is from that land.'

It took the rest of the afternoon to explain everything to Seboth, Lallia and Olam, during which time the baby was despatched to the nursery and the group transferred from the pleasant sitting room to the library. Seboth got up and down, finding various texts, while Elyssa deplored hthe non existent system of ordering his shelves.

After an argument, Olam left to take Seboth's place in the great hall to preside over the evening meal while the others ate in the library so as to continue their discoveries. Olam returned surprisingly quickly.

'I said I had the belly ache,' he grinned, and snatched the meat pastry from his brother's hand.

'Farn is back with Brin,' Tika announced. 'I must go down to them.'

'We all will come,' Seboth said generously.

For the first time, Lallia showed the timidity Tika had thought was the norm for Sapphrean females. 'May I come with you Seboth? It is almost dark and perhaps you could say that our guests needed a female escort?'

'Of course you can come,' Tika pre-empted Seboth smartly.

Making their way down Seboth's private stairway, Tika realised just how different Seboth was in his attitude, both to the way he treated females and in his eagerness to learn, and his openness of mind. If she had been raised in his household, perhaps she would not have run away. But then she would never have found Kija and Farn.

She looked down at Seboth, a few steps below her, and sent a tiny thread of power towards his mind. He faltered on the stair, putting a hand to the wall to steady himself. Tika grinned to herself. Unaware he might be, but old Valsheban blood still ran in his veins and the power was close to the surface. A little instruction and he would be able to reach it.

Farn and Brin had settled in an enclosed courtyard garden within Seboth's manor and were watching for Tika's appearance. As she was about to go to greet them she heard Lallia's gasp behind her. Turning, she saw that Lallia's eyes were wide: no trace of fear, only amazed awe. Tika reached for her hand, pulling Lallia with her. Farn's head lowered to Lallia's level and his eyes whirred many shades of blue.

'Another girl,' he exclaimed happily.

Olam departed that evening to reach the circle by the next day, taking extra koninas for the new arrivals. Seboth tried to appear nonchalant but failed dismally to hide his delight when it was suggested he go with Maressa on Brin's back to the circle outside Tagria. Farn would carry his two girls.

They had not waited long when the air trembled and two men stood upon the circle. One was older, short of stature and portly of build. The other was a slender, younger man with silver eyes and chestnut brown pupils. Lashek embraced Elyssa and Maressa, hesitating barely a moment before hugging Tika as well.

14

He introduced his companion as Ren Salar, an Offering from Drogoya.

The young man bowed politely and eyed the Dragons with caution. His relief at being offered a konina to ride back to Far was so plain that even Farn and Brin were amused.

'Have you flown on the back of a Great Dragon before?' Brin asked the stranger.

'I have not,' Ren replied. 'I have ridden upon a Plavat, a giant bird with unpleasant manners, and I did not greatly enjoy that experience.'

'I would take great care of you, should you wish to fly with me,' Brin said, his eyes sparkling with mischief.

Ren saw Tika's grin and bowed again to the massive crimson Dragon.

'Truly, I am greatly honoured by your generous offer, but I do prefer to be nearer the ground.'

Brin and Farn thought this remark extraordinarily amusing, and repeated it to each other all the way back to Far.

Chapter Two

In the settlement of Arak there was an air of bustling activity. Although a shelter had been provided to give the severely injured midnight blue Dragon Kadi some respite from the weather, Observer Chakar, Lorak and the ancient black Dragon Fenj were increasingly concerned. Kadi needed to be in a place secure from winds still bitterly cold. One of the Delvers' large growing areas was directly below where Kadi lay. The Snow Dragons using fire, and Delvers using hammers and hands, had enlarged the ventilation opening to a size enough to grant Kadi entrance.

What worried Chakar and Fenj most of all was the fact that Kadi remained silent although some of her wounds were beginning to heal. Her mind was closed and not even Fenj could reach her. Lorak had come up with the idea of moving Kadi and worked hard on the fulfilment of that plan.

Long lengths of rope were woven into a huge net, then heavily padded with whatever material the Delvers could lay hands on. Three Snow Dragons practised the manoeuvring they would need to do, over and over, until Fenj was satisfied. Now, in the early morning light, work began to ease the great net beneath Kadi's inert form. It took far longer than Chakar and Lorak had envisaged and they agreed to halt for a while to give everyone a much needed rest.

Mim and Ashta were to be the guides for the Snow Dragons and Fenj, and now Mim checked and rechecked the four harnesses. Lorak would ride Fenj, Chakar one of the Snow Dragons and Delver healers would be on the remaining Snow Dragons. Finally, Mim secured the last ropes to Fenj and stepped back.

'Stars guide our path now, old one,' he murmured.

Fenj bent his head to Mim's.

'Indeed, let us trust that they will Dragon Lord. But there is no choice. She will die if we leave her here much longer.

16

Gremara's healing was weakened by her battle with the Forsaken.'

Mim scratched his talons along Fenj's long jaw then ran lightly back to Ashta. The four Dragons harnessed to the net, lifted slowly into the air until they were perhaps three man heights above the ground and the ropes tightened. There was a brief flutter of panic from one of the Snow Dragons as she realised just how heavy a load Kadi was going to be but, as quickly, she calmed. Mim watched, leaving Fenj to order the beginning of the lift.

With agonising slowness the net drew closer around Kadi and then, suddenly, she was clear of the ground. The four Dragons flew in precise formation, moving across to the plateau's edge. Kadi swung as a gust of wind caught her, then steadied again. Further out they moved. Still so slowly, they began to drop the two leagues down to the settlement of Arak. Ashta swooped down, flying below but to the side of Kadi, guiding the other four.

Delvers craned out of the enlarged opening as Kadi's body descended towards them. Willing hands reached to grab trailing catch ropes to pull the Dragon inside. This was the moment Mim had been dreading. Fenj and the Snow Dragons had still to bear Kadi's weight, but that weight was now unevenly balanced as she was drawn within the settlement. Fenj lurched and Mim's heart pounded in sudden terror, but the old Dragon righted himself, murmuring reassurances through their minds.

The Delvers called out that Kadi was secure, and instantly the riders on the four Dragons released the harnesses, letting them fall to the waiting Delvers. Fenj slowly manoeuvred his great bulk through the space beside Kadi and paced further from the entrance to allow the Snow Dragons passage. He reclined against a side wall, tremors rippling through him, his eyes slate grey with weariness. The three Snow Dragons settled nearby, trembling worse than Fenj. Lorak and the Delver healers concentrated their attention on these four while Chakar began organising the removal of the ropes and netting from Kadi.

Mim came hurrying to Fenj's side, the tension easing in his stiff shoulders as he heard Fenj rumble: 'Splendid fellow,' and saw Lorak move on to a Snow Dragon, flask in hand.

There seemed no change in Kadi's condition. Chakar, with

many willing helpers, continued to apply ointments to the multitude of injuries, but although Kadi's breathing was regular, her eyes stayed closed and there was no contact with her mind.

A few days after the moving of Kadi from the exposed mountain to the settlement, there came a loud melodious call from outside the opening. Fenj woke with a start, about to trumpet in reply until he thought better of doing so inside the confines of the Domain. Chakar looked at Lorak across Kadi's outstretched wing. After a glance at Fenj's sparkling eyes, he shrugged.

'Whoever it is, Fenj is glad they're here.'

A flurry of wings outside and a Great Dragon peered within. Lorak grinned. Chakar could only stare at the huge, beautiful golden Dragon who now paced towards her. Honey coloured prismed eyes whirred, and Kija lowered her head to press her brow to Chakar's.

'I thank you for your work on my beloved Kadi. I will help you all I can. I am Kija, of the Broken Mountain Treasury.'

For the first time for longer than she could recall, Chakar found herself truly speechless. Light glimmered and flashed on the gold scales as Kija turned to press her brow to Lorak's. Clearly the Dragon spoke to Lorak's mind because his gap-toothed smile split his face and he chuckled softly. Kija studied Kadi for a few moments before moving to Fenj's side. Chakar's breath caught as golden and black faces touched, then the golden neck twined briefly round the black in affection.

'They Dragons be better than your old feather pillows any day, don't you think then?'

Chakar glared at Lorak and refused to answer, but in truth the beauty and intelligence of the Great Dragons had completely captured the Observer's heart and mind. A whimper, quickly suppressed, came from Kija. Lorak shook his head when Chakar would have moved.

'No, no, m'dear. Fenj, he be telling Kija about Gremara and Jeela. Did you not know Jeela is Kija's baby daughter?'

Later Kija lay beside Kadi, watching Chakar stretch and massage the shattered wing.

'You wear an egg such as Mim and my daughter Tika wear. I understand from Fenj that it is – changing?'

Chakar sat back on her heels, wiping oil from her hands on a piece of cloth. She lifted the pendant out of her shirt, holding it up for Kija's inspection. Kija's eyes glittered, whirring faster as she focused on the pulsating oval.

'Place it beneath Kadi's head,' she said suddenly. 'I do not know why, but I feel it may help her.'

Chakar did not hesitate, slipping the chain of obsidian links over her head and gently lifting Kadi's face to place the pendant near her throat. Kija's mind tone was a little embarrassed.

'I do not know what it might accomplish. I just thought it might help her a little.'

Chakar came awake, thinking someone had called her. She crawled up from the pallet the Delvers had put for her near her patient and froze. It was just before dawn and she saw Lorak, Kija and Fenj all awake, all looking at Kadi. The midnight blue Dragon's body seemed to be drawing the pale outside light into herself. There were not enough lamps in the cavern to account for the flicker and shine that danced over her great back. Chakar forced herself to her feet and took a step towards Kadi. For an instant she imagined she heard singing but the sound was gone at once. And so was the light. Again, there was only the murkiness of pre-dawn and Kadi's body a dark silhouette against the sky.

Chakar shivered, reached back to her pallet and wrapped a quilt round her shoulders. She crossed to Kadi and knelt, feeling the breath steady against her hands when she held them to Kadi's nose.

'I know not your name, but I thank you for your great care of me.'

The voice was a whisper in Chakar's mind which she almost disregarded. Then, with a surge of excitement, she crouched lower over the Dragon's beautiful face.

'Kadi? Kadi? Have you come back?'

She sent the thought carefully to the Dragon mind. She was aware of Lorak's hand gripping her shoulder as he peered down at Kadi, and of Kija and Fenj pressing close to the blue Dragon's body. Chakar heard Fenj's voice.

'Her name is Chakar my dear one. You have been so ill, yet this Chakar would not give up tending you.'

'Thank you Chakar.' The faint whisper came again.

Then Chakar's mind reeled when Fenj's bass voice pealed out in joyous relief, Kija's harmonising as they sang health and strength into their friend. Lorak's arm went round the Observer's shoulders and she realised with surprise that she was crying. Lorak drew her away and sat her on her pallet, producing the inevitable leather flask while Snow Dragon voices joined Kija and Fenj, their song filling minds throughout the Domain.

Whether it was the effects of Lorak's restorative before breakfast, or the cumulative effects of so many days and nights of constant nursing, but Chakar fell sound asleep, waking to find Mim squatting by her bed.

'You have missed the midday meal,' he grinned at her.

She saw just how very young this Dragon Lord was in his exuberant relief at Kadi's recovery. Remembering, she sat bolt upright, looking to Kadi. The Dragon's head had been raised on a great heap of pillows and her eyes were closed. Chakar began to climb out of her covers in alarm but Mim's scaled hand pressed her back.

'She sleeps, my friend. She will heal now. No one can tell me what you did to restore her, but I bring you this in thanks and replacement.'

He held out his other hand to the Observer and she saw an oval shape filling his palm. Mim's head touched Chakar's as they both bent over the egg.

'Gremara spoke to me and said that she knew you had given yours to Kadi, which was the right thing to do.'

Chakar looked across at Kadi again and saw that someone had slid the obsidian chain over Kadi's head, allowing the egg to rest high at her throat.

Mim laughed. 'Lorak did it earlier when we raised her head a little. Anyway, Gremara told me to go to the Delvers' egg cave and when I unsealed the door they were all shining, brighter than before. Gremara said I would know which one was to be yours and I went straight to this one.' He frowned. 'I keep thinking I can hear singing – but it must be my imagination. This is to be yours.'

Chakar accepted the egg, cupping it between her palms. The back of the oval was a deep amethyst and within the transparent, faintly gold front a tiny shape twisted and glimmered. A chain of silver was attached to the egg and Chakar glanced questioningly at Mim. He shrugged again.

'The chain was there when I picked it up,' he said, 'although I had not noticed it when I reached for it.'

A small furry creature crept onto Chakar's lap, nosing at the egg, making a pleased buzzing sound. It was black, except for splashes of white on each paw and tail tip. He squeezed between Chakar's hands and her chest and stared pleadingly up at Mim. The Dragon Lord reached out with one taloned finger and touched the Kephi's head.

'Would you be prepared to care for Rofu?' Mim asked softly. 'He came first to me. He has a loving but timid heart and would be far happier with you, as he is showing now.'

Startled, Chakar looked down into bright blue eyes.

'May I stay?' Rofu asked her wistfully.

'Of course you may, if you are sure that is what you want.'

Rofu nearly choked himself as his buzzing intensified.

'You are acclaimed throughout the Domain, Observer!' said a voice above them. Imshish, Nesh and Daro stood beaming at Chakar. 'We have come to carry on your work if you trust us to do so properly,' Nesh explained. 'The Lady Thryssa wishes to visit Gaharn before returning to Vagrantia but would like to speak with you before she leaves. And your friend Ren Salar has disappeared with Speaker Lashek.'

They laughed at Chakar's horrified expression.

'I'm sorry, we only tease you,' Imshish apologised. 'Lashek and Ren have travelled through the circles to Sapphrea.'

Kija insisted on carrying Chakar to the Stronghold. Rofu travelled inside Chakar's shirt, nestled close to the amethyst egg and refusing to open his eyes. Mim and Ashta flew with them. Chakar slipped from Kija's back, thanking the Dragon for the ride. Again Kija touched her brow to the Observer's.

'You have my gratitude Lady Chakar. You have but to summon me and I will answer your call.'

Kija moved into the Stronghold's great hall and reared erect, giving formal greeting to the two strangers sitting with Kera, Dessi and Jal at a table. Thryssa and Kwanzi stood and bowed deeply to the magnificent golden creature before them.

'I am so glad your friend Kadi is beginning to recover at last,'

Thryssa said at once. 'We were much distressed at the terrible state we saw her in on the mountainside.'

Kija's eyes whirred softly, appreciating the true feeling behind Thryssa's words. Before more could be said, Mim came sprinting down from the upper levels, his expression outraged. He glared at Chakar.

'One of those great birds is in the room I chose for myself,' he said furiously.

Chakar was taken aback. 'Baryet? In your room?' she repeated helplessly.

'I don't know which one it is, but it hissed at us and it tried to peck my Ashta!'

As he spoke, Baryet himself stilted into the hall, settled in his usual spot and waggled his head.

'You disturbed my wife,' he accused Mim coldly.

Mim gaped but Chakar caught his sleeve.

'Baryet, the room Syecha is occupying is the private – nest – of the Dragon Lord. It is a great rudeness to move in there in such a manner. Why is Syecha there anyway?'

Baryet tilted his head, one gold rimmed eye glaring over the black hooked bill.

'My wife is with egg,' he said.

Mim caught Chakar's eye and spun away, his shoulders shaking. For some reason, the five at the table all had their hands over their mouths and their eyes appeared to be watering. Mim kept his back turned. His voice sounded strangled.

'She may remain there for now in those circumstances, but it would have been more polite if you had asked permission first.'

Baryet stuck his head under his wing in an offended manner. Kera put both hands over her face, trying to keep from laughing aloud. Chakar joined them at the table, glancing anxiously at Mim.

'I do apologise. I am not sure that we could actually get Syecha out now that she has apparently made up her mind to nest there.'

Mim shook his head. 'It is not really that important,' he said. 'Especially if she is – with egg.'

Dessi snorted and that sent everyone into gales of laughter.

'I do believe he has more conceit and far less humour even

than Brin,' Kija's voice commented in their minds. The golden Dragon reclined near the table and was regarding the pile of dishevelled feathers with disbelief.

Kera sobered. 'Chakar, will Baryet leave Syecha to fly to Drogoya again? Clearly, Syecha will not travel so far in her present state.'

Dessi giggled helplessly.

'You have been preoccupied with poor Kadi,' Kera continued. 'Thus you may not be aware that something occurred?'

Chakar was listening closely, conscious that the amusement had vanished from the faces around her. Quickly Kera outlined the supposed death of Rhaki in Serim's body in the Asatarian circle, and of the distress it caused Daro here.

'Emla reports the same distraction in Elyssa and Tika. Ren was also discomfited and it was he who suggested the appalling idea that Rhaki's spirit is in Drogoya. If that is so, Rhaki allied with your Cho Petak is not something we dare ignore.'

Chakar tugged at her long white braid, Rofu batting at the feathery end of it.

'It would be possible for a strong Dragon to fly to Drogoya. The longest space between islands was a full day and a night. The islands are small but large enough for a Dragon to land on and rest.' Chakar was thinking aloud. 'I will ask Baryet to fly, order him if necessary. I am still his "parent" and thus have the right to insist if I must. I think it better that the Dragons do not attempt the journey until we are more sure of what may be happening there. If you would find me paper and pen, I will write at once to Babach.'

Kera dug in her ever present satchel and produced paper, pen, a small jar of ink and sealing wax.

'I will write what I think best, then you must tell me of anything other that you wish me to pass on.'

The chamberlain Yoral appeared with several servants loaded with trays to set the supper ready and Guards began to emerge from their labours in the lower levels.

'Perhaps we had best not mention Syecha's condition to Lorak, Lady Kera,' Jal said thoughtfully. 'He constantly grumbles that none of the hens sent from Gaharn have begun laying yet.'

23

Mim chuckled. 'Can you see Lorak trying to steal eggs from Syecha?'

'Unfortunately, yes,' said Kera grimly. 'You are right Jal – not a word to Lorak.'

'How long do the eggs take to hatch?' asked Kija.

Chakar glanced up. 'About a season.'

'Stars preserve us,' Kera groaned.

It took Chakar some considerable time to persuade Baryet of the necessity of another flight to Drogoya and back but outrageous flattery finally convinced him. The scroll tube was strapped beneath his wing and he departed the Stronghold.

'I felt quite ill, hearing all that,' Kwanzi teased Chakar gently.

She smiled. 'I know. But I would rather persuade him than resort to ordering him really. He is a little unbalanced due to the fact that I brought him up, and I am not a Plavat.'

Kwanzi patted her back and plied her with spice tea.

Next day, Thryssa and Kwanzi went through the circle to Gaharn. From there, they planned to go directly back to Vagrantia. A warm friendship had grown between the Vagrantians and the tiny Drogoyan Observer. Thryssa and Kwanzi had watched how hard Chakar had toiled over the injured Dragon Kadi, which earned her their respect and admiration. Thryssa urged the Observer to visit Vagrantia soon and assured her she would be a most welcome guest.

Thryssa had also taken the time to explain the exact working of the circle's pattern and the words of the chant – something only previously divulged to Emla. Chakar was touched by this evidence of Thryssa's trust and promised she would visit Vagrantia in due course. She voiced some surprise that Ren had gone through the circle with Lashek, given his aversion to any form of travel other than his own two feet or horseback.

Thryssa laughed. 'He was not exactly sanguine about it,' she admitted. 'He eventually decided it would be slightly preferable to flying on your birds or on a Dragon.'

The great hall seemed empty once Thryssa and Kwanzi had gone to Gaharn, but Dessi kept Chakar company. Dessi told her much of the Delvers' history, and Chakar began to teach Dessi of the Order of Myata. Mim listened to many of these sessions and both he and Dessi became increasingly drawn to Myata's surprisingly simple teachings of love and respect for the land, and the magic therein.

Reports came daily from Arak of Kadi's slow improvement, but Chakar felt she should stay at the Stronghold until Baryet returned. He would be impossibly irritated if she was not patiently awaiting his reappearance. A ten day passed, and nearly a second when a Snow Dragon warned of Baryet's imminent arrival.

Kija had just returned from visiting Kadi and was describing in detail to Chakar how each and every injury seemed to be mending. Her eyes began to whirr in consternation as the great bird stilted into the hall.

'I do not know what is wrong with him my Chakar! It is through no fault of mine!' Baryet sounded afraid, sending a chill of terror through Chakar which Kija picked up at once.

Chakar, Mim and Dessi were already hurrying to Baryet as he sank down onto the floor, his head twisting anxiously. They saw a shape among the thick plumage on the bird's back and reached up to help the rider free.

'Voron!' Chakar exclaimed.

'Help him Chakar. He is burnt so badly. I could think only to bring him here when Baryet arrived.' Voron helped to ease Babach's heavily wrapped body into the arms of Motass and other Guards who had been taking their ease in the hall.

Delver healers came running, already summoned by Kija. Voron staggered and Jal held him until Mim came to support Voron as well.

Voron's voice was hoarse. 'He was conscious until two days ago. Baryet flew magnificently Chakar, I thought he would never tire, but he said he must get Babach to you. I do not even know if Babach still lives.'

Voron would have fallen if not for Mim, and Jal called other Guards to carry the Drogoyan to pillows by the fireside. The healers and Chakar were unwrapping the bundle that was apparently Observer Babach. There was a screech and Sava fluttered free, clicking his beak in agitation. Finally the hood of a second cloak was pulled from Babach's face. Even the healers gasped involuntarily. The face revealed was a mass of weeping blisters, no eyelashes, no brows or beard remained.

Slower now, the healers uncovered his body and found his back untouched but his front was a mass of raw flesh.

Chapter Three

Cho Petak had long awaited the arrival of Rhaki and Mena. He was aware, where they were not, that two creatures of the Void had insinuated themselves within not just the bodies but the minds and spirits of the two. The creature which inhabited Mena had waited through generations of her ancestors and was extremely annoyed on finding Cho's plans were coming to fruition when he was in a very young female body in this male dominated world.

At least that creature had learnt to adapt, whereas the one who had entered Rhaki had become complacent over the near thousand years of Rhaki's bodily existence. The one within Rhaki had been terrified when Rhaki became unbodied: it was a reminder of the countless ages the creature had spent trapped Beyond in blinding light.

Cho Petak now opened the way for the other creatures who clamoured for release from their long confinement. This had always been the most dangerous part of his plan: if he had miscalculated and there was even one creature who held back a little and considered his actions in this world, as had Cho, then he might face a serious challenge.

Cho Petak sealed himself within his secret room, where not even Rhaki, unbodied, could enter without permission, and released his kindred. Outside the Menedula, in the town of Syet, buildings burned on in the morning light, the heat distorting the air above them. Screams rang out as the students Cho had modified continued to hunt and rend any inhabitants they found. The red eyed killers would die soon themselves, their bodies consumed because of their raised metabolisms.

A river seemed to erupt from the sky, a river of darkness mixed with scarlet pebbles, cascading down to the land. It widened from the place it seemed to spring from, spreading out like flood water. Cho Petak waited, his knuckles whitening where his hands clenched the arms of his chair. He allowed himself to relax a little, smiling with satisfaction. None of his brethren had hesitated long enough to think of usurping Cho's position and they would not get another chance half as good as this one.

The dark river's volume dwindled, disappeared, and Cho leaned his head back against his chair. He would allow them their freedom for a while: they would be grateful that he had not asserted his will upon them before they had sated their all but forgotten appetites. Cho reached for the jug of water he had brought in here with him and poured some into a black crystal beaker. Sipping, he let his mind play with the thought of Mena and Rhaki.

Once, they had been his closest companions. Grek, whose spirit now resided within Mena, Cho recalled as a laughing boy, only too willing to please his many friends, following Cho's lead until he was too deeply mired to extricate himself. Cho could not remember ever hearing D'Lah laugh. Within D'Lah there had always burnt a fierce desire for power, and more power. When the Grand Master Cheok discovered what these three had already achieved and surmised their future plans, he had struck fast and without mercy.

Cho Petak had escaped his wrath only by coercing D'Lah and Grek to offer him their combined strength. Their howls of rage followed him through time and space, tormenting him ceaselessly. His first task on finding himself on this world, had been to gain the release of his two accomplices from the Void.

Cho Petak had appropriated the body of a farmer's son in the hot lands far to the south of Drogoya. It amused him to use his own name for this body once he had worked his way north to the seat of power which was the Menedula. It took many years to calm Grek and D'Lah into coherence. Then, he encouraged them to search through the captives within the Void, choosing those who would prove useful to them once freed. Using his own magic, harnessed to the magic of this land, he had freed Grek and D'Lah who raced to the beacon of his mind.

Grek had learned much of adaptability during his sojourns in various bodies, but he was still willing to please Cho Petak. D'Lah had learned much of power, through his long tenancy within one of the strange race who had arrived on this world a thousand years after Cho Petak. But he was too used to the one mind, the one body which had been Rhaki, as evidenced by his panic when Rhaki was unbodied. Cho would need to watch them both but especially he would be careful of D'Lah.

Cho had spent these long years in preparation. He knew how to nullify a large proportion of the natural magic within this land itself. He had worked under a considerable handicap: a great deal of his energy had to stay focused first on D'Lah and Grek, and then on the position of the Void until this moment, when he could release the chosen ones. For the first time since he had arrived here, his whole mind could be turned to making this world what he chose it to be.

Cho Petak watched with his mind as the kindred, bodied again, forced human limbs into impossible contortions in wild excitement at their freedom from the Void. He smiled. Let them have their fun unchecked for now. His mind ranged further afield. He saw the Chapter House in Radoogar, from whence he had chosen Krolik to become Master of Aspirants. All was quiet there, working to his instructions on the themes he had devised before Cheok tried to destroy him.

Cho's mind searched south and found the other Chapter Houses. Some were in uproar, some were as calm as Radoogar. Finally he reached to the north western House of Oblaka. He frowned. There had always seemed to be a faint blurring around Oblaka. Cho had put it down to the fact that Oblaka held strongly to the teachings of Myata, subtly different from those of her father, Sedka. He probed a little harder and jerked upright in his chair, his eyes widening.

There was a hard shell around the most northerly part of the complex. He analysed the composition of this shell and then sat back again, amused at his own concern. It was a particular amalgam of rock, well known to be impervious to magic. There were small deposits scattered throughout Drogoya and they had been well documented.

Once more he viewed the House of Oblaka and saw that his servants there had done well. Most of the buildings were unrecognisable, and charred bodies were strewn everywhere. Cho nodded. This part of his plan had gone very smoothly and easily:

he would be tested when he attempted to draw the kindred away from their present amusements.

But for the next few days, Cho would explore Rhaki's recollections of his land of Gaharn. He would have to allow for Rhaki's narrow view of those who shared that land, but D'Lah would be able to enlarge on many of the matters Rhaki had disregarded. Cho next considered Mena. If he was so inclined, he could think of many interesting things he might do with the child. She was attractive in a way: the short cropped, blonde hair, the large eyes, reddened now of course.

He frowned. It had been more difficult to get her physical body to Drogoya than he had anticipated – those great lizards had been most unreliable. Perhaps it would be best to order Grek from the girl's body now. She could stay here, in the Menedula, a sort of pet. It would entertain Rhaki, Cho was quite sure.

There was a core within the child, utterly resistant to any mind probe Cho had used. Grek had warned him that even he, within the child's mind since she was a new-made foetus, could not reach inside that core. Cho dismissed any worry from his mind. A female, alive only a handful of years, was no threat to him and his cohorts. Yes, he would order Grek to remove himself from Mena's mind at once.

By the time Cho had walked from his hidden room to the main apartment, Mena came dancing in from the outer hall. Her eyes shone blood red, flame flickering in their centres.

'Leave her Grek,' Cho ordered quietly.

Briefly, Grek's mind battered at Cho's in fury – he had grown to enjoy this body and where was he to go if he left it?

'Unbody, as has D'Lah,' Cho repeated his order calmly.

The child's body stiffened to an inhuman rigidity as Cho watched with an academic interest. The red of her eyes slowly faded and became a dark blue that was almost purple. Her body slackened and she stared up at Cho Petak in confusion. Frowning, she looked around the large room with its row of tall narrow windows. Then her eyes rolled up and she folded bonelessly to the floor.

A quivering of the air alongside Cho made him raise a brow.

'Does she still live, Grek?'

'Yes she lives,' Grek laughed.

How well he remembered that laugh, thought Cho.

'May I choose another body Cho?'

Cho Petak shrugged. 'If you must. But I believe you will find the unbodied state far more useful for our purposes now.'

On the floor below the apartment where Mena lay unconscious, a tiny spider spun a thread. It swung from the top of the cupboard, on which it had spent hours in terror, to the wall. Finding cracks too small for a human eye to see, it scurried to the window sill. Thank the Light no one had shut the window. A glow surrounded the spider and swelled, until it encompassed not a spider but a pigeon. The pigeon rested briefly, its head sunk low on its breast. Then it fluffed out its feathers and flew, away from the Menedula towards the north west.

Chakar had organised a careful watch of the Menedula from the Oblaka. Students devoted to the Order of Myata and gifted in air magic, took turns, day and night, waiting for they knew not what to occur. Chakar had told them only that they were to summon her whatever the hour, if anything at all out of the ordinary touched their awareness.

So it was that Lyeto alerted Babach in Chakar's absence. Babach cursed wildly, struggling up the steep path to the main complex. He could smell the burning and knew they were too late. Lyeto turned to the old man, his silver eyes wide with horror in the moonlight.

'We have looked to the Menedula when we should have watched here more closely.'

Babach shook his head and pointed on up the path, too short of breath to argue now. About five hundred lived and worked in the Oblaka and of those, barely one hundred escaped the inferno that night. Many of those who survived were Chakar's particularly promising followers and they had been talking late in one of the dining halls. They had already organised themselves into groups, some trying to pull victims from the fire, while others began the first attempts at treating horrendously burnt flesh.

Dawn eventually revealed a grisly scene: the buildings reduced, resembling the stumps of rotten teeth amidst the debris of fallen masonry. A young student handed Babach a mug of tea at which he stared in astonishment.

'Some of us with little skill for healing have tried to find some ways we can be of use.'

Grey pupils in silvered eyes looked up at Babach. The tracks of tears trailed down ash smudged cheeks.

'You can have no idea how very useful this tea is to me at this moment,' Babach replied, his voice hoarse from the smoke. 'Will you start telling everyone to begin making their way to Chakar's cottage? I fear I do not know your name child?'

'Melena sir. But is there room for us all there – it is so tiny?'

Babach drained his mug. 'Just tell them to make their way there. I will go on to prepare the rooms.'

Babach found Voron pacing, frantically worried, in the lower sitting room. The Observer slumped in Chakar's armchair. He allowed himself only the briefest of rests then climbed back to his feet.

'Come along boy, we must open the ways down here. There are many to shelter, although nowhere near as many as I would have wished.'

Voron did not speak as he watched Observer Babach move along the passages. A finger raised, a murmured word, and rock dissolved into doorways. Room after room appeared, large and small. Finally Babach turned back to Voron, a sad smile on his face.

'Chakar had long prepared for something like this, while always hoping it would never be needed.' He tilted his head. 'Go and open the doors Voron, and bring them down here. The worst injured will go in the first large room on the right.'

Voron wrote down the names of all who came down the ladder, through the tiny cellar and into the underground world. Lyeto did not seem as surprised as any of the others at the extensive cavern he saw under Chakar's cottage. He noticed Voron's speculative eye on him and gave a tired smile.

'I guessed there was a cellar of some size here, but I did not know how great it would be,' he said.

Melena and two boys began to prepare a meal in one of the larger rooms Babach had designated as their common room. The first sitting room, where Sava guarded Chakar's armchair, was left by unspoken agreement to Babach and Voron. Babach gathered the mobile survivors into the common room.

'Many of you have learned from Chakar, the fact that the long serving Sacrifice is not worthy of your trust. More than that, I have to tell you, impress upon you, that he is our enemy. Beneath these rocks he cannot trace us – he will believe all at the Oblaka died in the fires set by the three minions he placed among us.'

While there were several shocked murmurs, many others in the room nodded in understanding.

'Chakar and I have spent years trying to ascertain from whence Cho Petak came. All we have discovered points in the same direction. The Lost Realms.'

In the deep silence that followed, a wailing cry came from the room where lay the desperately hurt ones, quickly cut off as a door was closed.

'But where is Observer Chakar?' a young voice asked tremulously.

Babach lowered himself to a stool and bent his head for a moment. Then he looked up again.

'Observer Chakar and the Offering, Ren Salar, are in the Night Lands.'

This time there was no silence only an increasing buzz of questions. Babach raised a hand.

'Voron, fetch the scrolls if you would. I will explain all I can before we sleep. And I will continue to sleep above, in the cottage. Let Cho Petak know the Oblaka does not lie deserted.'

Voron promised himself he would argue the old man out of that decision as he hurried to fetch the maps and documents received from the Night Lands. Voron had nothing but admiration and respect for Babach as he explained, repeated, answered questions, without once raising his voice or showing anything other than a serene patience. Voron knew the old man was exhausted, angry and worried, yet no sign did he give of those feelings. Finally it was Voron who could take no more.

'Enough for now,' he said, standing up, his hand on Babach's shoulder. 'We will all try to sleep and begin again tomorrow. You must remember though, none of you can leave the shelter of these caves without betraying your presence to any who may be far watching. I will come to check the injured throughout the night. Tomorrow we will arrange rotas for necessary work – cooking, cleaning and so on, and the healers among you must also work strict shifts. We are few: we must find the best ways of living and working down here as quickly as we can. But now, we all need to rest.'

He caught Lyeto's eyes and the student nodded, getting to his feet too and herding the knots of young people out to their allotted sleeping quarters. Voron helped Babach up, thinking how very young these survivors seemed. He was only just past thirty and yet none of these could be even twenty five.

After a broken night, checking the badly burned patients and fretting over Babach's obstinate insistence on going up to the cottage, Voron rose before dawn. He went quietly to the washing cave, then on to the viewing ledge, his mind already occupied with what he had to do this day. He turned onto the ledge and stopped abruptly.

A naked woman, long grey hair tousled around her shoulders and back, lay slumped along the inner cliff wall. Cautiously he approached and knelt beside her. Strands of hair rippled as she breathed. Voron carefully pushed her hair back and stared in disbelief at the unconscious face of the Offering, Finn Rah. He raced back to his cubby hole room, grabbed a quilt from the bed and rushed back to the ledge. He wrapped the quilt over the woman's shoulders, rolled her gently towards him then scooped her up in his arms. She weighed next to nothing as Voron hurried along to the first sitting room. Holding his burden to his chest, he pulled cushions from the armchairs, laid them before the fire and put Finn Rah upon them.

Poking the fire until it brightened, he swung the kettle over it and turned back to the woman. He laid the back of his hand to her cheek and frowned at the chill he felt. He sped off for more covers from his own bed which he piled around her, then sat waiting for the kettle to boil. He was making berry tea when she groaned. He went back to her side, raising her head and shoulders and pushing more cushions beneath. Her face was drawn with exhaustion, her closed eyes shadowed and dark. The eyelids fluttered open and green pupilled, silver eyes stared up at him blankly.

'Hush. You are at the Oblaka. What's left of the Oblaka that is,' Voron heard himself babbling and stopped. 'How came you to be on the ledge? What can I do to help you?'

'You can give me some tea, unless you have something stronger which would be preferable.'

The voice was faint but still held the acerbic tone Voron remembered from lectures he'd attended in the Menedula.

'I have nothing stronger, I'm afraid,' Voron apologised, fetching the mug of tea he had just poured for himself.

A thin hand reached eagerly for the drink but trembled so violently that Voron had to hold the mug as Finn Rah drank.

'Where are Babach or Chakar?' she demanded, her voice stronger.

Voron sat back on his heels. Clearly the Offering knew this system of caves beneath Chakar's cottage, but what should Voron tell her?

'The truth please, at once.' Finn read his thoughts with no difficulty. 'And more tea while you're about it.'

Slowly at first then with gathering speed, Voron told her everything: everything from the time of his close questioning by Master Krolik, and his subsequent flight from the Menedula with Ren Salar, to the burning of the Oblaka the previous night.

Finn Rah struggled upright in the cocoon of covers Voron had wrapped her in. A quilt slipped from her shoulder and she belatedly realised her nakedness.

'If you could find me a shirt, trousers?' she raised a brow at him.

'Oh. Oh yes.' Voron went back to one of the many shallow caves he had seen packed with just such items. He picked up two shirts at random and a pair of soft woollen trousers. The first sounds came to him of others beginning to stir in the newly-opened rooms further on as he trotted back to the sitting room.

He found Babach in Chakar's armchair talking earnestly to their newest arrival. Finn took the clothes without a glance at them and dragged a shirt over her head. Babach and Voron politely averted their eyes as she pulled on the trousers. She stood up but swayed perilously and Babach caught her, forcing her to sit back on the heap of bedding by the fire.

Babach went to the table, retrieving the maps and papers he had shown to the gathering last night, and handed them wordlessly to Finn Rah.

'We must check the injured,' the old man said to Voron.

Three of the eleven most dreadfully burned had died and Babach gave murmured instructions to Lyeto. He mentioned only vaguely that the Offering Finn Rah had arrived here a few hours ago. He stressed that Finn Rah was a deeply-loved and trusted friend of both himself and Observer Chakar when he glimpsed a few suspicious faces.

Voron and Babach returned to their sitting room to find Finn Rah making more tea and hooting companionably to Sava, who swayed from foot to foot in delight on Chakar's chair. Quietly, Finn recounted what she had seen and heard in the Menedula before she fled. She told of several burning farms and an entire village in flames.

'How did you get here?' Voron asked, feeling he was missing something.

Finn met Babach's eyes and sighed. 'I used the oldest magic that Myata taught. I became a pigeon, and I flew here.'

Voron could only stare, knowing she spoke the simple truth.

'Babach it is dangerous for you in the cottage above.' Finn turned her attention to the old man. 'Cho Petak will surely check more than once. It is too dangerous.'

Babach smiled sweetly and tugged his braided beard. 'I have to be there in case the Plavats return.'

Finn sat cross legged on her nest of covers and considered. 'If Chakar and Ren came back and saw the destruction, would they still check inside here?'

Babach lifted his hands. 'Perhaps. Perhaps not, if Chakar could not find my mind.'

'I will take turns with you.' It was a statement leaving no room for any argument.

Babach slept above for the next two nights, while Finn spent some hours in the cottage during the days. Two more students died of their burns and a daily routine was established among the eighty new residents.

Baryet arrived with the dawn on the third morning, left the scroll case and announced he had family matters to attend to some leagues up the coast. He informed Babach that he would be back in two days time and would then leave at once for the Night Lands. That night, Cho Petak did check the Oblaka once more, and he found Babach's mind signature. The Sacrifice in his high rooms in the Menedula smiled, raised his left hand and pointed the little finger to the north west.

Finn Rah found the Observer when she went up to the cottage the next morning. He was alive, barely, conscious only through a huge effort of will. Finn summoned Voron and Lyeto and they smothered the deep burns with cooling salves. Babach seemed to sleep then and Finn told Voron she thought he should leave.

'When that Plavat comes back, you must take Babach to Chakar.'

Voron nodded although he was appalled at the idea of five days on Baryet's back with a desperately sick Babach.

Lyeto nodded too. 'She is right,' he told Voron as though Finn wasn't there. 'Cho Petak will now believe that no one survives here. It will give us a little more time. Babach will die within days if he stays here I think,' he glanced at Finn and she tightened her lips in silent agreement.

'They may have healers in the Night Lands who can better deal with these injuries. Voron, you must take him. And warn them of what has befallen us. It may be our only chance to survive, and theirs too.'

Chapter Four

Lashek was delighted to have the opportunity to be one of the first Vagrantians to set foot on their ancient lands again. He resembled a prosperous farmer rather than a leader of his people and Lord Seboth found himself warming to the Speaker of Segra Circle.

On the second day of his visit, Tika found Lashek alone in one of the many small gardens hidden within Seboth's sprawling manor. He was kneeling, bent over a tired looking plant, brushing his fingers lightly over its drooping leaves and muttering softly. He glanced up at Tika and beckoned her to join him. She knelt at his side and heard more clearly the words he spoke. She looked from Lashek to the plant and back in confusion.

The Speaker was saying a nursery rhyme, very similar to ones Tika herself had heard in the women and children's quarters in Return. Lashek sat back, smiling with satisfaction. Tika glanced at the plant. She gaped. The leaves now positively bristled with vigorous life. Tika regarded the plant thoughtfully.

'I was hoping to speak with you Lashek,' she said. 'Do you know the story of my soul bonding with Farn, and how Lady Emla's friends, Kemti and Iska, may the stars guard her memory, freed my mind from its restrictions?'

Lashek stood up, holding out a grubby hand to Tika.

'Mim told us something of it.'

He led her to a bench and they sat on the sun warmed stone.

'Have you noticed anything about Seboth and his brother?' she asked casually.

Lashek chuckled and waited for her to say more.

Her silvered eyes flashed briefly up at him, the pupils green as the new shoots in the garden around.

'I thought, perhaps, you might know how to free the power they have within them.'

'That would be a serious matter my dear. Sapphreans today

still regard power, magic, with the greatest suspicion.'

'But Seboth is very different from most. He is also held in high regard by the other Lords.'

Lashek pondered a while. 'If you can find me some of those exquisite pastries we were given yesterday, you might persuade me to discuss the matter with Lord Seboth,' he said solemnly.

Tika grinned at him and jumped up. 'As good as done, Speaker Lashek.'

She raced off into the building and Lashek closed his eyes, turning his face up to the sun. Perhaps the child was right. If one of the Sapphrean Lords was shown to have the magic in him, and used it as it should always and only be used? Feet pounded back along the flagged path and Lashek opened one eye. He inspected the dish Tika held beneath his nose and beamed in pleasure.

'I do believe I am quite persuaded, dear child.'

Gan, Sket and Riff became most friendly with Olam, Seboth's brother and Armschief. They gave him many details previously omitted, in long talks about the battle for the Stronghold. Olam told Seboth that he would be glad to have three such men beside him in a fight. Neither Seboth nor his brother missed the fact that the three were, even now, constantly protective of Tika and, by association, of Elyssa and Maressa. Seboth had accepted the presence of the two armsmen, after his initial surprise, as equals and friends of Tika and Gan.

Kephis being unknown in Sapphrea, Khosa, Queen of the Kephis of the Golden Lady's Estate, was given great attention. She stalked the corridors and rooms of Seboth's manor, orange tail regally upright, and expected doors to be instantly opened for her. She avoided most of the children, who evinced a distressing delight in pulling the royal tail. This evening, she was arranged upon Lallia's knees before the fire, buzzing contentedly as Lallia kept up a constant stroking of her back.

Tika broached the subject of power, carefully watching the reactions of the three Sapphreans. The conversation dodged and twisted around the main point until Khosa sat up, giving an enormous yawn.

'What the child is trying to say, is that all three of you have the potential within you to use the power.'

Maressa and Elyssa closed their eyes. Tika glared at the

Kephi. Lashek, Gan and Ren kept their gaze fixed on the Sapphreans. Mixed emotions warred on all three faces, Lallia and Olam both turning to Seboth to provide a reply to the Kephi's outrageous statement. Eventually, Seboth gave a nervous laugh.

'It must be obvious to you all that I am not sure whether to regard this news as a blessing or a curse.'

'Discuss it between you, think about what it might mean. Make no decision now about whether you wish to learn more or not. But just let me demonstrate something.'

Lashek rose to stand before the Lord of Far.

'If it helps you, close your eyes. But try to see with your mind's eye: look through my forehead and see what you will.'

Lallia closed her eyes but Seboth and Olam kept theirs open, staring hard at Lashek's lined brow. Lallia suddenly tightened her grip on Khosa who slitted her eyes in annoyance. Olam's jaw sagged while Seboth's eyes widened in surprise.

'It is like a jewelled web that I see,' Seboth whispered, Olam and Lallia nodding agreement.

'Enough.' Lashek returned to his chair. 'I swear to you that I did nothing except open my own mind to yours. It was the power, or magic, within you that, for the first time perhaps, you consciously focused. I must tell you that we do not crash into each others' minds. If I tried to enter your minds you would know at once. One of the first things we teach our children is to respect the privacy of others' thoughts.'

Seboth nodded then glanced at his wife and brother. 'It grows late and Lashek has given us plenty to think on. We will speak more on this matter tomorrow. Now we will leave you to yourselves.'

Goodnights were exchanged and the door closed behind the Sapphreans. Elyssa giggled.

'I wager they will be practising that half the night!'

Gan grinned. 'No wager, Lady Elyssa.'

'Gan, I feel drawn to the west,' Tika said abruptly. 'Is it possible for us to go into the salt lands?'

'I have made some enquiries. I also feel we should go in that direction – stars know why.'

'It is where the Valsheban cities lie buried,' Lashek said softly. 'And I wish I could accompany you, but I promised Thryssa that I would join her in Gaharn. I was allowed four days only here,' he said mournfully.

'Brin has flown over to the Bitter Sea several times. He says there are occasional patches of green. He stopped at one and found clear water.'

'What did you find out Gan?' Lashek asked.

'Hunters do occasionally go two or three days on foot, and they report no fresh water.'

'I will ask Brin to check as accurately as he can,' said Tika.

Lashek smiled. 'Why not ask Maressa? After all, air mages are taught to estimate distances rather precisely.'

Tika blushed. 'I'm sorry. I forget how differently you use the power. Would you do it Maressa?'

'Of course,' Maressa replied calmly. 'On condition that I can come too.'

'I had assumed we would all go,' Tika sounded indignant.

Ren cleared his throat. 'On horses – I mean, koninas?' he asked warily.

Gan patted Ren's shoulder. 'I think we would take at least six koninas: Sket and Riff are quite happy with them. If Seboth is agreeable to our journeying to the coast, I do not doubt that he will send at least two of his own armsmen with us.'

'Thank the stars you brought good news of Kadi with you Ren. We had no notion of where she had gone. I wonder if she has yet told Kija and Fenj of what befell her and Mena. Navan told us that Rhaki had expressed an interest in the child.'

'Things seem much calmer since he vanished though, don't they Lady Tika?'

Tika smiled at Sket. 'They do indeed, but –'

'No buts for now.' Gan rose to his great height. 'The hour grows late so let us all get some rest.'

The group dispersed, Tika, Elyssa and Maressa retiring to the large bedroom they had chosen to share. Tika lay still, waiting until the other two were asleep, before sliding from the bed and creeping to the door. Sket got up from the floor outside and silently followed her. They ghosted down the stairs and along dimly lit passages before reaching the courtyard Brin and Farn had appropriated as their own.

Sket felt the affection surge from the Dragons as Tika

approached. He grinned when Brin's great head pushed gently at his chest. Tika settled herself in the curve of Farn's shoulder. His eyes flashed in the starlight when Khosa settled in turn on top of Tika.

'I heard you say we will go to the Bitter Sea,' Farn murmured in Tika's mind. 'Shall we go tomorrow?'

'We will go when Lashek leaves us for Gaharn. He is a nice man.' She yawned hugely.

'This Lord Seboth, he is not like Lord Hargon at all, is he?' Sket asked from his place against Brin's chest.

Tika roused. 'He isn't is he? None of the lords is as strongly against using the power as Hargon. And it is only Hargon: Navan has no such hatred as Hargon shows.'

'Is it because of what's happened to his lads?' Sket wondered. He thought Tika had fallen asleep but just as he was beginning to doze himself, she replied.

'Losing his sons has made him even more resistant, but he has always hated it. I remember several times in my life in his compound, that he ordered the killing of certain people. It is only now that you remind me, that I realise they were ones who, probably accidentally, revealed they had some remnant of power through their old blood.'

Only a snore answered her, and Brin's chuckle. But Tika stayed awake much longer, wondering why it was that Hargon should nurture such an enduring hatred for magic.

Lashek departed for the circle on Brin's back. He carried with him separate messages from those left in Far, for delivery in Gaharn and the Stronghold. He had spent some time with Maressa and Ren trying to ascertain the location of two of the coastal cities of Valsheban days. Tika was stunned when Elyssa told her she would travel to Gaharn with Lashek. She argued, begging Elyssa to stay in Sapphrea.

'As you are drawn to the west, I am not. I sense that I must go to the Stronghold,' Elyssa said gently. 'But see, I have drawn a circle and I will show you how to read the pattern and teach you the words, and how to identify the different ones. Maressa will go over it all with you on your travels.'

Farn also could see no reason why Elyssa should leave and

added his arguments to Tika's. But Elyssa remained steadfast in her determination to leave with Lashek. Farn carried his two girls to the circle in silence on the morning of departure. Elyssa hugged Tika hard.

'I promise we will soon meet again Tika, but I must go to the north for now.'

Tika nodded. 'It is just that it seems such a short time to have known you.'

Elyssa hugged her again then turned briskly to the circle. Lashek put his arms round Tika, resting his chin on the top of her head.

'Find what you can of our old world, my child. I long to be with you as you go searching.' He held her from him and smiled down at her. 'You must promise me to add your thoughts to Maressa's reports on all that you discover.'

Tika managed a smile, then reached into a pocket. 'A little squashed I'm afraid.'

Lashek raised the package to his nose. His eyes rolled in delight. 'You didn't manage to wheedle the recipe from that dear Lady Lallia, did you?'

Tika handed him a folded paper. Lashek smacked a kiss onto her brow and joined Elyssa on the circle clutching parcel and paper to his chest. Elyssa glanced once across the circle into Tika's silver eyes then looked down at the pattern she was about to walk. Seboth, Gan and Tika heard her low murmur as she began the chant. There was a soft gulp of air and the circle was empty.

Gathered in Seboth's library that night, Tika asked if he had any strong objections to their searching the salt lands for the lost cities.

'None at all,' Seboth replied promptly. 'I only wish, like Speaker Lashek, that I could join you. Unfortunately, the reports from Return make me chary of leaving Far at the present.'

Gan frowned. 'Is Hargon ill – in your honest opinion Lord Seboth? I know he was sorely disturbed by the recent events concerning his sons.'

'No.' Seboth sighed. 'Since the Ganger Wars ended, cycles past now, most of us Lords have enjoyed the chance to get on with our lives in our own areas. We keep a force of armsmen, trained and ready, but we enjoy our peaceful ways now. Hargon has always been the sole one of us to fret about keeping our men battle ready. He is also the only one of us who tries to keep alive the old fear of the power users – as I am sure you must have noticed.'

'I have been wondering about that,' said Tika. 'Sket made me think of it the other night.' Silver eyes gleamed when Tika turned to face Seboth. 'Do you kill any of your people who show they have some unexplained way of doing something? Healing perhaps, or making plants grow?'

Seboth looked shocked. 'Of course I don't.' Understanding dawned. 'You mean Hargon does?'

Tika shrugged. 'I know one of the old women "died" just before I – left – Return, half a cycle ago. She taught me to read and write, and she had also shielded my mind somehow. She tried to protect me, Seboth.'

Seboth scowled and began to prowl the room. 'I heard from Hargon this afternoon.' He swung away from the window and squatted beside Tika. 'He summons me to a great council as he calls it. Summons me – a Lord of the same standing as him.' Seboth took Tika's hands. 'He ordered me to kill any Merigs I might see around Far. He has killed several, he says.'

Breaths were drawn in all around the fireside. Seboth's hands tightened on Tika's.

'Lashek has freed the power within Olam, Lallia and myself. He said you could help us make progress in understanding just what we might be able to do. But I went out anyway this afternoon, after I read Hargon's words, and I called to a Merig with my mind. He had heard of Hargon's killings. I begged him to tell all his kind to beware Return and any armsmen in Hargon's colours.'

Tika continued to stare at the Lord of Far.

'The Merig was good enough to accept my word that his kind could find refuge here. I had thought that he would not listen to me, let alone speak to me after what has passed at Return.'

Tika laughed without humour. 'Most of the creatures I have encountered who use the mind speech, judge each case as it arises. It seems only humans judge one and condemn all.'

Seboth released her hands and moved to sit on pillows near his wife.

'When would you like to begin your search?'

Tika glanced at Gan for his suggestion.

'I think as soon as possible. I do not think it safe to stay too near Hargon now.'

Seboth nodded, scrubbing a hand across his face wearily. 'I must leave tomorrow. Olam will go with you, and an armsman as token escort at least.'

'For the first day or so we will far speak you each sunset, Lallia. I would not risk trying to reach Lord Seboth while he is in Return.' Tika hugged her knees to her chest. 'We will leave the morning after tomorrow. That gives Gan time to arrange supplies and will allow the three of us –' she indicated herself, Maressa and Ren – 'to begin your instruction in the use of power. Lord Seboth, if you choose, we will work with you for a while now, before you must leave for Return?'

The room emptied of all but Lord Seboth, looking a trifle apprehensive, Tika, Maressa and Ren. Ren's silver eyes regarded the Lord of Far.

'We think you need to learn to shield yourself, quickly and thoroughly. That is most important. And if you can learn that readily, there are a few smaller things that might be useful in Return.'

Seboth was amazed at his exhaustion after only a short period of working with the power. Tika and Maressa threw mind probe after mind probe at him, until Seboth could slam a shield into place the instant he sensed their presence approaching. Ren finally smiled.

'You were right Tika – he will be strong indeed, given time and training.'

Tika stretched. 'I will go to Farn and Brin now.'

'I will go to bed.' Ren stood, bowing to Seboth before leaving in Tika's wake.

'And I will begin to show you how to far speak,' Maressa told Seboth quietly when they were alone. 'Tika is with Farn and they are holding their minds closed. Now, open your mind to mine and watch closely what I do.'

Seboth had a mild but persistent headache by the time he went to bid farewell to his guests. Farn's sapphire eyes flashed and sparkled as he bent his long, beautiful face towards the Lord of Far.

'May the stars guide your path Seboth,' he intoned. His eyes whirred faster. 'Only summon me if you believe we should do something interesting with this Hargon.'

Seboth blinked. Tika elbowed Farn sharply in the chest.

'But Tika, this Hargon is not a pleasant creature – I knew so when I first met him,' Farn objected.

'Be that as it may Farn, we do not want to encourage trouble where it might not appear.'

Tika met Seboth's eyes and knew they shared the same thought: trouble was already nearby and Hargon would be at its heart.

The visitors watched as Seboth, at the head of a full escort of armsmen in their green uniforms, rode from the outer court of Seboth's manor. Several women, including Lallia, also watched, but from half shuttered windows, as the riders wound out into the town's narrow streets.

A flash of silvery blue and Farn swooped above the contingent when it emerged from the town gate. He spiralled and pirouetted, then swerved back towards the manor. Tika muttered under her breath. Ren raised a brow in question.

'He is encouraging Seboth to do something awful to Hargon,' she explained irritably. But watching Farn's graceful flight over the manor roof, she was unable to restrain a smile of complicity.

A large part of that day was spent working with Lallia, who showed great promise in the talent of far speaking and also for far seeing. As with her husband, Tika and Ren taught her first to shield herself, then Maressa took over. Maressa was impressed with Lallia's abilities and told the others so.

'She would be an air mage among my people and a powerful one too. In this short time she has learned what it takes years for many to comprehend.'

'Perhaps she just somehow remembers?' Tika suggested. 'I still do not know quite what I can do or how I do many things.' She shivered. 'Farn's healing for instance. I have no real idea of what I did then.'

They were gathered in Seboth's library with a new face among them: Olam introduced Pallin, a grizzled man who reminded Tika strongly of Lorak. It was made plain that both Olam and Lallia had a fondness for the elderly man. Gan later explained that Pallin had played the part of father to Seboth and Olam when their true father was killed in the Ganger Wars. He had devoted his life to serving Seboth and Seboth's family but had reached an age when he should be retired from strenuous duty.

'Where do you hear all this gossip?' Maressa asked Gan with admiration.

Gan laughed. 'Armsmen are the worst of all for gossiping. Seboth has tried to give Pallin lighter duties but the arguments have been heard halfway into the town apparently. And he never won any of them.'

Next morning, the party assembled in the inner court. The three armsmen, with Olam and Ren, were mounted on koninas, and all except Ren led a spare animal which carried supplies. Maressa and Gan climbed onto Brin's crimson back while Tika bade a last goodbye to Lallia within the manor.

'We will make no attempt to contact Seboth,' Tika told her, 'and nor must you. But once he is home again, it will be safe to do so.'

'I wish I could come,' Lallia said wistfully.

Tika grinned. 'Would you bring the baby and a couple of nursemaids too?'

Lallia laughed. 'I know, I know. But one day, I swear I will leave this town and see something else of this world.'

She spoke so forcefully, Tika could only hug her in delight. Running out to the court where Farn waited impatiently, Tika chuckled to herself. She had a feeling Lady Lallia would achieve her ambition.

Chapter Five

In Gaharn, Emla found Ryla icy with rage. The very idea that two Discipline Seniors should attempt a virtual coup within the Asataria seemed preposterous and infuriating. Secretly, she was also upset and worried that these two had been joined by roughly one hundred other Discipline Seniors and Seniors. A mere handful of students remained in the building – those who excelled at fawning and toadying. The vast majority had been ordered to leave. Some of these had returned to their homes laden with books in the hopes of continuing their studies unsupervised, while others had made for the Golden Lady's great House.

And fortunate it was that the House was so large with so many students moving in to it. The great hall was put out of bounds, the students relegated to the fractionally smaller chamber in a distant wing of the House. All three Pavilions were also forbidden to them, although one was at present unused – Ryla deemed it best to forbid entry to any. Many Discipline Seniors and Seniors decided to move out to Emla's House too during this emergency, abandoning their own perfectly pleasant houses in Gaharn City, as Ryla acidly remarked.

One good thing about this influx of students was that they relieved Hani of much of the arduous duties of keeping her two eyes on five young Dragons. Ikram and Nya, Farn's brother and sister, had fully recovered from both shock and injuries caused by Gremara's mad screams. Mischief was their lifeblood and they had inveigled Hani's daughter Deeba into becoming part of their many plots.

Hani's other daughter Lilla was as shy as her mother and, with Shar, preferred to learn than to play constant pranks. Farn's sister Shar was also glad to know the students were willing playmates of the three youngest Dragons. She was very like her mother Kija, by far the most responsible and serious of this brood.

Emla, Bagri and Soran closeted themselves in Emla's study to determine the best and speediest way of evicting Fayet and his followers from the Asataria. Various Discipline Seniors had already been reprimanded for leaving the City and promptly sent back to their own homes. They were instructed to move among the local people, assuring them that the Golden Lady would bring this unprecedented situation to a rapid close.

Generations of humans had lived and worked in Gaharn with never a hint of any sort of trouble among them or the People of the Asataria who governed them with such a light hand. Tension had grown during the cold season with unconfirmed rumours spreading through the City of monsters, created and loosed into the world by the Grey Guardian of the North. No monsters had been seen in Gaharn City, but many families had leaned of their menfolk's deaths in a great battle with the forces of the Grey One. Many more now had crippled husbands, brothers and sons to support, albeit a task made financially easier with the generous pensions paid by the Asatarians.

Soran reported that the City Guards still answered to his authority but the corp of Guards maintained by the Asataria were within that building under Fayet's control. Soran had a plan of the Asataria complex laid out on Emla's table. He pointed to various places as he spoke.

'These seven entrances are all well guarded,' he said. 'All windows at ground level are heavily shuttered. Lady Ryla says that there are ways in from here, and here, which she remembers from her student days. I sent men to check. They found nothing at all here, but there is a door at this point, half its height buried under soil and shrubs.'

Emla pulled her lower lip with long fingers. 'Would it be worth risking entry that way?' she asked.

Soran sat back in his chair. 'Lady I had a thought last night. If I put a squad of men to gain entry there, as a diversion, how many might we get through on the circle?'

Emla stared at her Captain of Guards. Bagri coughed politely.

'Jilla has told me that Fayet asked about moving armies through the circles just before he stormed out of Ryla's presence. If he is still ignorant of how the circles may be used, he would surely keep a large force of guards around the one within the Asataria?'

Soran scowled. 'You are quite right of course. Perhaps we could send some men in both ways, hoping to split Fayet's forces while we made an assault on the main doors?'

'The main doors were specifically built to withstand any attack Soran.'

Soran sighed. 'How well is the Asataria supplied Lady?'

'Far too well I fear, Soran. They could hold out in there without needing any more provisions for another half cycle easily. And there are four wells within too. No Soran, this must end quickly. I will ask Ryla if she can remember any other possible ways in or out, from her wicked student days. Come in,' she called as a knock sounded on the door.

Shan entered and saluted smartly.

'Lady, Elyssa and Speaker Lashek are in the hall, just come from Sapphrea.'

Bagri grinned. 'I am surprised Lashek has actually returned so promptly. Thryssa must have threatened him with something truly dire to make sure he would be here.'

Emla smiled back at the Vagrantian. 'What of the Drogoyan Observer, Ren?'

Shan shrugged. 'He was not with them Lady, or Maressa.'

'I will be down directly Shan. I am sure Speaker Lashek will be in great need of sustenance.'

'He brought a recipe which he has already copied and asked the cooks to make up so we may all marvel,' Shan told her mistress as she closed the door behind her.

Emla rose and went to one of the windows. Snow still lay in sunless corners but most of the gardens were clear now. A student dashed across a stretch of lawn and was knocked to the ground by a mauve blue Dragon. Emla heard shrieks of mirth in her mind as Nya planted herself firmly across the student's back. She turned back to the room.

'I must welcome Speaker Lashek and Elyssa. The High Speaker and her husband will also arrive soon too. Come back here after the noon meal Soran. We must have a firm plan of action drawn up this day.'

Soran saluted.

'I am meeting with my officers as soon as I leave you, Lady. But it would most certainly help matters if Lady Ryla could recall any more ways of sneaking in or out of the Asataria.'

Emla laughed. 'I feel Lady Ryla would most strongly object to your use of the word "sneaking" Soran, but I will see what she might remember.'

Emla greeted Lashek and Elyssa warmly, aware of an air of resolve about Thryssa's young aide. Elyssa handed her the letters from Tika and Gan, which Emla in turn passed to the two ancient ladies enthroned by the fireside.

'I am glad that Tika is going to seek the lost cities,' Nolli announced. 'Even if they find nothing, I believe the child needs some time to accept all that has befallen her. We are apt to forget that she lived as a slave less than a cycle past.'

Jilla looked shocked, as did Lashek.

'I had not heard that, Nolli. A slave? I did not think slaves were kept here?' Jilla sounded perturbed.

'They only keep slaves still in parts of Sapphrea.' Elyssa's tone was matter of fact. 'More specifically, Return has a high population of slaves and I gather they are never given their freedom. Lord Seboth of Far still has "slave families" – descendants of slaves taken during their Ganger Wars – but they were given their freedom over ten cycles past when the Wars ended.'

'From these letters, the news is not good of Lord Hargon's attitude to any of us from outside his lands?' Emla queried.

Lashek shook his head. 'Did they tell you that he has ordered any Merigs in his territory to be killed? Seboth was not pleased to be "summoned" to a council in Return any more than he was that this Hargon also ordered him to destroy any Merigs around Far.'

Hani's head peered anxiously round the side of Nolli's chair and the small Kephi on Nolli's knees chirruped in distress. Tears shone on Nolli's cheeks and Elyssa knelt, putting an arm around the tiny woman's shoulder while her friend and maid Lanni clucked and patted.

'The Merigs are kindly souls. They have long carried messages willingly between the creatures of this land. This is a dreadful thing to hear.'

'Hush,' Elyssa tried to comfort the Delver. 'Seboth called a Merig to him and warned of the danger.'

51

'Seboth did?' Emla asked in astonishment.

'Yes he did.' Lashek tried to look modest. 'He and his Lady wife and his brother Olam are all strong in the power. Or they will be when they are properly instructed. All three had been shielded.'

'Shielded?' Emla felt she was becoming an echo. 'But who might have shielded them?'

Lashek smiled. 'Who knows? But they are being taught to guard themselves even now and will be safe for a while yet.'

Ryla had heard none of the conversation, her mind had been back in the long distant days of her studentship.

'Five more places I can remember,' she now said suddenly. 'Where is the plan Emla?'

Emla nodded to Shan, who sped off up the wide staircase to fetch the plan of the Asataria from Emla's study. Before Shan reappeared, six Guards escorted High Speaker Thryssa and Kwanzi into the hall. Emla went to them, arms outstretched. Thryssa's gaze went quickly round those present and she could not hide her relief at seeing Elyssa, still kneeling by an extremely tiny, extremely old, Delver woman. Retaining Emla's hand in hers, Thryssa greeted the other Vagrantians on her way to the two great chairs by the hearth. She bowed deeply.

'I am Thryssa, High Speaker of Vagrantia,' she said before Emla could introduce her. 'I am greatly honoured to meet the Wise One of the Delvers and you also, Lady Ryla. May the stars guard your souls.'

Kwanzi, behind her, bowed even more deeply.

Tears still glittered on Nolli's face but she gave her sweet toothless smile and reached up to Thryssa.

'Sit with me, child,' she insisted. 'Your Elyssa and Jilla have told us much of Vagrantia but we would always learn more.' Nolli's sharp dark eyes caught the quick exchange of expressions between Jilla and Elyssa and she crowed with laughter. 'Very well. No questions – yet. But sit with me anyway.'

Shan had given the plan of the Asataria to Ryla and now Ryla's voice cut across the greetings and chatter in the hall.

'These are the places. I think at least one of them should still be accessible – this one surely.'

Emla was bending to look when Soran entered, a black scowl

52

on his face. He saluted Emla.

'Seven killed, Lady. Random arrows from high in the Asataria. Seven market people, and two of those women.'

Emla had explained in cogent detail, the problem that had arisen among her own People whilst she was absent in Sapphrea.

'Your difficulty is winkling them out of this building then,' Lashek concluded helpfully when Emla paused for breath.

'May I speak with you privately?' Elyssa murmured to the High Speaker, the change in her eyes still causing Thryssa disquiet.

'Of course child. Would you excuse us briefly Emla?'

'Look!' Lashek exclaimed. 'Lallia's pastries! We must eat them with the reverence they deserve if only your cooks can match Lallia's, Emla!'

Everyone obediently took one of the great pile of pastries and they were all suitably appreciative. Lashek picked up one of the heaped dishes and moved to sit beside Nolli. He had seen her look of true bliss when she took her first taste. Thryssa and Elyssa returned from the doorway whence they had moved for some privacy. Kwanzi saw his wife was troubled and was immediately watchful, unable to rid his mind of the memory of her recent despair.

'Elyssa and I would go to your circle here Emla. I will be able to tell if the circle within your City has been used.' She paused. 'I agree with Bagri that it seems obvious your rebels would set a guard about that circle, whether they are able to use it or no. I think Elyssa has already mentioned that we are able to travel without using the mosaic circles?'

'But it is extremely dangerous!' Kwanzi expostulated, and Lashek nodded, his face serious for once.

Thryssa flicked a hand in dismissal of Kwanzi's objection.

'It can be dangerous, yes. But for this short distance, and using one circle at least, the danger is lessened.'

Emla, Soran and the two old ladies listened closely. Thryssa sat down on the cushions, drawing Elyssa down with her.

'The point is, one must know exactly – and I mean exactly – the place one wishes to reach. A slight error and one could find oneself within the stone of a wall for example.'

Shan was not the only listener to swallow hard. Thryssa frowned, trying to find a way of making herself fully understood.

'Without a circle, I must hold two images, crystal clear in my mind: of the place I am at present, and of the place I wish to transfer to. Absolutely clear – every small detail of both places, whilst saying a chant and moving round as though I stood on a real circle.'

Lashek was leaning forward: he had known nothing of this.

'It is less dangerous,' Thryssa sent a brief smile towards Kwanzi, 'If one of the locations is a real circle, as is the one here Emla.'

There was a silence while Thryssa's words sank into her audience.

'But neither you nor Elyssa knows the Asataria building,' Kwanzi said finally.

'No, but Emla does. An image from her mind to mine, would work satisfactorily.'

'How many could you move in this manner Lady Thryssa?' enquired Soran.

Thryssa shrugged. 'Probably twenty five at most. If I took one group through, Elyssa could follow with the same number. But I think twenty five would be the maximum at one time.'

'If I had even just twenty men and we could reach Lady Kera's rooms, we would have a good advantage, even over the sixty Guards Fayet now commands.' Soran looked to the Golden Lady for her opinion.

'Sixteen Guards on the first transfer and sixteen on the second then,' Emla decided firmly, giving herself no chance to have second thoughts.

'When?' Thryssa asked,

'During the night.' Soran's reply was crisp. 'Lady Kera's rooms are near the top of the Asataria. We will be going down – it is much more difficult to fight trying to climb up stairs. Many if not most will be asleep – they believe they are unassailable. All points are in our favour.'

Bagri nodded, his face alight. 'I shall accompany Elyssa,' he said. It was half statement, half question as he turned to Thryssa.

A slight smile tugged at her mouth. 'I suspected you might,' she agreed mildly.

'Shan and I will travel with you first, Thryssa. Soran, begin selecting the Guards and tell them what you think they need to know of this plan.'

Soran hurried from the hall, his thoughts busy running over each of his Guards' merits among those he would pick for this action.

'As soon as we reach the room you select, Emla, all of us must stand against its walls, leaving as much space as possible for Elyssa to envisage her circle therein.'

Emla nodded her understanding. 'You and Elyssa must come back here at once after the transfer,' she said.

'I think not,' Thryssa replied. 'If the Lady of the Asatarians is fighting there, then the High Speaker of Vagrantia, new allies though we may be, will remain in the room chosen as the transfer point.' She raised a hand to prevent argument from both Lashek and Kwanzi. 'If wounded are brought there, it will be much easier to bring them through with a proper circle at this end to focus on.'

'Then I come too,' Kwanzi insisted. 'I am a healer Thryssa, at least I can offer first treatment.'

'I would join you too,' Lashek pleaded.

Thryssa reached across to catch the earth mage's hand. 'No Lashek. You are the next most senior Speaker. You take my place if needs be. And you will give strength to Jilla here.' Thryssa turned to look up at Nolli and Ryla. 'Jilla is a gifted air mage. And she has been to your City and within the Asataria. She will easily find Emla's force and will watch what befalls. You can see what she sees quite simply by linking your minds to either her or to Lashek.'

Nolli and Ryla nodded, Ryla's transparent skin flushed with excitement.

'Have you any questions regarding my part in this? If not, perhaps you have a room where Elyssa and I may get some rest. It is tiring work we will be doing, unlikely as that may appear to any who watch us.'

Jilla smiled. 'Use my room. I will show you the way.'

'It would be best if you rested too, Lady Emla,' said Lashek gently. 'And I do not know if anyone has discussed with you our abilities with the power? Although long unused in this kind of context, I can assure you we will help as we can.'

Ryla studied Lashek with growing interest although Emla frowned a little.

'Why don't you go to your room, Emla – a most sensible suggestion. Speaker Lashek can help us eat up all these very delicious pastries.'

Emla regarded the ancient Discipline Senior with suspicion but got to her feet anyway as Jilla came down the stairs.

'I trust Thryssa and Elyssa will be comfortable? Come then Shan, we must find some suitable leathers and a rest might be a good idea.'

Following Emla to the staircase, Shan grinned over her shoulder at Bagri.

'Captain Soran will have spare leathers for you, I am sure.'

Bagri rose with alacrity and hurried to find Soran, leaving Jilla and Lashek to an inquisition by two very determined old ladies.

Eventually Hani took pity on Lashek and Jilla, firmly ordering Shar to escort the Vagrantians out for a breath of evening air. They escaped to the sound of Nolli and Ryla arguing fiercely with the pale green Dragon.

'Stars above,' Lashek groaned. 'I am sure we must have missed our supper. Do they never run out of questions?'

Jilla laughed heartlessly. 'I haven't noticed that they do.'

'It is just that they want to know everything,' Shar tried to explain.

Lashek stopped halfway down the wide flight of steps outside the huge main doors.

'Of course they do, and quite rightly so,' he apologised. 'But I will fade away without regular meals do you see?'

Shar's eyes whirred in alarm at the prospect of Lady Emla's guest fading away. Jilla gave Lashek a glare of annoyance and then tried to explain what the earth mage meant. Shar refused to allow Lashek to wander the gardens. Instead, she insisted he and Jilla return at once to the house through a side entrance and search for food to keep Lashek healthy. She sat outside the door to make sure the two Vagrantians could not slip back out, and Jilla muttered beneath her breath.

'Really Lashek, that dear Dragon is truly worried now that you will vanish. She is only half a cycle old, it is quite unpleasant of you to upset her so.'

'I am sorry.' Lashek sounded genuinely contrite. 'But I am also hungry.'

'When are you not?' Jilla snapped, pushing him into the small dining chamber.

A maid appeared almost as soon as Jilla tugged the bell rope, and then rushed away to fetch food for them. Soran's head poked round the door when Jilla had finished her meal and Lashek was, she judged, approximately halfway through his. Jilla smiled at Soran. She had found him pleasant company since she arrived here. He had not a scrap of magic about him and Jilla found that fact very restful. She poured him a mug of tea and waved him to a chair.

'Have you picked the men for tonight?' she enquired.

He nodded. 'Some men have gone into the City with word from Lady Emla to the Discipline Seniors and Seniors who are in their own homes. She says they will use power against the few of their colleagues who have chosen to side with Fayet. The townsfolk have been warned to keep within doors until instructed differently. The Seniors who are healers are ordered to be ready at Lady Emla's summons.'

'Emla could have mind spoken them, surely?' Jilla frowned.

'She fears that those within the Asataria could overhear her should they have set a watch for such things.' Soran shrugged. 'I know not how such matters work, but if my Lady orders word taken personally to the City, so shall it be.'

An air of expectancy pervaded the Lady's great House as the night deepened. Students had been told that something was to happen and they were to be ready should they be called. The household staff were still busy: they remembered the House filled with wounded Guards brought from the mountains but a scant time before.

Emla and Shan came down to the hall, both wearing hardened leather jerkins over their shirts. Swords hung from their belts and dagger hilts protruded above. Suddenly Ryla seemed lost for words, as if she only now realised that this was no game. Kwanzi appeared with the High Speaker and Elyssa. Soran came in from the main doors and saluted.

'Thirty-two Guards are outside Lady. I have posted extra

57

Guards around the Pavilion.'

Emla nodded. She opened her mouth to say something to the two old ladies, then shut it again. Stooping, she gave each a quick hug and a kiss on each withered cheek, then spun away, marching towards the door, Shan at her heels. Bagri waited outside and walked with Kwanzi and Shan behind Thryssa and Elyssa. The Vagrantian women had the image of Kera's room starkly clear in their minds, even to the layer of dust Emla remembered from her last visit.

The second group halted with Bagri and Elyssa outside the Pavilion, while the first group went in. Emla touched Thryssa's arm lightly.

'You do not have to do this Thryssa. While I am more grateful than I can say for your help and support, you do not have to do this.'

Thryssa smiled. 'Friends are there to help each other, are they not? In truth, I am interested in this situation.' She grimaced. 'I fear I face a similar problem when I return to Vagrantia.'

Emla stared at the High Speaker, unable to decipher her cryptic remark. She shrugged, took her place with Soran at the head of the double line of Guards and followed Thryssa and Kwanzi onto the circle.

Chapter Six

Berri, the acting Wise One of the Delvers during Nolli's absence, came from the Domain to add her lesser strength to Dessi's. Four of their most accomplished healers were to help Dessi focus her power on Observer Babach's worst injuries. The burns he had suffered were, in many parts of his torso, deep enough to bury a fist inside. His body and mind were severely shocked, his pulse weak and erratic.

Fenj and Kija were horrified at the sight of such wounds and they willingly offered their strength to the healing process just begun. Mim and Ashta had gone again to the hidden cave in the Domain, on Gremara's instruction. Once more, so she told the Dragon Lord, he would know which egg to take back to help Babach's mending. Now Mim leaned against Ashta, his gold scaled arm draped across her shoulder. He had no part to play in this, other than to watch.

Chakar knelt at Babach's head, aware of the tremendous surge of magical force rising around her. She watched the tiny Delver girl Dessi lean forward, her hands held flat above a blackened hole high in Babach's chest. Chakar felt the child falter and she held her breath. Then she felt Kija's mellow voice murmuring to Dessi in a soothing hum of sound.

Dessi steadied, drew a deep breath and allowed her mind to sink within the man's ruined chest, as once she had watched Tika healing Farn. Chakar watched in disbelief when slowly the gaping hole turned from black, to red, to pink, and began to close. Chakar was only aware of the long passing of time because her legs and back started to cramp as they had when she had worked so long over Kadi. But dreadful as she had thought Kadi's wounds, they were as a child's grazed knee compared to what Dessi was trying to mend.

The Delver shuddered, moving her hands and revealing a patch of new flesh that looked sore, but was at least whole. Berri pushed a flask of water at the child, urging her to drink. Then Dessi knelt straight again and moved her hands to the next great pit in Babach's body. The day passed unnoticed by all those watching in the great hall of the Stronghold until, finally, Dessi toppled bonelessly to one side. But Mim was there, waiting it seemed for the moment Dessi reached the end of her strength.

All who had witnessed this feat of healing seemed to exhale their long-held breath in gusty sighs that swept around the hall. Other healers came now to assist the four who knelt still at Babach's side. Imshish and Kera came to help Chakar to her feet, but her legs screamed in agony and Imshish simply carried her to a chair. Lorak appeared silently at Chakar's elbow and without a word, she held out her hand for his flask.

'Kija's all right, but the old fella, he be a bit shaky,' Lorak frowned. Chakar had a firm grip on his flask. 'Well then, you keep that 'un. I've more in my workroom.'

Chakar managed a wobbly grin as Voron bent over her.

'Try some,' she suggested.

Voron sniffed cautiously and politely declined. 'The Offering Finn Rah would no doubt appreciate it better than I,' he smiled.

'I will hear all your news later Voron.' Chakar groaned, straightening her legs carefully and bending them again. 'For now I have Babach to tend and I cannot concentrate on anything but that.'

'No, Observer.' A quiet voice spoke above her head.

She twisted and saw the Vagrantian boy with the silver eyes smiling shyly at her. 'There are more than enough of us to care for Observer Babach now. You must sleep and be fresh for your turn of nursing tomorrow.'

Chakar's mouth opened, closed, and so did her eyes. Imshish caught her before she slid off the chair.

'What have you done to her?' Voron asked in panic.

But Imshish chuckled, gathering up the small body in his arms again. 'An extremely good example of a sleep suggestion,' he told Voron. 'Or Lorak's restorative.'

Daro bowed and moved across to Fenj where the massive black Dragon reclined against the wall.

Imshish stood watching Daro murmuring to Fenj and Lorak, then smiled at the still frowning Voron.

'Somehow the silvering of Daro's eyes has accelerated his abilities. I understand that he seemed an average boy until this change in his eyes. Now, he could equal Maressa in air magery I would guess – he has been working with Dessi a great deal. But he seems able to do much more than just work with air.'

Voron followed Imshish towards the fire where the four Delver healers and Dessi already lay on pallets in the deep sleep of total exhaustion. Voron thanked Imshish for his kindness and settled beside Chakar. He saw the boy they called the Dragon Lord sitting cross-legged at Dessi's side, the pale green Dragon who seemed his constant companion was curled against another Dragon.

Despite Voron's weariness, panic and confusion, he had registered that Dragon when he arrived here as being one of the most beautiful creatures he had ever seen. Now he found himself staring at the gold scales glittering in the lamp and firelight until his gaze was drawn to the many faceted honey coloured eyes. Kija's voice spoke in Voron's mind.

'The stars must surely have lent strength to Baryet's wings, Voron of Drogoya, to bring your old one here so swiftly. I think only Dessi or perhaps my daughter Tika, could have effected such a healing.'

'Is she your daughter?' Voron asked, looking at Ashta.

Laughter rippled through his mind.

'No. This is Ashta, Hani's daughter. She is soul bonded to the Dragon Lord. Sleep now Voron and I will tell you stories tomorrow such as you will find hard to believe. But they are true nonetheless. Sleep, Voron of Drogoya. You are safe here.'

And so Voron slept while Berri and other Delvers watched over Babach's unconscious form.

Berri had accompanied Mim to the hidden cave in the Domain and watched when the Dragon Lord moved directly to one niche. His taloned fingers closed around an egg and a gold chain winked as it swung loose from his hand. Now that egg, its back shelled in black obsidian and its front filled with a bright yellow topaz, nestled at the crook of Babach's neck and shoulder, pulsing in unison with the Observer's own heartbeat.

Mim's still-smooth palm closed round the pendant hanging from his neck. Gremara refused to tell him of these strange eggs, but this was the second time they had been used in a great healing. Observer Chakar had brought her egg from the land of Drogoya, saying it had belonged, once upon a time, to Myata, the founder of the Order of which Chakar was now the head.

Dessi was strongly attracted to the teachings of Myata, in which Chakar had been instructing her. Mim too found the ideas of great interest: they felt somehow familiar to him, as if he had heard them long ago and now nudged at his memory. He knew though, that no Nagum in his village had spoken to him of such things.

There were similarities of course between Nagum beliefs and the Drogoyan Myata: both cared for growing things, revered the life-giving land, and abhorred violence. But Mim could see clearly still the devastation wreaked by Linvaks – his village destroyed, himself the sole survivor. And he knew that he could never stand by and allow such murder to take place – he would fight now, fight and kill. He glanced down at Dessi, glad to see some colour tingeing her ashen cheeks, knowing she was undamaged by the great effort she had expended save for the need for a long sleep.

The Dragon Lord appeared relaxed but part of his mind travelled his Stronghold, touching a Snow Dragon's thoughts within the Domain of Asat, drifting lightly over Kadi. Briefly, his thought flared far to the south east and the Circles of Vagrantia. Instantly, Gremara was alerted to her Lord's presence.

'Is all well my Lord? The healing was successful?'

'Yes,' Mim replied. 'All rest here now. What of the trouble in Vagrantia?'

He felt a tremor of amusement pass through their linked minds.

'Worry not of Vagrantia yet, my Lord. I watch carefully, un-known to their mages. Rest now yourself Lord, and all will be well.'

In the morning, Kera and Nesh busied themselves helping the chamberlain's staff distribute mugs of tea to the many who had slept in the hall. Pausing by Babach, Kera looked anxiously at the Observer's blistered face. Berri smiled.

'We are keeping him asleep, Lady Kera. His body will fully heal more rapidly while he is still. He will wake in a while then we shall make him sleep again, and so on for the next days.'

'Those great holes,' Kera ventured, still unable to believe that Dessi had managed to close them.

Setting down her mug, Berri gently raised the light, dampened cover over Babach's chest. Kera stared in awe at the smooth skin which looked healthy although tender. She shook her head in wonder and Berri replaced the cover.

'Kija touched his mind twice during the night and she told him what had been done. He understands the need for rest now – he is old, even by Dragon reckoning so Kija says.'

Kera's next call was to Lorak. The gardener had just emerged from his workroom, Bikram bleary-eyed at his shoulder. In answer to Kera's question Lorak gave a brief nod.

'Fenj sleeps now. That young lad Daro, he came and sent him to sleep. Best thing for the old fella.'

Lula tiptoed down Fenj's neck and wound herself around Lorak's ankles. He scooped her up and she buzzed urgently, butting her head under his chin.

'I know. I'll find you some food, don't you fret.'

Guards who had fallen asleep where they had sat watching Dessi heal the stranger, now roused themselves and went quietly to the tables where breakfast had been set. Gradually the hall emptied, Guards going down to the lower growing areas with Bikram and Lorak, and many Delvers returning to the Domain.

Mim and Ashta left to fly to Arak to visit the slowly recovering Kadi. Voron sat with Kera, Imshish and Jal while Nesh spoke with the first awakening Delver healer. Lula suddenly chirruped and raced down Fenj's back to sit in front of the long black face. His eyelids lifted and prismed eyes whirred the shadows on snow colour.

At the same moment, Kija moved towards the low pallet on which Observer Babach lay. Her golden head lowered to study him closely. The first thing Babach saw in the Night Lands, was the most beautiful face he could ever have imagined.

High on her favourite ledge in Talvo Circle, Gremara lay soaking up the warmth of the sun. She rejoiced that she should be sane again after so very many cycles. Tilting her silver scaled face against the black rock, she watched Jeela indulgently. The small ivory Dragon was playing in the air currents, occasionally swooping to frighten a small flock of lumen from their grazing.

They were so young for the tasks ahead of them. That was the one thought that brought back a touch of melancholy to Gremara. Her long-awaited Dragon Lord was a child, even allowing for the much lesser span his kind could expect. He would live far longer now, with his new Dragon blood but he was still a scant sixteen or so cycles old she judged.

And this little Jeela – only half of one cycle! Gremara marvelled at the workings of destiny, fate, the old gods' will, that such children would hold the Balance between them. Unknown to Mim, she had bespoken Kija and had learned of the other soul bonded child, the one Kija named as her daughter. That child too carried one of the precious egg pendants, and Kija told Gremara that her eyes were silvered. Gremara understood a great deal since her flight to the limits of the air that surrounded this world. Her memories had become unmuddled, and she exulted in her clarity of thought.

There was so much to teach Jeela. She could transfer the memories, as had happened to her, but Gremara was reluctant to take that step yet. Although Gremara had straightened everything in her head, or at least those Beyond had done so for her, she was still apprehensive of giving Jeela all the information she held. Jeela would absorb the memories intact and concise, as had the first few silver Dragons. Then the increasing tendency to lonely madness had destroyed the coherence in their minds.

If the Dragon Lord had not come now, young as he was, Gremara suspected that the plans of those Beyond would have been cast into irrevocable disarray. But he had come, and so had Jeela. Jeela would succeed Gremara in due time here at Talvo and out in the wider world. There would be no need for a silver Dragon to live in solitude, waiting for the day of reckoning.

Gremara stretched luxuriously. She had fed well yesterday, her body was warmed by the sun and her heart by the sight of Jeela spinning over Talvo Circle. She sent a wisp of her attention right across the adjoining Circle of Parima to the Circle of Fira, where dwelt the water adepts. She noted that the gateways had been sealed in Fira, the entrances closed and heavily barred which should give access to tunnels leading to both Parima and Kedara

Circles.

Gremara's thought drifted across the lakes and pools of Fira and picked up the rumours of Speaker Kallema's intentions. Gremara withdrew, tucking the small items of information into a corner of her mind for later consideration and peeped into Kedara Circle. So many air mages' thoughts were swirling into the upper atmosphere that she pulled back at once. But there was no undercurrent of menace there, as she had felt in Fira. She did not bother to spy on Parima or Segra, knowing already that there was nothing to give rise to her concern within them.

Gremara yawned, giving a rare glimpse of the curved fangs that could inflict fearsome damage. She twisted her long sinuous neck over her shoulder, resting her head between her wings. The silver Dragon slept, while the ivory Dragon danced on the breeze above her.

Thryssa's new first councillor, Pajar, sat scowling over a parchment recently arrived through the circle from the Stronghold. He rested his head on one hand, letting the scroll slowly re wind. One full cycle was all the time he had spent training directly under Alya for this position, and it was usual to spend at least ten times that long in training.

Thryssa wrote of some rebellion in Gaharn and that she personally had allied Vagrantia formally with Lady Emla's People. She was about to participate in some sort of action alongside the Golden Lady: she failed to specify exactly what that entailed. Thryssa listed several topics with which she had been involved prior to the appearance of, first the affliction among the Vagrantians and second, the Lady Emla's unexpected arrival here.

She explained to Pajar how she had intended to conclude these many and varied issues and, in the event of her not returning to Parima, all such information was to be presented to Speaker Lashek of Segra when he returned. Lashek was the senior Speaker who would naturally assume the rank of High Speaker on Thryssa's death. It was at that point that Pajar clutched his head and stopped reading.

Stars be merciful – but what was Thryssa up to? She must have put herself in a perilous position to send her councillor what was virtually a document dictating her final wishes. Pajar raised his head at a light rap at the door. Speaker Orsim of Kedara came into the room. Uninvited, he sat opposite Pajar, glancing briefly at the loosely wound scroll secured under Pajar's hand.

'News from Gaharn?' he enquired.

'I have not read it all, but the High Speaker is in what sounds dreadfully like a battle situation.'

'What? May I see it?'

Pajar did not hesitate. Orsim was as trusted as was Lashek: it was merely tradition that barred air or water mages from the High Speakership.

Pushing the scroll across the table, he admitted: 'I was too shocked to finish it at once.' He blushed, the colour in his face clashing unfortunately with the flame of his hair.

Orsim raised a brow, flattening the parchment under his hands.

'I reached the part where she designates Speaker Lashek formally as her successor.' Pajar clutched his head again while Orsim bent over the familiar, close written script.

'Hmm.' Orsim sat back, the scroll whispering into a curl again. 'Well Pajar, there is absolutely nothing we can do to influence whatever is happening in Gaharn, so I suggest you try to put it from your mind for now. But remember, Thryssa was raised High Speaker because of her many strengths and her wisdom. She is most certainly not a fool. Now, I am here because of new reports from Kedara.'

Orsim crossed his legs and regarded the young first councillor of Parima shrewdly.

'Chornay, Daro's friend who chose to come with him here to the Corvida, has made friends with those three poor creatures Thryssa had removed from Fira Circle.'

Pajar nodded. He had been appalled to learn that Speaker Kallema had ordered the virtual imprisonment of the three whose eyes had silvered.

'They were all severely frightened, both by their confinement and by the deluge of hatred directed at them by the majority of Fira's adepts.'

Pajar nodded again. 'I heard that even their parents turned against them.'

'Well, Chornay was outraged at things they began to tell him of their treatment within Fira.' He paused thoughtfully. 'I would have said that both Daro and Chornay were average students Pajar, but Daro showed a great increase in ability when his eyes changed.' The Speaker shrugged. 'Some of that seems to have affected Chornay – he is far in advance of his standard now. I had to reprimand him, mildly of course, but he sent his mind into Fira last night.'

'We know that the access tunnels to Parima and Kedara are closed,' Pajar interjected.

'Yes, but Chornay said the waters of the two larger lakes within Fira were agitated, bubbling. Almost as though they were being heated.'

Pajar looked alarmed. 'The volcanoes are long dead surely? There are still the hot springs but no molten rock has ever been seen here in all our time of occupation.'

Orsim wandered over to the window. The Corvida was two leagues from the tunnel to Fira Circle, and four from Kedara's tunnel. He looked to his right, across the expanse of Parima, to the rim which bordered Talvo.

'I consulted Pachela. She says there is no activity beneath the earth at present.'

Pajar's face showed only incomprehension. Orsim restrained a sigh and sought patience. Pajar would do very well as first councillor once he had more confidence in himself, but Orsim found him still far too nervous of his position.

'Pachela thinks Kallema is planning something, quite out of our experience. I agreed with the child once I had gone over all the facts she could produce. I have ordered that the water supplies for Kedara, Segra and Parima be checked at once.'

Pajar stared at him. 'But what could they do?'

'Pachela says – and the three from Fira agree – that Kallema's mages could redirect the water sources from our Circles, or conversely overload them, or even open more.'

'So either drought or flooding would result.' Pajar's brain at last began to work in the manner which had first brought him to Thryssa's attention as a future councillor. Water had always been in abundant supply, even when the air mages reported parched conditions beyond Vagrantia's towering walls.

'Flooding,' Pajar concluded. 'A much quicker way to ruin our crops, and, depending on the amount of water Fira can redirect, more damage to houses and, stars forfend, to the people.'

Pajar went to the door leading to a larger general office where several scribes sat at work. He murmured something and returned to his chair.

'I have asked for Shema to join us,' he told Orsim, 'and for Chornay to bring the three Firans.'

The Segran councillor arrived first and listened in silence while Orsim outlined their concern. He had just finished when Chornay came in with the three silver-eyed youngsters from Fira. Pajar was immediately aware of both Shema and Orsim projecting calmness throughout the room, although he suspected the three Firans were still too upset to notice.

The two girls and the boy had not the typical appearance of most water adepts. All three were shorter and stockier than the average Firan and even more unusually, one of the girls had dark brown pupils in her silver eyes rather than the normal pale blue or grey. The other girl and boy both had blue pupils, made even more brilliant set as they were against the surrounding silver.

Shema smiled at them and suggested they made themselves comfortable. Pajar followed the earth mage's lead offering tea or berry juice, which offer they accepted.

'We hear worrying news of Fira,' Shema began smoothly. 'Speaker Orsim and Pajar believe the Speaker and Assembly plan to raise the waters of the Circles against us. Would you think this is either likely or even possible?'

The shorter of the girls, Graza, glanced at her two friends, then nodded.

'They spoke of nothing else when they had shut us in that barn.'

The other girl, Mokray, interrupted, 'We were so afraid, suddenly dragged from the infirmary and thrown into that place. Kralo suggested that we concentrate on trying to hear them to stop us from being so scared.'

Shema's gaze moved along to the boy. 'Were you not afraid too, Kralo?'

He looked startled. 'Of course I was, Councillor Shema, but it seemed to be the most sensible thing to do. If we were very careful, we could find out what they planned for us without them being aware. We could not get out: the door was barred and guards stood all around the building.' He shivered slightly. 'Before this happened to our eyes, we had all asked the Assembly for permission to come to Parima for assessment, but we were all refused.'

'And we were not the only ones,' Graza added. 'Quite a number have asked to leave, during the last two or three cycles.' She dropped her gaze to her hands, twisted tightly in her lap.

Mokray stared straight at Shema. 'They just disappeared. We thought they must have gained permission and come here, but Chornay has checked for us. There is no record of them ever being here, yet they are no longer in Fira.'

Chapter Seven

The few members of the Order of Sedka who escaped the killing frenzy made their way to various Chapter Houses in the hope of finding sanctuary. The crazed bloodlust seeped outwards from the Menedula and paused for a few days to ensure the total annihilation of the town of Syet. That pause gave some of the fleeing Observers, Aspirants and Kooshak hope that they might escape completely. A handful of such refugees made their way on foot and horseback to the north-west, towards the House of Oblaka.

Two Kooshak who were travelling healers met on the shoulder of the Gara Mountain and together made their way down to the town of Valoon. They found an inn where they could obtain a much needed meal and, for a price, horses to carry them on to Oblaka. There were few customers in the common room when they arrived in mid afternoon, but the innkeeper, a barrel of a man, agreed that he could supply both meal and horses.

He brought the food himself, introduced himself as Volk and looked pointedly at the obsidian beads the Kooshak wore at their throats. The woman gave him a wan smile.

'I am Kooshak Sarryen, and my travelling companion is Kooshak Arryol.'

Volk nodded. 'In a bit of a hurry are you?'

There was the slightest pause before either Kooshak replied, which could be accounted for by the fact that they were eating.

'Yes, Goodmaster Volk. We need to reach Oblaka at all speed.'

Volk nodded again. 'Trouble all ways,' he pronounced.

Forks halted midway to mouths. 'All ways?' Arryol queried.

'Aye. Word came yesterday that Oblaka House and town both be afire. People gone crazy.' He studied each Kooshak shrewdly. 'Trouble where you came from then?'

Sarryen laid her fork on her plate and reached for her bowl of tea.

'Goodmaster Volk, there is very bad trouble on the other side of the Gara. If it reaches here, you will not be safe even in this well built stone inn of yours.' Her silver eyes held Volk transfixed. 'We believe that the only hope for any of us is to reach the Oblaka.'

When Volk would have protested and repeated his tale of madness and fire in the Oblaka area, Sarryen raised her hand. She glanced quickly at Arryol, then back to Volk. 'We, who follow Myata closer than we do Sedka, have been taught, and so we believe, that there is always a place of safety at the Oblaka. So there we must go. And I strongly urge that you hide your valuables, pack up your family and join us at once.'

Volk rocked gently back and forth on the balls of his feet for a moment.

'Know an Observer called Ren Salar do you?'

Arryol frowned. 'Yes, I do. Except he is an Offering, not an Observer. Why?'

'Offering is he?' Volk pursed his mouth in a soundless whistle. 'I thought it strange that an Observer be travelling without no badge of office and now you say he be an Offering. In a great hurry to get to Oblaka too, him and his friend.'

'Please, think about coming with us Master Volk. We leave as soon as you can ready the horses for us.' Sarryen spoke earnestly.

The innkeeper made no reply, only turned away and vanished to the kitchens behind the bar.

'So Ren Salar is in Oblaka. I had heard that he had suddenly left the Menedula. The message I received said that if any of us came across him, we were to tell him that his presence was urgently needed back there.'

Sarryen drank the last of the tea.

'I do not know him myself. I wonder who travelled with him. It seems most odd that he was wearing no insignia.'

Arryol counted some coins out onto the table to pay for their food. 'Maybe he heard something of what was to happen. I know he was a protégé of Babach's.' His eyes met Sarryen's. 'And Babach was from Oblaka originally I was told.'

'So, an Offering of the Order of Sedka could well be a

follower of Myata,' Sarryen suggested.

'Finn Rah never hid the fact that she believed Sedka's teachings had been corrupted. I attended her theory classes years past, and she strongly advocated that we study Myata's teachings much more deeply than we were expected to.' Arryol got to his feet. 'It was she who proposed me for acceptance within the Order of Myata.'

'Me too,' Sarryen said with a smile.

When Arryol rapped his knuckles on the bar counter, Volk appeared at once. He lifted a bulging pack onto the counter and propped a staff against it.

'Think you be right,' he said curtly, as a tall beanpole of a man came from the kitchens. The newcomer began folding shutters across the front windows, securing them with horizontal iron bars. Volk went out to the entrance and shut the heavy doors, locking them and also barring them.

'This way out.'

The two Kooshak silently followed Volk through the kitchens and emerged into the stableyard. A scrawny boy was leading a horse from a large barn.

The boy tied the horse he'd been leading to the rail and ran back to the barn.

A much younger version of Volk, and female into the bargain, came round the side of the inn laden with various bags and bundles. Two children carried more parcels at her side. Volk muttered to himself then spoke aloud to the Kooshak.

'Daughter and her husband Povar,' he nodded at the beanpole, who was trying to relieve the woman of some of her burdens. 'Their two children. And I won't leave Rivan. Don't know where he's from but he turned up here three years past and works hard.'

The ragged boy glanced at Volk at the sound of his name.

'Fetch another two, one for all those bundles and one for you Rivan.'

The boy raced again to the barn.

Sarryen and Arryol were surprised at how speedily they were mounted and their little cavalcade moving out of a small gate behind the barn. Volk led them up an alley and onto a wooded track behind the inn. Arryol looked over his shoulder and saw no one at all in the main street.

'Where is everyone?' he asked Volk quietly.

The innkeeper shot him a quick look. 'Most already gone up to the mountains to their summer cabins. People round here smell trouble quick though. Any still here, hiding themselves away.'

'How far to the Oblaka? – I have never been there.' Sarryen nudged her horse closer to Volk's flank.

'Three days,' was the short answer. 'And if you Kooshak be able to shield, that may be a good idea.'

Sarryen let Arryol move alongside. 'I will shield today – I should have thought of it before.'

Arryol nodded. 'Tell me if you tire and I will take over.' He looked unhappy. 'It is not something I have practised much, not having felt the need to do so before.'

Sarryen smiled wryly. 'Nor me, but I think we must now.'

They followed the same route taken earlier by Ren Salar and Voron, and encountered no people and no difficulties during the next two days. The Kooshak had found shielding tired them quickly at first but took turns every few hours. By the second day, they were much easier with the procedures involved and were more confident of their ability to shield the party. Dawn of the third day gave them their first glimpse of what was left of the town of Oblaka.

Volk had led them along a narrow trail a league or so higher than the more well-used track taken by Ren and Voron. As they came clear of the woodland, three creatures rose from the undergrowth bordering the path and attacked. Arryol was shielding them but only from prying minds, and Sarryen snapped at him to maintain the shielding even as she swung her horse round to protect his side.

Volk and his son-in-law Povar freed their staves and proved to have a great facility with the weapons, the wood humming through the air before crashing into an attacker's skull. Rivan pushed himself and the pack horse towards Volk's daughter and grandchildren and drew a wicked looking knife from beneath his layers of rags. Sarryen noted that their assailants were human, although their faces were contorted into bestial grimaces. And their eyes burned like coals.

Quite calmly, she pushed her magic into the one nearest to her.

He stiffened and started to turn towards her. Sarryen flicked her hand and he fell, his heart ruptured. Povar and Volk were finding that no matter how many blows they landed – which should have proved fatal to any ordinary being – did not even slow these creatures. Sarryen sat relaxed on her horse and burst the heart of first one, then the last. Volk and Povar looked at her. She realised she was shaking badly enough that she had trouble staying in her saddle. Arryol caught her arm, riding close to support her. Without a word, Volk moved into the lead again, Povar at the rear, and they rode on.

The town still smouldered but they saw no living creatures, human, animal, or whatever they were that had attacked them.

'I have not seen a case of the affliction before,' Arryol said softly. 'But that was what had happened to those poor souls was it not?'

Sarryen managed to turn a little to stare at him.

'Those "poor souls" would have killed all of us without compunction Arryol. And probably eaten us.' She faced forward again in silence, wracked with physical and mental trembling. Never would she have imagined herself capable of using her healer's knowledge to take a life. Never. Yet she had just done exactly that.

Volk skirted the town, all of them alert and wary of every breeze that ruffled a bush, or pushed a half charred door into motion. The two Kooshak looked up towards the Oblaka complex on the cliff top. They saw that it too was a burnt out ruin.

'You know where to go Goodmaster Volk?' Sarryen asked, her teeth chattering with her shaking.

'Aye.' After a few more paces, Volk glanced back at Sarryen. 'Delivered things now and then to an Observer. Lives away from the main House. Showed me a couple of ways up and down.' He turned away again.

They gave the horses their heads to pick their own way up the steep uneven hillside, on a faint path more suited to goats than to men or horses. They wound round a great solitary boulder and then on again, across a treacherous scree slope. A shout came from above them and someone waved. Then another head appeared and a grey haired woman stepped clear of what seemed to be solid rock.

'Finn Rah,' Sarryen managed.

'Yes. Come. As promised, there is safety in the Oblaka. Arryol release your shielding, others are covering you for the moment, and help Sarryen inside.' The Offering studied Volk and his daughter, the jade green in her silver eyes glittering with amusement. 'It may be a tight squeeze, but we will get you inside too, Goodmaster Volk.'

Sarryen woke to find herself in a tiny stone room, just big enough to hold the narrow pallet on which she lay, a small table and a stool. A lamp glowed on the table and looking round as she pushed herself upright, she realised there was no window. She rubbed her hands over her face and through her hair, finding that someone had undone her braid. Her disorientation vanished as memory flooded back. Finn Rah was here. Sarryen remembered seeing her outside, then she had been led stumbling, and at one point crawling, through cracks in the rock. Then nothing, until now. But she was safe. She was in, or rather under, the Oblaka. The door opened and Finn Rah squeezed into the tiny room.

'I thought you had awoken.' She smiled, handing Sarryen a bowl of tea. She sat on the stool and watched the Kooshak sip. 'You have slept two days. We thought it best, after what you had to do.'

Sarryen shivered, remembering.

'Stay in bed if you wish,' Finn began, but Sarryen shook her head.

'No thank you. I would like to know more of this place.'

Finn Rah smiled again. 'I suspected that you might. One of the students will come and show you where to wash and get more tea. When you have had a good look around, she will bring you to me.'

'Volk and his family?' Sarryen asked suddenly. 'They can stay here too can they not?'

'Well of course they can. Volk began doing various errands for Observer Chakar when he was a small boy – difficult as that may be to imagine now.' She grinned wickedly. 'We feared that he and his daughter were stuck fast a couple of times on the way in. But the joy of having an expert cook.' Finn rolled her eyes in bliss.

'Volk's daughter?'

'No, no. The beanpole. I swear he could make a feast from oatmeal and turnips.' Finn Rah rose. 'Melena will be along shortly, and I will see you later.'

The student Melena arrived with a pile of clothing, brushes and combs, small rounds of different coloured and scented soaps, and a shy smile.

'Kooshak Arryol is in the infirmary. We have five badly-burned patients still whom our healers are struggling to help. Already Kooshak Arryol has done a great deal for them.'

'While I have been lying about in bed,' Sarryen said in a tone of self-disgust. She pushed away the quilt and put her feet on the floor.

'Oh no. Oh Kooshak Sarryen, I was not criticising.' Melena looked aghast.

Sarryen studied the girl. She was very young indeed, yet her eyes were already silvered around grey pupils. Sarryen patted the bed beside her, and Melena sat nervously.

'You do not need to be formal child. I am a Kooshak, yes, but my name is just Sarryen, which is what I prefer to be called.'

'But you are Kooshak,' Melena argued. 'You could be an Offering.'

Sarryen sighed. 'Some have those kinds of ambitions child. I knew from the time I entered the Menedula as a student that I wished to be a Kooshak – to travel the land, meeting the people. I could never have endured being confined to the Menedula for years at a time – it was hard enough being a student enclosed there. So. I am Sarryen, and you are Melena. Tell me what is your field of study, then tell me what befell the Oblaka, while I dress.'

'Shall I brush your hair Koo – Sarryen?' Melena asked, watching Sarryen sort through the heap of clothes.

Without looking at the girl, Sarryen touched her mind gently and found a genuine need to be of service within the child. She handed her a brush.

'No one has brushed my hair for me since I left home for the Menedula,' she smiled. 'It would be wonderful if you would do it for me now.'

Sarryen was amazed by the extent of the caverns which Melena showed her. She encountered Volk in the common room, staring morosely into a bowl of tea.

'Had to leave my horses loose on the hill,' he grumbled. 'Probably get theirselves eaten.'

A student bringing Sarryen some hot food grinned. 'Master Volk is going to show us the arts of brewing later today,' he said.

Volk brightened fractionally. 'Which of these caves will I be able to use then?' he asked. He heaved his bulk out from behind the table and rolled after the student.

When Sarryen had eaten enough, Melena led her along the passages to Chakar's sitting room and left her at the door. Entering at Finn Rah's call, Sarryen joined the Offering beside the hearth. She smiled at Finn.

'I am truly astonished. I guess the whole cliff is composed of the amalgam which deflects magic?'

Finn Rah nodded. 'To any inquisitive minds, there is only a small area of the rock – where it is exposed to the surface directly above this room. The rest is hidden beneath a considerable depth of soil – thus undetectable.'

A silence fell between them. Finally Sarryen stirred. 'Cho Petak is the instigator of this turmoil, is he not?' she asked quietly.

Finn removed her gaze from the fire's twisting flames. 'He is, and there is a very great deal I have to tell you, my dear.'

When Finn Rah finally stopped speaking Sarryen sat, maps and parchments on her lap and around her feet, trying to grasp the immensity of all she had been told.

'You do not know if Babach survived?' was all she felt able to ask.

Finn stretched her arms above her head. 'No word from the Night Lands for sixteen days.' She grimaced. 'The Plavat, Baryet, said his mate was nesting, so it would be difficult even for Chakar to persuade him to fly here again.'

'And there really is no other way we could contact them?'

'No one can travel so far with their minds – at least, no one here. I have to assume that Cho Petak can either use mind travel so powerfully, or he has a way quite unthought of by us.'

'And he would know at once what we attempted.'

Finn nodded. 'To try mind contact, we would have to leave this shelter to escape the shielding thus exposing our presence instantly.'

Sarryen rescued a parchment that had rolled beneath her chair. 'Would these people send one of their Dragons? Chakar says they have a vast intelligence, including knowledge of much magic. Could one of them reach here in safety?'

'I would not dare to guess, having no idea of their capabilities other than what Chakar has written. Her owl went with Babach,' she added irrelevantly.

'Her owl?'

'Hmm. Sava. Chakar always had an owl, even at the Menedula. Odd birds. This one made such a fuss and eventually clung to the first cloak we had wrapped around Babach. We just wrapped another around them both. Poor thing was probably smothered on the first day.'

'Could no other bird make the journey?'

Finn put a log on the fire and added a few pieces of coal. 'Have you ever seen a Plavat?' she asked.

'Well, no. I know only that they are large, and predatory, and spend most of their lives in the air.'

Finn snorted. 'I can promise you they are very large. They have tempers as foul as a bear's breath, and why Chakar adopted one is beyond all rational thought.'

'Except at this moment, that misguided whim has proved to be our one piece of luck,' Sarryen pointed out.

Finn wiped her hands on her trousers and sat back in Chakar's armchair. 'Arryol has little gift for mind travel. He is a healer beyond compare, but that is also his limitation. Your talents are much wider Sarryen. I need you to work with me on all these appalling problems.'

Sarryen smiled ruefully. 'Where shall I start?'

'Everything relating to the Night Lands is in this room. I have two students trying to sort their way through the most hideous jumble of texts in one of the chambers along this passage.' She frowned in thought. 'I will send Lyeto to you. He is highly intelligent and I believe Chakar had hopes for him as her successor here. It is nearly supper time. Come with me to the common room and we will eat. I have made a habit of staying there for the remainder of the evenings and just talking with our few survivors. I will tell Lyeto to join you back here. He understands some of these papers far better than I do.'

Sarryen liked Lyeto immediately and understood why Chakar saw so much promise in the young man. The delay in ageing, which came into effect as eyes became silvered, would keep him looking young for many more years, as too would Melena. Sarryen guessed that she herself looked to be in her mid thirties when in reality she was nearer three times that age. Lyeto looked less than twenty, and Finn had told Sarryen he was only a year or so older in truth.

On entering Chakar's sitting room, Lyeto went straight to swing the kettle over the fire to make tea. He shrugged sheepishly when he caught Sarryen's raised brow and smile.

'Offering Finn seems to exist on tea, Kooshak Sarryen. Since I have been working with her, making sure there is a constant supply has become second nature. Although, she may be happier now that Master Volk is to begin brewing.'

Sarryen stared hard at him but his expression remained innocent.

'Where to begin?' She waved her hand at the table and its pile of books, scrolls and loose papers.

'Kooshak,' Lyeto began, saw Sarryen's scowl and inclined his head. He started again: 'Sarryen, we need to know what is happening in this land before we risk reaching out to the Night Lands. To do that, I need to be outside and Finn Rah expressly forbids any of us to leave this shelter. Kooshak Arryol will only say that a madness spreads through all of Drogoya, and Finn Rah has not said a great deal more.'

Sarryen chewed her lip. 'You had heard of the way many people's eyes became red and they became insane?

Lyeto nodded.

'Did Finn tell you what she witnessed in the Menedula?'

Lyeto nodded again, but more doubtfully. 'I think she did not tell us all of it. Chakar has long taught us to beware of Cho Petak, Sacrifice though he is.' He paused. 'Is Cho Petak truly the monster that both Chakar and Finn Rah have suggested?'

Sarryen's violet and silver eyes held his gaze. 'Far, far worse than either they or any of us could ever have imagined.'

Chapter Eight

Two days from Far, travelling north west, Tika's party could still see the last peaks of the Spine Mountains behind them. Farn and Brin flew on with their riders and checked a tiny oasis several leagues further, then turned back to where the konina riders had camped. They carried enough water for six days, if they used it sparingly, but confirmation of a place where fresh water could be found comforted them all.

Storm clouds had loomed during the evening of the first day, but no rain fell and the land around them began to have a strange ashen appearance. A few desiccated bushes clung to the thin soil, but there was a deadness, an eeriness, about the area they were entering. They made a fire, using some of the brittle bushes, but did not bother with tents, all except Ren and Maressa being used to sleeping under the stars.

'How far ahead is the water?' Pallin asked.

'A day and a half for you,' Brin replied. 'You could rest when we reach it for a day while Farn and I search ahead again.'

Both Gan and Tika regarded the huge crimson Dragon with suspicion. His eyes whirred an innocent rosy hue. Olam did not miss a thing.

'You would only need to be gone a short while of course?' he asked.

'Of course,' Farn replied before Brin could speak, his eyes gleaming in the firelight. 'We fly so much faster than your koninas can travel.'

Tika noted a certain annoyance from Brin, but made no comment. Whatever mischief he might have planned had been effectively curtailed by Farn's boastful comment.

Olam's group made less distance the second day than they had hoped: a wind raced up from the south, hurling thin soil, grit and sparkling salt crystals against them. They hastily erected two tents and crowded within, grateful for any shelter. The wind died away in mid afternoon and Olam decided they should ride on until full dark. The land was flat, they had seen no real obstacles in their path to cause the koninas to fall or stumble, so he reckoned it was safe to continue.

Brin had recognised the twirling dust tendrils and had led Farn quickly out of the storm's path. They watched and waited until it ceased, then flew on again. Maressa bespoke Ren to ensure that he and his companions were unharmed.

'Olam is riding on until dark, to make up the lost distance,' she told Gan and Tika.

Brin led them to a point he thought Olam was likely to reach by nightfall and Gan set about building a fire. It was crackling cheerily when Olam's party rode up, a light to welcome them.

Each sunset Maressa or Ren far spoke Lady Lallia in Far, and on the ninth evening, Maressa called the travellers together.

'All of you, listen to Lallia. Ren, help them to hear her.'

She closed her eyes again and they heard her call Lallia's name.

'Maressa? I feared you had gone too great a distance. There is uproar in Return. Hargon is killing many of his own people, saying they are tainted with ancient poisons, and he demands that the other Lords join him in wiping all such people from the face of the land. Seboth sent a message to warn me and instructing that Far begins preparations to defend itself. He hopes to be here tomorrow but Maressa listen! Hargon ordered the death of his own Armschief, Navan!'

Tika gasped and Maressa opened her eyes briefly to share a worried look with her.

'Navan fled Return. He stopped here long enough to confirm my Seboth's letter and eat a meal. I gave him supplies and a fresh konina, and he follows you now, into the bad lands. Will he be able to find you?'

'Worry not, Lady,' Brin spoke at once. 'I will fly back along our route tomorrow and find him, you may rest assured.'

They all felt the relief surge along the mind link.

'Be very careful Lallia,' Tika added. 'Remember the shielding we taught you. I fear that Hargon himself may have enough old blood to somehow sense it in others without realising how he does it. Please Lallia,' she repeated, 'be very careful, and Seboth likewise.'

Maressa broke the link and they all stared silently at each other around their little fire.

At dawn next day, Brin lifted into the air and arrowed towards the south east. He flew high, to gain the widest view of the empty land. The rest of the party put up two awnings: they had found the temperature rose rapidly in the day time on this strange plain, although the cold season had barely passed when they left Far, and then they settled in to wait.

Brin bespoke Tika as the sun beat down at midday. The glare off the grey white ground made them all squint. Brin told her he had just spotted Navan and would reach him in moments.

'You have flown a great distance in this short time Brin, will you wait and rest before bringing Navan to us?' Tika asked.

'It is hot Tika. I will rest a short while but I will fly through the night I think. It will be better for this Navan in the cooler time.' Tika relayed Brin's words as they all huddled away from the sun's glare.

Farn enjoyed the heat, basking, wings outstretched to soak in the warmth through every piece of his body. Pallin was the only other who seemed unbothered by the high temperature.

'Wonderful for elderly bones,' he explained to a wilting Maressa.

Olam had raised another canvas awning under which the koninas stood. The heat did not seem to worry them too much at present and Sket remarked that no flies had appeared to pester them, as he would have expected. Farn snored gently, and Tika, Ren and Maressa listened to the armsmen's talk of koninas and fengars. Sket gave an accurate if lurid description of the savage fengars, which Olam and Pallin clearly thought was pure invention. Eventually, Gan came to Sket's defence, agreeing that although very alike in appearance, koninas were far preferable to fengars in temperament.

Ren glanced at Tika. 'Fengars sound as bad as Plavats.'

Tika grinned. 'I do not recall that your Plavat attacked you, or tried to eat you, during your journey. At least, you didn't mention that it did anyway.'

'Fengars are really that dreadful?' he asked, doubt still in his voice.

'Look.' Tika made an image of the fengars that had taken them on that first journey into the High Lands.

Ren winced. 'You make your point.' He subsided into silence again then smiled. 'And this is a Plavat.'

He showed them a vision of Baryet standing in the great hall of the Stronghold, peering down over his hooked black bill at Mim, dwarfed in front of him. He allowed the image to fill everyone's minds and mouths fell open, heads turning to the Offering in horror.

'Are those a common sort of bird in your land?' Riff asked faintly.

Ren grinned in satisfaction. 'Fortunately no. They restrict themselves to the northern coasts.'

The heat gradually lessened and they were able to leave the shade and move around, gathering a pile of the near dead bushes for the night's fire.

'Why does it get so cold at night when it is so very hot in the day?' Riff enquired generally.

'It is to do with the physical laws,' Ren began. He studied the blank faces around him and shrugged. 'It is just one of those things,' he finished lamely.

They slept, knowing that Brin would warn of his imminent arrival, and most of the night slipped away. Dawn was fingering the sky with pale rose and lemon light when Tika and Farn both jerked awake. Tika coaxed the embers of the fire to a more enthusiastic blaze and carefully rationed some water into the kettle. The others were stirring as Brin landed some paces from the camp, the koninas only twitching slightly at his presence now.

Navan slid from the crimson Dragon's back, carrying saddle bags and a pack, and staggered. Tika and Sket ran to help him, exchanging glances at the Armschief's haggard appearance. He also wore the green uniform of Far rather than Return's dark grey, a fact noted by all the now-awakened party. Maressa had tea brewed to push into Navan's hands when he sank onto the ground by the fire. Olam stood over him for a moment.

'Sleep Navan. We know your news is not good. You can tell us all when you have had some rest.'

Gan helped Olam get Navan under the awning and he was asleep before they had straightened up. They turned back to Brin.

'He is deeply sad,' Brin told them mournfully. 'He spoke a little to me, but I will leave it for him to tell you later.'

The great Dragon yawned and stretched himself along the ground, but he did not seem particularly tired. Ren tried to work out the distance the Dragon had covered in the last few hours and could only marvel at the creature's stamina. They waited out another hot day while Navan slept unmoving, so exhausted was he. The air cooled again and they sat round their fire, waiting for Navan to rouse.

'This daytime heat is too much for us to journey in,' said Olam. Heads nodded in agreement. 'It does not bother the Dragons, so I have thought that they might scout ahead for the next water hole and ensure that the way remains without hazard. We could then begin to move once the heat cools and ride through the night.'

'It will take another five or six days to reach the coast,' Brin told them. 'There are two places for water between here and there. The last is only a small way from the great water.' His eyes whirred in excitement.

As always, Brin was ready to wander in search of new places, new things, wherever the wind or his mood chose to take him. Farn had yet to see this ocean of which Brin had so often spoken, and his eyes too sparkled at the prospect.

'I am glad I have waited,' he announced. 'I will see it first with my Tika.'

Tika hugged him, then went still as Navan came from the shelter. The awful weariness was gone from his face but Tika saw new shadows in his eyes. Accepting food from Pallin, Navan sat between Tika and Gan.

'Lady Lallia said that she told you some of what has happened?' he asked.

'She did. But we have not contacted her since then,' Maressa explained. 'She told us that Seboth was due home and we felt it best to speak with you before putting either her or Seboth at any risk.'

'Hargon looks terrible. He has scarcely eaten since the news of his younger son's death. His eyes grow more bloodshot by the day.'

Maressa and Ren both became alert at Navan's words but said

nothing as he continued.

'He sent an order through another officer to start killing any townspeople suspected of either dabbling with power, or thought to have old blood lineage.' Navan put down his half-eaten meal. 'I knew nothing of it until the seneschal, Traff, told me. He was terrified, because his mother's sister had been known as a teller of fortunes. My second officer, Triss, came to tell me to flee. Traff had already been killed he said, by Hargon himself as he walked across the hall. I was to die because Hargon remembered my great grandmother told tales of a "magic circle" close by Return.'

'Mayla,' Tika murmured.

Navan nodded. 'Mayla,' he repeated.

Gan cast Tika a questioning look.

'I told them in Lady Emla's House when first I was there. An old woman taught me to read and write. Then she had me beaten so that I would never betray the fact that I had learnt such a forbidden thing from her. That was Mayla.'

Khosa had been extremely reclusive during this journey. She had enjoyed the heat for the first few days but quickly found it overpowering. So she slept throughout the days in whatever shade she found with Tika on Farn's back and latterly under the awnings. At dusk she wandered off exploring. She had scarcely spoken to anyone in the last ten days, so it was with some surprise that Tika now saw the Queen of the Kephis stalk out of the dark and into the circle of firelight.

She climbed daintily onto Tika's lap and began to buzz quietly. Olam was explaining their plans to travel at night to Navan when Khosa murmured to Tika alone.

'Something follows us.'

Tika's hand paused in its rhythmic stroking along Khosa's back.

'Some thing? Do you know what?'

'Something bad. It is some way back yet, but it follows our trail exactly.'

'Could it be Hargon, or men he has sent after us?'

Khosa yawned. 'None of you have bothered to watch behind you. Only I.'

'Yes, yes, yes. I am sure we have been very stupid not to do so. How far is this something?'

'It was ahead of Navan I think, so maybe a day or so distant.'

'Show me.'

Tika closed her silvered eyes and followed the faint wisp of pale thread that was Khosa's mind, and travelled out over the dark land. Khosa stopped.

'It is there.'

Tika could see nothing at all, but she sent a probing thought cautiously forward. And came up against a hard wall of shielding. For a moment the wall shivered and blazing red eyes glared out straight at her. Then they were gone.

Khosa was pushing at her mind. 'Back now! Back Tika, to the camp.'

Tika slumped over against Navan, causing him to spill the last of his tea.

'You should be asleep Lady Tika,' he began, but stopped as Farn's head snaked over his shoulder to peer anxiously into Tika's closed face.

Brin rattled his wings and Gan and Maressa were already at Tika's side.

'What happened?' Gan snapped. 'Tika! Who did you contact?'

Dark lashes fluttered while Sket propped Tika against his shoulder. When she managed to describe what Khosa had led her to, Maressa instantly sent her mind back along their route. Ren monitored her, ready to pull her away should the need arise. But Maressa found nothing at all.

'Show me exactly what you saw.' Maressa knelt in front of Tika. When she saw the red eyes that Tika had seen, she gasped. She looked at Ren. 'Like the affliction,' she said.

The Offering was deeply perturbed. He had seen no cases of the affliction personally in Drogoya. He had learned much from Maressa of those she had seen within Vagrantia. In Drogoya there had been no mention of any victims' eyes changing to silver, only to the red with its concomitant insanity. He had made no attempt to examine this child Tika's mind. Maressa told him that the golden Dragon Kija had assured her there was a very slight change. She was sure it was not harmful but more than that she was unable to say.

Ren was still trying to adjust to being here in what he had always believed were the virtually mythical Night Lands. The previous three years he had spent secluded within the Menedula, and just travelling with Voron to the Oblaka had been strange enough. Six days on the back of a Plavat, meeting great Dragons within the Stronghold of that changeling boy, the Dragon Lord, travelling the mysterious circles, and now riding these horse-like creatures across a barren land. Ren suddenly longed for his quiet rooms in the Menedula and old Babach's gentle company.

'I had thought to stay here another day, to allow Navan more time to recover.' Olam looked at Gan as he spoke. 'I think now that we should make what progress we can at once.'

Riff and Pallin were already saddling the koninas, redistributing the packs from one of the spare animals to give Navan a mount. After Sket had assured himself Tika was her normal self again, he hurried to help take down the awnings.

'Would the Dragons know of any defensive locations ahead?' Olam asked Tika.

A rumbling laugh echoed in their minds.

'Olam, you are able to mind speak me yourself you know,' Brin chided gently. 'But no. It is all open country until we reach the high cliffs along the coast.'

'Which is five days travel I think you said?' Olam attempted to sound as though he had always conversed with Dragons using the mind speech.

'Yes. The next water place is two days more from here, but it has no trees or large rocks from where you might make a fight.'

'And if we are caught between watering places,' Gan started to say.

'We would be in bad trouble.' Olam finished for him.

Brin went carefully over the route with Farn, using stars as sight guides. Farn was to stay close to the front of the armsmen and Ren, while Brin would fly at the rear. And so they proceeded each night, setting a watch during the day as well as relying on the Dragons or Khosa to sense any unwanted followers.

Ren had never been garrulous but during these days he became almost taciturn. The first time that he ignored a question from Olam, the Armschief was inclined to irritation. It was Sket who informed him that judging by the vacant unfocused look of

Offering Ren, he believed him to be either deep in thought or trying to far speak someone. Sket advised Olam to leave Ren be.

'Even my Lady Tika can be a little odd sometimes,' he admitted, but with a look which plainly said others might be ill advised to criticise Tika even thus far.

Shortly before dawn on the fifteenth day from Far, the party began their routine of raising their awnings, making a meal and preparing to sleep through the heat of the day. The temperature reached the highest yet and by midday they were all uncomfortably awake. Farn could scarcely contain his excitement, his eyes whirring and flashing as he stared at the western horizon. Light seemed to glitter all along the line where sky met land, and it was only slowly that Tika realised that the sparkling line must be the sea.

'How much further Brin?' she asked.

'If you left now, you would be there well before nightfall – it is truly not a great distance now.'

Tika called Gan and Olam to the edge of the awning. 'The sea.' She pointed. 'I think we should move on now, despite the heat.'

'It would be cooler beside the great water,' Ren said unexpectedly. 'There is usually a breeze at least.'

Gan nodded and turned to give orders to the armsmen. Farn's excitement was contagious: all of the riders, with the possible exception of Ren, sat their koninas straighter, staring eagerly ahead at the line of brightness. Farn's delight rang through their minds when he lifted from the ground, carrying Tika and Khosa higher, where they could see the narrow line broadening into a vast expanse of water.

Ren proved correct: half a league from rising cliffs, a breeze swept in over the land. It had an odd tang to it, a smell unfamiliar to all except the Offering. The water was hidden as they made the final approach. Although the land they had ridden across had appeared flat, in fact it rose and fell in gentle waves, and now they were angling down behind a sharply rising band of high grey cliffs. Now the travellers could hear a steady noise, a regular sighing and booming as though some monstrous creature slept on the other side of those cliffs.

There was a narrow split in the cliffs directly before them and while Brin and Farn swooped and soared over the beach and water beyond, Tika released Khosa from her carry sack. She joined Gan and Olam as they chose the best place to camp. Maressa had been unusually subdued throughout the previous night and this day, which Tika attributed to the heat. But now, as the koninas were led into a small curved section of the cliff, Maressa stiffened, turning to stare back the way they had come.

Ren spun round at the same moment and Khosa, every hair standing out from her small body, leaped onto a boulder, spitting and hissing. Olam looked round, his newly-awakened mind sensing the urgency filling the air. Tika sent her mind out into the quickly gathering twilight and once more hit a solid wall of shielding.

'Everyone back in here. Now!' Gan barked, even as Tika summoned Farn and Brin from their play.

She grabbed Khosa with one hand and pulled Maressa with the other, back against the cliff. Swords were loosened in sheaths and arrows nocked and ready to fly.

'Do you know what it is?' Gan asked calmly, his eyes never ceasing to scan the darkening ground in front of them.

Tika glanced at Maressa. 'It is almost like a huge ball, a round shield, but stars know what it may hold.'

The air quivered and there was a sound similar to fabric being torn. Pain lanced through Tika's head and she knew that Maressa, Olam and Ren, also felt it. She forced herself to stay where she was, Gan and Sket to either side of her.

Ten or maybe more, figures suddenly formed, solidifying as Tika watched. Eyes red as coals burned with hungry hatred when the figures swung to face the group backed against the cliff. Arrows hummed past Tika and half the number of creatures fell. The cheer died in her throat when she saw them rise, arrows protruding from necks and chests, and continue their shambling advance.

Ren reached for Maressa's hand, pushing his other hand between Gan and Sket to grasp Tika's shoulder. Immediately, Tika felt the immense power within the Offering, and she willingly linked her mind to his. Ten paces, and Riff danced forward, dealing a massive down sweep of his sword which almost cut one of the things in half. As Riff was jerked back by a scowling Pallin, the creature climbed back to its feet, its eyes redder than before.

Suddenly two of the things screamed, their bodies convulsing into positions impossible for a normal human form. Their comrades spared them not a glance, moving another step forward even as more screams ripped from two more creatures. Tika felt power surging through her from Ren and was also distantly aware of the pendant she wore beginning to burn her chest. She would have fallen if not for Sket's support and felt rather than saw Navan hold Ren's body upright. Her teeth were chattering as power such as she had never imagined shrieked through her again, and Brin and Farn dived from the sky.

Flames scoured the earth a mere pace from the defenders. Flames, and more flames, until nothing remained but a greasy black ash. Ren fell senseless and was laid gently against the cliff. Tika's head rang and echoed like an empty chamber. She saw Olam sitting on the ground, clutching his head in his hands, and Pallin carrying Maressa's limp form to lay beside Ren. Farn's long beautiful face wavered in front of her, then she too fainted.

Chapter Nine

Babach's recovery was slow but steady. The shock to his entire system was the main obstacle to overcome, although the major burns were now only tender patches of skin. He wore loose robes provided by the Delvers, which rested lightly on his frame. Sava had taken up residence in Lorak's workroom, from whence he emerged only when he was certain Baryet was absent from the hall. Lorak was highly amused by the owl, although both Kera and Chakar suspected he was encouraging Sava to develop a taste for his infamous restorative. Sava was seen to wobble rather more frequently in his erratic flights across the Stronghold's great hall.

Despite being much weakened, once the healers allowed him to sleep less, Babach insisted on being brought up to date on all that had happened. Chakar had gone into the Domain to visit Kadi the first day Babach roused properly so it fell to Voron to describe the appalling journey on the Plavat's back to this Stronghold. There were few in the hall at this time of day and Babach had assumed that he and Voron were quite alone. Then a long golden face lowered over his pallet and he recognised Kija. He stretched up a hand still wrapped in dressings to the Dragon.

'You spoke to me, before the healing was performed.'

Kija inclined her head, her prismed eyes whirring a soft butter shade.

'I did indeed, Observer. The healing was a mighty task and we could not risk you deciding to fight against us. So many minds had to help you, you might have feared they were attacking you rather than trying to help.'

'When might I be allowed out of this bed, I wonder?'

Kija's laughter was a joyful sound. 'I see no reason why you must stay helpless in your nest, but then, I am of a different race.'

'Speaking of nests,' a voice said from behind them. Mim and Ashta stood there, Mim smiling at Babach. 'Have you yet learned that Baryet's wife has occupied my chamber? She is apparently with egg.'

The pale blue eyes inset in silver sparkled, then Babach winced as his grin pulled at the tender skin of his cheeks. The grin grew no smaller though when Mim sat on the edge of the pallet.

'Ashta and I went to the chamber and Syecha made the most excruciating squawks and tried to peck my poor Ashta. Baryet was most annoyed that I had disturbed his delicate wife.'

'Oh stop,' Babach groaned. 'I can see it perfectly. I always thought Plavats the most ghastly birds ever created.'

'And I thought you liked the things,' Voron said indignantly.

'Are you all supposed to be bothering my patient?' Dessi came round the end of the pallet, a mock glare on her still-pale face.

Babach instantly held out both bandaged hands to her when she perched opposite Mim.

'And I have you to thank for my life,' he said softly.

Dessi rested her tiny hands gently on Babach's burnt ones and he lifted them to his brow.

'To use so much of your strength on this old man is a debt I can never hope to repay.'

Dessi studied him for a moment then, smiling, changed the subject.

'There is talk of Kadi moving up here,' she said.

Mim nodded. 'We saw her take her first flight a day or so ago. The space there is cramped and the Delvers need to plant their crops,' he added to Voron and Babach.

'Kadi is a great Dragon who was dreadfully injured,' Voron murmured as a quick explanation to the Observer.

'And she still has not told us how she was injured,' Kija remarked, 'or given any hint of where the child might be whom she carried on her back when last I saw her.'

Babach gradually regained his strength and pottered about the hall in the days that followed. He found a great pleasure in spending the afternoons sitting with Fenj, who appreciated Babach's conversation greatly. Lula so far accepted the Observer as to curl on his knees when he came visiting. He was surreptitiously introduced to Lorak's medicine and instantly agreed with Fenj's view that the old gardener was indeed a splendid fellow.

Voron noticed, trailing in the old man's wake, that Babach's bandaged hand rested frequently on the egg that hung at his chest. When the dressings on his burnt hands were changed on the fourth day since he had risen from his bed, the healers agreed that his right hand could remain uncovered. The palm was healed but scarred and he was told to be cautious in using it for a while longer.

That same day, as Babach sat with Fenj, a melodious call sounded from without the gate. Fenj pushed himself up to a sitting position, his eyes glittering with sudden excitement. Lula deserted Babach's knees and flew up Fenj's spine to perch in her usual place atop his head. Mim and Ashta hurried in from the gateway, a broad smile on Mim's face and happiness radiating from Ashta.

'It is Kadi,' Fenj murmured to Babach and Voron.

Hastily they stood, awaiting the appearance of this new Dragon. Voron caught his breath when the huge, midnight blue Dragon paced into the hall, Chakar trotting at her side. The Dragon came straight to Fenj, leaning her head towards him to touch his brow with hers.

'It is good to see you here Kadi, and to know you are strong enough to fly once more.'

Kadi's eyes whirred all shades of blue as she turned to survey Babach and Voron. Babach bowed formally.

'I am truly honoured to meet you Kadi. We have both been invalids overlong I think.' He smiled up at her then saw the pendant on its obsidian links that hung just below her long jaw. He looked back to her face and saw that she was staring at his pendant.

'You and I must speak, Observer Babach,' Kadi spoke to his mind alone before turning to greet Kera and Jal.

Babach watched her move towards the long tables where Guards were beginning to gather. He noted the many places on the great body where there were no scales, only dark blue hide. Lines ran down and across her wings, of a much lighter blue: surely scarring from her recent wounds. He sniffed. There was a faint scent of mint, he could swear to it. Perhaps it was being used in one of the supper dishes. He swayed slightly and Voron caught his arm, leading him to the table to join Chakar.

Chakar hugged the old man tightly, then sprang away, remembering his burns.

'Forgive me for marching straight past you, old friend. I was not expecting to see you vertical yet and I had a private message to give to Dessi. How are you feeling? I must say you look greatly improved compared to when I left.' She peered more closely, the dark green eyes surrounded by silver examining him minutely. 'Sit here with me.' She dropped her voice to a whisper. 'Have you discovered Lorak's restorative?'

Babach chuckled. 'I have indeed. He could make a fortune in Drogoya with it.' His face clouded. 'Probably not right now though.'

Daro and Nesh came from the upper levels to greet Chakar and conversation became general. Mim sat next to Babach but ate very little the Observer noted.

'Are you not hungry, Dragon Lord?' he asked quietly.

Mim tilted his head and looked at Babach. Equally softly he replied: 'I prefer less cooked food now, since my body began to change. Only Dessi knows, within the Stronghold, how sick I feel eating these cooked dishes.'

The turquoise eyes with the odd vertical pupils, surrounded now with gold scaling, stared at Babach almost in challenge. Babach placed his unbound hand on Mim's scaled forearm.

'It must be difficult for you and for your friends to understand and deal with what is happening to you Dragon Lord. If there is anything at all that I may help with?'

Mim continued to stare at Babach for a while longer, then smiled his sweet smile.

'To begin with, you must only call me Mim.' He raised a mug of water and drank it down. He frowned. 'Have you heard singing since you have been here?' he asked.

Babach frowned in turn and studied the various dishes scattered along the table.

'I have heard no singing Mim. But can you smell mint?'

Mim sniffed. Ashta, at his shoulder, sniffed. Chakar paused in her conversation and gave them a concerned stare. Kera coughed.

94

'Is there a problem?' she asked brightly.

'Hmm? Oh no, no. Nothing at all. We, erm, were deciding what spices might be in this delicious pastry.' Babach gazed innocently along the table, and the babble of talk resumed.

Chakar slid along the bench towards Babach. 'You never could lie to me and get away with it old man. What are you up to?'

Mim grinned but Babach merely looked hurt. 'I am still convalescent Chakar dear. It is most unfair of you to bully me.'

Chakar snorted in disgust and moved back down the bench.

'Are you weary Babach?' Mim asked. When Babach shook his head he added: 'Come to my chamber – my new and temporary chamber – when the meal is finished, and we will speak without interruption.' His strange eyes rested briefly on Chakar.

'Voron will not let me out of his sight,' Babach warned.

'Nonsense. He is about to be occupied with Daro and Nesh.'

Mim moved down the table, bending to murmur to Nesh then crossing to speak with the great Dragons, Kija and Kadi, who reclined near Fenj.

Sava was on Lorak's shoulder where the gardener sat with Bikram and some of the Guards when a shriek at the gate heralded Baryet's arrival. Sava hooted dolefully and burrowed under Lorak's jacket as the giant Plavat stilted into the hall. Baryet stayed on his feet, staring at the hall's occupants, head tilting one way then the other. He eventually spotted Chakar and stalked a few steps towards her.

'There are three eggs now, my Chakar.' The pride in his mind tone was quite unbearable.

Heads bent low over plates along the tables while Chakar got slowly to her feet.

'I am sure that is quite remarkable, Baryet. Do give Syecha our warmest congratulations.'

Baryet's neck feathers lifted into a crest, his chest puffed out.

'There will be more,' he confided, causing an outburst of muffled choking amongst his audience. He stilted back to the gate, ignored Lula's spitting and returned to his wife's nesting chamber.

Kera listened to the laughter ringing through the hall and

wondered how long it had been since such a sound had been heard here. She leaned across the table to Chakar, pitching her voice to cut through the noise.

'How many eggs do Plavats lay at one time?'

Chakar looked uncomfortable while the sound that emerged from Babach was unmistakably a giggle. Chakar scowled at him.

'I believe it is usually five eggs, but in favourable circumstances, I understand there may be twice that number.'

The laughter vanished as people tried to imagine five or, stars forfend, ten young Plavats strutting about the Stronghold.

'They will surely remove themselves,' Mim suggested. 'Find a nice cosy cliff to live on.'

Chakar sank back onto her seat. 'Baryet and Syecha both think that except for its absence of sea, this is a very pleasant place. They think they may well stay here.'

Chakar flinched at the wave of outraged disbelief that swept towards her from the Stronghold's residents.

Mim's personal Guard, Motass, escorted Observer Babach to the Dragon Lord's chambers later that evening. He walked deliberately slowly as he realised the old man was far from recovered. Babach conceded his exhaustion on arriving in Mim's rooms, sinking into an armchair beside a small fire and closing his eyes for a few moments. Motass murmured to Mim, then disappeared. He returned in short order and passed a small flask to Mim. The Dragon Lord pushed a goblet into Babach's unbandaged hand and obediently Babach raised it to his lips. His eyes opened and he smiled, sipping the drink appreciatively. They sat in silence for a while, Ashta dozing against the wall beside Mim.

'You recognised the egg that Kadi now wears as being the one Chakar brought from Drogoya, of course,' Mim finally commented.

Babach nodded. 'The young man named Imshish told me that Chakar felt impelled to put it beneath the Dragon's head. And the Dragon roused soon afterwards.' He looked enquiringly at Mim.

'Kija suggested it in fact, but Gremara confirmed it. It was Gremara who told me to go to the place where several of these eggs are hidden and to find another that would be specifically

Chakar's. Again, Gremara instructed me to fetch one for you when your healing took place.'

'I still find it hard to believe I have been made whole. I saw my injuries when first I received them. I knew I could not survive them. Yet that tiny child healed me.'

Mim smiled. 'Dessi has a great power, but it was also the other Delver healers who assisted her, not to mention the Dragons lending their endurance, which all helped in your healing Babach.'

The faded blue in the silver eyes regarded Mim shrewdly. 'And something within this egg, you believe? And who is this Gremara of whom you speak? I have not met the lady I think?'

Mim laughed softly. 'Link your mind with mine and I will show you Gremara.'

Babach felt a total trust in all the people he had met within the Stronghold, and for this strange boy in particular. Now he leaned his head back against his chair. 'My mind is open, and yours to command.'

Mim locked his gaze with the Observer. 'This is Gremara.'

Despite himself, Babach gasped. The mind that met theirs was a brilliant dazzle of light. Mim briefly showed him Gremara's physical form and tears welled in Babach's eyes as the sinuous silver Dragon spiralled above an ancient volcanic crater. Then the dazzle filled his mind again.

'I am glad you are mending Babach. You have much to do in restoring the Balance of this world. Your task will be closely allied to my Lord's, so it is well you are with him in his Stronghold.'

Babach's right hand, resting on the egg pendant at his chest, tingled and grew warm. The brightness in his mind flared then dimmed again.

'The time is not yet when that will be of greater significance than you can guess. For now, let your body heal fully, and spend some of your days with Kadi.'

The brilliance winked out and Babach stared at Mim.

'But who is she?' he asked.

Mim sighed and began yet another explanation.

Motass, guarding Mim's door, eventually informed them that Voron and Daro were insisting that Babach be put back to bed, forcibly if necessary. Mim guiltily leapt to his feet.

'I am sorry Babach. I seem to need less sleep of late, and I forget that others do. You especially, at the moment. We will talk again when you have had time to consider my words.'

He helped Babach out of the chair and accepted the reproving looks delivered to him by Voron and Daro.

Kadi was not yet able to hunt for herself. The Snow Dragons had brought meat to her in the Domain and now Kija or Fenj brought her food. They preyed on the small herds of hardy grazing beasts that managed to exist this far north in the Wilderness. Servants were cleaning the vast expanse of stone floor in the hall this morning, leaving Kadi and Babach marooned by the great hearth.

'Gremara spoke to me, in Mim's company, last night,' Babach began.

Dark blue eyes whirred softly. 'I know. She spoke to me also.'

Babach waited when Kadi fell silent. She shifted her weight slightly and half stretched a wing.

'I am to tell you alone of what befell me and the child Mena, before I was brought down on Asat's mountains.'

Babach had not yet heard anything of Sapphrea, or Lord Hargon, or his children, and had no idea who Mena might be. But he asked no questions, simply waiting for the great Dragon to speak.

'We left Gaharn and flew west to Sapphrea. Tika believed that she was to face Rhaki and try to destroy him, remove him from this world. We met Lord Hargon on the slopes of the Ancient Mountains. He had three children, all of whom had talented minds.'

Babach nodded, understanding the gist of Kadi's words if not some of the terms she used.

'One boy child was already in Rhaki's thrall. The other had learnt hatred from his father, Hargon. The girl Mena...' Kadi fell silent again and Babach said nothing.

'I felt something within the child. She touched me in a way I cannot describe. Her mind had been deliberately shielded and I removed that shielding.'

Kadi's eyes whirred faster as she lowered her face closer to

Babach's.

'Briefly, there was a feeling of rightness, of wholeness, then…'

Babach felt confusion and distress flow from Kadi's mind. He put his bandaged left hand lightly against her neck, his right hand grasping the obsidian shelled pendant at his chest.

'Some of our party remained in the mountains while others went to Hargon's town. Hargon's elder boy died on the way, and I knew that Mena had contrived his death. I took her with me when I went to hunt next and I confronted her with my suspicions. Her eyes became red. It was as if flames danced within her and I feared I would burn should she stare too long at me.'

Kadi paused again. 'No. I just feared, Babach. Never have I felt such terror as facing that small female two legs. But then her eyes returned to normal and I thought I had imagined it all, although in my heart I knew I had not. I resolved to remain with her until I learned what was wrong with her, as something most surely was.'

There was a discreet throat clearing behind them and the chamberlain Yoral bowed, offering a tray of tea and pastries. Babach thanked him and after several more bows, Yoral left the Observer and the great Dragon alone again.

'That same day, the child's eyes changed again and power screamed from her. I could do nothing but obey her commands. She made me fly north. We took only the briefest rests and came north, flying on the Waste Land side of these mountains, rather than the Wilderness side. The child allowed one full day's rest about five leagues south of here, and ordered me to feed well and prepare for a much further flight.'

Kadi's head drooped lower still. Her voice in Babach's mind was the merest whisper.

'I had never flown beyond the coasts. Brin told tales that he had done so, but I never had. Twice Mena allowed me to make a landing on rocks that stuck out from the water. I think she realised that I could not go on without some rest. At last, I flew over land again. Mena made me fly high. It was cold and I was exhausted. I set her down – I know not where it was. She filled my mind with power and sent me forth again. I only remember flying until I truly thought my heart would burst, or my wings would fail, or both.

'After all the water became land again, I rested upon snow and ice – how long, I do not know. My mind did not seem to work: I felt as if I, Kadi, was shut in a dark corner and something or someone else made my body work.'

Babach was listening so intently he could himself feel the chill of ice where Kadi's body rested, feel her sense of terror and loss.

'I knew I would die in the cold lands I had reached, so I flew once more until, after I don't know how long, I felt the minds here in the Stronghold. I was so very cold that I flew to the south for a while, over the Wilderness. Then I heard a Dragon's challenge. I thought perhaps I had somehow encroached on the Silver One's territory, but it was Nula, the Forsaken.'

Babach saw the dark green Dragon storming towards the exhausted Kadi, saw the fire jetting from the gaping jaws, felt agony in his wings, and knew he was experiencing exactly what Kadi had suffered.

Kadi hesitated. 'I am not entirely sure, and I have not asked her, but I think Gremara was aware and somehow present. I fell out of the air and was fortunate to land where I did. I would have tried to rise, to fight back, but Gremara ordered me to lie still. I believe she made Nula think that I was dead, and made her leave me there.'

A huge sigh gusted from the massive blue Dragon. She turned her face to the Observer.

'I believe it is my task to fetch back the child Mena. It was your land of Drogoya that I took her to, was it not?' She rattled her wings. 'I remember pain and fire, fire and pain, flying over your land, Babach. And although I am sore afraid, I will have to go back there.'

'Know that I too am afraid, Kadi. But I will go with you when you return for the child.'

Chapter Ten

As soon as Thryssa had brought the Lady Emla and the first group of her Guards through the circle to the room high in the Asataria, she ordered them to move out to stand against the walls. Several Guards looked a little pale and dizzy, but they obeyed the order as promptly as those unaffected by their method of travel. A few moments passed in tense silence, then there was a soft explosion of air and Elyssa stood in the centre of the room with the second group of Guards.

Soran, in the first group, had placed himself by the door and was pressed to it, listening for any sound from without. Jilla and Lashek had fashioned a dozen glow stones, which gave a considerable amount of light. Small enough to fit in to the palm of a hand, the light was extinguished by the simple expedient of closing the fingers over it. Jilla told them that the lights would last for three days, then they would revert to being the plain round pebbles they had been before.

Many of the Guards chosen by Soran knew the Asataria building reasonably well, having escorted the Lady between her House and the City on numerous occasions. Discipline Seniors in their houses in the City were ready to shield three other forces of Guards who were to attempt entry by way of the places Ryla had remembered. The third force was clearly visible in front of the building's main gates. In all, two hundred Guards were deployed outside and Soran tried to be confident of the mere thirty two here under his command inside the Asataria.

Emla whispered her thanks to High Speaker Thryssa and moved to join Soran, Shan at her left shoulder. Soran eased open the door and strained to hear any sound from below. The room they were in was at an upper corner of the building: there could be no attack from behind them until they reached the first stairway. Shan twitched Emla's sleeve and the Lady turned her head, frowning. Her eyes widened seeing Thryssa and Bagri directly behind her. Glancing back into the room, Emla saw Kwanzi and Elyssa sitting calmly at the worktable. This was certainly not the moment to indulge in even a whispered argument so Emla could only shrug and follow Soran.

Only three glow stones were in use, just enough to see where they were walking. Reaching the first flight of stairs, Soran halted them. He motioned half the Guards up to him and murmured into Emla's ear.

'It is too quiet. They know we are here Lady. They probably wait for us directly below, assuming that we will take the quickest route to the Chamber of Gathering.'

Thryssa had pressed closer to hear Soran and she nodded.

'Is there another, less used way, Emla?'

Emla thought rapidly. 'The servants' stairs, about fifty paces further on the right, concealed by a door.'

One of the Guards ghosted away, returning almost at once to nod to the Captain. Two Guards remained by the door while the rest of the party crept down a narrow and steep flight of stairs. Soran recognised where they were as soon as they emerged from a second door at the foot of the stairs. He was signalling Guards forward as Emla and Thryssa reached the lower door. Light flared from the junior students' dining hall opposite and City Guards fell upon the Lady's men.

Bagri pushed past Emla until he was close to Soran who was defending himself against two swords. A strange quiet hung over the passageway, broken by the grunts and clatter of metal on metal, a quiet that seemed to expand. Bagri raised his left hand, the fingers slightly curled, and Soran's opponents reeled away clutching their faces. Emla blocked a side swinging sword, pushing it up and away as Shan darted forward, thrusting economically directly into the belly thus exposed. The rebel Guard gasped and fell, almost pulling Shan with him.

Emla grabbed the back of Shan's jacket, jerking her upright even as a spear of green flame whisked past her head. A group of City Guards, advancing from the left corridor, screamed as the green fire hit the first man and then bloomed out to engulf several others. Shouts could be heard from a lower level to Emla's left. Soran let out a bellowing shout in response and glanced quickly to the Lady, pulling his blade free of a body.

'Our men,' he gasped, 'from the first entrance.'

Emla nodded, ducking as a blade hissed over her head.

The fighting was swift and brutal: Thryssa and Bagri did not dare use their magic too much in the melee for fear of hurting their own side. Suddenly Soran's men found they had no more to fight, the few City Guards on their feet fleeing along the corridor towards the main chambers.

Three of the Lady's Guards were dead, and four had serious wounds. Soran detailed men to get the wounded back up to Kera's room as quickly as they could. Several others had taken minor cuts and everyone would no doubt have bruises, but Soran had twenty-five Guards still fit for action, and more approaching he hoped. Sure enough, about fifty men came from the left hand corridor, and their officer saluted Soran with a grim nod.

'Sir, they are fighting strangely. Almost as if they are sleep walking. Oh they still fight hard, but there is something amiss.'

Soran leaned on his sword to regain some breath.

'I noticed that too. And the ones here all ran back in that direction. Bait I would guess.'

'And do we take the bait Captain?' Emla asked.

Soran straightened and wiped blood from his blade onto a body near his feet.

'I think we have to Lady. You said you believed they would make the Chamber of Gathering the place they would try to hold against us.' He shrugged. 'That is in the direction we are being invited to follow.'

The party moved quickly through the corridors towards the great Chamber of Gathering, glow stones illuminating their way as none of the lamps were lit in their high brackets. The quiet that filled the usually bustling Asataria was affecting them all and as they crossed the last hall in front of the massive doors to the Gathering Chamber, the lack of sound felt smothering. They came to a halt half a dozen paces from the doors.

'This is the only entrance Emla?' Thryssa asked softly.

Emla nodded. Bagri moved closer to the two women.

'There is power being used in there,' he told them. 'Can you feel it Thryssa? And it is all around and through those doors.'

Thryssa narrowed her eyes. 'But extraordinarily primitive wardings, wouldn't you say?'

Emla studied the door, remembering the wardings in Rhaki's rooms in the Stronghold. What she could discern here was indeed much less complicated than had been Rhaki's.

'But there is something else I feel,' she said slowly. 'A mind whose type I do not recognise. Nearly human or Asatarian, but not quite.'

'Shall I remove the wards and let your Guards rush the room Emla? I can distract those within with some effective displays if you wish?' Bagri looked hopefully from Thryssa to Emla.

'It is your command Soran,' Emla said.

'Are we quite sure they cannot use the circle?' the Captain asked.

'Yes.' Thryssa's tone brooked no disagreement. 'This circle has been somewhat – tampered with – but there is no one here who has been able to use it properly in the last days at least.'

'In that case, the sooner we have control here the better.' Soran saluted Thryssa and Emla and turned to form his men up before the doors.

'Bagri.' Thryssa held him back when he would have followed Soran. 'Be ready to shield at all times. There is something very unpleasant here.'

'I can only sense something unfamiliar,' Emla said.

'Our knowledge has so long been confined within Vagrantia and we have had only our own histories to study and learn from. But this presence recalls something of that past to me. I sincerely hope I am wrong Emla, but I suspect I am not. Can you hold a shield for Shan and myself too? I will need all my energy focused on one thing.'

There was no time to ask Thryssa questions: Bagri and Soran were looking towards the women for the signal to begin the attack. Much as she hated her ignorance of Thryssa's fears, Emla nodded sharply to her Captain of Guards. She formed a mental shield around herself, Shan and Thryssa as Bagri raised a hand. Lines of light zigzagged across the huge doors and they seemed to shiver on their hinges, but they remained closed.

Soran reached for the handle of one half of the doors and Bagri for the other. Soran kicked at his side of the door, sending it swinging inwards. Officer Nomis plunged past Bagri to kick the other half of the door. Soran raised his sword, and a squad of the

104

City Guards trotted silently into the hall behind, three of the rebel Discipline Seniors with them.

Soran snapped orders. Nomis and half the Lady's men moved carefully towards the deep blackness within the Gathering Chamber while a dozen others raced to surround the Lady Emla and the High Speaker Thryssa. Bagri remained by the doors, sending a ball of multicoloured fire over Nomis's head to lighten their advance. He looked back towards Thryssa in time to see a Discipline Senior beginning to lift his hand. Another spear of green fire shot from Bagri's fingers to lance through the Discipline Senior and the men near him.

But then separate red flames, man high, danced across the hall, catching one of Soran's men in a hideous embrace. The Guard fell, writhing and screaming as the flame engulfed him. Emla watched in horror, still concentrating on keeping a shield about the High Speaker and Shan. Thryssa's face was expressionless and turned only to the open doorway to the Chamber of Gathering.

Within the Chamber, the creature that was using Fayet's body shuddered with anger. These useless fools! Millennia he had waited to be summoned again by Cho Petak. Millennia had passed since those promises were first made and look at this shambles. Those animals looked human, looked intelligent, but he was convinced now that they were neither. This body he was using: it became breathless at the least exertion, which had certainly put paid to some of the diversions he had dreamed of in his long imprisonment. He had destroyed Fayet's mind extremely quickly, if mind it could be called. Twittering and fearful, yet believing he was a genius. Oh no, that mind had to go at once.

He who had once been Rashpil, friend of Grek, allowed a tiny piece of his rage and frustration to escape and the tiered ranks of seats around the Chamber burst into flame. He watched a group of these pathetic beings scramble back from the doorway while he reviewed his options. Clearly this body was of no use to him. How had D'Lah found that tall intelligent body the very day he reached this world? Rashpil fumed: he was going to have to unbody and then spend some while in serious consideration of his next move. He had been too hasty and eager when released from

105

the Void

The only part of his thousands of plans that he had fulfilled was to reach this side of the world. His fellow prisoners also planned vengeance on Cho Petak but only he, Rashpil, had thought of distancing himself this way. Cho Petak was too clever. He would know those who wished him harm and would protect himself accordingly. Rashpil was craftier. By putting the world between himself and that accursed Cho Petak, he had thought to gain time to form the perfect plan for Cho Petak's utter destruction.

Only he had found himself here, in a place with appalling inhabitants, set in a grotesquely inconvenient land. Abruptly, Rashpil unbodied and what had been Fayet, slumped to the floor. The flames roaring round the sides of the Chamber vanished, the City Guards still fighting in the hall faltered, their faces becoming confused and uncertain.

Nomis shouted from the Chamber that Fayet lay dead along with several others.

'Keep the shield Emla,' Thryssa murmured.

Bagri hurried to the High Speaker, watching her intently. Emla felt Bagri's strength weaving into her shield and was aware not for the first time, how much more the Vagrantians knew of magic than did the Asatarians.

Soran's men were disarming the City Guards and forcing them to sit on the floor, arms behind their backs. Nomis came from the Chamber looking pale.

'The bodies in there are not fit for the Ladies to see Sir,' he said quietly to Soran. 'Fayet was standing on the far side of the circle when we first went in. He waved his hand at the galleries and they caught fire. When he collapsed, the flames disappeared. The seats are charred but not as damaged as they should be Sir.'

Soran nodded. He had absorbed every word Nomis spoke but his attention was on the High Speaker and the Lady Emla.

'Open the doors Nomis, then organise a complete search of the building. Get Lady Emla's Seniors to use power to check anyone you find worthy of suspicion.'

Unbodied, Rashpil drifted through the hall, looking down on the animals with distaste. He paused as he saw the brittle shimmer of a mental shield. He discounted the tall woman, but

106

the smaller one intrigued him. Despite the shield, he felt the power within her. He considered Thryssa for a moment. No, he absolutely refused to take on a female form, but to leave her thus untouched meant he may be leaving a serious opponent behind him. Not a good idea.

Rashpil drifted closer. He found it suddenly disconcerting to find the woman staring directly at his position. He was so astonished that he almost missed the slight movement of her hand and that of the man beside her.

He had time only to propel himself up, through the timbers and stone, out into an early dawn sky. His rage was terrible. What had that woman attempted to do? She had known he was there! She had known what he was! Rashpil soared beyond the Asataria, following the line of mountains westwards. He needed to think: about his revenge on Cho Petak, and how to deal with that woman and any others like her. The man beside her had merely been following her direction, Rashpil was sure, but she – she had known him!

He must hide himself away and consider what bearing this might have – on himself or any of the others of his kind, including Cho Petak. He was unaware of any others here – most had blindly rushed one after the other, to the place Grek, D'Lah and Cho Petak could be found. Nonetheless, Rashpil sank himself deep within the mountain rock, where it was most unlikely he could be tracked, and settled in for a lengthy period of meditation.

Discipline Seniors true to Emla, now came from their homes in the City and began working to help the many wounded of both sides. Emla and Bagri sat with Thryssa on the stairs. Several Seniors had already come to report a great degree of severe disorientation in the City Guards.

'It is as though they genuinely do not remember fighting against their brother Guards,' one Senior said, squatting in front of Emla. 'We know that can be done, but Fayet was not powerful enough surely, even with Harak and the others who joined him lending their support?'

Emla shook her head. 'I do not know. Let us just get this place cleared and the wounded cared for. There be time enough for talk later.'

Bagri leaned in towards the High Speaker. 'What was it Thryssa? I but followed your mind, I could see nothing.'

Emla shivered. 'I felt a malignancy all around, not from any one direction.'

Thryssa had been sitting, head sunk on her chest, but now she straightened. 'It is not to be spoken of here and now. We will talk when we are safe within your House Emla. Suffice it to say, it is gone from here. If someone could fetch Kwanzi and Elyssa – the circle here can be used to take us back.'

Soran, standing nearby, cleared his throat. 'There are several bodies within the Chamber Lady Thryssa, some on the circle itself. The – erm – remains are not pleasant to see.'

Bagri squeezed Thryssa's hand and stood up. 'Then let us see about clearing the circle Captain. It will not take us long.'

Soran raised a brow, called a pair of Guards to him and followed Bagri into the Chamber. It was indeed only a short while before Bagri and Soran recrossed the hall and Thryssa did not fail to note Bagri's waxen pallor. She said nothing, allowing him to help her up just as Kwanzi and Elyssa came from above.

'Soran, I will need no personal Guard now. Keep Shan with you,' Emla said as she followed the Vagrantians.

Soran smiled. 'In spite of the irregular training she has been able to do, I can tell you privately Lady that Shan is officer material.'

Emla returned his smile. 'Then make her earn her officer's badge Captain.'

Lashek and Jilla awaited them at the Pavilion in Emla's garden and seeing their weariness insisted they go to bed at once. Thus it was late afternoon by the time Emla joined Ryla and Nolli in the great hall. It was strange that they asked no questions, were in fact unusually subdued. Then Emla remembered that they had seen all that had occurred in the Asataria. The air mage Jilla had watched all the events, relaying them directly to the old ladies' minds.

Emla kissed each old cheek before sitting on her favourite stool by the fire. Lashek appeared carrying a large tray and was followed by two maids, equally laden.

'Lady Lallia's specialities! I suspect we will need sustenance through these imminent discussions.'

His beaming smile was answered with Nolli's toothless grin. She had become as addicted to these sweet pastries as was Lashek.

'You will get so fat that no one will be able to move you from your chair,' Ryla sniffed.

Nolli ignored her completely, already taking one of the pastries Lashek offered.

Elyssa came down the stairs next and was given a muffled but warm greeting from Nolli. She sat by the Wise One's chair and was promptly fed morsels of pastry. Kwanzi and Thryssa arrived together with Bagri and settled themselves on the heaps of pillows scattered around the hearth. Ashta's mother, the pale green Dragon Hani, reclined behind the old ones, but only Shar and Lilli were present of the five hatchlings. It was Nolli who asked Thryssa the question that was in all their minds.

'What was that "thing" that you forced from the Asataria, Thryssa dear? We saw no form, no shape, sensed nothing but a great unpleasantness.'

Thryssa was silent, marshalling her thoughts.

'I have to begin, I think, by telling you an old, old tale. It was old when our people first built the great cities of Valsheba.'

Her listeners waited expectantly. Thryssa sighed.

'The story tells of a wondrous place: a world of magic and amazing beasts, where all things lived in a Balance of Harmony. As with all such tales, there came a maggot to poison the heart of this beautiful world, and dreadful things befell the inhabitants.'

When Thryssa paused to sip her mug of spice tea, Jilla asked quietly: 'What was that world called, or had it no name?'

Thryssa smiled. 'It was called Nachalo, but who's to say where it was? Now, this maggot was spreading poison among some of Nachalo's best minds and they were crafty, keeping their evil plans most secret. But one of them suddenly became afraid of all the plotting and dreadful experiments he had got involved in. He fled in terror to the mage who ruled Nachalo with benevolence and wisdom, and he confessed all he had done, all he knew, and the names of those who had followed the maggot's path.

'The mage gathered those he trusted and they used their minds to capture the very souls of the conspirators. The mage was

109

appalled by the number of those who had fallen for the maggot's poisonous lies. It took all of the strength of the mage and his trusted ones to contain the wrongdoers. With their last effort, they constructed a great sphere around the many souls, and the mage cast the sphere forth to hurtle for eternity through the emptiness between the worlds. The sphere he made was called the Void, for within was nothing, nothing except the souls of the evil ones.'

The fire crackled in the silence that fell when Thryssa paused again.

'That is the story that I recalled when I sensed the presence within the Asataria. I fear the tale is true, and somehow the Void has been sundered and those evil souls so long imprisoned therein have found this world to settle on.'

'Who was this good mage who ruled Nachalo?' Elyssa queried.

Thryssa shrugged. 'He is not named in some versions, in others he is called Cheok.'

'And the maggot,' Kwanzi asked. 'Does the maggot have a name?'

Thryssa glanced round the ring of faces, her gaze resting last on Emla.

'The maggot's name was Petak.'

Chapter Eleven

When Tika woke, a new day was dawning. The instant she opened her silvered eyes, Farn's long beautiful face loomed over her, eyes whirring in agitation.

'Oh my Tika, are you well? I could not reach your mind all this time while you slept.'

Tika stared at him, remembering what had happened the previous evening. She sat up and threw her arms round his shoulders.

'I am sorry. It was so dreadful, I must have shielded myself against everything, even you. I am so sorry Farn.'

She felt his relief although she was also aware of the fine tremors running through his body. She sat back.

'I think we could both do with some of Lorak's medicines.'

Farn's eyes whirred faster. 'Oh yes indeed – the restorative.'

'Well, I think perhaps the strengthening medicine first, then a very little of the restorative.'

Tika ignored her soul bond's disappointment and searched through a pile of packs to find her own, which held several of Lorak's remedies. The one she sought, Lorak had concocted to calm and soothe Farn's recurring bouts of terror and distress occasioned originally by his near fatal injury. As she rummaged, she noted that one of the awnings had been stretched across the rocks, and that Maressa and Ren both lay asleep, or unconscious, on the other side of the shelter. Sket ducked under the low canvas, a look of relief on his face.

'Good to see you're all right, Lady.'

'I'm fine Sket. Where is everyone?'

'They've gone to look at all that water. I said I would stay and keep an eye on you.'

'You wouldn't have some tea brewed would you?' Tika grinned at the Guard, knowing he would be making tea all day given the chance.

'Just made some fresh.' He looked at the small pouches Tika had dug out of her pack and nodded his understanding. 'There is sweet water only a few paces along the cliff. They tell me that all that water out there has salt in it so we can't drink it. Did you ever hear the like?'

Farn had to wiggle a bit to get out under the edge of the canvas, but he was not going to let Tika out of his reach. His long lip wrinkled as she offered him a drink.

'You first,' he said sulkily.

Tika shrugged, turning to Sket as she raised the dish to her mouth and pretended to drink. She turned back to Farn and he drank the liquid down with much complaining. Sket produced a flask from his jacket.

'Only a sip,' Tika warned.

The taste of Lorak's restorative banished the acrid taste of herbs and Farn's good humour returned at once.

'Shall we look at the sea now, my Tika?' he asked hopefully.

Tika's gaze fell on a patch of darkened, greasy soil some paces beyond Sket's fire. She bit her lip.

'You go if you wish. I will wait with Sket until the others wake.'

Farn considered this proposal then settled himself beside the makeshift shelter.

'I will also wait,' he announced.

Khosa strolled down a sloping boulder and jumped to Farn's back, where she paused for a quick wash of her whiskers.

Tika sat cross-legged by the fire, sipping Sket's tea.

'How did you know of those things Khosa?' she asked, and winced.

She set down her mug and pulled her shirt away from her chest, peering down at herself. The skin between her breasts was red, blisters had risen in places and the inside of her shirt was singed. Sket vanished back under the awning, reappearing with a round pot of Lorak's salve. Khosa and Farn watched Tika cautiously smear some of the ointment onto the burn before Khosa replied.

'I could not see the thing as you could, but I could feel it as a nasty gap in the air.'

'Will there be any more of them?' Farn asked nervously.

Khosa's turquoise eyes met the silver and green of Tika's, and the Kephi refrained from her usual sarcasm.

'I would not think so Farn.'

Tika smiled gratefully at the Kephi Queen, knowing she lied.

Sounds of movement came from the shelter and Ren staggered into the open. He sank down opposite Tika and groaned, clasping his head. Sket busied himself pouring tea for the Offering when Maressa appeared and also accepted a drink.

'Shall we go and find the others?' Tika suggested when neither Ren nor Maressa seemed inclined to conversation.

Colour was returning to Ren's white face and he looked across the fire at Tika and Farn.

'I assume they are on the beach?' he nodded towards the narrow gap in the cliffs.

'Yes.' Tika hesitated. 'I think we should all hear what you can tell us about these things when we are together.'

Ren smiled suddenly. 'Of course. And I think that neither of you have seen the great sea?'

'I have seen the eastern sea,' said Maressa. 'But only when I travelled the air currents.'

'It is wonderful! It sparkles, and shines, and goes on forever!'

Five pairs of eyes regarded Farn's enthusiasm with varying degrees of scepticism, but then Tika laughed and got to her feet.

'In that case, why are we still sitting here?' She reached for Ren's hand, pulling him up. Maressa was already moving round the boulders towards the gap. Khosa hissed and spat when Farn rose suddenly, spilling her majesty on to the ground.

'Sorry,' he mumbled. 'I forgot you were there.'

'Are you coming Khosa?' Tika asked in a polite attempt to distract Khosa's fury.

'I think not. I watched it for a while earlier. It does not hold a great deal of interest for me.' She stalked beneath the awning, orange tail fluffed vertically in offended dignity.

Farn rose into the air, twisting and turning and generally showing off, as Tika explained to her companions. Climbing up to the gap, they saw Brin spiralling into the sky.

'Go and catch Brin,' Tika suggested. 'You can see us all the time, after all.'

Farn rocketed skywards, calling out in delight as he climbed

113

after the great crimson Dragon. Reaching the crest of the gap they paused and stared. Water heaved and sank as far as they could see, its edge purling onto a wide sandy beach. They saw the rest of their party perched on rocks some distance to their left and began walking towards them. The sand was dry and difficult to walk through at first, then it became damper and firmer. Maressa dawdled, picking up strange shells embedded in the damp sand. She licked her fingers and pulled a face at the strong taste of salt.

Gan reached down from his perch and hauled Tika onto their rock.

'It is amazing is it not, Tika?' he said. 'So many different colours and never still.'

Ren rather ostentatiously sat down with his back to the sea. Olam waved at the beach.

'Why is the sand wet for a certain width, then completely dry?' he asked.

Ren pursed his lips. 'The sea moves onto the land twice each day, then retreats again. It is called the tidal effect in Drogoya.' He looked at the interested but uncomprehending faces and sighed.

'Take in a deep breath,' he ordered.

Eight people drew in their breaths.

'Your shoulders rise as you do so – yes? Now, let out the breath. Your shoulders sink again. So it is with the water: it advances onto the land a certain distance, then draws back.'

The waves hissed and murmured while the group on the rocks pondered Ren's words.

'So is it a huge creature then, breathing in and out, but only twice a day?' Pallin ventured at last.

Ren drew a very deep breath himself then exhaled slowly. 'Possibly.'

'It is rather beautiful,' said Maressa.

'Not when it is stormy,' Ren replied shortly.

'Do you not find it soothing to look upon?' Gan asked.

Chestnut brown eyes framed in silver glared at him. 'I do not.'

'When will the beast breathe in again?'

'I don't know without keeping watch for a day or two Olam.'

Olam nodded thoughtfully.

'I believe I may watch this event.'

'I know very little of the workings of the sea,' Ren admitted, 'but I do know the waters can be very strong.'

Faces turned to him again.

'Some writers maintain that the waters are beneficial, health giving, and they recommend those with certain ailments to immerse themselves in the salt water. But one should never venture too far from the beach. You no doubt notice that the waves surge up, then drag back? When they move back, sometimes they can pull hard enough to tug a person with them.'

'And so the beast would feed,' Olam agreed with satisfaction. 'I shall see.'

Pallin's remonstrations were to no avail. Off came Olam's calf high boots, his trousers were turned back above his knees and he marched to the water's edge, the others trailing after him. They watched as the Armschief eyed the waves then took two firm strides forward. The incoming wave rose a little and slapped down on Olam's feet, flowed past and then rippled back. He laughed aloud.

'A little cold, and a little ticklish, but really rather pleasant.'

Maressa was the next to wait for a wave to flood over her feet. She squeaked at the chill but then laughed as had Olam.

'He is right – try for yourselves!'

Eventually, all but Ren, Sket and a scowling Pallin stood ankle deep in sea water. Ren had joined them but adamantly turned his back on the view.

'Makes me a bit dizzy staring at all that water swaying about,' Sket remarked.

Ren glanced at Tika's personal Guard with approval.

'It makes me feel positively ill,' he confided.

Farn swooped along the water line, very low and fast, pulling up and over the group and trumpeting with delight, while Brin lazily drifted high overhead.

'I'm going to start making a meal,' Pallin finally announced. 'By the time you have had enough of playing with water, it should be ready.'

He stumped back up the beach followed more slowly by Ren and Sket. Reluctantly, the rest of the party collected their boots and ambled back along the waves' edge in the direction of their camp. All at once, Brin was plummeting down, wings closed to speed his descent, his bass call echoing across the water. Hands reached for swords and heads turned in all directions, trying to discover what had caused Brin's alarm.

From the south, behind them, seven Dragons flew. Two broke away to rise to meet Brin, and Tika watched in horror as two others swerved towards a jutting headland in which direction Farn had gone. Tika started after them but Gan caught her arm.

'Wait. This may be some sort of formal greeting of these Dragons.'

'But Brin never spoke of Dragons here, I'm sure he didn't.' Tika tried to pull free of Gan's hand.

'Look,' Olam called.

Brin changed direction from head first to tail first, hovering above their heads and trumpeting at the approaching Dragons. He had manoeuvred so fast that the two who had flown up towards him were only now changing direction back down again. Farn glided back from the headland, a strange Dragon to either side. With huge relief, Tika sensed only excited interest from her soul bond, no panic or fear.

Slowly, Brin's enormous body settled on the sand in front of Tika's party and reared erect, great wings outstretched as he called the formal greeting of the Broken Mountain Treasury to these strangers. Farn dropped beside him and followed suit.

The seven Dragons landed twenty paces from Farn and Brin. Their voices rang in the minds of all who watched, shriller and lighter-toned than the voices of the great Dragons. Tika and Ren stepped cautiously up beside Brin. The female Dragon in the centre of the group tilted her head down to study first Tika, then Ren.

'I am Cloud, Sea Mother of the Northern Flight.'

Tika bowed. 'I am Tika, soul bond of Farn, both of us children of Kija.'

The sea Dragons shimmered in the morning light, their scales various shades of grey but with glints of rainbow hues scattered all over them. Cloud was the lightest, almost white, and Tika sensed she was aged, probably near to Fenj's antiquity.

'We have not seen your kind here before,' Cloud commented.

Neither Tika nor her friends could fathom Cloud's tone: it held no obvious menace, yet neither was it warm.

Brin's deep bass answered. 'We seek the places where once were great cities. Many buildings where dwelt the two-legged kind.'

Cloud turned to stare at Brin. 'Long are such places gone from these lands. We rule these parts now.'

Brin inclined his head. 'So we see. We ask therefore, your permission to search for whatever may be left of the old places.'

Cloud's eyes whirred. She was clearly communicating privately with her followers. 'I must ask if you know of the other strangers here – are they of your Flight?'

'Do you refer to the red eyed ones?' Ren asked smoothly. Seven sea Dragons fixed their eyes on the Offering. 'If so, then no. We were attacked ourselves last night, and were fortunate to destroy them with no loss to our own company.'

Prismed eyes flashed. 'Destroyed them?' Cloud sounded more than politely interested.

'You have been bothered by these creatures?' Ren enquired.

Again there was a pause while the sea Dragons conferred.

'The second Flight, some days down the coast, were attacked.' Cloud's mind voice was bleak. 'Seventeen of my kindred died and five survive with bad hurts.'

Tika's breath hissed through her teeth. 'Seventeen dead?' she echoed in disbelief. 'But why would they attack you?'

'That we do not know.' Cloud stared at Tika.

'Perhaps they were looking for us, knowing that Brin and Farn were of our company,' Maressa spoke aloud, glancing at Ren then back to Navan and Olam.

Gan nodded slowly. 'They may have simply located Dragons and believed they would find us as well.'

'So they hunt you?'

'It seems so,' Ren replied. 'Although we do not know why we are their particular prey.'

Cloud raised her head towards Brin. 'Do you hunt in the sea?'

Brin's consternation was instantly hidden but Farn asked in alarm: 'In the sea?'

Cloud laughed. 'I thought not. Your bodies are shaped differently from ours. We occasionally hunt food on the land –

117

there are small shoals of beasts who eat grass, further north a short flight. Sleet will show you where, if you wish.'

A smaller, clearly younger sea Dragon inclined his head.

'We would certainly be grateful,' Brin sounded relieved. 'We have not fed for several days and I was beginning to wonder if any beasts did live in these barren lands.'

The Dragon named Sleet lifted into the air, closely followed by Brin.

'You will be safe, my Tika? Would you prefer that I stay?'

Tika laughed. 'Go on and hunt. I will be safe.'

Farn pressed his brow to Tika's, his sapphire eyes whirring with affection.

The brief exchange between Tika and Farn had been closely followed by Cloud and her companions.

'You called him your soul bond – is it really true?'

Tika laughed again. 'It is a long story but yes, it is true.'

There was a stirring among the Dragons. 'We are extremely fond of stories,' Cloud began, then startled back as laughter erupted from the group before her.

Ren smiled. 'I believe everyone in the world loves stories, Cloud. Will you join us at our camp over the cliff there, and we can exchange a few such tales?'

'My kindred would be most upset to miss a tale telling,' Cloud said thoughtfully, although her eyes glittered with undisguised mischief.

Ren sighed. 'Perhaps you should summon your kindred then,' he agreed. 'We will go to our camp and have some food, then we will share stories.'

'Do you like fish?' Cloud asked suddenly. Her laughter at their confusion chimed in their minds.

Two sea Dragons rose and arrowed out over the sea then flew parallel to the shore. Tika's party gasped as one of the Dragons closed its wings and plunged into the water. Moments later, it emerged, water droplets spraying from its slender body, and it flew back towards them. It dropped a large, gasping fish onto the sand at Navan's feet and swung back out over the sea. Riff dealt the fish a blow and lifted it in amazement.

'I have never seen such a great fish.'

All nodded agreement: fish bigger than a man's forearm were

unknown in the lands from Sapphrea to Vagrantia, and this one was five times that length. Two more Dragons rose and flew to the south, presumably to gather the kindred of whom Cloud had spoken. The remaining sea Dragons flew to the camp and were being inspected by Khosa when Olam led the company back through the gap. The Dragons had never encountered such a creature and clearly had mixed views about her superior manner. Pallin, Riff and Sket had cleaned the fish on the beach and now set about baking all four that the Dragons had provided.

'What are you doing to them?' one Dragon asked in alarm.

'Cooking them,' Tika explained. 'We do not eat our food raw as Dragons do. Can you use fire like the great Dragons?'

'Of course,' a young Dragon sounded affronted.

Another had peeped beneath the awning and sent the koninas into hysterics.

'What are they? I get no response from mind speaking them. Are they food?'

'No,' Maressa said hurriedly. 'They carry us on their backs, much faster than we can walk or run.'

'But they can't fly,' the Dragon sounded smug. 'No wings,' he murmured to his neighbour.

Navan found himself grinning, for the first time for a very long time, as he caught Gan's eye. Clearly, some of these Dragons were as young as Farn, and as inquisitive.

'Do these fish use mind speech?' Olam asked Cloud.

'No, no. They live in vast shoals, countless numbers together. They have a sort of shoal mind, they cannot act individually.'

'Is there any creature in the sea who does use mind speech?'

Cloud's laugh pealed through their heads. 'Of course there are. The great shelled ones, the water giants and their smaller kindred. Oh yes, many speak with us.'

Ren regarded the Dragons reclining round the camp. 'Have you ever seen Plavats here?' he asked, rather too casually.

'Plavats?'

Ren envisioned Baryet and all the Dragons stirred in annoyance, to Ren's delight.

'Sometimes they try to take our nesting caves, but we are far stronger than they.' Cloud's eyes flashed with amusement. 'They become dreadfully upset when we singe their silly feathers.

119

Our hatchlings find it a most amusing sport.'

Ren felt himself warming greatly to Cloud and her kindred, beaming his approval at her. Cloud lifted her head, a clear call sounding from some distance. She called in response, upsetting the koninas once more, and nearly twenty more Dragons appeared above the cliff. They landed a little distance away and paced towards Cloud. Obviously, there was a considerable amount of communication between them all and heads turned to inspect the two legged strangers.

By the time Brin and Farn returned and had been duly welcomed by Cloud's kindred, Tika's company were replete with baked fish. The sea Dragons waited politely until dishes were cleaned and put away under the canvas shelter. Finally Cloud asked:

'You were going to tell us of your soul bonding.'

Tika, leaning against Farn's chest, stifled a yawn and began her story. The Dragons listened closely to the whole tale: from her fall into Kija's nesting cave, to the battle in the Stronghold, to her arrival once more in Sapphrea, where she had woken with her eyes silvered. When she finished there was a collective sigh of appreciation. Then the questions rained down upon her.

Eventually, she suggested that Maressa tell the story of Vagrantia and the affliction recently suffered there. Again, the Dragons were most attentive and asked many pertinent questions when Maressa ended her account. Then Ren told of Drogoya and of his arrival in the Stronghold, far north of Gaharn. He too suffered close questioning when he had finished. The subject of a Dragon Lord in the north seemed of great fascination to the sea Dragons, but of equal interest was the affliction in both Vagrantia and Drogoya.

'Is there nothing in your histories that might help solve this riddle?' Gan suggested. Many pairs of faceted eyes rested on his tall form. 'The great Dragons tell of their kindred back into the most long ago times, yet they have no memories of this affliction which affects people's eyes.'

'There are three of us left at the nesting caves, watching over the eggs. They are the eldest of our Flight.' Cloud paused. 'We will go back now and tell them your words. Perhaps one of them may know something. I am sorry, but I do not. We will come back to you tomorrow.'

The Dragon the company recognised as Sleet, murmured and Cloud continued.

'We are agreed that we will suggest to the three elders that you move down the coast and stay with us. There are several empty caves you could use.'

Ren cleared his throat. 'These caves. They would not be at a great height in the cliffs would they?'

Cloud's eyes whirred. 'Some are, but many are not,' she told him gravely.

Farewells were much less formal and the company watched as the Flight rose into the twilight and slowly flew south over the cliff. There was much discussion of the sea Dragons as they gathered round the small fire for a final mug of tea before they prepared to sleep.

'They are quite wild, in spite of their good manners here,' Khosa remarked.

'What do you mean?' Navan asked, long past feeling odd at addressing a small Kephi.

It was Brin who answered and surprisingly, he concurred with Khosa's judgement.

'They do not always have an easy life here,' he said. 'They have to endure great storms and hazards. I think there is a fierceness and wildness in them which is absent from us.'

On that more sober note people began to fetch blankets and settle for sleep, some under the stars, some beneath the awning. Tika sniffed, emerging from the shelter wrapped in a blanket. Gan raised a brow at her as she sniffed again.

'What is it?' he asked.

Tika frowned. 'Can you smell mint?'

Chapter Twelve

Cho Petak was studying charts. It had been his favourite occupation for centuries. He had found many likely places but had been unable to do more than note their locations. Now, his strength was no longer needed to keep in contact with the Void and he could do more. With the added strength of Grek and D'Lah, he could do very much more. And of course, there was Rashpil. Cho Petak had not bothered to try to find him yet. He suspected Rashpil was in the Night Lands, but for now that was not an important matter.

The air on the other side of his work table quivered and Cho raised his eyes. Flames flickered within them as he studied the air.

'You wish to speak to me Rhaki?'

His tone was cool. He wondered whether it might not be time to force D'Lah to untangle his mind from this Rhaki after all. There was an arrogance in Rhaki that had not been obvious in D'Lah. But D'Lah had perhaps spent too long with just the one host, and his soul was so tightly entwined now with Rhaki's that Cho was not entirely sure he could separate them.

'You said I must remain within this building.' Rhaki sounded petulant. 'I have explored it all, and I am bored.'

Cho controlled his urge to destroy this unbodied fool, but he could not afford to lose D'Lah as well.

'Then wander where you will my dear. But beware some of my servants. Those newly arrived here will be aware of your presence among them. Do not underrate them, no matter what form you might find them in now.'

He felt Rhaki's impatience and disbelief.

'I warn you, two or three of them together could destroy you,' Cho repeated. 'Is there anything else? I was working – as you see.'

'That female child. Why are you keeping her – you do not

seem to use her for anything?'

Cho leaned back in his chair, the flames in his eyes burning ever more brightly although his voice remained calm.

'It amuses me to keep her here. And while it continues to afford me amusement, she will be untouched by anyone else. Is that quite clear my dear?'

It seemed that even Rhaki finally realised that Cho Petak was somewhat irritated.

'Of course, of course. I shall go and see these lands of yours then.'

'You do so,' Cho nodded. 'I can contact you in an instant, you understand, should I need your presence here.'

He felt Rhaki's sudden uncertainty, his reluctant acceptance that Cho Petak's powers were infinitely greater than his own. The air quivered again and Rhaki's presence was no longer there. Scarcely had Cho calmed himself sufficiently to return to his contemplation of his charts than Grek was in the room, the air stirring with his mental agitation. Cho Petak sighed and pushed his charts away again.

'Are you sure of D'Lah still?' Grek demanded. 'At times that Rhaki creature seems to dominate entirely – I cannot believe D'Lah permits it!'

Cho watched as the air distorted in a jerky zigzag down the room. He waited until Grek settled by his table again.

'D'Lah is our old friend,' he said soothingly. 'He has spent too long within the body and mind of Rhaki – as you suggest. But D'Lah is still there. He will never let us down.'

'I wish I could feel so sure,' Grek worried on. 'Can he still separate himself, do you think? Tell me truly Cho, for I doubt he can.'

'D'Lah was made fearful when Rhaki became unbodied. I admit that I was surprised by that show of weakness. We have all experienced that state.'

'You haven't for even longer than D'Lah,' Grek pointed out. 'Would you be willing to unbody this instant?'

Cho considered the question. 'I see no problem making such a decision,' he said finally. 'Should it be necessary, it would be done. It has its advantages after all.'

'And its disadvantages,' Grek retorted. 'And I have had more opportunity than you to study both positions.'

'What is your worry, Grek my old friend? It will be a while before the time is ripe for the next stage of my plan. If you wish to take a solid form again, there are plenty of hosts still available out there.' He waved in the direction of the window.

'You miss the point Cho,' Grek sounded exasperated.

Where was the laughing boy now? But before Cho could reply, Grek was gone.

More disturbed than he liked, Cho walked to the window. Of late, he took what little sleep he needed around the middle of the day. No longer did he have to hide the fact that he greatly disliked the bright glare of daylight. Now, he stared up at the star-filled night, noting that the constellation of the Weeping Willow was lower in the west and that the Wolf was dominating the sky.

Many times had Cho congratulated himself on taking the body of that farmer's son in the far south lands when he first reached this world. He had been an average boy: average height, average looks, but it was the sturdy solidity which had appealed to Cho. It was a body bred for endurance, for hard work in the fields. Now it was nearing the end of its usefulness.

Cho had slowed the ageing process further than any of the then Sacrifice and Offerings would have thought possible had they known of it. But over the last years, he had more and more often to retreat from public life for a day, to restore some degree of function to the body's vital organs. The bones were fragile and broke with tedious regularity, again necessitating a day's worth of repair.

It would be some time before the resources of this world were utterly depleted by his servants from the Void – he should calculate just how long it would take them to reduce the place to barren ruin. So much to think of! Cho turned from the window and made his way slowly to the rooms next to his, traditionally reserved for the most important visitors to the Menedula. Noiselessly, he opened a door and entered. A single lamp burned on a table which seemed haphazardly piled with books. More books lay scattered on the floor around a large armchair. Silently, Cho moved in front of the chair, staring down at its occupant.

The female child who had hosted Grek since before her birth

124

slept, curled into the deep chair, an open book on her knees. Cho bent to peer at the book, glanced at a couple on the floor and smiled. Books with lots of pictures in them, pictures of plants, animals, birds. Grek had sworn the child had not been taught to read – how could she without his knowing? Cho had his doubts, and before he ordered Grek from the child's body he had tried a little experiment.

Consequently, he had not revealed to Grek just how simple it had been for one of Cho's ability to block Grek's awareness without Grek even suspecting such a thing had happened. He had touched the child's mind and come up against the hard core that even he had not been able to infiltrate. But he had proved to himself that a person of great power could have taught the child many things, without Grek's knowledge.

Yet each time Cho tried to catch her out, he found her only poring over pictures, oblivious to the written words. Silently as he had entered, Cho Petak left the guest apartment. When the door closed behind him, the child's eyes opened, the almost violet-blue dark against the tracery of silver under the long fair lashes.

For a moment, her lips trembled then her teeth clamped tight and she forced away the weakness. She glanced down at the page she had been studying. Cho was incredibly stupid. Not once had he moved any book she held, which would instantly have exposed the papers beneath. Yes, Mena could read, better than either of her brothers or many of the men in Hargon's service. Thanks to Mayla. A tear splashed onto her hand and she tilted her head back against the chair, refusing to allow any more to fall.

When she was first released from Grek's domination, she felt total horror and self-disgust remembering what she had done. A cool, calm voice, which reminded her of Mayla, spoke in her heart, chiding her that it was Grek's doing, not hers. She should have resisted more desperately she argued back, visions of the midnight blue Dragon Kadi's exhaustion and terror filling her mind. At that point she could not resist, the voice told her calmly.

She was meant to be here, and so she was. Mena had wept for Kadi, she had wept for being the cause of her older brother's death. But she had not wept for herself. The voice had said she was meant to be here although as yet she had no idea why. She

125

hated the feelings within this building. Somewhere, far back in her mind, she could see it differently: its blackness gleaming, reflecting the light which streamed through its many tall windows. But now, its blackness absorbed the light, sucking it all into itself.

The voice like Mayla's said that she was meant to be here, but why? She was only a small female child, ten cycles old. What could she be expected to do about these dreadful creatures she now found herself among? The voice spoke to her only occasionally and only briefly. It did not seem inclined to answer when she tried to summon it.

Mena's silvering eyes began to close in real sleep when she heard the voice again.

'Long ago you were here as a little child, Mena. Now you are here again. Like before, you must soon leave, but you will be shown the way.'

Mena slept, and the fragrance of mint filled the room.

Finn Rah stood on the viewing ledge looking at the same stars Cho Petak had seen from his window. Below, the waves boomed against the cliff and pebbles rattled as the sea drew back again. Finn liked to come here in the middle of the night when no one else was around. So many years spent as a senior Offering, secluded within the Menedula with her own spacious apartments, had made it difficult to adjust to this close communal life.

She retraced her steps to the room always referred to as Chakar's sitting room, and made some tea. She sat sipping the hot liquid, her thoughts still busy. The Observer Soosha, who had survived the burning of the Oblaka complex, had suggested that they try to plan for the long-term continued existence of this hidden enclave. Both he and Finn had been amazed at the extent of the caverns and by the amounts of supplies hoarded away over light knew how many years.

Food, preserved both traditionally and with the help of simple magics, filled several chambers, and already various plants were sprouting in shallow trays. Volk's horses had disappeared but someone, Finn strongly suspected Lyeto, had been outside and now several goats were tethered on the hillside below one of the entrances to the secret Oblaka. There were enough young men and women to produce children: Finn and Soosha estimated that the population of the caverns could easily be maintained at between one and two hundred.

All aspects of learning were represented among those here now: healing, teaching, weather and sky watchers, botanists, and archivists. But no one, not Finn, nor the two Kooshak or three Observers here, knew or dared to guess how long they might need to remain in hiding. Chakar and Babach might know, but they were in the Night Lands, and Finn feared that Babach was not even still living.

The large chamber packed solid with books and scrolls had only been half disinterred yet, even with all the students taking turns helping the two in charge. Finn very much doubted that they might find a parchment explaining clearly how long Cho Petak's nightmare would hold sway over this land, or detailing instructions on their survival here. She sighed, pouring more tea. She was glad of the appearance of the two Kooshak. She knew them both from their student days and they discreetly helped share her burden of worries.

Finn felt a mind touch hers and knew it was Lyeto. He asked her to come to the hillside entrance. Finn put down her bowl and hurried through the passages. He must have been outside again and this time had given himself away so that she would have to reprimand him. She lifted a lantern from its hook to light her way through the final twists and turns until she felt air blowing, strong and cold, into her face. Lyeto was just within the entrance and thus shielded by the rock all around him.

Three shapes huddled beside him and Finn raised her lantern higher, peering at them.

'They survived in the countryside,' Lyeto murmured. 'They are free of the affliction but hungry and frightened.'

'Take them on through to the common room then.' Finn waited until Lyeto had spoken quietly to the three huddled figures then followed behind when he led them into the tunnels.

The first and the last of the three walked with odd gaits: the first with a rolling movement, the last with a hitching shuffle. The one in the middle walked straight but holding tight to the first one's arm. Lyeto settled his charges on a bench by the banked fire and busied himself making some tea. Finn perched on a stool opposite the three and studied their wrapped and huddled forms. While Lyeto waited for water to boil, he came and stood by the Offering.

'These two are husband and wife,' he said, gently pushing back the hoods of the first and second figures.

Finn stared. The second figure, the woman, had a face disfigured as though melted. Her eyes were sightless and her nose non existent. The man at her side took her hand.

'Fell into a tub of hot tallow fat when she were a tiny one.' His voice was hoarse but he spoke with the local accent. As his tattered cloak slipped from his leg, Finn saw that one of those legs was a wooden post. The man followed her gaze and tapped the post on the stone floor.

'I were a fisherman till an accident ten year gone.' He shrugged. 'Despite she can't see, she makes the best bread and pastries in town. I do odd jobs. We get by. Then the other night, whole town goes crazy. I got her and me out, up into the woods. Saw some folks we knew but their eyes were all funny, so I kept us low. We waited till it seemed quiet enough and come back. Nowhere else to go, see?'

Finn's gaze moved to the smallest shape on the other side of the woman.

'I be Giff, and she be Teal. That one we met when we come back. Don't know his name.'

Lyeto crossed to the bench, bending over the third member of the odd trio. It was a boy, around twelve years Finn guessed, but then she gasped when Lyeto pulled free the cloak. Blood soaked the boy's side from his left armpit to his foot. Finn was already on her feet to fetch dressings from the infirmary when the door opened. The bean pole cook came into the room, took in the scene at a glance and bent to stir the fire to life.

'I'll feed these while you see to boy.'

Povar had proved to be even less garrulous than his father in law. But despite his lack of conversational skills, Finn thanked the light for his cool efficiency now. He already had several pots over his stove and a large kettle over the fire. The smell of broth was soon warming the room as much as the newly blazing fire. Kooshak Arryol had been in the infirmary keeping watch over the two surviving burns patients when Finn had rushed in for some dressings. Now he followed her, a satchel containing instruments and various herbal potions in his hand.

Lyeto had been trying to reassure the boy who was clutching his cloak about him. Arryol stooped over the boy and placed his middle finger lightly between the boy's brows. Lyeto caught the child as he toppled forward off the bench. Laying him before the hearth, Finn and Lyeto quickly stripped the ragged clothes from the thin figure. The lacerations all down his left side were deep and filthy. Povar moved beside them to reach the kettle.

'I'd say bear, 'cept they be too narrow.'

'No bear,' said Giff, 'just the local people.'

Povar helped Giff move with his wife to a table, placing bowls of thick soup in front of them. Finn and Lyeto assisted Arryol when needed as the Kooshak cleaned out the deep wounds with his obsidian bladed knife to get the poisoned flesh out. Finn washed each freshly bleeding wound with an astringent herb wash and Lyeto stitched it closed. Students started to arrive for breakfast and exclaimed at the sight of the boy being worked on by Kooshak Arryol and Offering Finn Rah. Povar placed a screen between those by the fire and the rest of the room and calmly served out breakfasts.

The usual chatter and laughter was much subdued this morning and instead of lingering, the students quickly left to go about their duties. Volk poked his head round the screen, scowled, and vanished again. Finn heard his growling voice talking to Giff and Teal, then there was silence in the common room again. At last Arryol sat back on his heels and reached for a clean rag from the pile Povar had left beside the boy.

He wiped some of the filth from his hands and studied Lyeto's needlework. He shuffled on his knees back up to the boy's head and felt for the pulse in his neck.

'Be all right then, you reckon?' Povar stood at the side of the screen.

Arryol sighed. 'Some of those wounds were very deep and I had to make them even deeper.' He spread his hands in a helpless gesture. 'If they become inflamed, I will have to open them again.'

'What's his name then?' Povar asked.

Lyeto laughed softly. 'It should be Lucky don't you think?'

129

Arryol gave him a weary smile. 'If he survives, Lucky would do,' he agreed.

He got to his feet, kneading the small of his back and then stretching until his bones cracked. 'I will get someone to help move him into the infirmary. Then I will get clean and sleep for a while.'

Finn smiled up at him. 'That was good work Arryol. At least the poor child has a chance now.' She turned to Lyeto. 'I want to see you as soon as you are cleaned up.'

Dressed in a clean loose robe for once, Finn was sipping her perennial tea when Lyeto rapped at the door. She waved him to help himself to tea and then to a chair opposite hers.

'I ordered that no one leave the shelter of these caves,' she began in a mild tone.

Lyeto had the grace to look a little abashed, but only a little.

'I was looking for some hens,' he admitted. 'I thought it might be a good idea to find a few.'

'And that would mean going right into the town of course.' Finn's sarcasm was not wasted. She saw the colour rise in Lyeto's cheeks with some satisfaction. 'You clearly found no hens.'

Lyeto cleared his throat. 'No. But I walked straight into those three, and when I heard some of Giff's tale, I brought them back here.'

Finn's hand slammed down onto the arm of her chair with such force that Lyeto flinched.

'And what would you have done supposing they had not been the three helpless wretches they are, but were three afflicted ones? Do you think you would have survived an attack by three? Tell me please Lyeto. Kooshak Sarryen was able to deal with three – just. Are you already as strong as one who is so much older and so much more talented than you?'

The flush had drained from Lyeto's face under Finn's lashing words. He swallowed audibly.

'I go out shielded, Offering. I have a talent for altering the way shields may work. Observer Chakar had been supervising my experiments.' He met Finn Rah's jade and silver eyes squarely. 'I was alert for anything unusual – not for just plain ordinary people,' he ended lamely.

Finn let him sit and squirm a little longer before she held out her bowl to him and nodded at the teapot.

'Lyeto, when I order something I expect that order to be obeyed. By everyone here. Everyone. And that does actually include you, whether you were a favourite of Observer Chakar's or not. I would have expected you to come to me, to ask my permission to go outside and to state your reasons for such a request clearly and logically. By sneaking out, you have implied that I could not properly evaluate such a request. I resent that implication.'

Lyeto had dropped his gaze to his bowl of tea. 'I confess I had not considered how my actions might appear. I most truly apologise, Offering Finn Rah. But I must tell you this: after tonight, I feel I should go outside again – even more frequently than I have done. How many others might there be, wandering lost and hurt? Is that not what the Oblaka means, Offering – a safe sanctuary for any who need it?'

Finn sipped from her newly-filled bowl. 'I take your point Lyeto. But I must insist that you remain within these caves tonight, and you will report to me again tomorrow. I will then tell you my decision on this matter of your – excursions.'

Lyeto bowed, realising he was dismissed from the Offering's presence. His hand was on the door latch when she spoke again.

'Lyeto, you did well with the stitching of that child's wounds today.'

He flashed a quick smile of gratitude over his shoulder then hesitated, the door half open.

'Offering, did you hear singing while we worked on the boy?'

Finn Rah frowned. 'Singing? Light, no!'

Chapter Thirteen

Babach was an immediately popular figure around the Stronghold. He had that facility to remember which names fitted which faces, so that when he spoke to anyone, servant or Guard, he always used the correct name. His serene smile was returned by all he encountered. Mornings found him pottering with Lorak and Daro in the growing areas. For the midday meal he often sat among different groups of Guards. The afternoons were spent with either Kadi or Fenj, often both together. At the evening meal he sat with Kera, Mim and Chakar at the table tacitly reserved for the highest members of the Stronghold.

Babach had not spoken privately with Mim since the first day of his recovery, but he had thought deeply on the things told to him by the young Dragon Lord. He longed for the great library in the Menedula and the lesser library, now lost, in the Oblaka. He was sure that he had once read of a Dragon Lord, but wrack his memory though he might, he could not recall any of the details.

Chakar knew nothing when he asked her, but admitted that she had read very little outside of her chosen fields of study. Imshish shook his head when he was consulted.

'Segra Circle hoards many ancient texts, as does Parima. I had never heard of any Dragon Lords until Gremara called to Mim.'

Kera remembered Kemti's discovery in a book of children's tales, references to the Delvers and she proposed he enquire in Gaharn.

'The last scroll told of Emla's recovery of the Asataria,' she said. 'Why do you not travel the circle to Gaharn? The Asataria has an extensive archive and Emla also has a library of some size.'

'Perhaps I could write a request for someone to spare the time to look for me,' said Babach. 'I feel I must stay here for now.'

Kera gave him a quizzical look but Babach merely smiled and she asked no questions.

Baryet had decided to move in with his wife. It would be rather a tight squeeze for two Plavats in Mim's small chamber, but Baryet announced that it was the correct thing to do. One evening he had stilted into the hall to tell them of his intention.

'I know you will be bereft of my presence here, but I feel it is the proper thing to do in this sensitive situation.'

Mim buried his face against Ashta's shoulder, refusing to look round or to reply. Baryet's neck feathers crested.

'I knew you would be distressed,' he said with satisfaction.

Mim's shoulders shook and Chakar glared at him.

'We will miss you then Baryet,' she said. 'But, as you say, it is for the best I am sure.'

'There are six eggs now, my Chakar,' the Plavat said in a whisper heard by everyone.

'Perhaps that might be sufficient?' Chakar suggested weakly, aware of the irritation rising in the hall around her.

'Oh no.' Baryet's tone was shocked. 'As many as possible. There is plenty of food here for many children.'

A yellow rimmed eye settled upon Lula. Lula went into a frenzy of spitting and back arching and neither Lorak or Fenj could calm her.

'Plenty of food,' Baryet repeated, stilting from the hall.

'We will have to keep the gate closed,' someone called from a group of Guards.

Chakar looked at Mim's back. 'I do wish you did not find Baryet quite so amusing,' she said crossly.

Mim turned, wiping tears of laughter from his scaled cheeks.

'I apologise Observer Chakar.' He resumed his seat at the table. 'That might be a good idea though – keep the gate closed with a Guard to open it for the Dragons?'

Lula was snuggled between Fenj's upper arm and his chest, her blue eyes still blazing with fury.

'No one will harm you Lula.' Mim spoke to the tiny Kephi's mind.

She blinked but made no reply. Dessi slipped onto the bench between Kera and Nesh.

'Did I miss something?' she enquired. Mim chuckled.

'Do not set him off again,' Chakar ordered.

Ashta's eyes whirred. 'It was a visit from Baryet,' she told the

Delver girl.

'Aah.' Dessi nodded solemnly. 'You need say no more.'

Mim leaned his elbows on the table. 'Why are there these two Orders in Drogoya?' He looked from Chakar to Babach. 'If you follow one, is it permitted to follow the other as well, or are they exclusive?'

Babach's hand moved to tug at his now vanished beard, then dropped to rest lightly on his egg pendant.

'The Order of Sedka was the first time a detailed pattern for living was encoded. It worked quite well for a very long time. The Order of his daughter Myata complemented Sedka's. The difference between them eventually was that Sedka decreed while Myata suggested. If Myata's suggestions were not taken up, then she wasted no time on argument or recriminations. She taught that each one had to choose for him or her self the manner of their living. Sedka's Order became insistent, inflexible. Increasingly, when people were discovered not to be following Sedka's rules to the letter, they found themselves publicly rebuked, and worse.'

'And then the Sacrifice before Cho Petak introduced the idea of taxes and fines, which quickly grew to become imprisonment and death,' Chakar added. 'There was little difference in the beginning, when Sedka and Myata still lived. Only later did Sedka's followers organise into an Order, with Sacrifice and Offerings and so forth. Myata's followers had a communal system, not a hierarchy, where the lowliest or youngest had as much right to speak their views as any other within the community.'

Babach nodded agreement. 'My mother told me that is why the Oblaka complex was a collection of separate little houses gathered around the first house. Anybody could build their cottage close by, whereas in the Menedula, rooms are allocated strictly by rank within the Order and so on.'

'You have told us of a place called Sedka's Meadow, where he lived with his wife Dalena and their daughter Myata. Did Dalena go to the Oblaka when her daughter moved there?' asked Dessi.

'There is no mention of Dalena once Myata left the Meadow.' Babach frowned. 'No report was ever discovered as to whether Dalena lived on alone there, with Sedka travelling the lands of Drogoya and Myata far to the west.'

'Sedka died relatively young, attacked by the great desert cats in the southern hot lands. Shortly afterwards, the Order became much more formal and rigid,' said Chakar.

Daro raised silver eyes to the two Observers. 'Is Sedka a common name now in Drogoya?' he asked curiously. 'Has it a meaning?'

'Perhaps strangely, it is never given as a name,' Babach replied. 'We do not think it was Sedka's birth name, but we have no evidence for or against that idea. Sedka is an ordinary word in the old tongue, meaning a plantation. Clearly, he planned for Drogoya to become an orderly plantation and thus took that word as his name.'

'And Dalena?' Daro asked.

'That is quite often used to name girls in the country areas, less so in the cities or towns. It means a valley or a glen,' Chakar replied promptly.

Babach started suddenly then smiled at those gathered round the table.

'I wonder if I might have some paper and writing materials? I will send my questions to Vagrantia and Gaharn and, hopefully, some unfortunate student will find references to Dragon Lords in their archives.'

Kera supplied Babach's requirements and the conversation turned to the completion of the second growing area beneath the hall.

The days passed and Babach's strength continued to improve although his loss of weight made him appear older and more frail. He received messages from Vagrantia and Gaharn informing him that several hapless students had been set to searching through antique texts.

Lashek and Elyssa appeared through the circle one afternoon, Lashek still clutching Lady Lallia's recipe. He and Babach were drawn to each other at once and spent many hours, heads close together by the hearth, a dish of Lallia's pastries between them. Lashek was fascinated by the account of Babach's healing. After he had seen images from Chakar's mind of the terrible wounds burnt through Babach's torso, he insisted Babach remove his robe there and then so that he could see what had been achieved.

Kera had been talking with Fenj and Kadi before the evening

135

meal and her eye was caught by the old Observer and the Speaker of Segra chortling together. She shook her head.

'Have you any idea how many pastries they eat each day? They will become too fat to move.'

'Nonsense,' Fenj rumbled. 'Those pastries melt in the mouth and just vanish, so how can they possibly make you grow fat? They are both splendid fellows.'

Lorak grinned at Kera's expression. 'Fond of my restorative too, they are,' he informed her.

Kera laughed. 'I heard you have been making much more of your – restorative. Something about needing a bigger room to expand production?'

'Aah.' Lorak looked shifty. 'Well, no one weren't using that particular chamber see, and now Bikram shares my little place, I needed a bigger workroom, d'you see?'

Kera gave him a look of wide eyed innocence. 'But of course I see, Lorak dear. You must be so dreadfully cramped in that tiny room.'

Lorak's expression was suspicious but he deemed it safer to drop the subject.

'Plants are coming up well already, Lady Kera, in that there first area.'

Kera accepted the change of subject with a grin. 'I know. I had a look at them earlier. You have done extraordinarily well there Lorak.'

Lorak blushed. 'Well, Bikram, he helped a lot. And so did the Delvers and the Guards of course,' he mumbled.

Fenj's eyes whirred the shadows on snow colour.

'Splendid fellow,' he murmured fondly.

Thryssa and Kwanzi were the next arrivals and were glad to meet Babach and Voron. They were delighted also to see Kadi, not yet fit to hunt for herself but flying more strongly each day.

Thryssa spent the first evening of her return to the Stronghold telling of the rebellion of Discipline Senior Fayet in the Asataria to everyone in the hall. The Guards listened, avid for details of the fighting and then going over it all amongst themselves. Then, more quietly, Thryssa related the final events in the Asataria, her awareness of a being which radiated malevolence. It had fled just as she was preparing to use a great magic against it, but she had a deep foreboding as to whether that was the last they might see of it. She also told them the old story of Cheok and of her instinctive feeling that the story was in fact a true one.

'Obviously, I have no proof, but I feel in my very bones that being in the Asataria was a creature from the Void. No other solution strikes me so positively. But whether it is alone or others have escaped too, I could not guess.'

'Others are freed,' said Babach heavily. 'I sense that is what has descended on poor Drogoya. A few may have come to this land for who knows what reasons, but many more would have been drawn to Cho Petak.' He sighed, looking across the table at Thryssa. 'I did not miss the fact that Petak was the name of the maggot in your tale, but I am interested that you described him as "coming to" Nachalo rather than arising there. I know of no comparable tale in my land.'

'Nor I,' Chakar agreed.

The silence threatened to become gloom, and Mim decided to lighten the atmosphere. So he related Baryet's recent decision, announced so portentously in this hall a few days past. His telling brought laughter and did indeed lift spirits again.

'I must return to Vagrantia almost at once,' said Thryssa when they rose to seek their beds. 'Jilla and Bagri remain in Gaharn with Emla. Imshish must return with us.' She rested her hand lightly on Elyssa's shoulder. 'Elyssa says that she must be here at your Stronghold, Dragon Lord. I accept her intuition in this – may she stay?'

'She is welcome,' said Mim instantly. 'But before you leave, I would show you something, High Speaker. It will take up much of the day tomorrow, but it is of great import.'

Thryssa nodded. 'Very well.'

The residents of the Stronghold were astir early as usual and Mim announced that he and Dessi would be taking Thryssa, Lashek and Babach into the Domain of Asat. As Delvers reckoned distance it was half a "walk", so by mid morning, they had reached a narrow side tunnel. It was a mere slit in the mountain wall rather than a tunnel and Mim cast an amused glance over Lashek's portly person.

'We will not leave you stuck, Speaker Lashek.'

He lifted a glow lamp from a hook, handing it to Dessi and took another for himself, leading them into the narrow space. Within moments Thryssa and Lashek lost all sense of direction as the passage twisted back on itself then turned yet again. Even Babach confessed to being completely disorientated by the time they reached what seemed to be a dead end of seamless rock.

Dessi squeezed past Lashek, placing her lamp on the floor beside Mim's. The Dragon Lord faced the wall of rock and lifted a taloned finger. The wall slid silently aside and light blazed out from the chamber thus revealed. Mim stood aside, letting the three visitors move closer. They stared in awe at the small round chamber, its floor completely filled with a mosaic circle set with crystal, gold and jet. But the light came from hundreds upon hundreds of small niches set all around the chamber. In nearly every niche sat an oval shape and each oval pulsed with light.

In silence, Mim moved onto the circle, paused a moment and then went without hesitation to one of the niches. The oval felt warm when he placed it gently in Thryssa's hand. Twice more he went unerringly to a particular niche and returned with an oval, first for Lashek, and lastly for an astonished Dessi. Still in silence, they stared a little while longer into the chamber. Then Mim stepped back and the rock slid across the entrance. Mim slipped a pack off his shoulder and sat down on the floor.

'We can rest here for a while before we start back. I did not think you would be much inclined to be sociable right now, but we can walk on a little further and ask hospitality from the Delvers if you wish?'

'No,' Thryssa replied at once. 'You are quite right. I would far sooner rest here, just us, and consider these marvellous gifts you have given to us.' She sat cross-legged next to Mim.

Their eyes took time to adjust to the dimness of the glow lamps after the radiance of the chamber but they all sat patiently, Mim handing round dried fruit and cheese.

Lashek turned the egg in his hands, bending towards the lamps. It was backed in dark garnet and filled with a smoky topaz. A tiny shape flickered within, light softly pulsing from it. Lashek placed the silver chain around his neck and stared at Mim.

'Why did you give these to us Mim?'

Mim smiled. 'Gremara told me that you would have need of them,' he said simply.

Dessi had already looped the gold chain over her head and was gazing at the pendant in her hand. Hers had turquoise backing and a pale honey front. She could only stare at it wordlessly.

Thryssa suddenly leaned sideways and kissed Mim's cheek.

'Gremara suggested we have these, but you are the one who gave them to us. It is something I shall never forget.' In an odd gesture, she handed the oval back to the Dragon Lord. He took it, studying the jade shelling and olive-filled front as though he had not really seen it before. Then, with his sweet smile, he lifted the silver chain over Thryssa's head and kissed her cheek in turn.

'I wonder what your Gremara means when she says that we will have need of these?' Lashek sounded thoughtful.

Mim shrugged. 'When Kadi and you, Babach, were so badly hurt, one of these eggs was placed nearby. Tika wears one, she was wearing hers when she healed Farn. Clearly there must be a link – they help the healing, or help focus the healer? But I believe they are much more than aids to healing. Gremara knows, I think, but has not seen fit to tell me more yet.'

Mim regarded Dessi with affection. 'Have you nothing to say Dessi?'

The tiny Delver tore her gaze from her pendant to look at the others sitting on the floor of the narrow passage. She shook her head and went back to staring at the oval in her hands.

'I know how she feels,' Babach murmured, lifting his own pendant from his chest. 'We believe we have been given treasures beyond price.'

'Again, I thank you Mim.' Thryssa slipped her pendant inside her shirt and climbed to her feet.

Mim heaved Lashek upright and Thryssa gave her hand to Observer Babach. His silvered eyes glittered in the faint light of the glow lamps.

'I believe you have the right of it, Lashek,' he said. 'Let us pray that we prove worthy of our treasures.'

Mim noticed that all the pendants, including his own, had vanished beneath clothing, yet there had been no charge of secrecy put on them. Gremara had never suggested that they were to be kept hidden, but it appeared almost instinctive that the wearers of the strange oval pendants keep them hidden. Or keep them directly in contact with the skin? Mim pondered the question as an unusually quiet group retraced their steps back to the Stronghold.

The chamberlain Yoral had surpassed himself in galvanising the cooks into preparing a magnificent feast for the High Speaker of Vagrantia's farewell meal in the Dragon Lord's Stronghold.

'Where he has found eggs, I just dare not imagine,' Kera whispered to Thryssa.

The High Speaker swallowed the wrong way and was pounded vigorously on the back by Lorak. He had just offered her a new flask of his restorative as a parting gift, so he was best placed to offer his assistance. Several Guards rose to toast their Vagrantian allies and friends, and Kera promised herself she would make a definite point of investigating the exact extent of Lorak's increased brewing activities.

At last Thryssa stood up. Cheers rang round the hall and Lorak avoided meeting Kera's eyes by the simple expedient of retreating to sit with Fenj.

'I thank you all for your good wishes. I and my companions have been truly touched by your kind treatment of us on this, our first visit to a world that we forsook over fifteen hundred cycles past. I am sure you all understand there are dark troubles not too far away from us. Know that you can call upon Vagrantia for whatever aid we may be able to supply.'

She bowed to rapturous applause, whistles and booted feet stamping on the stone floor.

It appeared that everyone intended to see the visitors on their way until they reached the guarded Chamber where lay the circle. Only a few were allowed inside and Kera shut the door behind Daro with a groan.

'I promise Lorak will be taken severely to task tomorrow. What has he been brewing?'

Kwanzi laughed. 'An occasional party –'

Kera snorted in disgust.

'An occasional party can be most beneficial. You must take my word Lady Kera – I speak as a healer!'

Thryssa clung to Elyssa briefly then stepped onto the circle. Lashek kissed everyone he could reach.

'We made our farewells to the Dragons earlier,' he said, 'but oh, I do hope to be back with you soon.'

Chakar handed him a napkin full of pastries which cheered him a little as he followed Kwanzi and Imshish onto the circle.

A soft implosion of air, and the circle was empty. Kera turned to Jal and Nesh.

'Let's get back down to the hall and make sure it is still intact.'

She turned on her heel and strode from the Chamber. Nesh and Jal exchanged glances and trotted after Discipline Senior Lady Kera, trying to wipe the grins off their faces. Mim caught Babach's arm.

'A word before we sleep, old friend.'

Babach sank into the armchair, watching Mim poke at the fire until it began to brighten.

'I had intended to speak to you tomorrow anyway,' said the Observer.

Mim laughed and Babach noted the Dragon Lord's side teeth had lengthened. He wondered absently how far the physical changes to the Nagum body would go.

'About the Orders of Sedka and Myata?' Mim raised his brows. 'I noticed that you changed the subject rather suddenly. All that fussing for paper and pens, and busily scribbling your letters.'

Babach nodded. 'Quite so. But I needed to think, you see, as it had only just occurred to me.'

Mim sighed. 'You told us that Sedka was an ordinary word, not really a name, and that it meant plantation. Then you said that Dalena meant a glen, but was still used as a name for country girls. Then you changed the subject.'

Babach rested his recently unbandaged left hand on his egg pendant. It was scarred far worse than his right hand had been, but he noticed that the scars faded much more rapidly if he kept contact with the pendant. Now, he smiled at the Dragon Lord.

'Do you recall asking me if I had heard singing?'

Mim frowned. 'Yes. You said you had not. But then you asked if I could smell mint.'

Babach's smile widened. 'Well Dragon Lord, Myata in the old tongue simply means, mint.'

141

Chapter Fourteen

Pajar was crawling into his bed when a scribe knocked at his door to inform him of the High Speaker's arrival. He scrambled back into his clothes and reached Thryssa's study at the same moment as Thryssa herself. Lashek immediately offered him a rather squashed pastry, which Pajar took without noticing.

Thryssa sat at her table with a sigh of relief. 'It is good to be home, but the things we have seen Pajar! We will bore you to tears with our tales.'

She studied her new first councillor's anxious face.

'Should I hear your reports now, or can they wait till the morning?'

Pajar saw the weariness etched round the High Speaker's eyes and shook his head.

'I came only to welcome you back. It can all wait until tomorrow.'

Kwanzi smiled approvingly from behind Thryssa's chair. Pajar turned to go back to bed, absently biting into the pastry he discovered in his hand. He stopped.

'Where did you get this, Speaker Lashek? It is amazing!' he mumbled through the pastry.

'Ah hah,' Lashek beamed. 'A wonderful lady in what was once Valsheba. And – I have the recipe.'

Pajar waited next morning until a scribe came to tell him that the High Speaker was now in her study. Entering, he saw papers he had worked on neatly stacked to her left. So she must either have worked last night after all, or before breakfast today. He had an enormous respect for the High Speaker's capacity for work. She worked far harder than most people would have believed, overseeing every administrative detail of Vagrantian life.

'Good morning Pajar. I am most impressed with your efficiency in my absence. You dealt with that dispute in Kedara's main market very well indeed.' She smiled at the young man.

'And you have been most discreet regarding my last wishes.'

Pajar blushed, his red face clashing abysmally with his flaming hair. 'I was most worried, High Speaker. But Speaker Orsim was here and he spoke kindly and wisely to me of my fears.'

Thryssa nodded. 'I am glad that you were sensible enough to discuss your concerns with him. I do not approve of secrecy between the Circles and especially not between the Speakers or Councillors. But this worries me greatly.'

She tapped the documents before her. Pajar knew at once that she referred to Fira Circle and Kallema's arbitrary closing of all access to that Circle.

'The gates to Parima and Kedara were blocked the day you left, but the reports I received from Chornay regarding Fira's treatment of its residents came a few days later.' Pajar frowned. 'There is no way of knowing how long Kallema has authorised this "culling" of her people – which is what it amounts to.'

Thryssa shuffled through the papers to find the one she wanted. 'The three young ones who I ordered to be brought here. They refer by name to several who are on the census lists. As they are apparently no longer in Fira Circle, and there is no record of them residing here or in either of the other Circles, what is your conclusion?'

Pajar did not hesitate. 'They have been murdered and disposed of,' he replied.

Thryssa nodded. 'There can be no doubt of it,' she agreed. 'The question remains, how long has this been happening? These children mention names of students two and three cycles in advance of them. Has it only been happening for three cycles, or will we find it began much earlier?'

'Kallema has been Speaker for nearly twenty cycles. But I have made some enquires. There was nothing out of the ordinary until about seven cycles ago.'

Thryssa raised a brow. 'Is there a significance there?'

Pajar shrugged. 'Prilla became first councillor at that time.'

Thryssa pushed her chair sideways and stared out of the window, the rim of Talvo Circle a black line in the distance against the blue sky. After a while she turned back to Pajar.

'I was trying to think back,' she said, 'and I do believe that Kallema became more withdrawn then. I will ask Lashek and

Orsim what they can remember.'

'Speaker Lashek left at dawn for Segra, High Speaker.'

Thryssa nodded, then grinned. 'Did he take his precious recipe?'

Pajar smiled back. 'He has given it to everyone here, not just the cooks.' He fished in his shirt pocket and drew out a scrap of paper. 'I had to copy it too.'

'Gremara seems to speak with the Dragon Lord in the Stronghold frequently. Has there been any problem from Talvo of late?'

'No, High Speaker. But several people have said there is another Dragon with her, smaller and cream coloured.'

'She is Jeela, daughter of the most beautiful golden great Dragon, Pajar. In the Stronghold, they believe that Jeela will be Gremara's successor.'

'Pachela speaks very often with Gremara. She says the silver one is no longer mad?'

'So Mim believes.' Thryssa sat in silence. 'Gremara told the Dragon Lord to give myself and Lashek each one of these.' She lifted a silver chain free of her shirt and held the pendant across the table towards Pajar.

He stared in astonishment at the beautiful thing. It swung slowly on its chain, just below Thryssa's hand, first the jade back catching the sunshine, then the olive front seeming to trap the light within itself.

'Look closer,' said Thryssa softly.

Pajar leaned forward, his vision enhanced as he concentrated. The tiny shape within the oval turned and quivered. Pajar sat back with a thump and looked at the High Speaker. She hid the pendant beneath her shirt again.

'Mim told us that Gremara said we would have need of them. But we have no idea what she might mean. We know that they have been beneficial in healing situations, but what more they might help us with, we cannot guess.' She reached behind her and tugged a bell rope. 'But you say that Pachela speaks often with Gremara, and yet you did not know of Jeela?'

'Pachela chose to stay here in the Corvida.' Pajar could still see the tiny twisting form within the pendant as he answered Thryssa. 'According to first councillor Shema, Pachela was an average student, like Daro, although their assessors said she had the capacity to be extremely powerful in both earth and fire magic.'

He paused while a maid brought in a tray of tea, setting it at the end of the table. Once they were alone again he continued.

'Since Pachela's eyes silvered, she still seems shy of people but there is a confidence within her and an awareness of her own abilities.'

'I will speak with her alone later I think, Pajar. What of these three Firan children?'

Pajar sipped his tea. 'I would recommend that you see them separately, perhaps with Chornay present throughout to offer familiarity. I would suggest that you tell him he may not intervene at any point but must give you his impressions when each has left you.'

Thryssa considered Pajar's advice, eventually nodding her agreement. 'But I will leave you to explain to Chornay. Send him and the first Firan to me shortly, Pachela after the midday meal.'

Pajar got up and walked to the door.

'Pajar? I do appreciate that it is very difficult for you to be plunged into this position with so little training but I am sure it is the right decision. These last days you have shown yourself capable of the rank of first councillor and I am grateful to have your help.'

Pajar blushed again, mumbled his thanks and fled. Thryssa poured herself more tea, wondering if Kwanzi knew of any remedies against blushing. In Pajar's case, the result was most unfortunate.

By the time Thryssa went through to her private rooms at midday she was already exhausted. The interviews with the three young Firans had taken much of her strength. Kwanzi frowned as she poked food around her plate, rearranging it rather than eating much of it.

'Kwanzi, I would like you to attend the Firan children. They are deeply afraid of something, even knowing that they are safe here with us. Graza burst into tears at my first question. The boy, Kralo, has a confident front but it is egg-shell brittle just beneath.' She abandoned her food and reached for the jug of water. 'They

145

depend on Chornay quite heavily – he is their friend among all these strangers. But Chornay told me their minds have not been investigated as have all the others whose eyes silvered. Kallema imprisoned them at once. No healers went near them. And when they arrived here they were upset and shocked, so our people only offered reassurance – no assessments have been made.'

'Of course. I will arrange it this afternoon. Are you going to eat any of that food?'

Thryssa looked down at her plate then up to her husband apologetically. 'I'm sorry. I promise I will eat my supper. Those children bothered me Kwanzi, there is something badly amiss. Be careful when you try to work with them and make sure you have the best healers with you.'

'Yes, High Speaker. And what have you to do this afternoon?'

'I am seeing Pachela. Then I will spend some more time with Pajar. Which reminds me.'

Kwanzi hooted with laughter at Thryssa's query about a cure for Pajar's blushes.

'I will think about it,' he said, 'but I can make no promises.'

Pachela entered at Thryssa's call and sat in the offered chair by the window. Thryssa had decided to make this meeting appear more informal, so sat with her back to her work table.

'I am sorry I had no chance to speak with you before I left Vagrantia, my dear. I felt we should acquaint ourselves at once. Tea?'

Pachela accepted with a faint smile. Thryssa sat back nursing her own mug.

'Tell me first something of yourself.'

Pachela blinked her silver and grey eyes in some surprise and Thryssa congratulated herself on putting the girl a little off balance.

'I am Segran, as you know. I am drawn to earth and fire.' Pachela hesitated, then met Thryssa's stare. 'Fire calls me ever more strongly.'

Thryssa sipped her tea. 'Is that because of the connection between yourself and Gremara which has developed lately?'

Pachela looked out of the window, across Parima's vastness to the black wall between Parima and Talvo. She nodded slowly. 'I think it probably is, High Speaker. May I ask you something?'

'Of course.'

'Did you meet the great Dragons of the north?'

Thryssa relaxed. She felt none of the wrongness about this child as she had with the Firans. Then she chided herself: she really must stop seeing anyone under the age of thirty as a child.

'I rode on the back of a Snow Dragon and a great Dragon,' she admitted. 'And they are the most beautiful, kindly creatures in the world.'

Questions bombarded her, to all of which she gave honest answers until finally she laughed, raising her hand for mercy.

'Enough for now my dear. But tell me, why have you not told anyone of Gremara's new companion, Jeela?'

Pachela looked astonished. 'Is that her name? Gremara said that her successor had come, but spoke no more on the matter.'

Thryssa nodded in satisfaction: she had concluded as much.

'Pachela, I have a suggestion – a suggestion, not an order. Will you come with me, into Talvo Circle? Gremara will do no harm now. She instructed the Dragon Lord in the north to give me this, so I think she intends that we be friends.'

Thryssa drew out the egg pendant, watching Pachela carefully. The girl focused her sight, then her mouth rounded in amazement and tears poured down her cheeks.

It took three days to traverse Parima. The people who farmed the western end came out to greet their High Speaker with delight and warmth. Thryssa realised how many cycles had drifted by while she had remained shut up in the Corvida and resolved to find the time somehow to come out to talk to her people more often again. As they neared the entrance to the tunnel into Talvo, Thryssa glanced at Pachela. She was pale with excitement but there was no trace of fear. Kwanzi had fumed at Thryssa and Pachela going alone to Talvo, but for once Thryssa became angry with him.

'I can surely fear nothing in Parima. If I take an escort, it tells people I am afraid to be among them. Of course we travel alone.'

Now the two women, one very young and one far older than she appeared, walked steadily through the twilight of the tunnel towards the early morning light in Talvo Circle. Emerging, they paused, staring around them at the lush creepers clinging to the walls, the many-toned greenness everywhere. Hot water suddenly soared up from a pool veiled in steam some distance to their left. Thryssa grinned and reached for Pachela's hand.

'I think we should watch our path rather carefully, do you not?'

By late morning the rampant vegetation had retreated to the sides of the widening crater and they walked on thin soil from which only coarse grasses grew. Pachela's hand tightened on Thryssa's. Thryssa looked up quickly and smiled. A small ivory Dragon spiralled lazily above them, sinking lower with each turn until at last she landed in front of the women. She reared erect, faceted eyes whirring cream flecked with gold, and spoke in their minds.

'I am Jeela, daughter to Kija and heir to Gremara of Talvo. May the stars guide your paths.'

Thryssa bowed, Pachela copying her, and returned a formal greeting. At once Jeela dropped to the ground and lowered her brow to touch Thryssa's.

'You are one of the honoured,' she said. 'I am glad you have come. Have you news of Kadi, and Ashta, and Kija, and Fenj and –'

Thryssa laughed, placing her hand along Jeela's face. 'I will tell you everything, but you must meet Pachela, she who speaks with Gremara.'

Jeela turned her face to Pachela, her eyes whirring faster. 'I could talk to you too if you like,' she said. 'It sometimes seems a little empty here.'

Pachela followed Thryssa's action and raised her hand to touch the small Dragon's face. Jeela's laughter rang in their minds and then the Dragon was in the air again, curving and swooping above their heads.

'Gremara awaits you. This way. I will lead you.'

This time, it was Pachela's hand that reached for Thryssa's. After a glance at the girl's face Thryssa spoke not a word, letting her experience the real magic of walking beneath a dancing, laughing Dragon.

They walked for some time before Pachela stopped in her tracks, staring up to her right. Jeela's amusement rippled through the air and she swung back towards the high ledge which was Gremara's favourite place. The women waited as Gremara slid

148

from the black rock into the air and glided down towards them. The midday sun flashed and dazzled off each silver scale and her eyes sparkled with rainbow colours.

As on the mountainside above Arak, she did not raise herself upright in the formal greeting of the great Dragons but reclined gracefully on the ground before them.

'I am glad to see two legs in my Circle again.' Her voice was slightly higher in pitch than other Dragons, Thryssa noted. 'I have no food to offer you, but fresh water is only a few paces away.'

Thryssa took the pack off her shoulders and sat on the ground facing the silver Dragon. 'I have food for us should we need it. I am not hungry.' Thryssa offered the pack to Pachela who shook her head, dropping to the ground beside Thryssa.

There was an interval of comfortable silence while Gremara scrutinised the two women and they in turn, feasted their eyes on the Dragon's beauty. There was a flurry of wings and Jeela landed near Gremara.

'I would see what you carry, High Speaker Thryssa. I have only seen such things in my memories and I have long desired to see one in truth.'

Thryssa got up and moved closer to Gremara, drawing her pendant from under her shirt. She knelt by the silver Dragon's head and held up the oval for her to see clearly. To Thryssa's complete surprise Gremara made no comment but her voice rang out in sudden song: a song without words but with which Jeela joined in a treble harmony. At last Gremara's song faded into silence.

'I thank you for letting me see this wondrous thing. In small return, I tell you to beware the water Circle. There is a badness growing which will try to join with another, and between them they will seek to destroy all the Circles. I cannot interfere, not yet, but the trouble grows faster than I had believed it would. You will have to act, and act soon High Speaker.' Gremara flexed her wings in preparation for flight. 'We would welcome visitors sometimes – I fear Jeela grows bored occasionally.'

Jeela's eyes whirred, darkening to amber as she protested Gremara's comment.

'Again, I thank you for bringing the egg for me to see with my

149

own eyes. You will discover its meaning for yourself: I may not reveal it to you.' She leaned forward, her brow pressing first Thryssa's then Pachela's in the lightest of touches.

'Know that you both have a part to play in what will come. May the stars guard your hearts.'

They watched the silver Dragon rise, spiralling higher, and higher, until she was the merest speck far above Talvo Circle.

Jeela sighed. 'She can fly higher than any other Dragon – nearly to the stars themselves I am sure. She will not permit me to try though. I will guide you back to your tunnel, and you did promise you would tell me all about everyone in the Stronghold, High Speaker!'

Re-entering Parima Circle, it was but a short walk to the farmhouse where they had stayed the previous night. Twilight was thickening to darkness as they reached the black stone building, its windows spilling welcoming lights onto the path. Again they were treated as honoured guests and well fed before being left in the small bedroom they had shared last night.

Pachela blew out the candle on the tiny dresser between their beds.

'I can scarcely believe today really happened, High Speaker,' she murmured, pulling the covers over her shoulders.

Thryssa yawned. 'I promise you it did child. Now sleep, we leave at first light.'

'Good night, High Speaker.'

Thryssa was almost asleep when she heard Pachela turn over and sniff. Could the child have taken a cold?

'Are you all right Pachela?' she asked softly.

'Yes thank you, High Speaker. I just thought I could smell mint.'

Thryssa had a day of paperwork with Pajar when she got back to the Corvida and then next day the Segran and Kedaran Speakers and first councillors were arriving for an official meeting. Orsim of Kedara arrived first, with his councillor Dashka, and listened to a general account of the Stronghold and Gaharn from Thryssa. He had been intrigued rather than annoyed that one of his councillors, Maressa, had gone off to Sapphrea, the lands that had once been Valsheba.

'I would never have thought Maressa would take it into her head to go adventuring so far,' he said, smiling at Thryssa.

The High Speaker shrugged. 'Elyssa announced that she felt she had to stay at the Stronghold. Our young women are all becoming adventurous it seems. Your own daughter is quite captivated by the Wise One of the Delvers and a Lady Ryla of the Asatarians. Jilla was adamant that she remain in Gaharn with Bagri. And I must tell you, Orsim.' She drew him towards the window, leaving Pajar talking to Dashka. 'I understand from Pajar that you helped him through a brief bout of panic soon after I left here?'

Orsim shook his head. 'I just happened to be here. He would have managed without me. He is very young for first councillor but he has the makings of a very good one.'

'Well, I thank you anyway.'

Lashek came bustling in with his first councillor Shema, and Thryssa took her place at the head of the table. She immediately raised the subject of Kallema's activities in Fira Circle.

'As you probably heard, I visited Gremara four days ago. She explicitly warns us of serious trouble from Fira. But before I left here I asked Kwanzi to investigate the three Firan children whose eyes silvered. You were here of course when I ordered an escort to remove them from Fira, where we found they had been forcibly held, against their wishes, and against all our codes of conduct.'

She looked at the attentive faces turned towards her.

'I have Kwanzi's report here. All three Firans resisted investigation by his team. The combined efforts of the healers could not render them unconscious. After four days, Kwanzi stopped the testing. He reports that they are now working to find some way of reading these children's minds, which they will then use on them. The children showed no distress or discomfort at any of the tests. The boy, Kralo, found them amusing apparently.'

She laid the paper she had been referring to back on the table.

'I interviewed them myself earlier and felt a great wrongness about all three which is why I asked Kwanzi to arrange for the investigative procedures to be made.'

'Has Kallema had them blocked, or shielded, in some way?' asked Orsim.

'Would it be possible, or likely, that three such young students could know anything of importance about Fira's assembly or Kallema's intentions?' Councillor Shema sounded sceptical.

'Have you considered that the whole episode could have been arranged? We all know that Thryssa would never stand for a child being incarcerated, let alone three of them.' Lashek's left hand rested in the middle of his chest, over the egg pendant, Thryssa realised.

Pajar nodded. 'So now Kallema has three possible spies or worse, comfortably within our midst perhaps?'

Chapter Fifteen

The distance to the caves of the sea Dragons, referred to by Cloud as being "not far", took Tika's party nearly three days to travel. Tika, Gan and Maressa walked most of the way as their route followed the beach rather than the rough ground behind the cliffs. There was much debate about why the water crept slowly up towards them and then crept slowly away again: debate from which Ren Salar remained stubbornly aloof. He agreed with any theory suggested to him until eventually they stopped asking his opinion.

Gan and Sket had commented between themselves of the gradual change in Tika. For the first time since she had run away from Return, she could relax a little. No messages could reach her here, by way of a circle or by a Merig, and while she occasionally wondered how her friends fared back in the world, she revelled in a sense of freedom. Always at the back of her mind was the thought of the strange creatures who had attacked them on their arrival at the coast. She also wondered why her eyes had changed so strangely, but thoughts of Elyssa's acceptance of the fact for herself, and of Ren's considering it a normal part of life, kept any concerns to a minor form.

Seeing Farn's delight in flying above the sparkling waves gave her great pleasure: he was but a baby, and yet until now he had missed so much of the fun and freedom Dragon hatchlings usually enjoyed. Storm, one of the younger sea Dragons, accompanied them and Tika smiled, watching Farn chasing after him as he plunged beneath the water. So far, Farn had allowed only his feet to dabble on the surface and his wingtips to brush the waves, but had not been foolhardy enough to follow Storm under the water.

The rest of the party sometimes rode the koninas on their slow amble south but also spent a large part of each day paddling along barefooted at the edge of the water, with the firm exception of Ren Salar, Pallin and Sket, who all regarded the vast expanse of sea with the greatest suspicion.

Towards the middle of the third day, Farn reported that a freshwater stream cascaded from the cliff top a short distance along the beach, and the party rested there. Storm flew on to the south and Brin floated down to land near them. The great crimson Dragon found huge enjoyment in just drifting up and down on the air currents along the line of cliffs.

They began walking again but came to a halt as they rounded a rocky promontory. The sea waters had carved a small cove, half ringed by the grey cliffs. The cliffs were pocked with dark shadowed caves, but in front of many of the caves, the sea Dragons lay along their ledges. One of them slid from the ledge and glided towards them. Tika recognised her as Cloud and bowed politely as the Dragon settled on the sand.

'There are several empty caves here, along this side. You are welcome to choose whichever you wish.'

'Thank you for your hospitality. We will see which best suits our needs if we may.'

'We will wait while you decide and then I will introduce you to our Elders.' Cloud lifted back towards one of the highest caves.

Ren moved up beside Tika, staring up at the vacant caves with dislike.

'I knew they would all be far too high,' he said with disgust.

Khosa poked her head out of her carry sack on Ren's chest.

'Not too high,' she commented. 'But far too wet.'

'There is just enough room for us to take the koninas back through these cliffs,' Pallin reported smugly. 'And a couple of caves level with the ground.'

Ren brightened. 'Then I shall assist Pallin tomove the koninas to the far more sensible caves out of sight of all that.' He waved dismissively at the water already rushing in to fill the cove.

Tika grinned. 'We will climb up to look in these, then we'll see how our comfort compares with yours.'

Ren snorted and turned to help Pallin and Riff with the koninas. 'There will be no comparison dear lady.'

The rest of the group stared up at the caves offered by Cloud.

154

Navan moved forward onto the rocks and began to pick a path up to the first one.

'Well, we might as well all go and look,' said Maressa and followed Navan up the side of the cliff.

It proved to be less difficult than it had appeared. After peering into five caves, all far deeper than expected, they decided on two next to each other. Gan poked around at the rear of one cave and discovered it bore down the further back he went. He returned to the main part of the cave without reaching the end of the passage.

'This one for sure Tika,' he told her. 'I cannot see without a lamp, but I suspect this one may well exit behind the cliffs.'

Tika nodded. 'Let's go and fetch some of the packs and something to make a fire up here.'

Olam had taken a liking to the cave slightly above the one Gan had chosen and now joined them on their climb down to find Pallin.

'It must have been a tight squeeze getting the animals through here,' Maressa remarked.

Olam grinned. 'No problem at all, if Pallin was determined to get them through.'

It was as if a giant had hit the cliff with a might hammer and caused an uneven crack to split it apart. The narrow path turned left after only three paces, then right again almost immediately, then left and finally right. Gan looked to his right as he emerged from the gap and nodded with satisfaction.

'I am fairly sure that the cave I have chosen ends down in one of these.'

'Always useful to have a back door,' Olam agreed.

Pallin had the koninas beside a wide faced but shallow cave. It looked large enough to offer protection for the animals should the weather change. Riff came out of another cave which opened about waist high, a few paces further along. Pallin's scowl had disappeared and he was very nearly cheerful as he and Ren unloaded packs and saddles.

'Fresh water pool down there,' he told Olam. 'And this grass is not bad, a great improvement on what we've seen so far at any rate. If we are stopping here a while, it will save on grain for the beasts.' He slapped his hand on a flank as he moved round one konina to begin unloading the next.

Navan bent to pluck a blade of grass. 'The fresh water must be seeping through the ground all around here, or just beneath.' He bent down again. 'Tubers there, look.' He straightened and climbed onto a boulder. 'Quite an area of better vegetation.'

Khosa stepped daintily from the second cave and surveyed the scene. 'There are squeakers here,' she announced. Turquoise eyes glittered. 'Soon there will be less.'

Gan had vanished into the shallow cave and now came out frowning. His gaze landed on the orange Kephi.

'Khosa, is there a space from either cave, that might lead to one above?'

'Possibly. I may investigate for you, after I have eaten a squeaker or two.'

'That would be most kind of you,' Gan agreed.

'Where will the meeting with the Elder Dragons be held do you suppose?' asked Maressa.

'If it is on one of those ledges, I am afraid I am indisposed,' Ren told her.

'I thought you were an Offering in Drogoya. Isn't that a high and responsible rank?' Tika snapped at him.

'There is nothing in the rules as I recall them which states that I am expected to perch at ridiculous heights. My presence would merely be an embarrassment.'

'Why?'

'I would be sick.' Ren's reply was succinct.

Somewhat discomfited, Tika turned to sort through the piles of saddles and retrieved her own pack and rolled cloak.

'We will take some of our gear up to our cave and enquire about this meeting,' she told the Offering.

'I will be delighted to attend at ground level.' He inclined his head.

She glanced sharply at him but could find no sign of sarcasm or amusement. Tika sighed. 'You do not like heights, or the sea. What else makes you ill?'

'Certain foods in Drogoya,' he shrugged. 'I truly cannot help it Lady Tika.'

Tika glimpsed Sket's grin and reluctantly smiled herself. She headed back through the narrow gap and climbed up to the cave

Gan had picked out. She put her pack some way back from the entrance then stood on the ledge, looking up to where Cloud reclined watching them.

'Sea Mother, some of our party do not enjoy being above the ground too far. Where will we meet your Elders?'

Cloud's eyes whirred and Tika knew there was discussion between her and several other Dragons. But before Cloud could give a reply, a Dragon came from the shadows of another cave. This one was much larger than Cloud, of a dark slate grey, and Tika knew beyond doubt that it was the most important of the Elders by the sheer power it radiated. The watching Dragons became alert, their wings shivering in anticipation of the Elder's flight.

A body slimmer than Brin's but nearly as large slid smoothly into the air above the cove and drifted over Tika's head to settle on the beach beyond the promontory. Farn and Brin were already raised in greeting to the sea Dragon who responded in like fashion. Ren, Sket and Olam came through the gap and joined the others facing the new Dragon.

With screams and high calls, the rest of the sea Dragons landed around the Elder. One of them was also clearly an Elder.

'My name is Salt, Eldest of this Flight,' a low musical voice said in their minds. 'You are welcome guests within our caves.'

The dark grey male lowered himself to the dry sand and reclined opposite Tika. She bowed then sat cross legged, the others following suit.

'Is it polite to call you Sea Father, or Elder Salt?' she asked.

Salt rumbled with amusement, the sound reminding Tika with a sudden pang of old Fenj.

'We have no Sea Fathers, only Sea Mothers. Call me Salt, as I am known to all. 'This is Ice, second Eldest of this Flight, and my sister.'

Salt's head dipped towards the much paler grey Dragon beside him. 'You have come in search of ancient places, I believe you told Cloud?'

'Yes.' Tika took a deep breath. 'Long ages past, a great catastrophe overtook these lands. The people who caused it lived in cities hereabouts. We seek for any signs of those long-lost places.'

157

'Your words are difficult to follow,' Salt remarked. 'We do not know cities.'

Tika formed a picture of Gaharn in her mind and there was much murmuring among the Dragons.

'Do these things grow from the land?' Ice asked curiously.

'No, people build them, from stone or wood.' Tika picked up a handful of pebbles and stacked them one on top of another.

Dragons watched intently. 'Are there no caves for them?'

Tika was not sure who had asked the question but realised she was in serious danger of being side-tracked.

'There are many people but few caves,' Ren intervened smoothly. 'We will tell you all you wish to know of cities – later.'

Eyes whirred and flashed and Tika shot a grateful smile at the Offering.

'Do you have no memories of such a place as we have just shown you?' Ren continued.

Salt considered the question. 'We know of the catastrophe of which you speak. Our Flights lived further to both north and south long ago: we had no dealings with the two legged ones.' His eyes flashed like an angry sea. 'Even so, many of us died. There were great waves, greater than ever seen before or since. And the earth moved as easily as if it too was water. The sea poured over the land from whence you have come, and all the trees were gone. Fires burned, even from the water itself, and left the land as you see it now.'

'And you have no idea where the cities might have stood?' Ren pressed.

There was a silence before Ice replied. 'One such place may have stood here. When the great winds blow, the sands move. We see rocks that are not as these rocks.'

She envisioned large, tumbled blocks of dressed stone. 'Mostly, they are in the sands beyond our caves.'

'Will it inconvenience you if we search in that area, Salt?' asked Maressa.

'It is of no matter to us. We hunt the sea and have little interest in the land. It provides us only with caves in which to rest and to hatch our children.' Salt lowered his head to study Tika, then looked towards Farn. 'Cloud told of this soul bonding.

158

I have never heard of a hatchling bonding with another kind.'

'No,' Tika agreed. 'Nor had the great Dragons. I was bonded to Farn, and a Nagum boy bonded with a female hatchling at near the same time.' She held Salt's gaze steadily. 'The boy, Mim, is called Dragon Lord now by order of the silver one, Gremara.'

There was a flurry among the sea Dragons at this statement.

'Show us a Dragon Lord and a silver one,' Salt demanded.

Tika obediently pictured Mim as she had last seen him, leaning against Ashta, the scales shimmering gold on his face and arms. Then she gave them a sight of Gremara, explaining that she herself had not seen the silver Dragon. Khosa chose that moment to stalk across the sand. She sat firmly in front of Salt for an instant then rose and wound herself over his forearm and rubbed along his side, buzzing softly all the while. Salt's eyes followed the tiny orange shape in some bemusement.

'She has exceedingly sharp talons,' Farn warned nervously.

Salt swung his head to Farn then peered back down at Khosa.

'Show me your talons,' he commanded.

Khosa extended her claws onto his forearm and he studied them carefully.

'A very dangerous creature, I suspect,' he said solemnly.

Khosa's buzzing increased and she tucked herself tidily into the crook of Salt's arm.

'It is nice to be appreciated,' she murmured.

Farn was aghast that Salt should seem to be deceived by the treacherous Kephi but Tika hushed him. Salt could squash poor Khosa in an instant if he so chose and Tika did not believe for one moment that he considered the Kephi a dangerous threat to himself or any other Dragon.

'If you should need any help that we might provide, do not hesitate to ask,' said Salt.

Tika smiled. 'We enjoyed the fish the other day.'

Salt rumbled softly. 'Then more will be provided whenever you wish.' He settled more comfortably, making sure not to disturb Khosa as Tika's party all noticed with amusement.

'You said you would tell us things we wish to know.' Salt's eyes fixed on Ren. 'It is now later, so we shall listen to your tales.'

Tika grinned.

159

'I think Cloud will have told you all she heard at our first camp. What particularly would you like to know of?'

It seemed that Dragons never tired of stories, and were never lost for questions, or so an exhausted Offering Ren Salar decided as the moon rose. He lifted his hands pleadingly towards Salt.

'We are weaklings compared to Dragons. We need rest, Elder Salt. I promise I will speak again, but now we really must sleep.'

Maressa discreetly nudged Tika. Tika looked casually round at the Dragons and saw several of the younger ones, heads back between their wings, fast asleep. Brin was still awake, but Farn was sound asleep against his side.

With polite apologies, the sea Dragons rose in a flock and curved round the cliff to their caves. Belatedly, Tika realised that Khosa too had vanished. Irritating as the Kephi could be, Tika hoped that Salt did not decide to drop her. Brin roused Farn and they followed the sea Dragons. Brin had found that the cave next to Olam's had a wide ledge, suitable for his bulk, while Farn settled at the entrance to the one Gan had chosen.

Ren retreated with Pallin and Sket to their cave behind the cliffs. Sket busied himself brewing yet more tea in the kettle which simmered among the embers of the small fire. Pallin joined him and they peered into the darkness for the Offering.

'Nothing mentioned about those red eyed things,' Pallin muttered to Sket. 'All so busy talking of things long past, when it's now we should be worrying about.'

Ren appeared and sat by the fire, accepting the tea Sket handed him.

'Wondered had you got lost,' Pallin grunted.

'No. It was just that as we came from the gap to here, I could swear I smelled mint, yet I had not noticed it grew here. Remind me to look in the morning will you?'

Navan was first down to Pallin's cave next morning and found Sket and Ren prowling abstractedly around the edge of the small pool of fresh water. Pallin was poking in a large pan over the fire and wore his usual scowl. He looked up as Navan reached him.

'Fools are looking for plants.' He jerked his head in the direction of Sket and the Offering.

Navan nodded and took a bowl of the oatmeal leavened with a few dried fruits which was what Pallin considered a suitable

160

breakfast. Olam and Gan appeared, trailed by Maressa and Tika deep in conversation. Both girls declined the oatmeal but accepted the tea.

'Not much left in the way of supplies,' Pallin announced.

'I was thinking of that last night,' Tika replied. 'If we work out exactly what we might need for a few ten days – the quantities as close to exact as I am sure you could estimate – perhaps Brin could go back to Far?'

'I could go with him to mind speak Lallia or Seboth from a sensible distance,' Maressa volunteered.

'And what if Hargon has decided to besiege Far, or something equally nasty?' asked Gan.

They all knew he was thinking of the creatures in the shielded sphere.

Maressa shrugged. 'I would recognise the signature of anything similar if I met one again. But we were on the ground when they attacked us before, and from what Cloud has said, they attacked the sea Dragons when they were sleeping in their caves.'

Gan chewed his lip. Brin and Farn descended to land close by and Gan glared at Tika. She had obviously called them, to hear Brin's views on this idea.

'How long would it take you to fly to Far from here to replenish our supplies Brin? Carrying Maressa as well?'

Brin's eyes whirred with a rosy glow. 'Four days at the longest,' he replied promptly. 'And then four back.'

Gan scowled, a mirror image of Pallin across the fire.

'Eight days alone, Maressa. I do not think it wise.'

Maressa snorted. 'I am not entirely helpless Gan.' She lifted her hand slightly and dust swirled up by Gan's feet, whirling into the fire which blazed in the sudden gust of air.

Navan swallowed, but the look he gave Maressa was more of admiration than suspicion. Gan raised one shoulder, indicating that he still had considerable doubts for Maressa's safety.

'I would allow no harm to befall Maressa.' Brin sounded indignant and smoke wisped from his nostrils in annoyance.

'I know you would not Brin. I meant no insult. But I fear for you both, not just Maressa.' Gan was quick to soothe Brin's ruffled temper.

'I will permit no danger near us,' Brin repeated.

'Of course he wouldn't.' Farn was most upset that anyone should criticise his hero.

Gan shook his head ruefully. 'I apologise, truly I do. If anyone could fly to Far and back then you would surely be the fastest and safest of Dragons, Brin.'

Tika grinned at him. Gan was at last learning how to wheedle and flatter: a much better strategy with either Farn or Brin than issuing orders. Something she had long since discovered.

Maressa produced a scrap of paper and went into a huddle with Pallin to decide what would be most needed. They could survive here as they were with fresh water, fish provided by the sea Dragons and the occasional green shoots that resembled some of the salad plants of Sapphrea. It had taken them fifteen days to travel from Far to this coast with the koninas, and to make the journey back they would need more than a few fish.

Tika leaned back on her elbows and saw Olam drawn into Maressa and Pallin's discussions. The young sea Dragon, Storm, appeared above the cliffs, tilted his wings sharply and settled beside Farn.

'I will show you where the rocks usually come out of the sand,' he told Tika.

She sat up. 'We will come shortly. Is it really close by?' Her silver and green eyes narrowed at Storm. 'Cloud told us that your caves were "not far", and it took us three days to get here.'

She felt Storm's laughter. Prismed eyes stared at her outstretched legs.

'One hundred, two hundred, of your steps,' he suggested.

Tika moved across, leaning to hug Farn and reaching to touch Storm's face. 'If it turns out to be leagues and leagues, I might become very annoyed.'

Both Farn and Storm shivered in glee, recognising that Tika was teasing them.

'Go on then, we will follow.'

Storm lifted at once, closely followed by Farn. Tika turned to Brin.

'You will be careful old friend?' she asked softly.

Brin's eyes flashed with affection as he heard the genuine concern in her mind tone.

'You know I will, dear child. We will be back before you

162

have time to miss us.'

Tika put her arms around as much of Brin as she could reach and he rubbed his long face gently against her head.

'May the stars guide your path and guard your heart then Brin.'

She turned, coming face to face with Maressa, who carried a pack containing a handful of dried fruits, an end of flat, tough travel bread and two flasks of water.

'I promise there will be no risks taken. We will leave now – I dare not start looking at any ruins or I would never leave them!'

They hugged each other, Maressa climbed between Brin's great wings and they lifted into the sky. Brin circled once, then climbed higher and arrowed towards the east.

Chapter Sixteen

Finn Rah decided that Lyeto was correct: if there were refugees from the terror still wandering about outside, it was the duty and the obligation of Myata's followers to offer them sanctuary. Lyeto had gone out on several more occasions, each time bringing one or two shocked, frightened or injured people back with him. The worst time for Finn, and for the rest of the community, was the night that Lyeto returned with five terrified children, the eldest of whom was a mere seven years old. The four younger ones clung to the eldest, refusing to let him go until he gently persuaded them that these strangers were trustworthy.

That night, Finn saw more of the hidden Oblaka community in tears than ever before, including the night that their House had been destroyed. Strangely, it was the disfigured blind woman, Teal, who seemed best able to calm the children. Three of them recognised her: their mothers had often gone to buy Teal's bread from the market, and so her face, scarred as it was, was reassuringly familiar.

Finn was in Chakar's sitting room with Observer Soosha and Kooshak Sarryen.

'The last two adults Lyeto brought in came from just west of Krasato,' Soosha was saying. 'I wonder what impelled them to flee so far in this direction, particularly?'

Sarryen joined them at the table with a fresh pot of tea. 'I have to say that I have noticed increasing whispers of Myata over the last few years as I wander the lands,' she said thoughtfully. 'Perhaps the people remember the stories of her promise of welcome for all within her House?'

'It is interesting you should say that – I have heard fewer and fewer students mention her of late.' Finn looked over the rim of her tea bowl at the Kooshak.

Soosha grunted. 'I suspect that Cho Petak may have examined would be students far more closely than in the past. He would not want any other than blind devotees of Sedka's Order and, by extension, of himself as Sacrifice.'

'That makes sense within the Menedula. But why the sudden interest in Myata in the countryside?' asked Sarryen.

'The Balance?' The Observer suggested.

Finn nodded slowly. 'I remember some ridiculous cases about thirty years ago. People were planting onions among their beans, as they always had. They were accused of flouting Sedka's fourth law, or some such nonsense. Do you remember? It caused an unusual stir at the time then it all seemed to disappear. I should have checked out the matter more closely.'

Soosha patted her arm. 'We can all be more knowledgeable with hindsight, my dear Finn. No doubt the evidence is all there if we could but connect the various pieces which would then prove Cho Petak to be the foulest sort of impostor.'

'Strong words Soosha.'

'Indeed. But only the truth Finn. I have always worked best with earth and fire. Cho Petak is stronger with earth and fire than he is with air and water. Yet I have never felt the affinity with him that I would expect. On the contrary, I have felt a strong aversion to him, which is why I returned to the Oblaka after only the briefest of sojourns in the Menedula.'

'Chakar is greatly gifted in air and water, yet she used nearly the same words in a message to me some time ago,' said Finn.

'Neither Chakar nor I saw any way of overcoming him alone,' Soosha spoke heavily. 'We thought we would need a minimum of four Observers to combat each of his four talents. And there are not enough of us here to attempt it.'

Finn pursed her lips. 'You really think it would take four each?'

'No,' Soosha corrected her. 'That is what we estimated before this affliction beset the land. Melena told me that Babach said he believed Cho Petak to come from the Lost Realms.'

The two women stared at him.

'No one mentioned that to me,' Finn said at last.

Soosha nodded sadly. 'And several of us attuned to the earth, together with a few who are gifted in air, felt something happen some days past.'

'Felt what?' Sarryen spoke quietly but her face expressed her alarm.

'A sort of shuddering, a revulsion. As if earth and air across this land had been violated in some way.'

'But,' Finn began, then stopped to gather her thoughts. 'I was taught, and have since so believed, that the Lost Realms were light knows how far distant? They were encapsulated, the ones who contrived the overthrow of the First Age.'

'It would appear to me that Cho Petak escaped that fate somehow, and in turn has located and freed some of his ancient followers.'

'Then what hope have we?'

Soosha patted the Offering's arm again. 'There is always some hope, or so Myata taught. But we have to sit tight here, keep this community safe, alive and hopeful.' He paused. 'And wait for further news from the Night Lands.'

'If Babach survived with Voron, then they and Chakar would be foolish to try to return here now.'

Soosha laughed. 'So you say Finn. But in their circumstances, given the slightest chance, would you not come home?'

A knock at the door sounded before Finn could answer and Soosha and Sarryen were already getting to their feet.

'I have students to instruct,' Soosha said, opening the door to reveal Lyeto.

The young man stood aside to allow the Observer and the Kooshak past him.

'Come in Lyeto.' Finn moved from the table to the hearth.

'I did not intend to interrupt you, Offering. Volk suggested you might like to sample this.'

He held out a tall narrow dark blue bottle.

'Aah.' Finn took it from him and broke the wax seal. She sniffed cautiously, then with more enthusiasm. 'I shall try this I think. And you did not interrupt me Lyeto.'

A colourless liquid came from the bottle as Finn poured it generously into a mug. She sipped, swallowed, and waited. A smile spread across the Offering's face.

'A vast improvement on the last lot,' she announced. 'Have you tried it?'

'Oh no, thank you,' Lyeto said hastily. 'I find such drink just gives me a headache without the pleasure most seem to derive

166

from it.'

Finn glanced across at him. 'Well, sit down if you want to talk. You haven't come to suggest that you go outside tonight have you? Because I will not permit it. You work hard during the day with all the new arrivals, and you have been outside each of the last three nights. Tonight you will sleep. That is an order Lyeto.'

He gave a faint smile and stared into the fire. Finn frowned.

'I know I am not Chakar, but you can talk to me you know.'

The young man looked uncomfortable. Light, what could he have done now, she wondered. He drew in an audible breath.

'You remember when I brought in Teal and Giff and the boy?'

'I am hardly likely to forget.'

'I asked if you heard singing and you said you did not.'

He had Finn's full attention now.

'I have heard the same singing now, each time I come back from outside with refugees.'

Finn noted his long fingered hands were knotted on his knee, the knuckles white.

'What sort of singing do you mean, Lyeto?'

'That's just it.' He sounded exasperated. 'There are no words, but it is singing not humming. It is full of a joyous gladness. I do not recognise any tune, yet it is familiar. Am I touched with the affliction do you think?'

Blue silvered eyes regarded Finn with something close to panic.

'No Lyeto, you are neither touched with the affliction nor any other kind of madness.' She took another sip of Volk's latest brew while she considered what Lyeto had told her.

'Has anyone else heard any singing?' she asked.

'I mentioned it to a few people but they had no idea what I was talking about.'

'Does it stay in your mind, or just vanish when it ceases?'

Lyeto frowned. 'It is still in my mind.'

'Would you allow me to hear it?'

'Oh yes please. It is beginning to worry me, Offering Finn Rah.'

'Then relax and open your mind to me.'

Finn's jaw slackened as Lyeto's mind played the singing back from his memories. She stared hard at him.

'Have you heard such singing before Offering?' he asked hopefully.

'No. I have not.' Finn swallowed the remains of her drink and had a brief fit of coughing. 'Have I your permission to speak of this to the Observer Soosha and the two Kooshak? They may ask to hear it, as I have done.'

'Whatever you think best. Do you think it is something harmful?'

'Oh no,' Finn laughed. 'Something as beautiful as that singing could not be harmful. Well – it could,' she corrected herself truthfully, 'but there is something just too – joyous was the word you used I think? No Lyeto, it is not harmful to you I am quite positive.'

Lyeto relaxed visibly and soon afterwards Finn sent him to his bed with strict orders to sleep soundly. Finn sat thinking for a while then went in search of Soosha, Arryol and Sarryen. Soosha was delighted with Volk's newest brew and joined Finn Rah in her choice of beverage while the Kooshak brewed themselves berry tea with a faintly righteous air.

'Lyeto came to see me. He has heard voices singing. Have any of you?'

Soosha and Sarryen looked puzzled and shook their heads, but Arryol frowned. Finn waited.

'Well I thought it was just when I am very tired – my imagination playing tricks.' He looked at the other three warily.

'Would you let us into your mind so we might hear it?' Finn asked quietly.

Arryol shrugged. 'If you think it important.'

'Oh I do, Arryol. I think it is very important.'

A few moments later, Arryol shifted uneasily in his chair, the astonished expressions on the faces of Sarryen and the Offering quite unnerving him.

'It is the same as Lyeto hears. He said he first heard it when you worked on the boy he brought in with Teal. He hears it now each time he brings in people from the outside. He feared it was a form of madness.'

Soosha chuckled at Finn's words.

'No madness,' he said. 'The most marvellous of signs.'

Three faces turned to the Observer.

'It is a sign that we are not abandoned, that we may yet find help from a long-forgotten source.'

Krolik, Cho Petak's chosen Master of Aspirants, was now Cho's menial. It was Krolik who cooked the light, easily digestible meals that were all Cho's body could accept. He brought the same meals to Mena but with the addition of bread, cheese and fruits. Krolik no longer possessed a mind fully his own and moved only on Cho's orders.

Cho visited Mena twice each day. Sometimes he simply sat watching her; occasionally, he spoke or asked questions of Sapphrea. Mena had told him that, as only a worthless female child, she knew nothing of the government of Return and very little of the surrounding countryside.

This morning, Cho came silently to Mena's rooms and stood by the table looking down on the drawing she was copying from a large book propped up in front of her.

'That is a fair copy,' he remarked. 'But why do you choose to draw a Plavat?'

Mena's expression was innocent when she turned her face up to his. 'Is that its name?' she asked him. 'It is very hard to tell how big to make these things.'

She pushed some other drawings towards the Sacrifice. He picked them up, smiling faintly. She had drawn an owl as large as the tree beside which it stood, a cow was the size of a rabbit against the square block of a house. Cho increasingly thought it unlikely that Mena could in fact read: these simple drawings proved that she had not read the descriptions of the various creatures.

'A Plavat is a great sea bird, as large as the Dragons of your land,' he told the child in an avuncular fashion.

'Do people ride on them?' Her violet eyes seemed huge against the silver scaling.

Cho's smile broadened. 'Oh no. They are foul tempered birds. See this hooked bill? They use it to tear flesh.'

Mena shivered involuntarily. 'But what is the sea?'

Cho's smile vanished and he studied the child carefully. 'You came over the sea on the back of a Dragon child. The sea is an immense body of water.'

Mena shook her head in apology. 'I remember little except making the Dragon do what I wanted it to.' She frowned. 'I think perhaps there was a lot of water.'

Cho stood silently watching her, then his faint smile returned. He inclined his head.

'I will visit again at dusk. Perhaps you will have more drawings to show me.'

He moved to one of the bookshelves and opened a drawer. He rummaged among its contents then opened another. Cho brought out a box and walked slowly back to Mena.

'There are coloured inks if you wish.'

Mena opened the box, exclaiming at the rows of tiny pots arranged inside, and the pens and brushes held in its lid. Cho Petak nodded benignly and went to the door.

'Sir?'

He paused.

'May I go outside?'

Cho frowned again. Mena forced herself to keep utterly still while Cho Petak considered her request. Finally he nodded.

'There are three secluded gardens that you may use. Krolik – the creature who serves you – will show you where they are.'

The fire in his eyes flickered and danced as he stared into Mena's.

'You will go only in full daylight to these gardens. There are certain – dangers – to you should you venture there in darkness, or even twilight.'

He turned back to the door. 'I will instruct Krolik to take you there later.'

When the door closed behind him, Mena did not leap from her chair and jump with delight as she very much wanted to: she kept her head bent over the book and her hands occupied with the box of coloured inks. She did not think that she was constantly watched, but she knew that Cho Petak could overlook her with his mind whenever he chose. Which is why she took such pains to conceal her reading.

She sat, controlling her impatience, until at last Krolik opened the door. He merely stood there, waiting for her to join him. As soon as she got to her feet, he walked out of the door and she ran to catch up with him. Along a wide corridor and down a broad flight of stairs, Krolik keeping to the sides while Mena trotted in the middle of both corridor and stairs. There were scorch marks everywhere and Mena sensed the echoes of agony burnt into each mark.

Krolik suddenly turned down a much narrower way, then down seemingly endless stairs dimly lit by windows high above. Finally Krolik unbolted a heavy door and swung it open. Mena shot past him to stand just outside, feeling the sun warm on her head and fresh air filling her lungs. Slowly she stepped forward, looking about her. Fruit trees marched in rigid lines, pruned and shaped into tight uniformity.

Glancing over her shoulder, she saw that the door was still open but that Krolik had gone. Mena walked all around this oblong garden of trees, following the black stone path. Tiny buds were beginning to show on the grey twigs but she found little to interest her here. High hedges of some sort of evergreen surrounded the garden but then she discovered a gate tunnelling through the hedge. She peered over the top but the hedge was as thick as she was tall and she could see little.

She went through the gate and blinked. Sunlight flashed from a series of pools in this garden and she followed the path towards the first. A fish jumped a little way above the water, vanishing again amidst expanding ripples. There were pale leaves lying flat on the water and Mena knelt for a while, watching fish dart in and out between the wavering white stems. She walked all around this garden and found no gate other than the one through which she had entered. Closing it carefully behind her, she walked on along the rows of trees.

Another gate appeared when she turned the last corner and could see the door into the Menedula, still open, ahead of her. Unlatching the gate, Mena walked through the towering hedge and found herself in a familiar sort of garden at last. They grew herbs and medicinal plants in sheltered courts in Return and she had spent many hours in one such with Mayla. Insects buzzed and droned in the sun, which felt almost hot to Mena.

The cold season had barely ended at home, yet it felt much warmer here. A butterfly whisked past Mena's nose and she sighed. There was a feeling of peace and safety in this enclosed garden which, she now noticed, was quite circular. The plants did not seem to grow in precise rows in here, but haphazardly: a group of tall plants sheltering more delicate, smaller plants.

She wandered slowly along a sanded path, stooping to brush her fingers over some leaves that seemed kin to those she knew in Sapphrea. She came to a small wooden structure, like a tiny house, and eased open its door. The pungent smell of earth came out to meet her and she saw rakes, and hoes, and spades, neatly ranged along one wall. Without stopping to think, Mena picked a small hand fork and turned back to the garden.

She sat on the warm ground and began gently loosening the soil around the nearest plants, teasing out the weeds. There was lavender, just like at home, sage, mint, and lemon balm. She worked contentedly until the sun was high overhead.

'I do not know how long I am permitted to remain outside,' she told a young rosemary bush. 'Perhaps I should go in again for a while. But I promise I will be back tomorrow for sure.'

She stroked the thin aromatic spines, admiring the tiny blue flowers shyly emerging, then got to her feet. She cleaned the little fork she had used and replaced it in the wooden building, closing the door carefully.

Mena slept the afternoon away, due no doubt to the fresh air and sunshine after days shut up in the Menedula. Through the open door of her bed chamber, she saw Krolik putting a tray of tea on the small table by the window where she always sat to eat. He left without a word as usual and Mena yawned, rolling off the bed. She washed her hands and face at the strange basin affixed to the wall and went into the other room.

Krolik always brought her tea and flat biscuits in the late afternoon. She surmised that the biscuits had been made before the cooks disappeared: they were harder each day. She poured a bowl of tea and sipped it. It was different from tea she was accustomed to in Sapphrea, milder and with a fruity tang to it. Mena tapped one of the biscuits against the table, grimaced, and dunked it in her tea in an attempt to soften it a little at least. She realised she was hungry for much more than these horrid biscuits. But as she had no idea where Krolik prepared the food, and no inclination to wander around the vast, near empty building, she ate the biscuits and ignored the rumblings of her stomach.

172

Mena climbed onto the chair by the large table and looked at the drawings she had done. She opened one of the books beside her elbow and found the place she had been reading before. She held the page upright, ready to let it fall should Cho Petak appear. If he did, and came to see what she had been looking at, he would find the book open to a picture of something very similar to what she knew as a konina.

Meanwhile, Mena read of the Order of Sedka with a growing irritation. If this was truly what Sedka had believed and taught, then Mena concluded that he was not a very pleasant or intelligent person. Why did he want everything in Orders? She let the page fall closed and considered the herb garden she had found today. It was not ordered at all: was that permitted, in spite of Sedka's explicit instructions to the contrary?

She lifted one of the pens from the lid of the box Cho had given her and chose a bottle of dark green ink. Concentrating closely, she began to draw the little rosemary bush she had seen in the garden. In spite of his noiseless entry, Mena was instantly aware of Cho's presence in the room. She looked up and forced a smile.

'Thank you for allowing me to go in the gardens. I enjoyed it very much Sir.'

Cho nodded, approaching the table. He stopped abruptly, his nose wrinkling in distaste.

'What is that foul smell child?'

Mena stared at him. 'I smell nothing, Sir.'

'Have you been touching any of the plants?'

'Well, yes Sir. They needed weeding and I –'

'Wash yourself thoroughly if you do so again. The smell is most offensive to me.'

Mena sniffed her washed hands and could smell nothing. Cho was already retreating to the door.

'I cannot bear this taint,' he told her. 'Make sure it does not happen again.'

When Krolik brought her supper, Mena ate every scrap and could have managed the same again. She went to bed and lay watching the stars through the unshuttered window. She yawned and turned onto her side, thinking of the herb garden. In her heart, she heard peals of laughter.

Chapter Seventeen

In the days that followed the Vagrantians departure from the Stronghold, Chakar found Babach unaccountably elusive. She never managed to encounter him on his own and her suspicions grew. He was jovial at supper times, chatting and laughing with all, but became somewhat vacant if she tried to question him.

Chakar's owl, Sava, was seen more often in the hall since Baryet had elected to move in with his wife, and he seemed a little happier, even venturing into the growing areas in search of Lorak a few times. No information had been discovered pertaining to Babach's written requests to both Vagrantia and Gaharn as yet, but the Observer did not appear overly concerned.

Chakar finally cornered Babach in the great hall. All the Dragons were absent, Guards were busy in the lower levels, and Babach was dozing by the fire. Chakar planted herself squarely in front of him.

'You do not move from here until you tell me what is going on, old man. You have been avoiding me,' she accused him, 'and your wide-eyed innocence does not fool me a jot.'

Babach surveyed the small stocky figure, then he grinned.

'Make yourself comfortable then. What exactly did you wish to know?'

Chakar was taken aback by this instant capitulation. Eyeing him suspiciously, she hooked a stool closer and sat by Babach's knee.

'One, you changed the subject appallingly obviously the other evening when we spoke of the Orders in Drogoya. Two, you closet yourself with Mim for hours on end, yet make no comment at all on anything you may have discussed.' Chakar gave him a glare of frustration. 'You cannot have been talking secrets all the time, for light's sake Babach.'

Babach chuckled to himself for a moment while Chakar continued to glare. He stretched out his left hand and lightly touched the pendant she wore beneath her shirt, his right hand resting on his own.

'Have you noticed – differences – since Mim gave you that?'

'What kind of differences?' Chakar sounded wary.

'Do you hear anything odd, smell anything, feel anything unusual?'

Chakar was fully aware that despite Babach's relaxed expression and almost casual tone, he was concentrating his attention on her very closely. She clasped her hands round her knees and tried to think what he might mean. A vision of Kadi popped into her head. That early dawn, when starlight had seemed to dance over the great Dragon's damaged body. Chakar met Babach's faded blue and silver eyes.

'When Kadi first woke,' she began, speaking softly although they were quite alone.

'Yes?' he encouraged her.

'I thought I heard singing, but I am sure it was because I was so very tired.'

She studied Babach's smile. 'It was not my imagination?'

'No, I think not my dear Chakar. Mim also hears singing, whereas I smell mint.'

Chakar looked baffled.

'I have not yet decided what the singing might imply – nothing harmful, of that I am convinced. But the smell of mint.' He stopped, waiting for Chakar to deduce his meaning.

She scowled at him, thinking quickly back over her earlier questions and all that had been said so far. Babach closed his eyes while Chakar's mind raced: the Orders of Sedka and Myata – and then something fell into place. She leaned even closer, shaking Babach's arm.

'You think you smell mint because somehow Myata is influencing events?' Her voice began to rise and she forced it to a lower tone again. 'How long since Myata died, Babach? Died and was given funerary rites within the caves under the Oblaka complex, before witnesses? Are you saying that her ghost, her spirit, has come merrily back from wherever the dead go, to dabble in our present problems?'

Babach opened his eyes. 'I see no reason why she should not. And as I recall, the caves were then sealed for many years, yet when your predecessors reopened them, did they find her body, even a few bones? Did someone creep in and move her?'

Dark green eyes set in silver stared into faded blue, as thoughts scudded through Chakar's head. Loosening her grip on Babach's arm she sat back a little.

'No. No sort of physical remains were found. Only the pendant where her body had lain.'

'The pendant?' Babach sounded surprised but then he nodded. 'Of course.'

'Why of course? Babach, you cannot keep this to yourself – why of course?'

'I believe the pendants are linked not only to Myata, but to something else. The smell of mint would indicate a separate connection with her alone, but the singing … the singing comes through the pendants from that "something else".'

'But you are the only one to smell mint Babach. You wear a pendant yet you have heard no music or singing.'

Babach pursed his lips as he thought. 'I suspect that this is only the beginning. Wearing these eggs may – amplify – these sensations. But now they have begun, it would not surprise me to find others experiencing these things.'

'But how will we know? Will we put up a notice in here, asking if anyone has heard any voices or smelt mint?'

Babach smiled. 'That might be an idea for later. Now, I think we should contact Vagrantia – there are two pendants there although none in Gaharn.'

'There are?' Chakar asked in surprise.

'Mim gave Thryssa, Lashek and Dessi a pendant each the day that Thryssa left here. He said that Gremara had told him to do so, and that they would have need of them.'

'The child we have not met, Tika, she wears one I think Mim told us.'

Babach nodded. 'She is the only one out in the world to have one. There are two now in Vagrantia and five here in this Stronghold.' He paused. 'There are hundreds, resting in a cave within the Delvers' Domain.'

The two Observers sat in silence for a considerable time until they turned at the sound of light footsteps approaching. It was Elyssa, Thryssa's young protégée, whose eyes had silvered when the affliction fell upon Vagrantia. She smiled shyly and, without invitation, drew another stool close to the Observers.

'I felt you speak of the pendants,' she said softly. 'I have been in the settlement of Akan in the Domain, working in their archives. They have some amazing texts, wonderfully preserved.'

'Texts referring to the pendants?' Chakar asked.

'Indirectly.' Elyssa laughed. 'Whoever arranged all these things had a dreadful sense of humour, I think – there are riddles, and then you find that their answers simply make up more riddles.'

'You said you "felt" us speak of the pendants child. What did you mean?'

Elyssa hesitated, looking from one Observer to the other. 'The singing grew louder,' she said simply.

Babach smiled, reaching one still scarred finger to touch Elyssa's cheek.

'You hear it, yet you wear no pendant,' he said happily. 'Just as I had thought.'

Elyssa caught his hand. 'And there is a faint scent of something in the last few days, since Thryssa left. I think it is mint.'

'Hah!' Babach sat up with an air of triumph. 'You are the first to experience both sensations child. And she does not have a pendant,' he repeated.

Chakar left Babach to explain his theory of the connection with Myata as the Dragons arrived back from their hunting flight. Kadi was trembling and reclined beside Fenj.

'I hunted for myself Chakar.' The midnight blue Dragon's mind voice was low with exhaustion, but also held a note of satisfaction. 'It will not be long before I am fully restored.'

Lorak appeared, so opportunely that Chakar knew Fenj must have summoned him. The old gardener dived into his workroom, emerged with a familiar flask and tripped over Lula. The tiny Kephi, who regarded herself as the protector of the ancient black Dragon, was in her usual paroxysm of delight at his return from hunting. Chakar swore to herself that she would prise the exact recipe from Lorak for his restorative. Sure enough, Kadi's trembling ceased after only two small doses from Lorak's flask, and the blue deepened in her faceted eyes.

177

'Splendid fellow,' came Fenj's inevitable rumbling comment.

Lula had climbed onto the old Dragon's head and from that perch she crooned contentedly.

'Do you know when Lady Kera might be coming back 'ere then?' Lorak asked Chakar, his tone far too casual.

The Observer grinned. 'No I don't, but she will be sure to find you when she does return. Where did you hide anyway – purely as a matter of academic interest you understand?'

Lorak scowled. 'I were very busy elsewhere. I weren't ahiding.'

'Aah. My mistake.' Before she could tease Lorak further, Guards began wandering into the hall for the midday meal and Lorak took the opportunity of disappearing again. He was very good at that, Chakar thought in admiration.

Kadi slept all afternoon but woke when the hall again began to buzz with people gathering for the evening meal. Babach spoke with both her and with Fenj before going to sit at the head table. Voron slid along the bench to Babach's left.

'Perhaps you ought to have a word with Daro, Observer. He says he smells mint everywhere we go.'

Babach smiled, taking a piece of bread from the dish before him.

'Indeed. Maybe later Voron.'

Towards the end of the meal, Babach banged a spoon against the wooden table and rose to his feet. Heads craned towards the Observer.

'There is no call for any alarm, but there have been reports of one or two odd phenomena here of late. If anyone has smelled a particular herb – spice, or mint for example, or heard any music, no matter how far away it seemed, would they please be good enough to inform either myself or Observer Chakar? Thank you so much.'

He sat down and leaned across the table to Chakar as talk began to rise around the hall again.

'Any who arrive, do try to keep them apart – we want genuine instances, not conspiratorial dramas.'

The servants cleared the tables and the Guards broke into their usual evening groups, but five made their hesitant way towards the top table.

'I wish young Mim was here,' Babach muttered to Elyssa who sat at his right side.

She smiled at him. 'Don't worry Observer. Both Gremara and Mim know exactly what is happening.'

'A message scroll from the Stronghold, High Speaker.'

Pajar held out the sealed cylinder towards Thryssa. She pushed aside the papers she had been checking and took the scroll case. As Pajar turned to leave, she called him back.

'Wait, in case Babach has come up with some more ruses to occupy students in the archives,' she said with a wry smile.

The papers slid into her hand and she spread them on the table, reading the topmost one. Then she frowned and picked up the scroll case again, peering inside it.

'Aah. Babach says there is other information – it was caught up – look.'

Another roll of paper slid from the case but this was sealed, unusually for a document carried within an already sealed case. She read all the first papers and passed them across to Pajar without comment. Then she broke the seal on the second scroll. When she had finished reading, she leaned back in her chair and looked across at her first councillor. He was frowning down at the papers in his hands. He glanced up.

'Erm, I do not wish to sound rude, but is Observer Babach quite sound of mind? He suffered terrible injuries I believe,' he ventured.

Thryssa gave a grunt of amusement.

'Observer Babach is very like to our Speaker Lashek. Both can give the appearance of seeming vague and foolish, although kindly old men. You should have learnt by now, Pajar, that Lashek is kindly but neither vague nor foolish. So with Babach.' She tapped the second scroll. 'You had best read this one too.'

Pajar read the paper slowly, then handed it back to Thryssa. She smiled.

'Before you ask, no, I have heard nothing and smelt nothing.' Her smile faded. 'But Pachela said that she smelt mint, the night we came from Talvo Circle. I have been too busy to see her since, but will you ask her to come to see me later this morning?' Thryssa sighed.

179

'It is such a nuisance, being unable to mind speak Orsim and Lashek, but I still think it would be unwise to do so at the moment.'

Pajar nodded. 'I have taken on twelve new runners in the past eighteen days.'

'I lose track Pajar – when were Lashek and Orsim due back here?'

'The day after tomorrow, High Speaker. Do you wish them here sooner?'

'No. The poor men are dashing back and forth enough. Leave it as it stands. Keep your ears open for any rumours about this.' She placed her hand on the documents from Babach. 'I will discuss it with the Speakers before taking any steps to enquire more generally.'

Pajar got to his feet, picking up the papers which Thryssa had approved and signed.

'Any further developments on our three Firan – guests?'

Pajar's worried look returned. 'We have moved them, with Chornay, to the other guest quarters, as you suggested. Various instructors, assessors and healers are keeping them occupied under the guise of "continuing their studies". Kralo was the first to object. He said that he knew all that the instructors could offer him on the first day. Then he calmed down and said that he was willing to "go along with our little games – for now".' Pajar shrugged. 'The two girls reacted similarly the following day.'

'They are shielded at all times, are they not Pajar?' Thryssa asked sharply.

'As you instructed High Speaker.'

Thryssa drummed her fingers on Babach's papers.

'I would speak with Chornay, I think. Send him to me directly, before Pachela, if you would. And I will call you again this afternoon.'

Thryssa continued to go through the routine papers that she was still trying to catch up on after her absence from Vagrantia until Chornay was shown into her study by a scribe. She smiled and waved him to a chair.

'How are our guests today?' she asked blandly, noting his immediate discomfort.

He hesitated then plunged into speech. 'High Speaker, I am

not sure why they decided to cling to me as their one friend here in Parima. I am increasingly worried, High Speaker. I have done as you asked and maintained my role as their friend and they do seem to believe it.' He looked distressed.

'Continue Chornay. I am fully aware you have been acting under my orders to befriend these three.'

'More and more, when there are no others present, they jeer at the Corvida, at Parima, and Segra, and Kedara. They scoff at you yourself, High Speaker.' Chornay's head had lowered, as had his voice.

'Chornay, there is no blame attached to you at all in this. Tell me what they have said please.'

'It is as you thought. They are devoted to Speaker Kallema, but more so, it seems, to first councillor Prilla. High Speaker, are you quite sure the shield you implanted protects me still? Their powers are greater than mine, despite they are younger than me.'

'I assure you, you have been guarded whenever you have been with or near them.' Thryssa regarded him with sympathy. 'You have also done more than enough. You will attend them no more.'

Seeing the relief on the young man's face increased Thryssa's feeling of guilt. 'They will be told that you have been reassigned, back to Kedara. In fact, I would prefer you to remain here in the Corvida. I must be honest with you Chornay, I suspect they may try to locate your mind.' She spread her hands, palms up. 'Let them waste their time searching Kedara for you.'

'They have begun to frighten me badly, High Speaker,' Chornay said in a rush. 'There are times when I know they are mind speaking but I do not know to whom. I feel strongly it is the first councillor of Fira and at such times I can barely contain my terror.' He raised his eyes to Thryssa. 'I am sorry to be such a coward, High Speaker, but will I be safe here?'

Thryssa sat back in silent thought. The boy was right of course. Sooner or later, and Thryssa feared it was likely to be sooner, his mind signature would be discovered. She made her decision.

'I do not believe you are any more cowardly than the rest of us Chornay. Would you go through the circle – to Gaharn, or to the Stronghold?'

181

Chornay's face revealed complete astonishment. 'Daro is at the Stronghold, High Speaker. We have never been apart since our first days at school. I would go to him.'

Thryssa nodded briskly. 'Then it shall be arranged later this very day.' She pulled the bell rope behind her chair in three sharp tugs and Kwanzi appeared almost at once.

'Would you keep Chornay with you in our apartments until I can come to you, please Kwanzi? We must get him away from the Firans, with all haste I fear.'

Kwanzi asked no questions, merely smiling at Chornay and inviting him back through the door with him. Thryssa sat still for a while then reached for pen, ink and paper. She wrote rapidly for several moments, reread what she had written and then rolled the paper, slipping it inside the scroll case that still lay on her table. She sealed the catch, impressing the symbols of Vagrantia on the wax and went to the outer door of her study.

Pajar was in the workroom beyond and she gave him the case, instructing him to send it through the circle immediately. Thryssa had just resumed her seat when there was the lightest of knocks on the door. Pachela came in at the High Speaker's call and sat quietly where Chornay had sat but moments earlier. Thryssa gave her a warm smile. She waved her hands over her paper strewn table.

'I have not had an instant to speak to you child. I apologise but this is one of the worst aspects of life as High Speaker.'

Pachela returned her smile. 'I am sure I can guess how busy you must be High Speaker. I have been busy too.' Her smile became wider. 'I have been working with Healer Chalo and Temno.'

Thryssa's own smile faded. 'I had forgotten Temno is still here. He was summoned back to Fira was he not?'

Pachela frowned. 'Yes High Speaker, he was. But he forswore Fira while you were away and he bound himself to Parima, the Corvida and to Healer Chalo himself. Chalo stood surety for Temno's honest intent High Speaker.'

Thryssa shook her head. 'No doubt someone would have told me eventually, or perhaps there is a note of it amongst this lot.' She pushed at the clutter of papers in disgust. 'Thank you for telling me at least, but what are you doing with Chalo and

Temno?'

'Well of course Chalo is the greatest healer in all the Circles, but Temno is considered second only to Chalo now. I was specialising in botany before my eyes changed, but I have become particularly interested in medicinal herbs now. And I thought – who better to learn from?'

'Would this new interest have anything to do with your smelling the aroma of mint?' Thryssa's voice was calm, but Pachela looked first startled, then embarrassed.

'I have spoken of it to no one High Speaker, but yes. It seems to happen much more often, although it must surely be my imagination.'

Thryssa studied the girl, then sighed. 'Read these while I find us some tea child. Then tell me what you make of it all.'

Pachela was standing by the window when Thryssa brought in a tray of tea, the papers she had been given to read stacked neatly on the edge of the table. Thryssa poured two mugfuls and sat looking at the girl's slender immature figure.

'Your tea grows cold,' she said finally.

Pachela stirred and turned slowly from the window. She picked up her mug of spice tea, the grey of her eyes suddenly dark against the silver.

'I do not understand very much of what the Observer writes – the Order of Myata?' She faltered over the unfamiliar name. 'But it seems right to me, High Speaker. I know nothing of this woman he talks of, yet it feels as if I do.'

'You could go through the circle and speak of it with Observer Babach if you wish?' Thryssa suggested.

'No!' The negative was immediate and decisive. 'I cannot leave here now.'

Pachela looked at the High Speaker as though surprised by her own vehemence.

Thryssa raised a brow and waited, a tactic that had rarely failed her in a multitude of situations. It did not fail her now. Pachela leaned forward earnestly, clutching her mug to her chest.

'I can give you no sensible reasons High Speaker, but I have to remain here.'

'Is this to do with Gremara – can you at least tell me that much?'

Pachela sat back in her chair and sipped her cold tea. She grimaced and set the mug down on the table.

'It has something to do with Gremara. It also has to do with my sense that I must learn from Healer Chalo as much, and as fast, as I can. I sense too that I must be here when the trouble finally erupts within Fira.' Grey silvered eyes met Thryssa's steadily. 'And that will be all too soon High Speaker.'

Chapter Eighteen

After only a few days of her mind being unshielded and the intensive instruction from her strange guests, Lallia was amazed at feeling so bereft once Tika's party were beyond mind speaking her. The Lady of Far was no fool, and she took heed of the repeated warnings they had given her regarding using the power. Especially with Hargon of Return in such a bellicose mood. It was only two days since the Vagrantian Maressa had bid her farewell with the news that Navan was close to their company after his escape from Return.

Now Lallia paced a high balcony, anxiously watching for the arrival of her husband, Lord Seboth. She had dismissed her maids: she hoped that there were none who might be disloyal, but she preferred them not to see how worried she was. At last! Lallia stood on tiptoe, pressed against the lattice work screen to peer down into the stable yard as the sound of hooves clattered on stone.

She hurried down the winding stairs until she arrived at the side entrance as Seboth strode in with two officers beside him. He glanced at his wife and she bowed low in greeting. Seboth crossed to where she stood and put his hands lightly on her shoulders. Bending to kiss her cheek, he listened to her rapid murmur. He stepped back.

'I shall join you later.'

Lallia bent her head again. 'I have moved into the sun tower in your absence my Lord. If it displeases you, I will return to our old apartments.'

Seboth paused then nodded. 'No doubt those rooms could do with a good cleaning and repainting.'

'My thought exactly, my Lord.'

He nodded again and headed for his work room, his officers at his heels. The house steward approached.

'Will my Lord need a proper meal, Lady?'

Lallia shook her head. 'Bread and meat will do Meran. But plenty of it. And a dish of pastries in the tower rooms later, if you please.'

Drawing her shawl closer around her head and shoulders, Lallia climbed back to the balcony. Stars glimmered through the lacy metal grill and she watched them for a moment, before entering the apartments she now used. This whole section of the huge, sprawling house of Far was the oldest part. It had once stood as a solitary tower until buildings grew round it like chicks clustered about a hen. Another lower tower stood squarely at a distance from this round sun tower, but was used mainly for storing things – old furniture in its upper floors, weapons below.

The top two of the sun tower's five floors were hers alone. A later building adjoined the tower's middle floor and her maids had the use of that floor. Lallia had remembered hearing Seboth and Olam joking about being able to bar the access doors and make the sun tower impregnable. The two lowest floors had no windows and for ages past had been used, like the square tower, as a repository for unwanted furniture. But there was a well in the basement: Lallia had made an opportunity to investigate and discovered the water was still there, still sweet.

Now Lallia settled herself on a heap of great cushions and waited for Seboth. She had braziers heating the room, she had not bothered to have the small fire lit as the weather was warming unusually quickly. Meran entered and put a wide platter of pastries on the low table near Lallia.

'Thank you Meran.'

The man hovered and Lallia raised her brow at him.

'Some of the armsmen have spoken of Lord Hargon's madness Lady. They disapprove quite strongly of some proposals he has ordered that all the towns carry out.'

'Proposals such as?'

Meran shook his head. 'I did not hear. Shall I enquire further Lady?'

'No Meran. Lord Seboth will tell me, I am sure. But thank you as usual.' She smiled up at the elderly steward.

He allowed himself the faintest of smiles in return and retreated to the door.

'I have ordered extra armsmen to watch your doors Lady.'

'Do you think that necessary Meran?' Lallia felt the stirring of alarm within her.

'I am afraid that I do Lady.'

The door closed behind the steward and Lallia chewed at her thumb nail. By the time Seboth joined her, Lallia's nail was beyond repair. The Lord of Far dropped onto the cushions beside his wife with a groan. He slipped his arm round her shoulders and hugged her close, then released her.

'It is much worse than we feared,' he said at once. 'I could not decide if Hargon is overtired and distraught, or if he is suffering from this affliction of which the Lady Emla and Maressa both told us. His eyes are reddened more than one could think normal due to grief or tiredness.'

He reached absently for a pastry. 'He ordered us to kill anyone we suspect might carry the old blood. He ordered us to kill all Merigs we see. He ordered us to have no contact with Lady Emla and "her cronies" as he so delightfully phrased it. He "ordered" us Lallia!'

'But did any agree with him?' Lallia clung to his sleeve in her urgency.

'Raben of Tagria lost his temper. He said that no one gives Tagria orders except for himself, and Hargon's orders were mad anyway. That was not well received, as you might guess. Raben stormed out, saying that the circle near his town was his and it would be well protected if Hargon had any foolish ideas of appropriating it.'

Seboth helped himself to another pastry and bit into it thoughtfully.

'I have never seen Hargon so angry. But the anger was all within – he did not shout back at Raben. His rage was cold, and perhaps more frightening because of it.'

'What of Andla?'

Seboth shrugged. 'You know Zalom as well as I. He tries to please both sides in the hope that they will leave him alone to go his own way.' He frowned. 'I believe he will not join with Hargon, or with us, until he absolutely has no alternative left. Hargon was annoyed that none of the lower towns representatives to his council. Raben has sent men to warn the southerners to beware Hargon – he told me before he rode out.'

'I presume we stand against Hargon?'

'Yes of course we do. But whether he will try to change my mind, or attack both Far and Tagria, I couldn't guess. Although his words greatly angered me, as always I tried to lighten all his worries. Eventually, I had to admit that I did not share a single one of his views and thus I would hold aloof from any of his "orders".'

'So he may believe it worth his while to try and persuade you to join with him?' Lallia studied her husband thoughtfully. 'What if he comes here with a full complement of armsmen, on the pretext of further discussions? Before, they would have been housed within the town and within this House. Could we risk that now?'

Seboth considered Lallia's question carefully.

'No,' he decided. 'Hargon, his Armschief and two officers would be permitted within the town and thence here. His men would have to wait outside the town walls.'

He struggled up from the cushions. 'I will order it so right now. Who knows when he might choose to descend on us.'

Lallia settled back to wait again for her husband, then sat up suddenly and stared around. Tubs of cream and blue flowers, grown from bulbs, stood against the walls beneath the shuttered windows, but it was not their heady perfume she could smell. She frowned. Surely it was mint?

Three quarters of Hargon's force of armsmen were encamped at a way station in the low hills less than half a day's ride south east of Far. The men were unusually quiet, wary of this new Hargon. Their old commander had been harsh but fair in their opinion. Now Hargon was as unpredictable as an untrained konina. There had been mutterings when the armsmen heard that sentence of death had been passed on Navan. The men had willingly followed Navan in everything, whereas to follow Hargon had been merely their duty.

Those who muttered overloud, vanished. They just disappeared from the barracks and were seen no more. The mutters became whispers breathed softly into another's ear, and to all outward purposes the men obeyed their officers. Navan's second officer, Fryss and the veteran officer Tarin, wore similar expressions of blank obedience, but they had let it be known that they were extremely doubtful of Hargon's command now, and especially of his new Armschief Trib.

The ordinary armsmen found Trib an offence. He was from their ranks, so they knew him rather too well. In various squads he had been known as lazy, brash, quick to put blame on another man rather than admitting a wrong of his own. Now, as Armschief, he was above officers and men, and took great pleasure in underlining that fact at any opportunity.

This night Hargon paced. He planned to ride on to Far at dawn, just himself and a minimum escort of twenty armsmen with his officers and Armschief. The main body of men, under third officers, would follow, keeping themselves from view until the last, open league to the town. When the sun reached its zenith, they would attack. He intended that he would have killed Seboth by then and the armsmen of Far would surrender swiftly enough. He needed time to speak with the fool Seboth first though.

He had heard rumours that some of those strangers, including his slave Chena, were still in Sapphrea. He needed to know where they were lurking so that he might dispose of them next. Then he would ride west to destroy Tagria and, more importantly, smash the cursed circle to pieces as he had already ordered done outside Return. None of these fools realised the danger they were in. Hargon knew beyond question that he had to unite this whole land under his rule and stamp out, once for all, the verminous blood of those who had once nearly destroyed Sapphrea completely.

Hargon turned back into the shelter of the way station. In the dimness, he saw officers Fryss and Tarin sitting silently, staring into the small fire. Trib was not present: no doubt he was throwing his weight about among the men. Hargon had no illusions about Trib's qualities. For now, he was suitable. He had loyalties only to himself, which was fine with Hargon. For now. Hargon sat down, leaning against the wall by the hearth.

'You will accompany me at first light,' he said flatly.

Tarin and Fryss looked up at the Lord of Return and somehow kept their faces expressionless when they saw the flames dancing in his eyes.

Tika followed the others in the direction Storm and Farn led them. It was in truth only a short distance from the caves but further back behind the cliffs. They saw at once that the boulders half covered with sand and salt crystals were not natural rock formations. The lines were too sharp, too straight, for them to have been shaped by wind or water.

Ren knelt by the first tilted block and began shovelling sand clear of its base. Riff and Sket joined him, scooping handfuls away from the sides. Olam and Navan watched, then moved over to help too. Pallin grunted and ambled further along, vanishing behind further boulders. Tika grinned. She would wager he would find himself a cosy place to doze the morning away. She wandered over to the other men and saw that the dry sand had been moved sufficiently already to reveal the darker, damper sand below.

Olam had got to his feet and was running his hands over the upper part of the block. Tika went round the kneeling men to his side.

'Feel it, Lady Tika,' he said. 'It is almost like metal or glass.'

She put her hand on the smooth black surface and found that Olam was right. It did not feel like any stone she had ever touched.

'What is it made of?' she wondered aloud. 'It must have been carried here from far away. And do stop calling me "Lady", Olam. It makes me wonder who you are talking to.'

'Oh. Erm, well – Tika, I know of no place where such stone as this might be found.'

'It could well have been changed if there was an explosion and tremendous heat close by.' Ren's voice was muffled and they craned round the block to see what he was doing.

The Offering's head and shoulders were out of sight down the hole they had dug out. He wriggled up and wiped damp sand off his face.

'It is but one block on its own,' he announced. 'I shall try another.' He trudged on to the next block, but examined the way it protruded from the sand before shaking his head and moving further on among a more densely jumbled heap of odd-shaped boulders.

'What exactly is he looking for?' Navan asked discreetly as he

190

followed Ren with Tika and Olam.

Tika laughed, green and silver eyes glinting up at him. 'Stars know, Navan. But we had better help him I think.'

She looked round for Gan, spotting him eventually on top of a pile of blocks that resembled a huge version of nursery toys – a tower built with great care, then sent crashing down with a wave of a child's hand.

Ren was on a patch of ground surrounded by the blocks, talking to Gan who still perched two man lengths or more above him.

'I will have to see from above,' Ren was saying.

Tika nudged Navan in glee. 'Farn would be happy to lift you, however high you wish,' she offered innocently.

Ren glared. 'Although I am not as strong with air as Maressa, I am still capable of doing it that way.'

'But will you not get ill?' She sounded most concerned.

'No I will not,' he snapped. 'Watch. You might learn something.'

Sket scowled but Tika smiled. 'Very well, we will all watch you, Offering.'

She sat on a block and cast her mind outwards, netting the awareness of the five men, then smoothly linking with Ren. Navan and Olam hastily sat beside Tika as, through Ren's mind, they saw the ground drop beneath them. More unsettling was the fact that they could see themselves, sitting around Ren's central figure while they floated high overhead. Olam's mind was suddenly agitated.

'Calmly, Olam,' Tika's mind murmured to his. 'What is it you have seen?'

'I have seen houses laid out in just this way. A few cycles past, I went to one of the further southern towns, and they showed me such a place. They said that the earth had trembled and shaken and most of the houses in one villages fell down.'

'Come higher.' Farn joined the linked minds and Ren ducked instinctively, sending Farn into shrieks of amusement.

Ren's ire simmered briefly through the link then his equable nature reasserted itself.

'That was most alarming, Farn. Why should I go higher?'

Farn sent a panoramic view of the area and Ren caught his

breath. Without another word, he sent his mind to Farn's height and they all just stared. What had seemed like a few scattered blocks, stretched for leagues inland, and south along the coast.

Tika released the link and stared at Gan. 'It must have been vast.'

Gan nodded. 'A dozen times larger than Gaharn,' he agreed.

Ren opened his silvered eyes and drew a breath.

'Did you notice anything odd?' he asked.

'All fallen the same way,' Sket volunteered.

Ren beamed at Tika's personal Guard.

'They did indeed. The explosion or whatever it may have been, came from the south and everything would have been blown away from it.' He stared thoughtfully at the block in front of him.

'These all lie parallel to the coast, so the event would have surely occurred directly south along this shore.'

'Maressa said there were four big cities by the Bitter Sea,' said Tika.

'Did she say what they were called?'

'The same as the Vagrantian craters – this must be the furthest one north – Segra.'

'Lashek was the Speaker of Segra Circle was he not?' Olam enquired. 'He would love to be here now.'

Farn settled on some of the blocks near Tika.

'Will you dig in the sand all day, my Tika? Why do you not come and play with the water?'

Tika clambered across to the silvery blue Dragon and swung onto his back.

'A good idea,' she agreed, then added aloud: 'Farn wishes me to see something. I will not be long.'

Farn settled upon the wet sand at the water line and Tika slid from his back.

'Look my Tika! It is not quite as pleasant as the hot pools in the Domain, but it still feels good.'

As Tika watched in some alarm, Farn paddled out several paces into the water. The waves were pushing against his chest when he sank out of sight. Tika shrieked in horror, bringing the men scrambling down the cliff, when Farn surged up, water cascading from his body. He stretched his wings and disappeared again. Gan and Sket reached Tika as Farn erupted once more, hurling the water on his wings, with great accuracy, straight over them. It was cold. Gan and Sket gasped, but Tika began to laugh.

Farn waded towards them, beating his wings and sending huge showers of water over all three again. Sket and Gan hastily withdrew, leaving Tika, soaked to the skin, giggling helplessly. Farn struggled out of the water and flopped rather than reclined on the sand, his eyes whirring in delight.

'It is cold at first, my Tika, but then it seems warm enough. It is wonderful fun.'

Tika pushed wet hair off her face and grinned at him. 'Your new friend Storm showed you this game, did he not?'

'He said he knew you would enjoy it.' Farn sounded hugely pleased with himself.

'I am sure he did. I think I may have to have a little talk with him later.'

'Oh you must,' Farn agreed. 'He has many such ideas.' He looked around the beach and out over the sea. 'I wonder where he is. He said he would love to see you enjoy this joke.'

'How very odd that he is not here to enjoy it then,' said Tika, giving Farn a soggy hug. 'Why do you not go and find him while we go back to the caves for some food?'

'I think I will.' Farn rattled his wings and prepared to rise. 'It was a good joke, was it not?'

'Oh undoubtedly, Farn, a most excellent joke.'

As Farn swept lazily towards the sea Dragons' cove, Tika walked up the beach towards the others. Sket was wringing water from his shirt while Navan and Riff attempted to conceal their amusement.

'It was all a joke, arranged by Storm,' Tika explained.

Sket merely grunted, but Gan smiled.

'I suspected as much. That water was very cold though.'

Tika nodded. 'And it feels sticky, not just wet.'

'That is because of the high percentage of salt contained in the water,' Ren told her. 'It will dry on your skin to tiny crystals – like it is on all the rocks.'

She noticed that the Observer kept his head turned towards the cliffs as he spoke.

193

'Do you think that Pallin will have got a meal ready?' Riff asked from behind Tika and Ren. 'Where did he go to anyway?'

'Perhaps he decided to go in search of the plants you and Sket were looking for? What were they by the way?'

Ren extended a hand to pull Tika over a heap of shattered boulders.

'We were looking for mint. I thought I could smell it the first night we were here, then Sket said he had smelled it as well.'

Tika stopped and stared at him. 'But I smelled it too, three or four days ago, when we had just arrived on the coast.'

Ren looked back at her for a moment then continued walking. 'So far we have not found any sign of the plant. But all three of us cannot be imagining it can we?'

Day followed day in similar fashion: the party went further into what was left of the shattered city, but found only endless black blocks. After six days, Farn had begun to fret over Brin's absence.

'He said it would be eight days Farn,' Tika told him for the tenth time that morning. 'Tomorrow he may be close enough to mind speak us.'

'I think Storm and I should fly to meet him and that dear girl.'

Tika looked at him sharply. She had hoped he had forgotten his penchant for referring to his dear girls.

'You will do no such thing Farn.' She thought rapidly. 'Who would protect us, protect me, if you were to go off like that?'

There was a long silence. 'I think you may be right. Unless you would like to come too?'

'My place is here with our friends Farn, I could not abandon them.'

'Oh.' He sighed heavily. 'Then I will wait with you.' He lifted into the air to join Storm who was zigzagging high above. 'I nearly forgot my Tika. The Elder Salt asks to speak with you.'

'With me, or with all of us?'

'With you. He said you may go to his cave whenever you wish or he will fly to the beach when the stars appear tonight.'

Tika watched her soul bond racing to intercept Storm. She dug her bare toes into the warm sand and wondered what the Elder might need to speak to her about.

Chapter Nineteen

Cho Petak was slightly perturbed: not worried of course, just perturbed. He had discovered that four of his minions were missing from Drogoya. He was aware that Rashpil was somewhere in the Night Lands – he had sensed his departure from the main part of the horde that descended in such a chaotic fashion days ago. But he had sensed no other such divergence. He sent Grek out a second time to try to locate the missing three. One truanting servant was quite enough.

He was also bothered by the continuing foul stench that appeared to emanate from the child. He had stood by her door on the second evening and had commanded her to strip and scrub herself clean in front of him. It had made no difference, and apparently neither Krolik nor the child herself seemed to notice it. He could find no disease within her small body, check as thoroughly as he had. On the contrary, she seemed quite disgustingly healthy, a point Cho resented when his own body was so close to disintegration.

Whenever he bothered to overlook her during the day, she was in an untidy garden which Cho did not recall visiting for very many years. Often she sang: nonsense rhymes and nursery songs. He toyed with the idea of forbidding her to go outside but decided against doing so. Her skill at drawing had improved dramatically, he had noted, and it amused him to see her growing skill with pens and brushes. She brought twigs, leaves, and odd shaped stones back to her room from the garden and then spent hours trying to copy them perfectly.

Cho had woken yet again from his increasingly brief naps. His mind viewed the town of Syet below the Menedula, then he checked for the child's mind signature. She was in the garden as usual and Cho dipped back into sleep again.

Mena had cleared a sizeable area of the choking tendrils of weeds and the plants thus freed were growing fast. The pale new tips protruding from the sage, quivered towards the sun. The young rosemary bush had thickened, her blue flowers fully opened now. Mena hummed and chattered as she worked and imagined that the plants answered her. She got to her feet and took the box filled with weeds to a pile of rotting vegetation she had found beyond the wooden house.

She stood there for a while, watching a fat bumble bee lurching in and out of the hedge. That was when she heard something fall within the little building. She held her breath but there was no further sound except for the drone of the bee as it swooped past her towards the open garden. Quietly, Mena moved to the door, which she always left open. Now, it was half closed. Slowly, she leaned to peep inside and saw a bare foot, not much bigger than her own, the toes clenched as if their owner was ready to run.

Mena crept back to where she had left the small fork and, humming quietly, moved close to the door again. She knelt beside the door and began to work loose the weeds matted around a very ancient sage bush. She put words into her humming, repeating them at intervals as she worked. Time passed and Mena weeded. Then out of the corner of her eye, she saw both bare feet on the threshold.

'Hello,' she murmured, without turning fully round. 'My name is Mena. What is yours?'

She waited patiently but eventually half twisted and glanced at the figure in the doorway, then looked back at her heap of weeds.

'I wish you would talk to me. You might tell me how you got in here because I surely long to find a way out.'

'Come here at nightfall usually. Safe place to sleep.'

The boy's voice was husky and low but Mena's heart raced. He had spoken to her, not just run away! Perhaps he would show her how he came and went. In the quick glance she had given him, he had seemed about her own age, thin beyond belief and extremely dirty. Unidentifiable rags covered some of his body although his legs were bare to the thigh.

'Have you nowhere else to sleep? No home?'

'Burnt. Bashed up. All the town went crazy when those students came down there. Eyes red as fire. Only a few of us left I reckon.'

'Why have you stayed then?'

'Don't know nowhere else.'

Mena bit her lip. 'Well, like I said, my name is Mena and I would like to be friends with you.'

'Why you here anyway?' The question came out in a belligerent tone.

Mena sat back and hugged her knees. 'I come from very far away. Cho Petak keeps me prisoner here.' She looked fully at the boy for the first time and he took a pace back inside the building.

'You a Kooshak?'

Mena frowned, shaking her head. 'I don't think so. What are they?'

'Why you got silver eyes then if you ain't Kooshak?'

Mena put her hands up to touch her eyes in bewilderment.

'I do not know what might be wrong with my eyes. Are Kooshak bad people then?'

'No. They're the best – help anybody anytime.' The boy stepped forward again. 'You really don't know about the Kooshak?'

Mena shook her head again. 'I told you. Cho Petak had me brought here from such a long way.'

The boy stared at her through a tangled mass of black hair. 'I'm Tyen,' he said.

Mena's smile was radiant and the boy continued to stare. He had never seen a girl like this: almost white blonde hair curling close round a triangular face. A face dominated by enormous violet blue eyes set in silver.

'Can you help me get out of here Tyen?' Mena whispered. 'I have to go in that direction.' She nodded to the north west.

Tyen shrugged. 'Expect so. But it's bad outside here. Specially nights.' He shivered. 'That's why I hide in here. Slept too long today because it was near day when I got here. Lots of those changed ones in the town again. You sure you ain't Kooshak?'

Mena smiled faintly. 'I wish I was, if it would help, but I don't think I am.'

The boy fell silent for a while. 'Can you get food?' he asked. 'There's not much out there.'

'Some. Not much. I am not given much and I don't know where it is kept. Will you be here tomorrow? I should go in now.'

'If I don't get caught then I will.'

'Have you no family?' The question was out before Mena could stop it.

Tyen's face closed tight. 'Not any more.' He turned his back and disappeared into the shadows within the small hut.

Mena collected up the weeds and took them to the rotting pile, cleaned the box and fork she had used and put them back in their places. Drawing the door closed as she left, she murmured:

'Stars keep you safe, Tyen. I'll be here tomorrow.'

Climbing back up to the top rooms of the Menedula, Mena deliberately walled off thoughts of Tyen, pushing the memory of him into the hard centre deep inside herself. She could not risk Cho picking up the faintest hint of the boy's presence in the garden. Briefly, she wondered how the boy had gone undetected: Cho regularly checked the building and its immediate surroundings, as well as the town in the valley. Not now, she warned herself. Think only of the plants you will draw.

When Krolik brought the hard flat biscuits, Mena caught his arm.

'May I have a little more food Krolik, please? I am very hungry when I have been working in the garden.'

The once Master of Aspirants released himself from the girl's grasp, but quite gently Mena noted. He stared at her with the same blank expression he always wore, then left the room. Mena sighed. She had no idea if Krolik had heard her, or understood her if he had. There was a small risk in asking for extra food, but she was confident that she could convince Cho if necessary that she was hungry all the time here. Because she was.

She was concentrating hard on getting a sprig of lavender exactly the right shade of grey green, when she felt the air stir close to her. She had felt it before and had been made uncomfortable by the sensation. This time, it seemed as though someone was standing close to her left shoulder – much too close. Her throat tightened in sudden fear. She knew that it was not Cho's thought checking up on her activities. It felt unpleasantly familiar though. She nearly jumped from her skin when the door

198

opened and Cho Petak stood there. Mena heard him use the mind speech, his tone icy with barely controlled rage.

'I understood that I had forbidden you these apartments, my dear Rhaki?'

Rhaki? Mena sat frozen in her chair. She had been completely unaware that the Grey Lord was here in this land. She remembered hearing the name D'Lah, but she had not realised that D'Lah and Rhaki seemed to be one being. The presence vanished from her side but Mena saw Cho's gaze move down the room as if following someone's movement. She did not hear any reply but then Cho snapped again:

'Your reasoning is but a feeble attempt to excuse your flouting of an explicit command.'

The flames leaped and writhed in Cho's eyes.

'Lord Rhaki, let me explain so that there may be no further misunderstanding on your part. It would be the simplest of things for me to unmake you. Do you follow me? I could take your mind apart, tiny piece by tiny piece, until it was completely unmade. And there is no restoring a thing so thoroughly unmade.'

Cold sweat prickled between Mena's shoulders as she listened to Cho's side of this conversation. She had no doubt at all that Cho Petak could do precisely what he had just described. Cho lifted a nearly transparent hand.

'I have warned you too many times already, my dear. This is the last time. Now go.'

Mena felt the unwholesome presence dissipate and realised she was trembling. Carefully, she laid her brush against the lid of the box of inks and hid her hands below the table, gripping them tightly together.

'I regret that you witnessed that unpleasantness child. He will not trouble you further I think.'

Mena swallowed, her mind devoid of any suitable reply. Cho moved closer to the table, lifting the drawing Mena had been working on.

'You improve daily, child. I commend your close attention to the detail.'

He laid the paper back in front of her and studied her bent head for a while. She had asked for extra rations and his

199

suspicions had been instantly alerted. But he could see that she was in fact thinner than when she had arrived here. He realised that her body was still in its growing stage and would thus demand more nutrition. He turned to go. He would instruct Krolik to improve and increase the child's diet. Where Krolik might find the ingredients to do so in the shattered ruin that was the town of Syet, Cho neither considered nor cared.

Sarryen had quickly adapted to this strange existence in the Oblakan caves, and took her turn instructing groups of students in history and botany. She also took her turn with the routine chores: sweeping the passageways, cleaning the dishes and helping with the laundry. One of Lyeto's refugees arrived in the caves with a dreadful cough and feverish cold, which swept through the community with enthusiastic speed. Arryol, in constant proximity to the victims, was the only one to escape the illness, and wore himself out caring for everyone else.

Finn Rah was most annoyed to discover she had the cold and she was unspeakably bad tempered for the next four days. Lyeto insisted that he still go outside and search for any survivors even though he returned with fewer and fewer people. Finn Rah sensed a certain relaxation among the students, as if they felt that here, beneath the burnt out Oblaka complex, they were impregnable. She fretted over this while she cursed the cold in her head in the privacy of Chakar's sitting room. Volk delivered her "medicine" each morning and evening, and in the common room later he swore he had heard the Offering singing one of the bawdiest tavern songs ever to burn his ears.

Sarryen had caught the cold days before and was recovered enough to resume her duties when Finn Rah succumbed. This evening, she tapped cautiously at Finn's door. Lyeto had reported that a mug had been thrown at him that morning. Taking the distant croak to be a call to enter, Sarryen opened the door a fraction.

'Oh come in, come in,' Finn snapped. 'You have all been tiptoeing around as if I was either mad or dying.'

Sarryen tactfully refrained from answering and Finn Rah's scowl turned to a reluctant grin.

'Have I been that awful?'

Sarryen smiled back. 'You have rather.'

'Aah. So apologies will have to be issued at once. Do I need to apologise to you?'

'No. I have managed to avoid visiting you.'

Finn laughed, which brought on a paroxysm of coughing. Sarryen pushed the Offering gently back into the armchair and set about making tea until Finn regained her breath.

'I have always detested being ill.' Finn spoke softly, careful not to set the cough wracking her again.

'I do not believe any of us much enjoys ill health,' Sarryen said. She smiled over her shoulder. 'Some of us are just a little more stoical perhaps?'

Finn's scowl returned but her eyes danced with amusement. 'What news since I got this cursed cold? Is anyone still standing?'

'Arryol is the only one immune it seems, but as everyone else has had it or is suffering with it now, it should be finished within a couple more days.'

'Perhaps we should keep any new arrivals segregated to begin with – light alone knows what disease could appear next.'

Sarryen nodded. 'Arryol has already suggested the same, and has organised two chambers near the entrance from the hillside for that purpose.' She handed Finn a bowl of tea and caught the Offering's glance at the bottle on the table. 'Tea will be more beneficial for you at present,' she said reprovingly.

'Nonsense.'

But Sarryen noticed that Finn made no effort to get up again to fetch the bottle. Indeed, she looked very tired and pale the Kooshak thought.

'Arryol has made a fine tonic remedy. It seems to work well on everyone. Why don't I get you some?'

'Oh very well. And ask Soosha to join us, would you – if he is fit?'

'His cough is lingering a little longer than Arryol likes, but he is teaching again.'

When Sarryen returned with a large brown bottle, an equally large spoon, and Observer Soosha, Finn's head was back against the chair and her eyes were closed. More concerned than she appeared, Sarryen poured a spoonful of Arryol's tonic and made

Finn swallow it.

'Really,' Sarryen scolded. 'You make more fuss than the children.'

Soosha sat in the armchair opposite and chuckled. 'You will recover almost at once Finn, if only to avoid taking too much of that stuff.'

'What have I missed while I have been lingering at death's doorway?'

Soosha looked into the fire. 'Someone walks in my dreams.'

Finn and Sarryen stared at him, not sure they had heard him correctly. Sarryen knelt on the floor between the two armchairs and waited for Finn to question him.

'Dream walkers are the stuff of legend, Soosha,' the Offering said quietly. 'That is, if you discount deliberate mind speaking when the recipient is asleep. I believe Babach spoke thus to Ren. Is that what you mean?'

Soosha sighed. 'No, Finn. It is the stuff of legends variety. I hardly dare guess who she is, but she walks my dreams each night of late.'

'She?'

'Oh yes.' Soosha grimaced. 'There is only one name that seems to fit her.'

'Does she speak to you?'

Soosha frowned. 'I do not think so Sarryen, not clearly in words at any rate. She seems to be warning me of something. No.' He raised his hand as both Sarryen and Finn were about to speak.

'Perhaps preparing would be a better word than warning. It is not of a danger coming to this community.' He shook his head. 'This woman is a blurred shape in my dreams. She walks a garden, or fields, and two children run beside her. She is calm but the children are greatly afraid.'

'How do you interpret these dream messages, Soosha?' asked Finn.

He shrugged. 'Two children are trying to reach us. They are under the woman's protection but there is still great danger for them.'

'Can you see the children clearly in your dream?' Sarryen was studying the Observer closely.

'Yes, I see them. I would know them should they find their way here. It is the woman I cannot see properly.'

Soosha looked down at his hands, clasped around the bowl of tea. 'When I wake, as I always do the instant this dream ends, my room is full of the scent of mint.'

Finn drew in a breath so sharply her cough began again. Sarryen took the bowl of tea from the Offering's shaking hands while Soosha moved behind Finn and rubbed her back. When Finn's cough slackened to a chesty wheeze, she forced out a question.

'Do you know where these children are now, or where they come from?'

Soosha went back to his armchair. 'From the east. The sun is rising behind them every time. How far they must come, I cannot tell.'

'Are those children who walk your dreams clear in your mind still? Lyeto at least, should be able to recognise them should they reach us.'

Finn nodded her agreement with Sarryen's suggestion.

'I can show you the children but the woman disappears. In my dream she is a vague shape but I cannot even see that blurred figure once I wake.'

'Show us,' Finn whispered.

From Soosha's mind Sarryen and Finn Rah saw the clear image of two small children. Light, thought Finn, how truly small they are! A thin boy with a wild mane of black hair, dressed in rags. But it was the girl who drew their attention. Nearly as frail as the boy, her hair gleamed white as snow. She was better clothed than the boy but not by much. In Soosha's mind, the girl turned her head, seeming to look straight out of his dream into their eyes.

An unusually shaped face for a Drogoyan, which appeared to be mostly eyes: dark lavender eyes surrounded by silver. Even as this strange girl child turned her head away again as if to speak to the boy, the fragrance of crushed mint filled Chakar's sitting room. The vision faded leaving the two women in stunned disbelief.

'Who is that girl?' Finn's voice was a croak, a discordant sound.

Soosha shook his head sadly. 'She most positively is not of the Lost Realms. I have spent much time pondering this – as you would guess. I have no idea how she could have reached Drogoya, but my feeling is that she is from the Night Lands.'

A brisk knock on the door made Sarryen jump even as Finn called: 'Come.'

Arryol entered, Lyeto at his back, both wearing frowns.

Soosha smiled suddenly. 'What brought you two here in such haste?'

Arryol glanced at his companion and then turned to Finn Rah.

'The singing began. Lyeto was in the common room and I was reading – not healing.'

'Join minds with the three of us,' Soosha ordered.

Lyeto gasped and Arryol caught hold of the edge of the table as the picture of two young children filled their minds. At the same moment, the two women and Observer Soosha were swamped by a crescendo of harmonised music. The image disappeared, the singing ceased. But the scent of mint remained.

'What, in the name of the light, is happening?' Arryol gasped.

Soosha explained his dreams and the conclusions he had so far drawn. Lyeto was on the floor beside Sarryen, amazement still plain on his face. Arryol listened but had moved to Finn's side and was feeling her forehead and her throat.

'I am quite recovered thank you. Listen to Soosha. Concentrate on that, not on me.'

'I was listening,' Arryol retorted mildly. 'And you are most definitely not recovered.' He turned to Soosha. 'According to the documents which Babach received from the Night Lands, they have no record of the eye changes which we have long been accustomed to here. If this child is from those lands, why are her eyes silvered? And have any of you heard tell of the silvering even starting so very early in life?'

Sarryen tilted her head to look up at her fellow Kooshak.

'I have not. But it seems to me we are barely keeping abreast of events. Things are happening, changing, without any warnings or apparent reasons. It is clear I think that this girl child is of great importance. Why else would she appear to be travelling under the protection of Myata herself?'

'And why else the sudden burst of sensation we have all just

204

experienced?' Soosha studied the four faces before him. 'Oh yes. This is indeed a special child and we must wrack our brains to find some way to help her reach the sanctuary which is the Oblaka.'

Chapter Twenty

'Do you know more than you have told me?' Mim asked Dessi casually. 'I mean, do the Delvers in general or the Wise One in particular, know more of the eggs than they have admitted?'

Elyssa had been working with Dessi, explaining some of the Vagrantian ways of working with the different elements for the last days, but she was spending today with the two Observers. Mim had taken the opportunity to climb up to Dessi's chambers, high in the Stronghold. Dessi turned on her stool to look at him. He was changing even more, she realised. His shoulders were much wider, but still tapered down to a narrow waist. He no longer hid the fact that he ate with the Dragons when they hunted and he made no more pretence of eating the food cooked in the Stronghold kitchens. Except for the pastries, Dessi remembered: he still had a great fondness for those.

'No.' Her dark copper curls shone as a finger of sunlight poked through the narrow window beside her table. 'I have tried to guess but I would not tell anyone, even you Mim, what my guesses are. I am just as likely to be utterly wrong as anywhere near the truth.'

Mim noticed that her left hand rested upon her pendant. He had also noticed that she alone wore her pendant openly now, not beneath her shirt as did all the others. Himself included of course.

'Sit down. I will make some tea – or would you prefer water?'

Mim waited until Ashta had squeezed herself fully into the room, closed the door and settled beside the pale green Dragon.

'Tea is fine.'

He watched the Delver girl busy with tea pot and mugs.

'Does Elyssa say why she has chosen to stay here?'

Dessi grinned at him. 'She does not know herself. Only that she felt impelled to remain here.'

There was a burst of deafening screeches and Mim winced

while Ashta's eyes whirred rapidly in distress. The tea was made and poured before the noise abated.

'How can you endure that din, Dessi dear?' Ashta murmured, her tone deeply concerned.

Dessi laughed. 'It is only that bad a few times each day. When Syecha returns from finding food and orders Baryet off of her eggs. I gather there are eight now,' she added.

Mim groaned. 'It would be most unwise to mention that fact beyond this room – Chakar would be thrown out of the Stronghold!'

'Is this all connected with Myata of whom Babach and Chakar speak, Mim?'

The Dragon Lord shrugged. 'Part of it. But the part that most closely involves me, is linked to Gremara. Of that I am sure.'

'I do miss Jeela,' Dessi said softly. 'I know there must be some special destiny for her, but I miss her a great deal.'

Ashta's eyes flashed the palest green with honey speckles. 'I miss her too.'

Mim reached his arm around Ashta's neck and hugged her, his face against hers.

'Have you any regrets Mim? So far from your Nagum forests, here in this cold stone place?'

Mim studied his scaled hands and flexed the taloned fingers.

'At first I longed only to be back there, but then I accepted that I could never return. My village was destroyed completely, my family, everyone, slaughtered by Rhaki's Linvaks.'

He met Dessi's sympathetic eyes.

'I have Ashta, and the Dragon Kin. I am called Dragon Lord. I like to spend time with Lorak, and working among the plants in the new growing areas here. This life is far better than lying dead in my village.'

'Will you tell me if Gremara explains about the eggs that have been so long safeguarded by my people?' Dessi asked.

Mim got to his feet. 'I promise I will Dessi. Although I am sure you will know before I do.'

When he and Ashta had left her, Dessi moved from her stool to crouch by the fire. She lifted the pendant on its gold chain for the hundredth time, and turned it, studying first the turquoise backing and then the honey coloured front. Light throbbed faintly but rhythmically from the tiny speck within, but Dessi could make no contact with any mind. She longed to discover the secrets she knew were sealed within each of these beautiful objects. She also understood that they would reveal themselves in their own good time.

Kera returned through the circle to report that all was peaceful once more in Gaharn. Discipline Seniors had been positioned in houses around the City and they watched for any sign of the creature High Speaker Thryssa had identified as a being from the Void. Chakar had told Kera of Babach's theories and she was aware of the Discipline Senior's scepticism. Chakar warned Babach that Kera had little belief in his ideas of Myata's intervention in the affairs of this world, but the old man merely smiled.

'Many will not believe,' he said. 'Myata taught that it was irrelevant whether people believed her lessons or not. What will happen will still happen. It is of no importance my dear Chakar.'

Somehow, word had spread that the Plavats now had nine eggs, and Chakar was blamed for bringing the birds here in the first place. The majority of the Guards liked the tiny Observer, but they felt she should have sent the Plavats back where they came from as soon as they had delivered her here. She quite understood, and even shared their feelings, but it was Mim who eventually ordered the Guards to stop their increasingly surly attitude towards Observer Chakar.

Sava ignored Chakar for the most part. The owl seemed to feel that she had betrayed him, leaving him behind and adventuring off with the hideous Plavats. So Sava was usually to be found on, or near, old Lorak, and his hooting became less doleful.

Elyssa spent longer each day with the midnight blue Dragon Kadi and with Observer Babach. The golden Dragon Kija also spent time with Elyssa, sharing her memories of Farn's hatching and of his bonding with Tika. Kija was aware that Elyssa had heard much of these things from Tika and Farn themselves, but Kija viewed these happenings slightly differently. Tika had spoken of the terror she had experienced when Farn was wounded near to death, but Kija let Elyssa see also the wonder of the

208

healing that was performed on her son.

This day, Elyssa sat with Kija in the great hall. Lorak had dragged both the Observers off to inspect his new gardens yet again and the other Dragons were flying in the, at last, slightly warmer air above the Stronghold.

'How much longer do you wait, child?' Kija asked.

'Until Kadi is strong enough,' Elyssa replied unguardedly. Then she looked up at the golden Dragon and smiled. 'Neatly done, dear Kija!'

Kija's laugh seemed to tickle Elyssa's mind. 'I am old, child. I will hatch no more children, but I am not an old fool. It has become clear to me that you and Kadi, with the old man, plan to go to Drogoya.'

Elyssa sighed. 'I do not think we dare say that we "plan" anything Kija. The thought was in each of our minds and it grows more insistent each day. But Kadi must be as strong as may be for such a journey.'

Kija rattled her wings. 'Where did Kadi take the child Mena? Even now she does not speak of it to us. She says only that something affected her mind and that she flew as if crazed.'

Kija felt a shield tighten around the girl's mind, then it melted away and bright blue eyes set in silver stared up at her.

'She took the child to Drogoya of course – as you have already guessed. Now, we must retrieve the child, bring her back here for a time.'

Smoke wisped from Kija's nose and her prismed eyes darkened.

'Mena is the child of Hargon, a so-called Lord in the western lands. He bred my daughter Tika as a slave.' Anger pulsed from her. 'Is his daughter worth the lives of my dearest friend and clan sister Kadi, as well as you and Babach?'

Elyssa held the Dragon's gaze steadily. 'Yes,' she replied.

Gold flared in Kija's stare. Elyssa got to her feet. She reached both hands to Kija's face and leaned her head against the Dragon's brow.

'Kadi must return the pendant to the child.' Her words were a bare whisper even in the mind speech.

Kija jerked her head out of Elyssa's hands, confusion spilling through her thoughts. Elyssa sat down again, watching Kija closely as the Dragon fitted pieces of the puzzle into place. Finally Kija swung her long face down to the girl who quietly sat at her side.

'Do you believe it to be so, or do you know it to be so?'

Elyssa's smile was radiant. 'I know it.'

Silence fell between them once more until Kija spoke again.

'Where is she truly from, this child Mena?'

Elyssa's head tilted to one side. 'Two places I think, and this I do not know for sure. But I think she is from here, and also from Beyond.'

Kija moaned softly and rocked from side. 'If she is who you say, why must she be brought here? Why is she but a child, untrained, when this world has need of a powerful, experienced being to ensure its survival?'

'Perhaps even the old gods of Valsheba can miscalculate?' Elyssa suggested. 'The child is at least born, and she will grow to her power very swiftly I suspect. Babach and I think that she is not strong enough yet to resist Cho Petak with all his newly arrived creatures. She must therefore come here.'

'Has this Cho Petak not discovered what she might be? He would surely destroy her so easily should he find her now and suspect her potential?'

Elyssa bit her lip. 'From what Kadi has been able to recall, she left the child close to the building which Babach calls the Menedula. It is where Cho Petak dwells. Therefore she may be with him at this moment.'

Kija was aghast. 'The child is under his control even now?'

'Babach thinks that she will find her way to the House of Oblaka,' Elyssa began but Kija did not let her finish.

'This Oblaka is the place the old man says was burnt, the place where he was so grievously hurt!'

'Kija, listen to me. You have heard both the Observers tell of hidden caves below the House of Oblaka. That is where the child will try to go, and once there, she will be safe, for a time at least.'

Smoke wisped again and Kija's eyes blazed with fury.

'I understood from the old man and the woman Chakar that it takes six days or more for them to ride some sort of animal from the building where dwells Petak to the coast. Will the child find animals to ride do you think? She will surely have to walk. How long then would it take a child, travelling unknown ways, and with dangers all around, to get to this safety you speak of with such frightening complacency?'

A scribe scratched at the door of the High Speaker's study and poked his head into the room.

'Forgive the interruption High Speaker, but the mage Pachela begs a few moments of your time – she says it is most important.'

Thryssa nodded and Pajar started to get to his feet.

'No, stay please Pajar,' Thryssa murmured as Pachela came into the study.

The girl bowed to both Thryssa and the first councillor and then sat on the very edge of the chair offered to her.

'Gremara spoke with me, High Speaker. She says she will have to leave Talvo, at least for a while. She has instructed Jeela in many things but by no means all the silver one's successor should rightly know.'

Pachela looked from face to face. 'Gremara said that Prilla is no longer Prilla, and one of the three Firans within the Corvida is likewise altered. She said what appears to be Prilla plans to move against Parima within days, and if shielding is to work, it will take every mage here working in concert to make it so.'

Thryssa had grown pale listening to Pachela repeat Gremara's warning.

'The three Firans,' she said slowly looking to her first councillor.

'Destroy them at once.' Pajar did not hesitate.

Pachela stared at him, gulped but nodded her head. 'Gremara said Speaker Lashek and Speaker Orsim are on their way here now?'

Pajar nodded.

'She said that they are in danger while – while the three Firans live.'

Without further comment, Pajar left the room. Thryssa looked at the closed door in silence then folded her hands together on the table.

'Dear stars, what is happening to us? I do not recall a death sentence being enacted in all the cycles since Vagrantia was found.'

211

'Gremara said it was necessary,' Pachela whispered, her silvered eyes fixed on Thryssa.

The High Speaker forced a tiny smile. 'I am sure she knows more than she has told us. But where is she going? Only once before has she left Talvo, and that only recently to reach Jeela and Kadi.'

Pachela shook her head but before she could speak, the Corvida rocked. Thryssa's hands clenched on the table, her mind flashing to find Pajar's mental signature. He was close to the apartments the Firans had been moved to, but he did not respond to her thought. Kwanzi burst into the study.

'What now?' he asked tersely.

Again, the Corvida building moved, a rippling sensation making the walls shudder. The window to Thryssa's left fell inwards, glass ringing on the stone floor.

'The three Firans,' Thryssa told him equally tersely as she hurried past him.

Kwanzi glanced at the girl already on her feet to follow the High Speaker.

'Pajar went to destroy the Firans in their chambers.'

'Destroy?' Kwanzi echoed in horror.

Pachela brushed past him. 'It was necessary. One is not truly Firan.'

She ran along the corridor in Thryssa's wake while Kwanzi was still gaping. Ordering the men standing watch at the end of the corridor to come at once, Kwanzi rushed after Pachela and his wife. He caught them up near to the apartment which the Firans now occupied. Thryssa had come to a halt outside the main door leading into this suite of chambers. The door glowed red, the heat from it reaching ten paces or more into the corridor. To Kwanzi's left, he saw three bodies sprawled on the floor, two in the brown and green robes of healers. The third body's flaming red hair identified him as first councillor Pajar.

Kwanzi hesitated only briefly. Pachela stood by Thryssa, her arm linked through the High Speaker's. More healers and armed guards were coming from corridors to either side and Kwanzi moved to bend over Pajar. He turned the first councillor onto his back and laid his fingers to the pulse in his throat. He could see no obvious injury but Pajar's mind was blanketed in deep unconsciousness. He stooped to check the healer lying by Pajar's feet and found her dead. Other healers had reached him now and Kwanzi quickly told all he knew: that Pajar had come here to destroy the Firans. Two older healers remained by Kwanzi and at his nod they linked minds and tried to penetrate into the rooms behind the glowing door.

The man beside Kwanzi swayed against him with a gasp but pulled himself upright again.

'Whatever is it?' the woman on Kwanzi's other side murmured aloud, her voice husky with fear.

'A creature from the Void, or so we suspect.' It was Pachela who answered.

She and Thryssa had crossed to join Kwanzi. The two women felt a surge of power as the three linked minds manoeuvred together against an unseen force. There came an ear-splitting scream of mingled surprise, anger and pain, then the heat around the door died away. Guards moved as Thryssa walked to the door and one, at her gesture, tentatively reached for the latch. When his fingers found that the metal was cool, he lifted it and pushed it wide, slipping quickly into the room, sword drawn and three comrades at his heels.

Thryssa found herself gripping her pendant which did not feel overly warm but throbbed insistently against her palm. Three more guards followed Thryssa into the chamber, the first four already searching through the adjoining rooms. A guard called from what Thryssa remembered was a sitting room overlooking the gardens to the side of the Corvida. She went quickly through to that room, aware that Pachela was close behind her. She heard Pachela's indrawn breath and nodded slightly. The velvet smoothness of the black walls was corrugated as though it had been heated far above any natural temperature. Thryssa's gaze moved from the walls to the floor where two of the young Firans lay.

One of the girls, Thryssa thought it was Graza, stared up with sightless blue and silvered eyes, her face twisted in a rictus of terror. She lay half behind an armchair, as if she had tried to find a hiding place. The boy Kralo lay under the window, his face pressed against the wall, his back to the room. A guard rolled him onto his back and Thryssa's mouth tightened when she saw a similar grimace of fear on his face. She bent, pushing up his eyelids and saw his blue silvered eyes were already dulled.

Thryssa glanced up at Pachela. 'I made a mistake. I was sure it would be Kralo.' The High Speaker rose. 'Where is Mokray then, we must find her.'

Guards emerging from other rooms, shook their heads: the apartments were empty other than this room. Pachela caught Thryssa's arm and pointed at a narrow low door at the side of the hearth. Thryssa frowned. It was merely a cupboard used to store extra cushions. She signalled a guard to open the cupboard and flinched as a body sitting sideways on the floor within, toppled out. The guard's sword was at the girl's throat immediately but he raised it after a moment. He turned to Thryssa, his face rather pale.

'Dead as well, High Speaker.'

Thryssa walked round a long low table to look down at the girl. Her eyes were no longer brown set in silver: they were burnt sockets, and blood smeared her face like red tear tracks.

Kwanzi came in unsteadily, his arm half supporting both himself and the woman healer at his side. They reached Thryssa and stared down at what remained of Mokray. The woman, Lori, pointed at the girl's hands and Thryssa swallowed hard. Mokray's fingers were curled into claws and were bloodied to the second knuckles.

'It was Neri who was working with you, was it not? Is he all right?' Thryssa asked.

The woman healer straightened her back with a groan. 'He is drained but will be himself after a good rest, as will we.'

'How did you destroy it?' Thryssa looked suddenly alarmed. 'It is destroyed I trust?'

Lori smiled. 'Some of us had heard rumours of these things from the Void making an unwelcome appearance on this world and had talked of ways of defeating them.' She shrugged. 'We unmade its mind. But the three of us were fully stretched. Six would have dealt with it quicker and suffered less than we. None of us will be able to call any power for several days.'

Kwanzi rubbed a hand wearily over his face. 'All three bodies must be burnt to ashes at once.'

'Why?' Pachela asked in surprise. 'They are dead, they are of

214

no danger now. Are they?'

Lori started to turn away, moving like an ancient crone. 'Their bodies could be reanimated for a while. They must offer no haven for any other such creatures.'

Pachela put her hands over her mouth, grey silvered eyes round with shock. Thryssa put her arm across the young woman's shoulders and moved them both towards the door.

'Take these bodies to the roof, burn them, and stay with them until the winds take the ashes,' she ordered the guard leader.

Another guard hurried in as she was speaking. He saluted.

'Speaker Lashek and Speaker Orsim have been brought in High Speaker.'

Thryssa's arm tightened about Pachela at the words.

'They seemed to have some sort of fit so their escort told us, about a league from here. They are not conscious but have been taken to infirmary three.'

Kwanzi and Lori had turned back to hear the guard's words. Kwanzi met his wife's stare.

'Lashek wears a pendant,' Thryssa murmured. 'I will go at once.'

Somehow, Kwanzi and Lori summoned a reserve of strength and followed Thryssa and Pachela down three floors to the infirmaries where the Speakers had been taken. Senior healers were already working over the two men when Thryssa arrived. Gripping her pendant in her left hand, she reached between two healers for Lashek's hand. She lifted it and placed it over his pendant, pressing the limp fingers around the oval shape. A healer moved aside, raising his brows at the High Speaker in mute question.

'Can you find any damage, any reason for this collapse?' Thryssa kept her voice low.

The healer shook his head. 'There is evidence of great shock – the sort we would expect to see following a major injury and serious loss of blood. But there is no sign of any physical injury.'

Another healer murmured something and the one who had spoken to Thryssa turned back to their patient. Thryssa moved to Orsim and heard the same conclusions. She studied Orsim's face, relaxed and unguarded as she had rarely seen it. Slowly, she raised the silver chain over her head and held the jade backed egg

215

in her hand. She put it gently in the curve of Orsim's neck then stood back, aware of the healers' curious stares.

'Let that not be moved from where I have placed it,' she commanded them and moved once more to Lashek's bed.

The healer who had spoken to her previously bent towards her.

'The shocked reaction to his sensory web is dissipating quite quickly High Speaker. Quicker than I would have thought possible.'

Thryssa drew a stool to Lashek's bedside and sat watching him. Colour had returned to his pallid face and suddenly his lips twitched into a wide smile, although his eyes remained closed. Thryssa had no idea how long she sat, healers coming and going around her. She was aware only of Lashek. His eyelids fluttered, and opened. He looked straight into the High Speaker's hazel eyes, the smile still creasing his plump face and the scent of mint suffused the infirmary.

Chapter Twenty-One

Tika decided that it might seem more polite if she made her way
to the Elder's cave rather than expecting him to fly to the beach.
She knew from Farn that the young sea Dragons such as Storm,
supplied fish for the Elders, who spent most of their days basking
on the ledges. Tika had not met the third Elder. She had seen a
massive body lying outside a cave near to Salt's but its colouring
was so like the weather streaked rocks that she saw only a blurred
shape with no definitive form to it.

The party spent the hottest part of each day within the lower
caves, dozing or chatting, until the heat abated enough for them to
venture forth to the ruins of the ancient city of Segra. A short
while after their midday meal was finished today therefore, Tika
announced that she was visiting the Elder Salt. She shook her
head when Gan would have escorted her.

'He has asked to speak with me, Gan. I presume he means
alone.'

Gan settled back against a small boulder.

'I will wait for you here then, should the others have gone off
to dig in the sand some more.'

Ren looked up from a sketch he was making on a large piece
of paper and scowled.

'It is serious research, not just digging about in the sand.'

Gan nodded and closed his eyes. Sket caught Tika's eye
questioningly. She grinned.

'You can wait here with Gan if you wish – just think of all that
water you would have to look at from so high up.'

Sket grinned back and continued cleaning and checking his
weapons. Tika walked round to the beach side of the cliffs and
began to climb towards the cave in which she, Gan, Navan and
Riff slept. She studied the cliff face and picked a route upwards
to Salt's cave. Halfway to her goal, the path became far more
tricky and took all her concentration. When she hauled herself

onto the ledge she sat for a moment, legs dangling, and sucked her sore fingertips. It was going to be even more unpleasant climbing down, she realised, and sincerely hoped that Salt would allow Farn to land here and carry her back to the beach.

She heard a dry rustling to her left and got to her feet, moving cautiously toward the cave. The bright sunlight and the glittering dazzle off the water made the cave seem even darker as she peered within. From the darkness the slightly paler face of Salt loomed towards her.

'Welcome child. I will lie outside then you may choose heat or shade in which to sit while we talk.'

Tika pressed herself against the rock as the huge body emerged from the cave to recline along the ledge. As she sat against the cave's entrance, head in shadow and legs out on the ledge, she realised how dark her skin had become. Her trousers were rolled to the knees and her legs and bare feet looked a tawny brown against the rock.

'You find your chosen caves suitable?' Salt asked politely.

'Oh yes, perfectly,' Tika answered. 'Brin will be back in a day or two we hope,' she added, wondering if Salt really wanted to discuss such details.

Salt rumbled quietly and extended a wing over the side of the ledge to better soak up the heat. His long grey face turned to regard the small figure beside him.

'Storm tells me there has been much searching for a particular plant?'

Tika noticed that his pale faceted eyes had dark green specks in them as she considered her answer.

'It is a herb, called mint. It is used in many ways, some of them in healings.'

'Hmm. We know of certain such plants, but we have to seek far to the north for them. We use plants that grow in the sea more often.'

'Those long ribbon things you mean?' Tika asked in surprise.

'Not those generally, but Ice can tell you more of such things than I.'

Salt regarded her steadily.

'Why do you need this mint plant – none of you are sick I think?'

Tika paused to think. 'It has a strong smell. Some of us believe we have smelled it, but look though we may, we cannot discover it.'

Silence fell. Salt swung his head to gaze out over the endless waters.

'Do you hear the singing?'

Tika stared at Salt's profile. 'No one has mentioned to me that they have heard any singing.'

'Hmm.' The Elder turned his gaze back to Tika. 'You carry something special with you.'

Tika's hand went automatically to the pendant under her shirt.

'It calls to me,' Salt's voice whispered in her mind. 'Might I see it?'

Tika pulled the gold chain free of her shirt and let the pendant swing freely below her hand. The red gold backing winked and shimmered in the bright sun and the amber front seemed to drink in the light. Salt's eyes whirred rapidly and he lowered his face close to the pendant.

'Listen child.'

Tika frowned then gasped as Salt opened his mind to her. Countless voices mingled in Salt's mind, their singing rising and falling in joyful cadence. Very slowly, Tika slipped the pendant under her shirt again but held it away from her skin when she realised how hot it had become. The singing faded and ceased. Salt sighed, a great gusting sigh.

'That is what I hear. Only myself and Mist hear them. It began on the day that you arrived at this shore.'

Tika realised that she was trembling and also that Salt was aware of her agitation. The Elder's eyes darkened, fixing on Tika.

'You have heard this before.' It was a statement not a question.

Green silvered eyes sparkled with unshed tears.

'When my Farn was near death, I think I heard something like that, but not so clearly, nor so close.'

Salt's mind tone softened. 'Go now and speak with Mist.' He glanced a little higher along the cliff face to an empty ledge. 'She awaits you now child.'

Tika scrambled up the short distance to the ledge that Salt had indicated. She stood at the cave's mouth and called in the mind speech:

'Elder Mist? Elder Salt told me that you wished to see me?'

Tika was unable to hide her shock when the sea Dragon came into the sunlight. One side of her face was still the long beautiful Dragon face that Tika had come to expect. The other was twisted by a burning of some kind. The left eye socket was empty, puckered grey hide grown across it. There were no scales on the left side of her face and, as Mist came fully onto the ledge, Tika saw great patches on her neck and shoulder were also bare of scales. Tika could not restrain her tears: Mist's left wing was half gone, clearly this Dragon could no longer fly. The single eye rested on her, pale greens and blues iridescent in the prisms.

'I appreciate your feelings child, but I am long used to my disfigurements.'

'Yes, but to be unable to fly!' Tika blurted before she could stop herself.

Mist laughed softly. 'I can manage to reach the shore on occasions. More often, I go to the cliff top, from whence I can get back here quite easily. I will admit that it is a struggle up from the beach.'

Tika could not believe that this huge creature of the skies could speak of her loss of flight so lightly. But Mist again answered Tika's thought.

'It was long ago child. I am accustomed now to my restrictions.'

Tika brushed her sleeve across her wet face. 'Forgive me, Mist. Your bravery makes anything I have heard of or experienced fade to nothing.' She drew a shaky breath. 'You wished to speak to me?'

'Yes indeed.' The Dragon settled herself more comfortably along the ledge. 'It will not surprise you to know that I listened to your stories through Cloud's mind? All of this Flight allow me to see and hear things through their minds since I am isolated here.'

Tika nodded in understanding.

'The hatchling you are bonded to – his mind is fragile. No, no.' Mist lowered her head to touch her undamaged right cheek to Tika's. 'I do not say his mind is weak – fragile is what I truly meant. I am surprised that his mother has let him travel so far

220

from her though.'

Tika was quick to Kija's defence. 'She went to visit an Elder – not too distant from us. Then she heard tell that her clan sister had been dreadfully injured a long way to the north. She flew to offer her help, not knowing that we would come across the barren lands to the coast. Brin is boastful sometimes, but he cares for Farn and would let no harm come to him. And I have some medicines which help if he becomes too upset.'

Mist listened carefully until Tika fell silent.

'Know that I can help him child. And as he is the one who carries you, and you have been Chosen to carry what you do, every Dragon of my Flight will defend and protect you should such need arise.'

Tika's jaw dropped in astonishment. Mist's words rang with simple truth and Tika believed them. But she had felt the independent wildness within the sea Dragons and had not thought that they would bother overmuch with the fate of two legged strangers. Again Tika revealed her oval pendant.

'Is it because of this? Is it so important? Mim and I do not even know what they really are.'

Mist's eye was glued to the gently revolving pendant and Tika stared at it too.

'Inside, there is –'

'I know what is inside,' Mist interrupted her. 'And I marvel that I have survived long enough to see such a thing.'

'Are they so very important?'

Mist shifted her weight to lean against the cliff side. 'Oh yes. We have stories that tell of their hiding long ages gone. Before the two legs built their strange cliffs here. And I knew when they were taken from hiding half a cycle past.' She tilted her head to see Tika clearly. 'More have been freed of late. There is one which is the most precious and that one too is in the world again.'

Tika had no idea what Mist was talking about. She knew the strangers from Drogoya had brought a pendant with them – she must ask Ren more of that.

'One of our company comes from the land on the far side of this world – you will have heard his story? The leader of the people who fled from here, she told of something called the Void. We think it was creatures from that place who attacked us when

221

we arrived here.'

'And attacked some of my Flight a few days before.' Mist's eye flashed with sudden anger.

'If you know of these pendants, do you know aught of these other things?' Tika pressed on.

Seboth's scouts had informed him of Hargon's arrival at the way station close to Far. He was told at mid morning of Hargon's approach to the town itself – with a minimum escort. Seboth quickly ordered two squads, already positioned in the thinly wooded hills near the way station to be watchful for the prearranged signal. Then the Lord of Far went down to the main courtyard to be ready to receive his visitors.

Lady Lallia waited above stairs beside a screened grill set high in the wall of the reception hall to which Seboth would invite Lord Hargon. Lallia heard the hooves ring on the stones of the yard and kept watch on the door below her. Armsmen in the green uniforms of Far entered and stood to either side of the doorway. Then Seboth walked into sight, Hargon at his side. Behind, but only by half a pace, slouched the newly appointed Armschief of Return, Trib, of whom Lallia had heard much and none of it pleasant.

Three paces behind him, walked officers Tarin and Fryss, and Lallia knew instantly how unhappy they were with the present state of affairs. Their expressions were blank, notice in itself of their confusion. They halted and stood smartly to attention, stark contrast to Armschief Trib's casual stance and crumpled dark grey uniform.

Meran stood by the inner door, overseeing servants who offered refreshments to the visitors. When dishes had been set for the men to help themselves and jugs of ale and water stood ready by a line of goblets, the servants disappeared with Meran.

'No females flocking about you Seboth?' Hargon's voice was cold and harsh. 'How can you bear to be parted from them – I thought they were always permitted to attend you in your house-hold?'

Seboth poured himself some water and sat down.

'My wife is unwell at present.'

'Unwell?' Hargon barked a laugh, although it sent chills down

Lallia's back. 'How opportune!'

Seboth studied the Lord of Return coolly. 'She is breeding again, so I command her to guard her health at such times.'

Hargon flinched and turned away at this subtle stab at his now childless state. Armschief Trib was already pouring a second goblet of ale for himself, Lallia saw, although the two officers had not moved.

'I come to persuade you from your foolhardy ways Seboth. All aspects of life in Sapphrea have become too lax in this generation, and you exemplify this laxness even in the way you allow such ridiculous freedoms to your females.'

To Lallia's practised eye, Seboth's mild expression had become somewhat strained and she clenched her fists, willing him not to lose his temper.

'There are no more Gangers to war with now Hargon. Our lands are secure. Some tolerance is but small reward for the hardships our people endured but a few cycles back.'

'Tolerance.' Hargon spat the word out. 'You have allowed the old blood to revive and strengthen among you – I could smell it from the moment I reached your town border. I tell you, you will cull it from your people, or I will.'

Seboth placed his goblet deliberately and carefully on the table and got to this feet. He stood easily, his hands loosely hooked on his belt.

'I give the commands in Far, Hargon, and never will I command that any man, woman or child be killed because they "might" have old blood in their veins. And you are no longer welcome here. You and your men will leave now, unharmed. But the instant that you clear my boundaries, we are foes.'

Hargon's hand slammed onto his sword hilt as he glared across the room at Seboth. Lallia saw her husband's face lose colour, his eye widen in surprise before cold determination clenched his jaw while he stared back at the Lord of Return. Hargon glanced at his Armschief, who was peering into the depths of the ale jug with an air of dejection, then at his two unmoving officers.

'You have let your armsmen grow soft, Seboth. My men will treat them as playthings ere they kill them. Come.'

Hargon strode to the door, Trib staggering in his wake. Seboth gestured to his own men to follow Hargon and then eyed the officers still standing before him. They dropped to their knees, unbuckling sword belts and laying the weapons on the floor in front of them. The veteran Tarin looked up at Seboth.

'Kill us now Lord Seboth. We cannot serve whatever has possession of Lord Hargon.'

Seboth raised his hand to silence the elderly armsman.

'This constant talk of killing grows tedious. If you ask for refuge in Far then be assured you are offered it. The price is information regarding Hargon's immediate plans for my town.'

Tarin did not hesitate. 'He has a large force at the way station. They will attack at his signal.'

For the first time, Tarin glanced at Fryss before looking back to Lord Seboth.

'I think he suspected that we would try to stay here – he did not tell us what his signal was to be.'

Lallia felt a sudden surge of power and realised that her husband was checking the truth of Tarin's words. He nodded slowly and beckoned the two armsmen who remained by the door.

'I think you had best change your clothes – that uniform will be inviting target practise from now on. Keep your daggers but for the moment I would have you leave your swords here.'

Seboth picked up the two swords and put them on the table.

'My men will get you other clothes,' he continued, but was interrupted by Fryss.

'We would both be proud to be permitted to take the uniform of Far, Sir Lord.'

Seboth paused then nodded. 'Very well. Take them to Meran when they have changed their clothes,' he instructed one of his armsmen. The other was ordered to fetch Seboth's first and second officers at once. The room emptied and Seboth looked up at the grill with a rueful smile.

'No worse than we anticipated my love,' he said.

'But what was wrong Seboth? Hargon had his back to me so I could not see his expressions.'

'His eyes. There were flames within them – did you not see how red they have become?'

'Do you think it is the affliction Lady Emla spoke of?'

An armsman came hurrying in and Seboth swung round to

hear his message.

'Sir Lord, the two officers say that Lord Hargon seeks information of the strangers who travel with Dragons. He has scouts ranging across most of the northern territories looking for them.'

'There is more,' Seboth stared at the armsman.

'Officer Tarin said Lord Hargon's methods of questioning folk is extremely unpleasant and it involves much torture Sir Lord.'

'If Officers Tarin or Fryss have any other details, tell them I will see them later. Meanwhile, begin the signal procedures at once.'

The armsman trotted away while a group of Seboth's officers came quickly into the hall.

'All defensive positions are manned Sir Lord.'

Lallia heard that one report as she slipped away from her watching post and climbed up to the floor which led to the sun tower. She stretched her hand to open the door to her apartments, and froze.

'Lallia? Is it safe to speak with you?'

'Maressa?' Lallia whispered both aloud and in her mind. 'Wait one moment and I will be alone.'

Lallia went swiftly into her maids' sitting room, heading for the winding stair up to her private chambers.

'No, no,' she assured the girls. 'I wish to sleep for a little while. I will call should I need you.'

Once in her own sitting room, Lallia sat on a heap of pillows. 'Maressa? How can you speak to me from such a distance as I believed the coast to be?'

Maressa laughed. 'I am but twenty leagues west of you Lallia. Brin and I come for some supplies. We hoped you would be generous enough to provision us once again.'

Lallia clasped her head in her hands. 'Maressa, listen.'

As quickly as she could, Lallia explained how the problems with Lord Hargon of Return had degenerated into a war situation. Maressa remained silent while she tried to decide on her best options.

'Maressa, you must not come any nearer Far, and Brin must not be seen – Hargon is determined to kill you all.'

Maressa described the area in which she and Brin were currently resting, relaying an image of sparsely wooded slopes and coarsely grassed plains stretching east and south.

'Seboth will know where you are. I will try to organise what you need.'

Lallia squeaked when Maressa began to recite a list of requirements.

'Wait! Let me write it down!'

When the list was made, Lallia studied it for a moment. 'None of this should pose any problems, but getting it to you may take a couple of days Maressa. I will try to speak to Seboth, but you can imagine he is a little busy just now,' she finished with wifely understatement.

She sensed Maressa's amusement.

'I will leave it to you to mind speak me when you can Lallia. I am sorry it seems unlikely that we shall meet for now.'

The link was broken and Lallia sat staring at the scribbled list. She went to the door and called for one of her maids to summon Meran. Meran arrived in a short while, suggesting to Lallia that he was keeping close personal watch on the sun tower. Rapidly she explained that Maressa had bespoken her and that she needed these supplies for the party who had travelled to the coast. Meran knew all that had transpired while the strange visitors had stayed in the House of Far and accepted all with equanimity. He had sworn his life forfeit to the wellbeing of Lady Lallia in her cradle at Tagria, and had been prepared to pay that forfeit every day of her life since.

'I shall gather these items in one of the empty stables,' he told her now. 'Do you wish me to tell Lord Seboth? He is at present checking that the people are secure within the town. Many farmers have come in the last few days seeking refuge, as you know.'

It was growing dark before Seboth appeared in Lallia's chambers. 'I cannot stay long. There is much fighting around the way station. According to reports I am getting, the Return men fight like madmen whenever Hargon is in their midst but seem to have no heart for it when he is elsewhere. They have taken heavy losses but still Hargon urges them to fight on.'

'Did Meran tell you of Maressa's presence but twenty leagues west?'

'Yes.' Seboth frowned. 'He has arranged for the provisions I understand so that two riders can leave at full dark. Show me the place Maressa pictured for you. Oh yes. I know it.' His frown deepened. 'It is too exposed there, particularly for such a very large, very red Dragon.' He chewed his lip. 'There is a ravine a few leagues south of that spot, they would be safer there. Call Maressa's mind and I will explain it to her.'

Lallia concentrated as Maressa herself had taught her. She concentrated harder. Then she looked at her husband in horror.

'I cannot feel her mind Seboth! Not there or anywhere near.'

Chapter Twenty-Two

Each time that Mena went to the small overgrown herb garden, her heart thumped against her ribs lest the boy Tyen not be there. Each time, she fervently thanked the stars that he was. In the five days since she had found him, Mena's food had improved: there was more of it and dried fruits and nuts had been added. There was apparently an inexhaustible supply of the hard biscuits and some of those, with nuts and fruit, she hid in her bed chamber.

She had also asked for a flask in which to take water outside, claiming that the water from an old pump she had found there, tasted unpleasant. Cho Petak suggested she might like meat but Mena assured him that she had never eaten meat, that it made her ill. In fact she had always eaten meat before, but she wondered exactly what animal the meat might come from here, and was not prepared to take the risk.

She always took a few fruits and one of the biscuits to the garden for the boy. He stayed within the wooden building when Mena worked at the endless weeding, but they talked, and gradually Mena built up a vague picture of the Menedula and what it had, until lately, represented. Tyen told her what he understood of the hierarchy of the Order of Sedka: the Sacrifice, the Offerings, the Observers, the Kooshak and the Aspirants. Much of what he said Mena had already read of in her chamber, but Tyen had learnt it by rote in his school and it was thus merely a string of words to him, meaningless as a rhyme.

Cautiously, Mena asked of the other Order, stumbling over the pronunciation of Myata's name. Silence followed her question.

'My father and mother said that Myata had the right of things,' Tyen finally replied. 'But you wasn't supposed to speak of her, except among others who you knew for sure believed the same.'

Mena weeded on, knowing that Tyen was still thinking.

'Some of the Observers and Kooshak were known to favour Myata and there was always a party at our house if a Kooshak visited who would tell more stories of her.'

Mena heard the hitch in his voice and began humming softly as she went to empty her weed box. She had nearly refilled it before Tyen spoke again.

'They say, the stories, that Myata gives a safe home to any who ask at her House in Oblaka.'

Mena paused in the act of winkling out a particularly stubborn and long rooted weed. That sounded like the name she had seen on a map upstairs, the place her eyes were drawn to each time she looked at it.

'I think that is in the direction that I need to go,' said Mena. 'Could you get us there?'

'Take us many days and it is dangerous out there now,' Tyen sounded dubious. 'As good a place as any I guess. Can't stay here much longer anyway.'

That evening, when Cho visited Mena, he found her drawing a map. She looked up in time to catch his frown.

'What is this place please Sir?' she asked, pointing to a marked spot in the centre of the page.

'It is the town of Krasato, where the Emperor lives. Lived,' he corrected himself.

He looked at the way in which Mena had copied the map and his frown disappeared. Mountains took up an inordinate amount of space, and the tiny representations of woodlands Mena had enlarged so that their branches trailed right across the page.

'An interesting interpretation child, but I think I like your other drawings better.'

'Yes Sir. I just thought this might be fun. Are all these squiggles towns as well then Sir?'

He stared down into guileless eyes. 'Yes. At least they were towns, but now they are returning to the dust from which they grew.'

Mena nodded solemnly and drew a clean sheet of paper towards her.

'I think you are right Sir. I do prefer to draw the flowers.'

Cho Petak watched for a while longer then silently left her. Mena slid out another paper on which the map was copied and checked yet again that she had everything in its exact position.

Cho had returned to his own rooms and was staring at the

charts spread out before him. Perhaps the child would develop an interest in such things, as he had so long ago. He glanced at the darkening window and sighed. These creatures had such extended infancies. It would be years before he could hold an intelligent conversation with that girl. He sighed again when the air shuddered, announcing the presence of Grek.

'Byess is destroyed,' Grek began at once.

Cho frowned.

'Yes,' Grek continued. 'Destroyed. In the east of the Night Lands. Taken apart completely.'

'What of the other three? Have you located Rashpil yet?'

'No. There is no trace of him at all, but I have found M'Raz and Zloy. Zloy is embodied in the eastern Night Lands, very near to where Byess was lost. M'Raz,' Grek laughed. 'M'Raz has taken the body of that child's father.'

Fleetingly, Cho enjoyed the sound of Grek's laughter. He so rarely heard it now, and when he did, it held a note of bitterness rather than the unalloyed joy Cho so well remembered.

'They can stay there for now,' he told Grek. 'But I begin to grow concerned by Rashpil's absence.'

The air flurried around the end of the table then stilled again.

'There was some disturbance in a city called Gaharn. I have a sense that Rashpil was there, but nearly met with the same fate as Byess has done. Perhaps he was damaged, or frightened. I think that he is deliberately concealing himself from us at present.'

'And you wonder, as I do, why he should feel the need to do so?'

'Cho, are you sure of all the ones now freed?' Grek asked earnestly. 'Have you seen what they are doing to this land of yours? I had not seen Drogoya until I came in the body of the girl, but it is a pleasant land Cho. Greener, more lush than the land of Sapphrea where I have spent all these long years. Do you really mean them to ruin it so totally?'

Cho shrugged. 'It is of no importance.' He tapped the chart in front of him. 'There is a world which will be within range and would suit us far better than this one. It is far richer in the elements we most benefit from. I have planned that we will move there within this year and remain there as long as it takes to increase our strength beyond belief.'

230

His eyes had begun to burn as he spoke and the unbodied Grek watched him closely. Conviction underscored Cho's words: he believed in the rightness of his plans.

'I will seek Rashpil once more,' Grek announced abruptly and left Cho's apartments.

But he went only to the roof of the Menedula, an unbodied spirit drifting with the slight breeze. Cho's words convinced him less each day and he feared that Cho was a far lesser being than he had seemed when Grek fell under his spell. In the brief time that Grek had been back once more in Cho's company, he had discovered far too many discrepancies in Cho's conversation.

Grek slid through the air particles, towards the east. He felt no strong urgency to find Rashpil, but he did feel a need to distance himself from Cho Petak while he struggled to decide his own course of action. Grek had once had true human form, unlike Cho Petak. He had been beguiled by Cho's talk, Cho's promises to all those who followed his path. Even now, Grek was not sure what Cho's true form might look like. Nor did he know from whence Cho had originated, whether he was the solitary representative of some distant race or the one survivor from an equally distant catastrophe.

Grek had been unaware that Cho was not what he appeared until shortly before Cheok's punitive attack on Cho and all who followed him. The unbodied spirit of the young man that Grek had been on that day drifted with the increasing wind, high above the eastern coast of Drogoya. He alone had lived in many bodies since his arrival here, all of them in Sapphrea in the western Night Lands. D'Lah and Cho Petak had each used only one body through all these years and Cho had killed the mind of his host within days of taking over that body.

D'Lah had forced his way into the body of an Asatarian woman at the moment she gave birth to a boy child. He had swiftly transferred to the new-born, and was now so closely entwined with that one's mind that Grek did not believe they could ever be separated again. He alone had experienced many bodies, many minds, and in so doing had learnt much more of the inhabitants of this world. Grek realised that both Cho and D'Lah could accuse him of over-sympathising with the resident people, and Grek knew they would be right.

The laughing boy, so fondly and frequently recalled by Cho, had done little harm in the centuries of his sojourn here. He admitted to himself that many times he had immersed himself into the life of his current host, enjoying the simple experiences through them as once he had enjoyed them for himself. He had been in Mena's blood line since he reached this world, when her ancestors lived in the coastal city of Parima. Three generations he enjoyed in that stupendous place, before the Valsheban cities were blasted into ruins.

He had escaped because his host was on a visit to the inland city of Kedara, north of present day Tagria. That was the first time that Grek interfered in his host's life, by blanketing the web of power which would have betrayed him to the vengeful farmers. All those lives he had shared, Grek thought as he idled along on the air currents over the endless sea.

Then, at last, the summons from Cho Petak, the excitement of reunion with his old teacher and master, the fury at being in a female child's body at such a crucial moment. Savagely, Grek had captured the unsuspecting Dragon's mind, his rage burning through Mena's eyes, and forced them to Drogoya. Yet he had felt the pain from them both seeping through into his mind. He had been aware of the child's anguish when he made her urge the failing Dragon to fresh efforts.

The lands of Drogoya were in the process of being devastated by Cho's minions. Grek had doubted Cho's insistence that some of those spirits within the Void should be released to serve him. Having seen the horror these same spirits had wreaked upon Drogoya and its people already, Grek's doubts were leading him to the only choice he could make. He would have to betray Cho Petak again. As he had before, to the Grand Master Cheok.

Volk was ecstatic. Four of his horses had reappeared, grazing placidly among the goats on the hillside below the caves.

'But what use are they, Volk?' Finn asked him that night in the common room. 'They could die of old age before it might be safe to venture out from here.'

Volk scowled. 'Always useful to have a horse around,' he insisted.

Finn abandoned the point as Melena joined them. 'The boy?'

she asked quietly.

Melena nodded. 'He died a few moments ago. Kooshak Arryol worked so hard on the poor child, but he believes the poison was already too deep when the boy arrived here.'

Volk's scowl became even more ferocious. 'Poor lad. Didn't even know his name. Cursed be that Sacrifice.' He got to his feet and rolled away to seek solace in his new brews.

Sarryen had come to sit with them. 'He is a good man, that Volk,' she said.

Finn snorted. 'For light's sake, never let him hear you say that – he would be mortally offended.' She shook her head at Melena and Sarryen's puzzled faces. 'Of course he is a good man, one of the very best. But he works so hard giving everyone the impression that he is a bad tempered, hard headed man of business without a heart, you would destroy all that effort if you let him know you can see through it.'

Finn stopped as she began to cough. Sarryen stared at Melena, silently warning her not to fuss, and after a quick glance of concern the girl got to her feet.

'I have lessons to write up for Observer Soosha, if you will excuse me.'

Before Sarryen could question Finn Rah as to whether she was taking Arryol's medicines rather than Volk's, Lyeto came into the common room with two other students. All were covered with dust. Finn's coughing fit subsided and she beckoned Lyeto over.

'What have you been doing?' she asked him.

'Observer Soosha asked some of us to widen the viewing ledge, Offering Finn.'

'Widen the – But why?'

Lyeto grinned. 'He believes that the Plavat will come back, and rather than have it perhaps seen wandering around in the ruins above, he wants it to be able to come in here.'

Finn gaped at him in horror. 'A Plavat? In here? The man's wits have gone. Where is he?'

'He said he was going to talk to you, but he was not aware that you would be in here I am sure.'

Finn was already striding out of the door, Sarryen behind her.

'Finn, slow down. You will only cough again. There. I told you so.'

The Kooshak put an arm around Finn Rah's shaking shoulders and helped her the rest of the way to Chakar's sitting room. Soosha was pouring tea when the two women entered and Finn was deposited in an armchair. He gave the Offering a bowl of tea and settled in the chair opposite.

Finn glared first at Sarryen. 'Those are the four most hateful words in the language – I told you so – you are most hurtful towards an invalid.'

Sarryen grinned unrepentantly.

Finn's glare shifted to Soosha. 'And what possesses you to think we should invite a Plavat in here? Plavats live along this coast – why would anyone think it suspicious if one began poking about above us?'

'Cho Petak is fully aware of Chakar's interest in birds, and that she raised a Plavat from a fledgling. But why would it stay around here if it could not find her fairly quickly? You know that Plavats do not have much patience, or a great deal of intelligence.'

Finn continued to glare while she mulled over Soosha's words.

'You may have a point,' she finally conceded. 'But they come only just inside that viewing area. I absolutely refuse to contemplate the idea of those foul birds stalking around the passages.'

'I hardly think they would particularly want to Finn, and they wouldn't fit through most of them anyway.'

Sarryen cut across the squabbling between her elders. 'You really think that a Plavat will return Soosha? Bringing Chakar?'

The Observer raised his shoulders slightly. 'Yes. I believe a Plavat will come, but whether it will bring Chakar, or Ren, or Voron, I have no idea.'

'You do not think Babach might be the one to return?'

'You did not see his injuries Sarryen.' Soosha spoke in a low voice.

Finn nodded, closing her eyes. 'He could not have survived the journey from here.'

'It feels as though we have been here forever.' The Kooshak clasped her hands round her knees. 'Everyone has adjusted extremely well, even the children seem content to stay down here.'

'Do not forget that those children have seen exactly what awaits outside, and I doubt any of them are in a hurry to go back out there.'

Soosha nodded agreement with Finn, adding: 'Teal is very popular with the children – have you noticed? And how she makes the dough for that delicious bread with those twisted hands amazes me.'

Finn sighed. 'Arryol looked at her hands, but he said far too much time has passed since the burning. He gave her balm to make the skin a little more supple and a tincture for when the pain is bad.'

Sarryen bit her lip then plunged ahead anyway. 'Finn Rah, you are the only one to seem restless, bothered by our confinement. Is there anything that might help you?'

Finn opened her green silvered eyes to glare at Sarryen but then gave a lopsided smile instead.

'Is it that evident? I do find so many people so closely confined difficult to adjust to, I admit. If I did not have this room to retreat to, I would surely have leapt from the viewing ledge before now.' She regarded her tea bowl. 'I had a small balcony at my apartments in the Menedula. I found a small forgotten herb garden I used to visit occasionally, but apart from a modest number of lectures, I was mostly alone.'

Soosha leaned forward. 'Finn you are gifted with the oldest of magics, and Sarryen's talent has a broad range. Could you perhaps arrange odd times to risk far seeking back towards the Menedula?'

Finn and Sarryen watched the old Observer get to his feet and pace round the table.

'The children are there, I am convinced. But they will begin their journey to us within days. We have to know where they are, and lend them what help we can.'

Finn sat in thought. 'Is there any way from your dreams that we could get the smallest clue to a mind signature for one or both of the children?' she asked eventually. 'Tracing two small children in the vast area between here and the Menedula presents one huge problem without a mind signature to work with.'

'I will try to ask in the dream,' said Soosha. 'I know of no precedent where identity can be confirmed through a dream though.'

'Well.' Finn got to her feet. 'We will have a try right now, from either the viewing ledge or the hillside – which would be best do you think Sarryen?'

'The hillside,' the Kooshak replied promptly. 'To begin with, all the dust no doubt hovering around the ledge, will make you cough enough to fall down the cliff unintentionally!'

'Oh you make such a fuss! It is a cough, remnant of that disgusting cold we have all endured. That is all.'

Sarryen said no more but caught a brief look of sorrow cross Soosha's face which sent her heart plummeting. She suspected that Finn was ill, really ill, with something far worse than the residue of a cold. She snatched a cloak from a peg on the wall and hurried after the Offering. It had grown late while they had sat talking in Chakar's sitting room and the passages were empty, the chambers quiet.

Squeezing through to the outer world, Finn sat on a flat rock and looked up at the sky. She could see only a fragment of the constellation of the Weeping Willow, while the Wolf glittered directly north. She turned to study the sky above the sea and saw the stars which formed the snout of the Resting Dragon were beginning to rise. Sarryen dropped the cloak over Finn's shoulders and sat beside her.

'I will far seek, Sarryen. You will accompany me if you wish but if you tire, pull back and lend me your strength. Do not try to keep up with me out of any misplaced pride.'

Her smile flashed in the starlight, removing any sting from her words. She reached for the Kooshak's hand and held it loosely between her own, wriggled her shoulders more comfortably against the lumpy rock, and sent her mind up towards the stars. Experienced though Sarryen was, she was astonished at the speed and skill of such an accomplished far seeker. She knew at once that she should withdraw, expend her own talent on strengthening Finn Rah rather than trying to keep pace with her. Finn Rah squeezed her hand, acknowledging Sarryen's decision, and raced eastwards alone.

Approaching more populated regions, Finn flinched. Pain groaned upwards from the very earth itself. The Offering saw the mass of the Menedula building brooding blackly in the star-filled

236

night. Thinning her consciousness to a hairsbreadth, she floated into the structure. Sarryen sensed that Finn was on the brink of great peril and poured ever more of herself into the link between them. The Offering sent tendrils through the corridors and found two humans. One lay mindless on a pallet far below. The other was close by, and was a child.

Finn's mind hung above the wide bed and saw a white blonde head resting on a pillow. Huge violet silvered eyes stared straight up at her.

'Who are you?'

'Finn Rah. You must try to reach us at the Oblaka child. We will do all we can to aid you.'

'I am called Mena.'

Then something snarled and snagged all around the room and Finn shot back along the line of Sarryen's mind. Behind her, she felt Cho Petak's fury blazing and flaming through the Menedula. She implored the Light to keep the child safe from Cho's demented wrath as she realised her own strength was failing fast.

Sarryen held Finn's limp body, waiting frantically for the Offering to return. Finn jerked in her arms then bent forward, the cough tearing through her chest. Lyeto appeared behind them and without a word lifted the Offering's small figure in his arms. He carried her through the passages to Chakar's sitting room where Arryol and Soosha waited. Arryol pointed to the narrow bed and piled pillows behind Finn's back. He held crushed leaves beneath her nose while Soosha brought a bowl steaming with a pungent decongestant.

Finn struggled to control the cough briefly.

'She saw me. Her name is Mena, and she could see me.'

Chapter Twenty-Three

Orsim and Lashek both recovered fully within two days of their collapse. Neither remembered much of what had happened, nor was there any residual memory for the healers to discover what might have felled them. Both Speakers agreed that they had experienced a sensation of burning within their very brains, followed by a noise like a great rushing wind. Then they had woken in infirmary three in the Corvida. Orsim was the more shaken of the two men. He was deeply affronted that such an attack could be made with absolutely no warning from either his own air mages, or from any in Segra or Parima.

Lashek was more sanguine about the episode and many people noticed that a faint scent of mint clung to him. Most put it down to the fact that both mint and lavender were used in the storing of clothes and assumed the aroma came from such a source rather than from Lashek himself.

On this third day since the killing of the two Firans and the destruction of the creature that had inhabited the third, the Speakers were in Thryssa's private sitting room. Orsim stood at one of the windows, watching the rain pouring relentlessly down outside. He turned back to the room.

'This is all wrong.' He brandished a paper as he rejoined the others by the fire. 'My mages say that these rain clouds are confined only to this area – Talvo and Fira are having no rain. It is obviously something to do with Kallema, but I would never have thought it possible that her mages could work the weather systems.'

Kwanzi handed him a mug of tea. 'I agree. Firans can do very small things with air, but to bring a rainfall such as this should be far beyond their capabilities.'

'But perhaps not beyond the power of Prilla now?' Lashek raised a brow as he spoke. 'I have seen through Lori's mind, as well as Kwanzi's, what they had to raise threefold power against.

If a similar creature inhabits the body of Prilla now, she would be able to do much, much more than even the most senior water mage.'

'Before you ask,' Kwanzi smiled at his wife, 'Neri is recovering well, but he is far older than either Lori or myself – thus he will take longer to regain strength.'

Pajar came into the room, his red hair on end.

'Water levels in the streams and pools are rising throughout Parima,' he said without preamble. 'I have ordered the people at the greatest risk of flooding to move out now.'

Thryssa frowned. 'Surely there has not been enough rain yet to cause such a rise.'

'Of course not,' Orsim snapped. 'Kallema is drawing water up from deep underground.'

Lashek looked thoughtful. 'And there are no exits to the outside world are there? Everything was carried in over the rim of Segra when our ancestors arrived here, as I recall from my history studies.'

'What does that imply?' Thryssa's alarmed expression showed that she had realised the implication only too well.

'The craters will fill,' Lashek smiled without humour. 'And there is no way we could get all our people safely out.'

Pajar nodded. 'The water is rising in the pools even as you watch – much too fast for it to be natural.'

'Is it worth trying to contact Kallema?' asked Thryssa slowly.

Orsim and Lashek exchanged glances.

'I would guess that Prilla is in control in Fira now,' Lashek replied. He shrugged. 'It may be worth a try.'

'I will do so now,' said Orsim. 'But I would feel safer if we joined minds.'

When the mind link was joined, Orsim sent out a call to Kallema. He became rigid in his chair as did the others in the link. They could see only a wall of fire, and almost believed they could feel its heat. The voice that came from the flames crackled and hissed with amusement.

'You soon come calling do you not, once you get a little afraid.'

Thryssa overrode Orsim immediately.

'We are not a little afraid.' Her mind tone was utterly calm.

239

'We are irritated.'

The flames roared higher.

'You lie. You fear you will all be floating in a world of water, slowly dying.'

'I repeat, we are not afraid. But to whom do we speak? You are neither Kallema nor Prilla, so who are you to presume to speak for Fira Circle?'

There was a pause during which they could hear only the barely restrained fire.

'You may call me Zloy. I intend to rule in this place. If you submit to my commands, I may reverse the flow of water.'

'I must have time to confer with my Speakers and also I need some idea of what your – commands – might entail, before I could agree to anything.'

The fire leaped and raged, its centre glowing almost white hot.

'You have until darkness to decide whether you live or die. I discuss my plans and intentions with no one.'

'Did you not discuss anything with your – comrade – whom you sent here Zloy?'

Laughter, loud and maniacal, ripped through their minds.

'Byess was ever a fool.' The laughter stopped abruptly. 'You may think he was easy to deal with. I am a very different opponent. You may tell me your choice when darkness falls.'

Thryssa waited but the creature had released the mind link. She looked at her husband, the two Speakers and Pajar.

'That was the same kind of mind as the one you dealt with Kwanzi?'

He nodded. 'But, as he said, much stronger.'

'Would the shields work against him, the ones made to protect us from the silver one's bouts of madness?' Orsim enquired.

Lashek was getting to his feet. 'We can try. They were formed to cover the four Circles – perhaps we can divert the extra energy from Fira to augment the shield over the other three. I will begin the preparations.'

Orsim turned to Thryssa. 'Do you think it is monitoring our mind speech? I need to contact my Assembly and if you say you think I should not do so with mind speech, then I must despatch runners at once.'

Thryssa smiled. 'Whether it can or not, if you keep your

240

messages cryptic enough it should be safe to do so. And at this point we do not dare waste the time it would take runners to reach Kedara or Segra.'

Orsim followed Lashek from the sitting room and Thryssa turned to her first councillor.

'Send Pachela to me please and order the scribes to begin moving the most precious of the archives up here.'

Kwanzi reached for her hand. 'I will go and arrange teams of the strongest healers – it will take more than six minds to destroy that thing.' He leaned to kiss her forehead. 'I could give Lashek nettle rash, for saying what fun it would be to live in interesting times!'

Thryssa chuckled. 'I believe you would, too.'

A knock heralded Pachela's arrival and Kwanzi smiled at her as they passed in the doorway.

'Gremara has gone,' Pachela said before Thryssa could ask. 'She bespoke me last night. She was worried by the creature that pretends to be councillor Prilla, but she said she had to leave as she has far to go.'

Pachela accepted the mug of tea the High Speaker offered her. 'She did not say where she was going, or why, or how long she might be absent from Talvo.'

'How much has she passed to Jeela I wonder?' Thryssa frowned. 'Jeela is scarcely half a cycle old – a mere infant in Dragon terms, or even in ours come to that. It is a terrible responsibility for one so young.'

Another knock on the door admitted a guard. With admirable aplomb, he saluted the High Speaker.

'There is a Dragon on the roof Lady.'

Pachela was at Thryssa's heels as the High Speaker raced up the two flights of stairs to the roof. Opening the access door, they saw Jeela sitting patiently in the rain.

'What is it my dear?' Thryssa said to Jeela's mind.

Prismed eyes reflected the light from behind the two women.

'You could come inside if you came down to the main entrance.'

Jeela laughed. 'I do not mind the wet. Gremara has told me more of this thing in the Firan Circle. She says that it is aware that alone, it will not be able to overcome the combined strength of your mages. She thinks it is more than capable of inflicting much damage before it flees. And it will flee. Gremara says that there are two others in these lands – that is partly why she has gone.'

Faceted eyes whirred, water spangled on the long pale lashes.

'She said that you must remember the story of Cheok.'

'Did she give no hint as to our best method of dealing with this creature – it calls itself Zloy,' Thryssa added.

'Only that you must combine your strength. Separately, the thing could destroy you easily. And she said that it fears fire, despite the fact that it uses fire to conceal itself.'

'You will be safe in Talvo, will you not Jeela?' Thryssa felt, with misgiving, mischief lurking in Jeela's mind. 'Jeela?' she repeated more firmly.

'Oh yes. I will be quite safe,' Jeela replied airily. 'Do not forget to think of Cheok, High Speaker.'

The ivory wings extended and the small Dragon lifted into the rain filled twilight, arrowing back towards Talvo.

Pachela urged Thryssa back inside and they stood, water dripping from their drenched clothes.

'Go and change,' Pachela ordered. 'I will tell Kwanzi what Jeela has said.'

'Little help though it is,' Thryssa shivered. 'I know that the archives will be in chaos now Pachela, but see if you can find a scribe who might know where a book called "Tales of Valsheba" might be found. It is a very worn copy, pages loose. I think a purple binding, or a dark blue. Have it brought to me if you can.'

Pachela returned with the book by the time Thryssa had changed into dry clothes, her braid loose and the dark red hair streaked with white lying damp on her shoulders.

'Stars, that was quick work,' she smiled at the girl.

'It was actually in the box they were packing at that moment,' Pachela smiled back. 'Unless you have need of me High Speaker, I should be attending Healer Chola.'

'Of course. It seems crazy, but I must read this closely even as darkness approaches and that creature expects his answer.'

The last light was draining away beyond the windows when Orsim and Lashek came to join Thryssa. A full dozen healing mages, old and young, also arrived, Chola and Pachela with them,

242

as the time approached when Zloy would demand their submission. Thryssa indicated the book lying open on her lap.

'Gremara said that we must remember the story of Cheok,' she explained to the assembled company. 'I have been over and over it. One thing pulls at my attention each time, but I do not see its relevance to our situation here.'

'And what is that?' asked Lashek.

'Petak was betrayed to Cheok by one of his closest followers.' She shook her head. 'I do not think Zloy is a close follower, rather, he is acting independently, and I also do not think that he could be persuaded from his present intent. So why should I feel there is a clue there?'

Gremara flew high, her slender body racing through the upper air. The voices sang wordlessly through her whole frame as she sped towards the west. She felt a small pang of concern that she must leave Talvo to cope with the entity that was Zloy, particularly with Jeela so newly and early come to the knowledge of the ancients. But Gremara was confident that others would watch over the events in Vagrantia and do what they could to help. She could feel neither the child's mind nor Grek's, but she had been told that he at least would soon reach Sapphrea. And M'Raz was already there, she had felt his mind for days. Untiringly, Gremara flew beneath the stars, lands she had never seen far beneath her wings.

In the Stronghold, Mim stood outside the great gate, staring up at the night, stars glinting and shivering against the blue black sky. He turned his head to the south west and sent out his thought.

'Good hunting, silver one.'

He walked slowly back into the hall. It was late. Only the Dragons, and Lula, were there, everyone else was abed. Fenj rumbled softly when the Dragon Lord paused beside him.

'Where does she fly to Mim?'

Mim tilted his head to one side, studying the aged black Dragon.

'To Sapphrea, Fenj, but whether to find Tika or for another reason entirely, I know not.'

Fenj rumbled again and rattled his wings. Mim waited: clearly

243

Fenj had something on his mind.

'I cannot remain here for my last days. I believe that I should journey to this Vagrantia, whence came Thryssa and her friends.'

Fenj's eyes whirred the shadows on snow colour when he felt Mim probe further than politeness dictated.

'I am fit and healthy for one of my age. The cold season has abated and there are wapeesh and lumen upon the grasslands, all the way south to Vagrantia.'

'What of Lula? And Lorak?'

'They wish to accompany me.' Fenj's tone held a note of puzzlement.

Mim smiled, laying a taloned hand on Fenj's massive shoulder.

'Of course they do. I will sorely miss you my friend, but if it is your wish to go, then go you must. I have been honoured and proud to have shared your company this long.'

Fenj lowered his head, carefully, for fear of disturbing the sleeping Lula, and pressed his long face against Mim's.

'The last message from Thryssa said they are in trouble. Perhaps I may be of help. I do not like to think of little Jeela being there alone now.'

Mim chuckled. 'You will say nothing to Kija of Gremara's departure, will you Fenj? Or she too will be rushing off to Vagrantia.'

Prismed eyes whirred faster. 'I will say nothing. But Kija could not go from here just yet.'

Mim frowned. 'Could she not then Fenj?' He sighed. 'Secrets within secrets, and riddles within riddles is all I encounter of late.'

'All things unfold in time,' Fenj murmured. 'I think often of Bark these last days. I would like to have known him before the Grey One damaged him so.'

Mim was surprised at this remark and also rather concerned. What was going through the old Dragon's thoughts to make him dwell upon the poor crippled creature who had rectified the Balance and died in Tika's stead?

'When had you thought to leave us?' he asked.

Fenj sighed. 'Tomorrow seems a good idea. Otherwise it will be put off for one excuse after another.'

'But Fenj,' Mim was openly concerned now. 'You do not sound as though you really want to make this journey?'

Fenj rumbled. 'Oh I do, but I have ever hated farewells.'

Mim reached his scaled arms around the thick black neck and hugged him tightly for a moment.

'Then this shall be our private farewell. May the stars always guide your path and guard your heart Elder Fenj. Our love and our thoughts will go with you wherever you journey.'

He felt affection – and something else – surge from the Dragon, then it was gone. Fenj moved his head carefully back to rest between his wings and Mim moved across the hall to where Kija, Kadi and Ashta reclined. Ashta's neck snaked across his shoulders with a sigh of contentment. She was warm, well fed, and her soul bond sat leaning against her: all was well in Ashta's world.

Kija studied the young Dragon and the changeling who was now called Dragon Lord, her eyes a buttery gold in the light of the dying fire.

'More changes then Mim?'

He looked at her sharply and heard her laugh chime in his mind.

'I heard Gremara call to you. I know my daughter must take on the silver one's responsibilities.' Her tone saddened. 'She is so young and so small. But – if Gremara has confidence in my child, then so must we all.'

'I too will leave soon, Mim,' Kadi spoke softly.

Mim nodded. 'You go with Babach to his land of Drogoya? I had thought that was a likely possibility.'

'And I.'

Mim stared at the great golden Dragon.

'Surely not Kija? Your children are here – will they not have need of you still in their growing?'

'Hani cares for the three in Gaharn with a patience beyond belief.' Kija sounded rueful. 'Jeela is under the care of Gremara, absent though she may be. Farn …' She hesitated, and Mim took advantage of the pause.

'We all know that Farn was hurt as much mentally as physically in the battle to gain this Stronghold. Is he truly safe, with only Brin to safeguard him? Brin is good-hearted and loyal, but he is also easily distracted by everything new. Are you sure Farn will be kept safe?'

When Kija's eyes began to whirr in distress, Kadi replied on her behalf.

'Mim, do not try to put doubts in our minds. It is a great and difficult decision that we have made – do not undermine it.'

'Babach's words have led me to guess that he would try to return to Drogoya, but I do not understand why either of you should need to go with him – surely Chakar could order the Plavat to take him?'

Kadi's eyes whirred all shades of blue. 'It is imperative that I go Mim, for reasons I choose not to give you.'

Mim was confused by the wave of shame and remorse that briefly came from the Dragon.

'And I go for my own reasons, only one of which I can tell you. That is the fact that Kadi is my clan sister and clan do not let clan fly alone into danger.'

The serious tone lightened.

'Surely you realise that Chakar could no more command the Plavat now than she could fly herself?' Kija's laugh rang again. 'I heard a whisper that Syecha has now ten eggs to hatch, and the first child will come from its shell before the next full moon.'

Mim groaned. 'They will move back to the coast won't they? Baryet said that they prefer to eat fish than meat.'

Kija chuckled. 'It takes half a cycle for their children to grow feathers and to learn to fly – unlike Dragon children of course.'

Mim caught a hint of smugness, which reminded him achingly of Farn's confidently sweeping statements. He knew he had not the faintest hope of learning more than the Dragons chose to tell and he gave up trying to tease more information from them.

'Fenj leaves tomorrow, so he says.'

Kija rumbled, her faceted eyes palest honey. Again Mim sensed a confusion of emotions from both adult Dragons: Ashta was snoring gently against his back.

'Ashta and I will remain here.' Mim shrugged. 'I still do not understand what my own role is to be. I am called Dragon Lord, but no one seems to have heard of such a one before, or to have a clue as to what a Dragon Lord's duties may be.'

There was no reply from either Kadi or Kija. Mim looked at

each Dragon in turn.

'If you have need of me, I would come to you. You do know that do you not?'

Warmth swept into his mind, warmth and affection.

'We know, Dragon Lord,' Kadi told him. 'We will not forget your words and if our need is great, then we will summon you to aid us.'

The dark blue of her eyes faded to muted sapphire.

'We will rest now Mim, to be ready to sing strength to Fenj in the morning.'

The two Dragons rose, Mim marvelling as ever at the graceful lightness and silence of their great bulks even on the ground, and crossed the hall to where Fenj lay sleeping. Gold Dragon and midnight blue curved themselves around the huge black shape and Mim heard Kija's croon. He frowned. He had heard it before. Then he nodded to himself as he curled against Ashta's chest. It was the song that Hani had sung over her three eggs on the day Mim was brought to her nesting cave.

Fenj slept on, both Kija and Kadi seeing in the misty blur of his dream his beloved Skay, long since gone Beyond. They were aware that Fenj's thoughts dwelt more and more often on both his mate and on the Asatarian Bark, long imprisoned here by Lady Emla's brother Rhaki. They understood his longing for Skay, but Fenj's preoccupyation with Bark was a mystery to them both.

High above the great hall of the Stronghold, in the rooms Dessi had offered to share with Elyssa, the Delver girl clung to the Vagrantian and sobbed out her terror of what was to come. Elyssa sat on the cushions by the small fire, Dessi's head buried in her shoulder. Blue and silver eyes stared at the narrow window where the glimmer of stars insistently drew her attention. Between their bodies Elyssa was conscious of the oval pendant Dessi wore. It was warm, not hot, and it pulsed in time with Elyssa's own heartbeat. Dessi raised her head, copper curls tangled on her forehead.

'Must you really do this thing?' she whispered, her throat thick with tears.

Elyssa's smile was as serene as Babach's as she kissed Dessi gently.

'But of course I must. It is the only reason for my being.'

247

Chapter Twenty-Four

Tika learnt nothing more from Mist than had Mim from Kadi and Kija. She returned to the ground level caves to find Gan and Sket awaiting her. Gan climbed to his feet, towering over both Tika and Sket. Pallin's snores came rattling from the shadows of the cave.

Tika grinned. 'At least his cooking is good, so I suppose he can be excused moving sand with the rest of us.'

Sket walked beside her as they followed Gan, winding between the fallen masonry.

'Easy to get lost in this lot,' he remarked cheerfully.

'Not if you are tall,' Gan said over his shoulder.

Sket pulled a face but made no reply. They walked for nearly a league, Tika estimated, until they found the rest of their party working on a horizontal block under Ren's instructions. He glanced up when Tika reached his side.

'This one had some sort of carvings on it,' he said, running his palm along the lowest part of the newly exposed side.

Tika drew her hand after his and felt indentations and extrusions in too regular a pattern for them to have been made naturally. She squatted beside him, squinting at the black stone.

'Was it a picture carved there, or words?'

'Words I think,' Ren began when there was a shout of alarm from behind the block.

Sket and Navan drew their swords even before Tika had straightened up, but Olam's voice called reassuringly.

'It is all right. Riff has fallen down a hole. He is about five man lengths down, but not hurt.'

By the time they had gathered about the opening in the sand, they could all hear Riff's steady heartfelt curses.

'The Lady Tika is here,' Sket called sharply and Riff fell silent.

'I will go back for a rope,' Navan offered and jogged off

towards the cliffs.

'Is there anything of interest down there Riff, or do you think it is just an old well shaft?' asked Ren.

The silence continued then finally Riff shouted back. 'Not a well shaft. There are steps. I landed on them,' he added feelingly.

'Just what I had hoped for,' Ren was practically rubbing his hands together in glee.

He dug in one of his many pouches and brought out a plain grey pebble the size of a plum. He murmured briefly and light flared from the stone just as Navan returned, sweating, with a coil of rope on his shoulder. Olam took one end of the rope and threw it over the end of a tilted block, tying it securely and testing his weight against it.

'It should be long enough,' he said, tossing the main length down the hole.

Curses, quickly bitten off, flew back up to those above.

'Sorry.' Olam shrugged guiltily. 'Should have warned him I suppose.'

Ren was already vanishing down the hole while the rest craned to see what they could.

'I'm going down too.' Tika caught the rope up and swung over the edge.

Olam looked at Navan and grinned. 'If they have found something more interesting than endless sand, then I want to see it too.' Turning to the hole, he saw the top of Sket's head disappearing.

'Will there be room for everyone down there?' Gan asked doubtfully. 'And I hope the walls of this shaft are stone, not just packed sand.'

Navan peered into the darkness. 'Stone,' he said, twisting round and taking hold of the rope.

As he too disappeared, Gan scowled, looked around at the thousands of tumbled blocks, shrugged and followed everyone else into the hole. To Gan's surprise, he did not land on top of anyone. In fact, there was no one at the bottom of the shaft. When his eyes had adjusted to the gloom he turned slowly round. He saw with some relief a faint light from Ren's glow stone some paces away along a horizontal passage. The floor was smooth, and stretching his hand to the sides, he found the walls too were without blemish or crack. The walls were high: looking up, Gan could see no ceiling, nor could he touch anything at full stretch. He looked back the way he'd come and saw only blackness.

'Ren,' he called ahead. 'I think we should be a little cautious before going too far.'

The blur of bodies in front of him separated into individuals as Ren came back towards him, glow stone on his palm.

'And I thought Riff landed on some stairs?' Gan finished.

Ren nodded. 'There are four steps, but they disappear under fallen stone both ways.'

'Was this passage open then? I would have expected it to be filled with sand.'

Ren tugged at his sparse beard. 'I was just lucky. I put my hands against the walls and must have triggered an opening mechanism which revealed this passage.'

Gan stared down at the Offering in alarmed exasperation.

'And might this mechanism possibly decide to close itself after a certain interval?'

Ren's silvered eyes shone in the glow stone's steady light.

'I should have thought of that,' he sounded apologetic. 'I was so excited to perhaps have found a way into a preserved section that I did not think as logically as I should.'

Gan turned back towards the shaft, Ren's glow stone revealing the complete lack of sand in the passageway. Gan was greatly relieved to regain the shaft, staring upwards at the circle of sky overhead. Ren passed him the glow stone and told him to hold it so that every piece of the door slab could be thoroughly scrutinised.

'Aah,' said Ren with satisfaction. 'This is how it opened.'

Tika and the other four men breathed heavily over Ren's shoulder while he showed them three dimples in the upper right corner. They were only visible when the glow stone was held just so, causing tiny shadows to expose the minute irregularities in the otherwise flawless block. Ren plucked the glow stone from Gan's hand and gave it to Olam.

'I will have to close the door to examine the other side. If I do not discover the mechanism by the time you have counted to – oh, say one hundred – then you must open it from your side Gan.'

Gan opened his mouth to object and Ren swung the slab closed. He found himself muttering some of Pallin's favourite oaths and controlling an urgent desire to kick something. Then he began to count. He had reached seventy three when the door swung wide once more to cheers from Tika and Olam. Ren beckoned Gan back into the passage and reluctantly Gan stepped across the threshold. Ren pulled the door shut again and showed Gan where three similar indentations were to be found two paces along the wall from the door's hinge side.

Gan put his fingertips against the small marks and the door opened, to his considerable relief.

'It is getting late in the day for too much exploring down here now,' Gan started to say, and glared when both Tika and Ren laughed at him. But Ren nodded.

'I agree. I can arrange some better light for tomorrow and I will also devise some way to mark the passages – it divides three ways a little bit further along.'

Tika paused on the way back to the cliffs to rub her hand across the block which Ren had been studying before Riff's accidental discovery of the shaft. Sket stayed with her while the others headed on. Farn descended, raising swirls of sand, to see what interested his soul bond. Storm spiralled above them before flying seawards again. Tika explained their discovery to Farn, who greatly disapproved. He went to look down the hole and returned even more concerned.

'I like not the thought of you down there, my Tika,' he announced firmly. 'I may not even be able to contact your mind through such sand or rock. How could I rescue you, should you find danger? Also, I think we should look for Brin and Maressa. They should have bespoken us by now – I think.'

Sapphire eyes whirred briefly. Farn's facility with numbers was not his strongest point and Tika was careful not to smile.

'Tomorrow Farn. Tomorrow will be the sixth day since they left and the day they might – might – be near enough to bespeak us.'

'Is that right?' Farn checked Sket's opinion.

Tika's self appointed Guard nodded. 'Six days tomorrow Farn.'

'Oh. Well. I still think it foolish to go down that hole,' Farn insisted.

'We will be very careful. There will be no danger.'

Smoke wisped from silvery blue nostrils and Tika sighed. She stood up and hugged the young Dragon.

'There is a door at the bottom of the hole,' she told him again. 'And we will leave it open whilst we explore a little way. I promise I will be most careful Farn. You will surely be busy with your friend Storm will you not?'

Farn lifted into the air, drifting above Tika and Sket as they walked towards Pallin's cave and their supper. They found Ren busy with what he told them were "scientific aids", and left him to himself. When he eventually joined them by the small fire, Tika asked for a scrap of paper. He obliged and watched as she drew misshapen letters upon it. She passed it back to him.

'That was the only whole group on the block you looked at this morning. But it doesn't make letters that I can understand, although I believe they are meant to be letters.'

Ren pored over the shapes Tika had drawn then he began to draw them himself, making a line taller here, longer there, holding the paper at a distance and once, upside down. They all watched him until he looked round the circle of faces with a triumphant smile.

'It says "master" I am sure, although the last letter is half erased.' Then he frowned. 'That is not a term of address that I have heard here.'

Olam shook his head. 'Lord, or Lady or Sir. They are the only special terms we use for those of high rank. One who trains armsmen is known as Master of Arms; everyone else is called by their own name.'

Gan nodded agreement. 'There are titles such as Senior, or Discipline Senior among my people, but not master.'

'And I do not think it is used in Vagrantia,' said Ren. 'I wish Maressa was here, but I am sure I am correct.'

'What about in your land Ren?' Tika asked the Offering.

'We would call someone "Good Master" as a form of politeness, or if we did not know their personal name – a farmer, or a baker, for instance. The only master within the Order of Sedka, is the Master of Aspirants. So why do we find the word here?' He brightened. 'Perhaps we will find something helpful

252

tomorrow.'

'What was that place we found?' asked Navan, stretching his feet to the fire. 'Was it a street or inside a building?'

'Inside a building.' Ren's answer was instant and positive.

'But it was level, not tilted or overturned like all those blocks.'

'The ground may have just sunk straight down in places, while in others it could have been thrust up, causing structures above to topple and smash. Any that sank could likely be well preserved. Which is what I am very much hoping we will find with this one.'

Maressa and Brin were on the western slope of a low hill twenty leagues from Far. Brin had been distraught when he realised that a band of armsmen had approached close enough to see them clearly before he had even sensed them. At his urgent warning, Maressa shielded them both, thickening the air in front of them. But not before arrows had been loosed and fallen rather close by. Maressa picked one of them up and scrambled onto Brin's back. Within the shield of distorted air, Brin took them south, finding by chance the ravine of which Lord Seboth had spoken to Lallia. Maressa set wards in the air all around for a distance of half a league, reckoning that should one be triggered, it would give Brin time to move them again.

She feared that Lallia would already have tried to bespeak her and could imagine the panic the Lady of Far would feel at not finding her mind signature, hidden as it was behind the shields. She herself did not dare use the energy needed to far speak Lallia, and forbade Brin to attempt it either.

'But we cannot just sit here,' said Brin reasonably. 'Tika needs those supplies, so we must try to get them.'

His eyes whirred, the rosy hue suffused with scarlet gleams. Maressa knew all too well that Brin was even now thinking what a splendid story this would make in the telling.

'Brin, someone in that group of men has some sense of the power, whether he realises it or not. That was why they were coming directly towards us. We cannot give away any hint that we are in friendly contact with the House of Far. It would place Seboth and Lallia in even greater peril. We must just wait for a while and hope they go off to search a different area.'

Brin rumbled but stayed quietly reclined beside her. She

examined the arrow in the light of the setting sun and frowned as she touched its head.

'It would appear that they came expecting to find a Dragon,' she murmured to Brin's mind.

He lowered his head to peer at the arrow in her hand.

'A sharp stick does not put terror into the heart of any Dragon,' he said loftily.

Maressa shook her head at him. 'The head is not metal, as have been on all the arrows in this land that I have seen. Look Brin, it is obsidian. It would cut through even your scales.'

Brin's eyes flashed in alarm and he extended his forearm.

'Show me.'

Very cautiously, Maressa applied the tip of the arrowhead to the edge of a crimson scale. A fine sliver fell to the ground.

'Hmm. So what is your plan?' Brin sounded a touch subdued.

'I can sense nothing through the shield, but I can go above it, at least long enough to scan our immediate vicinity. If the armsmen are distant enough, I will try to reach Lallia.' She shrugged. 'It is all I can think of to do.'

'I could easily deal with those few,' Brin suggested.

Maressa leaned against his great shoulder. 'I am sure you could, but let us not hurry to destroy any lives unless we absolutely have to.'

'Your plan is quite good,' Brin conceded, but Maressa heard the relief in his tone.

Brin had killed men and monsters in the northern Stronghold, Maressa knew, but she was glad that he found no pleasure in the prospect of such killing again.

'Keep watch on the shields for me Brin,' she murmured and sent her mind high into the darkening sky.

She looked first for the armsmen who had tried to attack them and found them camped much further northwards. She sighed with satisfaction: they had chosen the wrong direction to pursue the Dragon they had glimpsed. Maressa let her mind rise higher and orientated herself towards Far. Lallia's mind crashed into her like a thunderbolt.

'Oh thank the stars! Maressa, what has happened – I have been trying to reach you since mid afternoon?'

Maressa gave the briefest outline of what had occurred and

was jolted again as Seboth's thoughts slammed against her.

'I wanted Lallia to direct you to the very place you have found,' he told her. 'I have sent three men with pack animals loaded with your supplies. They should reach you by midday tomorrow. Maressa, when you have the supplies, please, please, get away from here as swiftly as you can. And Maressa, Hargon's eyes are frightening – could he have this affliction of which you spoke to us?'

Maressa felt ice form in her veins. 'No Seboth, something a thousand times worse. Do not attempt to go near him now. Do you understand me?'

She felt confusion and frustration through the mind link and repeated her demand.

'You must leave Hargon to those who are better fitted to fight what he has become. Seboth, I can tell you no more, but for stars' sake, keep well away from the man. Lallia, if it is safe, I will bespeak you when we leave here, but know now that you have our grateful thanks for your generosity. May the stars guard your hearts and your lives my dears.'

Maressa broke the mind link, slumping against Brin as she returned to her body.

'I saw what you saw,' Brin said gently. 'Sleep, while I keep watch. I think it matters not if the shields should fail while you regain your strength – those men are not close enough to worry us. I will waken you at the least alarm.'

Maressa reached for her cloak lying across her empty pack and wrapped it around her suddenly chilled body.

'I fear I shall have to sleep for a while at least, but do not delay in waking me Brin, if anything alerts you.'

She was asleep even as she slid down to the ground and Brin curved himself around her protectively.

Hargon had broken free of Seboth's too thinly spread armsmen and despite heavy losses he still had two hundred men at his back. He rode fast Tagria, his eyes blazing with rage at Seboth's defiance. The fool could not see how perilous a state these lands were in: those whose veins held traces of the old blood had increased too fast in even the last generation. Left alone, they would again become the scourge their ancestors had been.

A tiny fragment of Lord Hargon's mind understood that something encroached upon his very being and urged him to acts that he would not have contemplated even two ten days ago. Whatever it was that seemed to be influencing him appealed to those very opinions Hargon already held regarding those with the old blood, those able to use the evil magics and, to his great disappointment, even the magnificent Dragons had become corrupted and thus would need to be eliminated.

Magic, magic, magic. The word rang in Hargon's head, increaseing his fury. They had begun calling it "the power" in his father's time. As if changing the word would change its meaning! The power was still the filthy manipulation of honest life which was properly called magic.

M'Raz chortled within Hargon's mind. What a gullible fool this creature was, believing only what he wished to believe. M'Raz had simply encouraged his obsession against the use of magic, and look what had happened already! A few elemental beings had clung about M'Raz when he was freed at last from that cursed Void, and it had amused him to let them accompany him here. They had their uses, although half had been lost somehow, far to the west. He would have to investigate that occurrence shortly. But for now, M'Raz sat back and watched Hargon's mind collapse on itself. He was going to somewhere called Tagria and a patterned circle kept appearing in his thoughts. M'Raz had no idea what the circle might signify but he was content to let Hargon choose the way, for now.

Beside Hargon rode Trib. The brash young man was white faced with both exhaustion and fear. When Lord Seboth's men had attacked them at the way station, Trib had cut down the first men he encountered. Exhilaration filled him when he found how easy real fighting had turned out to be. Then he discovered that he had advanced too far and was a good fifteen paces in front of the line of armsmen. Exhilaration became panic as he hurriedly tried to move back to their supporting ranks, and he realised that the men harboured no protective feelings towards their newly appointed Armschief.

Time passed in a blur and it felt as though he was trying to lift ten swords rather than one, his own had become so very heavy. Men fell around him and it was only when he nearly dropped the dagger in his left hand that he found he had been wounded. Then Hargon was among them and after one glance at the Lord of Return, Trib kept his eyes on the armsmen still pouring out of the darkness in front of him. His body was drenched in sweat and blood, of which some was his own, although most was others', but he felt icy cold.

Hargon's face was twisted in a snarl, more bestial than human. And his eyes were living flames. One look had been sufficient for Trib to know that he had made a dreadful mistake. His first doubts had arisen when Fryss and Tarin had remained in Far. He knew Tarin's reputation: a veteran of the last Ganger Wars and devoted to the House of Return. In the barracks, Tarin would allow no slur, no jest, to be made against either the House or its present Lord. For Tarin to abandon Return, Trib knew there would need to be the most convincing of reasons. Having seen Hargon's face, even in the near darkness and so briefly, Trib knew that Tarin had the right of it.

But Hargon had ordered three quarters of his surviving armsmen to mount and ride with him for Tagria. The rest were to die delaying Seboth's pursuit, although Trib believed they would yield to Far the moment Hargon was gone. Trib offered to remain with those few commanded to die allowing Hargon's escape but Hargon had turned his awful face to Trib once more.

He smiled, which put more fear into Trib's heart than he would ever have believed possible – as if he knew that Trib would throw down his sword as soon as Hargon had ridden off.

'You ride at my side Armschief. You are too valuable to die with the dogs.'

Trib scrambled silently onto the konina held for him by an armsman and kicked it alongside Lord Hargon. And thus they rode, the body of men already tired from fierce fighting and now faced with a long gallop to Tagria. And apparently, yet another battle once they arrived there.

Chapter Twenty-Five

'But how, how, could the child see me?' Finn Rah's voice was a husky whisper.

Arryol and Sarryen had spent the night working over the Offering's suddenly feverish body. Her temperature had risen alarmingly after her mind returned from far seeking in the Menedula, and spasm after spasm of coughing had wracked her. Arryol sent Soosha away to bed: he was barely recovered himself and Arryol argued that he did not need two serious cases to deal with. Now, hearing Finn Rah's question yet again, Arryol sighed.

'You have asked that every time you have enough breath to do so throughout this night,' he said mildly. 'And we do not have an answer now, anymore than the first time you asked it.'

Finn turned her head against the high pillows.

'But it is impossible. Minds can be aware of other minds far speaking, but she *saw* me.' She twisted her head irritably away from Arryol's hand.

'Finn Rah,' he spoke sharply. 'You are behaving worse than any child I have treated. Surely you have not forgotten every piece of plain good manners since you were elevated to Offering? As your healer, I expect you to do as you are asked and stop acting like a petulant brat.'

Sarryen did not dare look at either Finn or Arryol, busying herself building up the fire, the noise she made filling the ominous silence behind her.

'You have the right of it, Arryol. There is no excuse for my behaviour other than my being uprooted at my age and flung into these awful events. I will do whatever you say and I will try my best to behave as I should.'

Finn sounded so humble that Sarryen's eyes burned with tears which she forced back before turning to the bed. She found Arryol and Finn staring at each other, then Arryol nodded and gathered up some of his healer's accoutrements.

'I will send Melena to you later with some medicines, and I will be back at suppertime.'

Finn gave him a wan smile and he quietly departed.

'Will you try to sleep for a while Finn, or can I get you anything?'

'You could get me the answer to my question,' Finn smiled wryly. 'It is really important to me to know how she could see my mind. Not just my mind, but my whole self. Seriously, I will sleep if I can. I am sorry I am such a nuisance when I should be in charge of all this.'

Sarryen stood watching as the almost transparent lids drooped over the green silvered eyes. She noted how thin the Offering's face had suddenly become, the hectic spots of colour on the cheekbones and the shadows like bruises beneath the eyes. A moment longer the Kooshak watched the too quick rise and fall of Finn's chest, then she went to sit at the table and began working through the piles of documents and books.

Melena appeared at midday and Sarryen slipped out to find herself some food in the common room. On her way back to Chakar's sitting room, she looked into the infirmary. Arryol sat at a table, his head propped on one hand while he turned the pages of a fat volume. Sarryen hesitated then closed the door behind her and approached the table. Arryol glanced up and smiled faintly. Sarryen thought he looked worn out.

'It is serious is it not?'

Arryol leaned back, stretching his arms above his head until the bones crackled.

'I fear so. She put herself under incredible strain using the old magic to change shape to get here. Then that cold sapped the little strength she had won back. And last night's effort of far seeing drained her utterly. There is a problem with her chest – without these recent stresses, there may have been no change for many more years. But now.'

'Is there nothing to be done?'

'I can alleviate some of the worst of the symptoms, but I can do nothing to affect or mend the root of the problem.'

'Does she realise?'

'Oh yes. That is partly the cause of the fuss this morning – a trivial matter blown out of all proportion to stop us from talking of the truth of her condition.'

Sarryen considered Arryol's words. 'How long can she survive?'

'In calm and normal circumstances, for a considerable time. If she exerts herself – far seeing again for example...' he spread his hands in a helpless gesture.

'She will feel that she must seek the child again,' Sarryen said anxiously. 'How can we stop her?'

Arryol had been watching Sarryen's face throughout and now he leaned forward, putting a hand over hers.

'I doubt that we could stop her Sarryen. And I rather wonder if we should. She is the most powerful far seer for generations, or so I heard, and she is an Offering, senior to us all. If she deems it useful or necessary to expend her life in this cause, have we the right to try to forbid her?' He squeezed her hand and released it. 'Think on it Sarryen, but my opinion, as her healer, is to take such care of her as she will accept. But the final choice and responsibility must be hers alone.'

Sarryen walked slowly through the passages to give herself time to think and to come to understand and accept Arryol's view. Melena opened the door as Sarryen was reaching for the latch. They exchanged smiles and Melena went on her way. Finn looked a little better in the short time Sarryen had been absent, the flush high on her cheeks faded to a more general rosiness.

'Loathe as I am to admit it, but Arryol's medicines seem to be quite effective.' Finn spoke in a whisper, fearful of giving the cough an opportunity to begin tearing her chest again.

Sarryen gave her a genuine grin.

'Surely you cannot be thinking of abandoning healer Volk's potent cure-alls?'

Finn managed a smirk and lifted a fragile hand to wave at the cupboard by the bed.

'He visited while you were eating,' she murmured smugly.

Sarryen went to inspect the squat green glass bottle. She uncapped it and sniffed.

'Light above! You could fell a horse or three with this Finn. Don't you dare even smell it.'

Finn dozed the afternoon away while Sarryen continued to study the selection of books discovered in one of the sealed chambers in the cave system. Most of them she had never heard of, nor seen references to them anywhere. Nearly halfway through the pile, she found a slim volume which purported to be Myata's "Last Teachings". To Sarryen's extreme annoyance, Myata seemed to take undue delight in the most elliptical phrasing and downright riddles. She must have been the most infuriating woman, Sarryen thought, sitting back for a moment.

Her gaze rested on the slight figure lying unmoving on the narrow bed. Just like Finn Rah in fact. The thought drifted through Sarryen's mind and she frowned. She turned a few more pages then set the book aside. Perhaps it would occupy Finn, although Sarryen could already see it hurtling across the room, thrown by an Offering irritated out of all patience. A rap at the door roused both Finn and the Kooshak and they were astonished to see the bean pole cook standing shyly outside. He held a tray before him and, after one glance, Sarryen waved him over to Finn's bed. She glared at Finn, daring her to be rude to Povar.

A lace cloth, delicate as cobwebs, was spread on the tray and a tiny pot held a cluster of violets. Two small, newly baked soft rolls sat between a bowl of broth and a dish of stewed fruits.

'Why, that looks delicious Povar. How kind you are,' Finn whispered.

Povar put the tray carefully across Finn's lap and twisted his hands together.

'Most don't care about food. Long as it be hot and plentiful. I like to make it look nice, but no one notices when I do.' He gulped another lungful of air as if unaccustomed speech used up breath far more quickly than just plain silent breathing.

'Children found the flowers. Teal made the bread.'

He nodded and marched from the room, leaving the two women gaping after him. Sarryen turned to Finn, expecting some comment and saw the jade green eyes magnified against the silver by huge tears. Sarryen wordlessly passed her a handkerchief and perched on the end of the bed.

'You had best try some of that broth before it cools.'

Obediently, Finn lifted the wooden spoon and took a mouthful. Sarryen watched until Finn had finished every drop and leaned back against her pillows.

'As delicious as it looked,' she whispered.

Sarryen replaced the soup with the fruit but Finn shook her head.

'I'll eat it later. Sarryen, I have never been a lovable person. It touches me more than you could guess that this gesture of affection should be made to me.' She touched a fragile violet with the tip of a finger. 'It also indicates that those children have been outside,' she said, the old glint back in her eyes.

Sarryen laughed then remembered the book she had found. She retrieved it from the table and handed it to Finn.

'I thought you might be able to understand some of this – Myata had a most devious mind.'

Finn snorted and tensed on the brink of a cough.

Soosha arrived before Finn could make the mistake of arguing further and Sarryen made a pot of tea.

'I have spent the day testing some of the students,' Soosha announced. 'Several are very capable indeed and more than able at least to give their support to far seers.'

Sarryen bit her lip. How could he suggest far seeing in front of Finn after her nearly disastrous experience last night?

'Not a one of them must attempt to get inside the Menedula.' Finn's words were flat.

Soosha nodded and smiled. 'Most definitely not Finn Rah. But there is no reason why they should not watch, at a distance of five leagues or so, outside the Menedula. They could then hopefully spot the two children once they are out of that place.'

Finn wrinkled her nose. 'I saw only one – the girl. I wonder where the boy might be?'

'I have also pondered why the girl could see you.'

Finn looked at the Observer sharply.

'And have you a solution?'

'I think it must be the obvious one. If she is who we think she is, or under the very particular protection of the spirit of Myata, then all things must be possible for her.'

'That simple?' Finn sounded sceptical.

'Finn, how many times have you worried at a problem only to discover the simple solution which you probably first thought of was in fact the correct one?'

Mena's store of food was lamentably small, but she knew that she had to make her move very soon. The boy Tyen had told her that the people still within the town of Syet were fewer in number now than ever since the night of madness and fire. He shuddered when he spoke of those who remained though, and Mena guessed they would have to be avoided rather than asked for help.

She sat in the late afternoon, drawing as always, and fighting to keep her mind empty of all but the plants in front of her. She allowed herself to think of the old lady who had said her name was Finn Rah only when she was outside in the garden. Mena had seen a small person, apparently floating close to the ceiling of her bedchamber. Iron grey braids were coiled around her head, and her eyes were such as Mena had never seen before: brilliant jade green surrounded by silver.

Mena asked Tyen if he knew the name Finn Rah and he had looked alarmed.

'She be the most senior of the Offerings,' he said. 'She would've got burned up or worse on that bad night.'

'She might have escaped,' Mena suggested.

'Nobody escaped,' said Tyen bluntly. 'I ran here when – when my house burnt down, and I saw such things. One of the Offerings was coming down the outer walk when one of those mad students got him.' He swallowed hard. 'Never seen nothing like it.'

'Then maybe she was away somewhere, visiting perhaps?'

'That one never left the Menedula, not since afore I were born.'

Mena had let the subject rest, only asking Tyen to work out the best and quickest way clear of both the Menedula and the town.

Now she sat patiently, outlining the whiskery leaves of a nettle while she waited for Cho Petak's usual visit. As soon as Finn Rah had disappeared, Mena had slept and woken again to find Cho standing by her bed, his face contorted and his eyes red fire. She felt him push into her mind, and withdraw none the wiser. He had said nothing, just turned away and left her to sleep again.

The door latch snicked closed and Mena lifted her gaze from her drawing.

'Good evening Sir,' she said politely.

Cho merely nodded, giving her current picture only a cursory glance. He went in his slow way to the window and stared out for a considerable while. Eventually he crept back down the room to Mena's table.

'I have not asked you anything of the disturbance the other night child. What do you know of it?'

Mena looked up at him, violet and silver eyes wide and innocent.

'I thought I had a bad dream Sir. Was there really something wrong then?'

Cho stared at her. It took an enormous effort for Mena to sit still and relaxed under that relentless gaze. At last Cho looked away, down at Mena's drawing.

'Nothing wrong, no. Perhaps it was just the ghost of one of the corrupt officials who dwelt here until lately.'

'Corrupt officials, Sir?' Mena managed to sound both confused and shocked.

Cho waved a hand dismissively.

'They are all dead. Do not be alarmed child. You are safe here with me.'

Mena smiled. 'Of course I am Sir,' she agreed.

Cho watched a little longer while Mena forced her hand not to tremble as she continued her drawing. Her hands were clammy by the time Cho left in his silent manner. Carefully, methodically, she cleaned the pens and brushes and put them away in the box of coloured inks. She straightened the pile of drawings and the books still on the table. She had discovered a worn leather satchel in the bottom of a cupboard in her bedchamber and hidden her cache of food in it. The map she had so meticulously copied was also there. Mena lay down, convinced she would never sleep, and promptly did so.

Krolik woke her bringing in her breakfast. By the time she had splashed water over her face, he was gone. She stared down at the tray. There was a stack of the hard biscuits, a large bowl full of dried fruits, a jar of nuts. Did Krolik know somehow that she was storing food? Had he guessed she was about to run away? Had he told Cho Petak? Mena suddenly heard that rippling laughter in her head again and shrugged.

She whisked most of the food through to put in the old satchel and then sat nibbling at some she had left on the tray. She had barely swallowed her first piece of fruit when Cho Petak was behind her chair.

'Good morning Sir.'

'I thought that Krolik was bringing you more food?'

'Oh he does Sir. I have eaten most of it already – it is far more than I was given before. I take what is left to the gardens with me, for later Sir.'

Cho considered the child then nodded and left her.

'Stars let that be the last time I need see him,' Mena thought.

She went into the bedchamber and fetched the satchel, putting the last pieces of food from the tray in with the rest. On impulse, she crammed the box of coloured inks on the top and looked once around the room. Straightening narrow shoulders, Mena marched out and down to the gardens. She paused at the gate into the herb garden. She had cleared quite a large amount of the ground and the plants now released from the choking embrace of the weeds reached to the sun, leaves and flowers burgeoning by the day.

Slowly, Mena walked around the path, bending to brush her fingers over some plants, murmuring softly all the while. She smiled when she reached the young rosemary bush, its pale blue flowers quivered with life and new shoots sprang from its base.

'Tyen,' she called softly.

The boy emerged silent footed from the wooden building.

'We must go now,' Mena told him, holding his stare.

He chewed his thumb nail and nodded, leading her along to the heap of rotting weeds. Mena settled the strap of the satchel more firmly across her back, leaving both hands free. Tyen glanced back at her as he stooped to pull aside a branch of the beech hedge.

'Very quiet, all the time,' he ordered, and ducked into the dark hole in the hedge.

Keeping at Tyen's heels, Mena moved in behind him. In moments she found herself crawling on all fours. Her trousers were torn at the knees by the time Tyen stopped and she banged her head into his back. In the dim light filtering through the thick hedge, Mena saw a grating ahead, raised on its edge. Tyen leaned back to her.

'Once we're in, pull it down over you.'

Mena nodded and Tyen disappeared. She wriggled round to go feet first as he had done and felt his hand guide her right foot to the rung of a ladder. She descended another rung and reached up to hook her fingers in the metal grill. She pulled, and nothing happened. She tugged harder and the grill fell with a dull thud. Mena wobbled on the ladder but managed not to fall. She had no idea how far down they had to go and no desire to break any bones this soon after leaving the garden.

Tyen touched her back and she found herself taking a last step down into ankle-deep water. At least, she hoped it was just water. Tyen gripped her hand, tugging downwards. She felt a roof brush her head and bent lower. Her free hand touched a damp wall of rough brick and the hand Tyen held occasionally bumped a similar wall on the other side.

Tears of exhaustion were trickling down her cheeks by the time Tyen stopped. He dragged at her hand in the total darkness and she realised he meant them to rest. He leaned close as Mena pressed her aching back against the curved wall, biting her lip to keep back a groan.

'We're half across the town,' he breathed in her ear. 'There's a way out just ahead and up, but we must go on, right to the river.'

'Right,' Mena whispered back.

She pulled the satchel in front of her and dug out a handful of dried fruits which she passed to Tyen. They ate in silence, hearing the drip of water behind and ahead and, every so often, a scuttering sound as of small animals.

'We have only been gone half a morning,' Mena thought, 'yet I do not know if I can go much further like this.'

The darkness did not especially bother her, but having to walk bent double for so long was an agony. Tyen sniffed and tensed. Mena turned in his direction and the scent of mint drifted over the two children. Mena breathed deeply and felt her panic subside. Of course she could go on! Half a morning's walk was nothing, but it was at least a start on the twelve or more days she anticipated to reach the Oblaka.

'What's that smell?' Tyen's question hissed into her ear.

'Just one of the herbs from the garden,' Mena whispered back. She sensed Tyen's doubts and whispered again to distract him.

'How far to the river?'

'About the same. The people who are still here, are usually

between this part of the town and the Menedula. Not so many to hear us in the next bit.'

He stood up, Mena scrambled up beside him and they continued through the drain. Mena was only conscious of the hot pain in her back when Tyen stopped abruptly. He pushed her back and put a hand over her mouth. She pushed his hand away, realising that there was a glimmer of light from high overhead. Faint cries grew louder until Mena could make out some sort of speech. High-pitched shrieks mingled with guttural howls, making it impossible to understand any words – if words they were.

Tyen drew her further back and held her arm tight. The voices grew louder, reaching a crescendo of dissonance, before fading again. Mena found that Tyen was trembling and could only guess at what meaning those strange cries held for him.

'Is it safe to go on now?' she murmured.

Tyen spat. 'I keep on telling you girl. Ain't nowhere safe.'

She felt his shoulders lift in a shrug against her arm.

'We'd best go on. How long before you're missed you reckon?'

'Late afternoon.'

Tyen grunted. 'Got to be out of here well before then. Come on then.'

Mena had not a clue as to how Tyen found his way in this dark warren. Several times her free hand felt a gap in the wall, suggesting other drains joining with this one. Surely the boy could not have learnt to travel this route in the relatively few days since the destruction of the town? Mena stumbled on, pondering Tyen's unerring leadership. At least it kept her mind busy with something other than cataloguing each new ache. Tyen slowed again, pulling her close to him.

'Round the next bend – the river. Left a boat there, but don't know if it will still be there.'

Wavering light began to glimmer as they approached the curve, then dazzled them. Mena threw her arm across her eyes, blinking against the glare of sun on water.

'Wait here.'

Tyen crept forward to the very edge of the brick-built drain and peered cautiously one way, then the other. He beckoned and

Mena joined him. What looked to her eyes much like a very small tree trunk, half hollowed out, nestled against the rim of the drain. Tyen was busy loosening a thin rope and pulling the tree trunk closer.

'Get in,' he ordered.

Obediently, but very dubiously, Mena climbed down to what Tyen had said was a boat, and stepped into it. It rocked alarmingly and she sat down with a jarring bump. Tyen grinned at her and dropped in front of where she had sat. He lifted a strangely shaped length of board and dug it into the water. Mena discovered they were moving, close to the bank, following the flow of the river. She clung to each side of this odd tree trunk and hoped fervently that they would not be travelling this way for too long.

Chapter Twenty-Six

Kera had made a carry sack for Lula, like the one her mother Khosa travelled in, and Lorak looped it about his neck. Guards, Delvers, the Stronghold staff and Yoral, the chamberlain, all came to bid farewell to the ancient black Dragon Fenj. The other Dragons waited outside on the still snow-covered crags above the Stronghold to sing him on his journey. Elyssa and Babach had been the last to say goodbye, and Lorak was already on Fenj's back, giving minute instructions to Bikram regarding the growing areas.

Fenj's massive bulk paced to the gateway. He turned his head for a final glance at those gathered in the hall. He moved through the gate, onto the span of rock bridging the Stronghold with its neighbouring mountain, and lifted easily into the air. Snow Dragons called and trumpeted, then joined in the song of the great Dragons. Kija and Kadi stood erect, their wings fully extended as Fenj flew slowly past them. He tilted round a pinnacle, heading south eastwards, and the pale green Ashta swung up by his wing tip, Mim on her back. Fenj said nothing, merely increasing the pace of his flight until Ashta swerved away, calling her last goodbyes.

Then it was just Fenj, and Lorak, and Lula, alone in the crisp mountain air. Lorak was content with the silence. A great affection had grown up between Lady Emla's irascible old gardener and the Dragon Elder. Lorak sensed a sadness in Fenj now, but also a determination, and he sat on the Dragon's back calmly, waiting for Fenj to choose his time to speak. Lula had burrowed deep into her sack after her first excited look at the land falling away below had turned to a squeak of horror. Lorak could feel several claws, even through his coat and three shirts.

Fenj flew on, his wing beats regular and powerful. The snow beneath them slowly thinned away and grasslands began. Lorak twisted to look back and was surprised to see how small the mountains appeared already. The sun felt warmer and Lorak turned his face up to its heat.

'Do you wish to stop, Lorak my friend?' Fenj's first words since leaving the Stronghold murmured through Lorak's mind.

'Yes!' Lula cried, before Lorak could answer.

Fenj's wings ceased their beat and he glided smoothly down in a spiral manoeuvre to settle on this vast stretch of grass land. Lorak dismounted and released the tiny Kephi. She sniffed at the rough grass, then caught sight of her tail out of the corner of her eye. She leapt wildly to catch it and rolled under Fenj's chest. He rumbled quietly.

'I think you do not enjoy flying after all then my Lula?' he asked.

Lula sat up straight and washed her ears briskly.

'Your mother seemed to love it,' Fenj added in an innocent tone.

Lorak grinned. Lula's eyes narrowed.

'I expect I will soon find it boring,' she announced.

Fenj's eyes whirred. 'Then I shall have to think of something better with which to entertain you.'

Lula studied her huge friend. She was not always sure about the nuances of teasing. She turned her back and prepared to stalk Lorak's feet. Lorak eventually caught hold of her and put her back in her sack, to the accompaniment of much spitting.

They flew for three days before Fenj sensed Jeela's mind ahead of them.

'We are nearly at the place where the Silver Ones have dwelt throughout ages,' he told Lorak as they sat at midday, watching Lula leaping after emerald butterflies.

'Aah. Is there something particular we're going to do there?' Lorak asked.

Fenj swung his head low to stare closely at Lorak.

'There may well be. I have spent much thought on the little we know of the thing Thryssa encountered in Gaharn. Her last message from Vagrantia said that another such had been destroyed there and one still threatened her people.'

'Do you think it were for the best then – that messages don't go through they old circle things to Vagrantia at the moment?'

Fenj reclined more comfortably and watched Lula dancing

through the longer grasses.

'Whatever it is, it seems stuck there in Vagrantia for now. If it found out how to use the circles, it could go anywhere.'

'I don't understand why it be stuck there Fenj.'

'Because it is inside one of Thryssa's people.' Fenj thought for a while. 'If it came out of that person, it could go wherever it wanted I suppose.'

Lorak frowned, then shook his head.

'It's no good, I don't rightly follow you m'dear.' He reached into a pocket. 'Drop of restorative?'

'Splendid fellow.'

It was nearing midday when Fenj and Lorak saw the five conical shapes clustered on the otherwise empty plains before them. Fenj flew higher until they came directly over the space between two craters. The one on the left, Fenj told Lorak curtly, was Fira Circle, home of the water mages, and which had been taken over by the unknown entity. Past Fira and adjoining that Circle, was Kedara, home of the air mages. The one on the right, was Segra, the Circle of which Lashek was the Speaker. Straight ahead was Parima and beyond Parima lay Talvo. They were too high to be more than flecks of darkness should anyone look up to the sky and, conversely, Lorak could make out no details as they overflew Parima.

When Fenj had taken them nearly past Talvo, he began to descend in a spiral. He approached Talvo from its furthest southern side, and crested the rim as Jeela called welcome. When Fenj landed and rattled his wings, Jeela dropped beside him, her ivory neck twining around him. All Lorak could make out was an overwhelming delight pouring from the tiny Dragon as she greeted old Fenj. Fenj's faceted eyes whirred the shadows on snow colour while he crooned gently to the excited Jeela.

Then Jeela turned to Lorak who was just freeing Lula from her carry sack. Lorak straightened and found himself flat on his back, the small but surprisingly heavy Jeela on his legs, her face close to his.

'I am so glad to see you Lorak of the Garden. You must tell me everything of the Stronghold. Is Dessi well? I miss her you know. And Ashta? You will tell me all, will you not?'

Lorak spluttered, pushing at Jeela's chest with both hands.

271

'I can tell you nothing while you sit squashing a poor soul so. Get off me, you impudent hatchling.'

Jeela backed away to let Lorak get up to a sitting position while Fenj's laugh rolled through their minds and Lula pranced across to wind herself around Jeela's feet.

'Why do you not look at the plants old friend?' Fenj suggested. 'Jeela and I will talk a while, then you can add your news.'

Lorak grunted and clambered to his feet. Jeela's eyes whirred.

'I am sorry to have knocked you down Lorak. There are many plants here that I never saw before which will interest you I am sure.'

Lorak scowled. Jeela's mind tone was not as apologetic as he might have wished, but he turned slowly around, studying the vegetation. It seemed most lush, he noted: creepers rampant along the ground and up the crater side ahead. He sorted out the several packs he had carried and put an empty one over his shoulder. Lula trotted at his heels when he stumped off.

'Beware the small pools that make popping sounds,' Jeela called to his mind as he plunged into what looked to him like a forest of gigantic rhubarb plants.

Within moments Lorak was engrossed in the multitude of new plants. Not for the first time in his life, he wished he could draw or even write better than he could. Lady Emla had lent him books from her own library which showed the most detailed pictures of plants, right down to their root systems. Most of the plants here seemed large, as if the warmth and moisture had forced them all to grow without constraint. Poke beneath huge leaves as he might, so far Lorak had found no little things – nothing like his favourite violets. Everything was on a grand scale here. Lula shot between his boots and sat in front of him, her blue eyes wide with alarm above her bristling moustache.

'Now what?' Lorak eyed her warily. Fond of her as he was, he regarded her as mischief on four feet.

'Come and see one of the popping things.'

Lorak frowned. 'Now don't you start your tricks young Lula. I be busy.'

'No, no, no. You must see. It smells a bit strange.'

He knew from past experience that Lula would get in his way, sitting on plants, tripping him up, unless he gave in to her demands. He sighed.

'Hurry up then. Show me.'

He caught up with Lula to find her crouched beside a muddy circle from which steam rose. He squatted beside the tiny Kephi and stared in surprise as the mud pushed up to form a dome. Another dome appeared, then more. The first one suddenly popped and Lorak clapped his hand over his nose as the acrid stench of rotting eggs engulfed him. Lula sneezed and backed away. Lorak too was stepping away when a thin jet of water erupted from the mud, rising many times Lorak's height. As he gaped up at it, drops fell on his upturned face causing him to flinch. They were extremely hot drops. He joined Lula some distance back and they watched as the water sputtered, faltered, than vanished again beneath the mud.

'Well I never did.' He stooped to pick Lula up.

'It does it often,' she told him.

So he waited for a while to see if Lula was correct. He was about to give up when the domes started rising in the mud again. Once more, water gushed skywards and then disappeared.

'Well I never did,' he repeated and pushed back through the thick vegetation to where he had left his pack.

He spent the rest of the daylight lifting various plants and studying them closely. Lula sometimes helped him, digging enthusiastically when he was trying to extract a root undamaged. When she grew bored she went hunting and brought him various gifts: an extraordinarily large and annoyed spider, a bright yellow worm, or it may have been a snake – Lorak was not inclined to look too closely.

Jeela appeared above him, saying he should return to Fenj. He could easily fall in one of the strange pools in the twilight, she pointed out helpfully.

'There are more of they?' Lorak asked in some alarm.

'Oh yes. Lots in this part of Talvo.'

'Lead on then,' he said, picking up his pack which now bulged with samples.

Stars prickled overhead as he sat with Fenj and Jeela. Lula slept in the curve of Fenj's arm and Lorak nursed a mug of tea, well laced with restorative.

273

'What shall you do with all those plants, Lorak?'

'I thought I'd make a little nursery bed up here tomorrow, and see if they take to being moved. Have you thought of something to do to help they Vagrantians?'

Fenj's eyes whirred, reflecting the light from Lorak's small fire as well as the starlight.

'Well now old friend, I believe I may have an idea about that.'

Teams of the strongest mages, most of whom were Kedarans, had formed and held the shielding continuously since Zloy's first contact with the High Speaker. The torrential rain had ceased, although water levels in pools and streams still rose steadily. Thryssa had felt the incredible force of Zloy's rage when he battered against the shielding periodically and she saw with sorrow how often her mages had to change shifts before they collapsed from exhaustion.

She stood at the window of her study gazing at the familiar scene stretching to the distant black wall which separated Parima from Talvo. She was wondering if she dared risk using the circle to get a message to the Stronghold or to Gaharn. Speaker Kallema and first councillor Prilla both knew that the circle in the Corvida was active again, but she did not think that either of them knew how to use it. If Zloy had drained their minds of all relevant information, he would know of the circle but, like the two women, not how to make it work.

Thryssa's gaze rested on that black rim, behind which dwelt Jeela, alone these past days since Gremara's sudden departure. Did Zloy fear the Dragons, or disregard them as unimportant? Thryssa rubbed her forehead, then let her hand drop to the comforting oval pendant. She was not entirely sure, but she thought it seemed warmer all the time now. She could not begin to guess what that might mean. She turned from the window, frowning. Raised voices were coming closer to her door. Thryssa waited. Stars forfend that there was no new trouble. Lashek opened the door, a huge beam on his round face and Thryssa stared speechlessly.

An indignant Lorak, escorted rather more closely than he felt necessary by four men at arms, stood on the threshold. To her own surprise, Thryssa found herself crossing the room to greet the

274

old gardener with a hug and a kiss on his weathered cheek.

'You didn't come through the circle did you?' she asked in belated alarm.

Lorak was confused: first he had been leapt upon by some very well-built farmers, then a bunch of armed guards had hustled him across Parima these two days, and now Lady Thryssa kissed him in welcome. Lula struggled to get her head out of her sack below Lorak's chin and Thryssa exclaimed in pleasure, helping the Kephi free.

'Lorak brings news from Talvo,' said Lashek. 'I have taken the liberty of asking Orsim, Pajar, Kwanzi and Pachela to join us Thryssa.'

Thryssa dismissed the guards and drew Lorak to a chair.

'So,' Thryssa leaned towards Lorak while Lula perched primly on his knees and stared around the room with interest. 'You come from Talvo. How did you get there? Is Gremara back?'

Lorak looked a little vague.

'Me and Fenj, we come for a bit of a visit to young Jeela, seeing as how she be on her own for a while.'

Thryssa sat back as those whom Lashek had summoned entered the study.

'Fenj is in Talvo then?' asked Lashek cheerfully. 'Wonderful character!'

Lorak grinned at him. 'He is that.' He looked at Pachela who had sat down on a low stool beside Thryssa's chair. Her grey eyes surrounded with silver, stared steadily back. 'You be Pachela? Jeela likes you.'

Pachela blushed in surprise.

'Couldn't you go and see her for a while? Not much to do in this old place I shouldn't think, not for a fair maid like you.'

Thryssa cleared her throat to try to regain control of the conversation, but Lorak had transferred his gaze to Pajar.

'My stars! Never seed hair the colour of yorn,' he said. 'Just like a poppy.'

Pajar also blushed and Lorak's admiring look faded somewhat.

'Lorak,' said Thryssa firmly. 'What news do you bring us? Has Mim suggested a way we might deal with Zloy?'

'Who be Zloy?'

Thryssa's lips tightened in exasperation. 'The thing that has

275

taken over Fira Circle.'

Lorak belatedly removed his battered hat and studied it minutely. Lula chirruped on his knee.

'Fenj had an idea,' she said in their minds. 'We will help him.'

Six pairs of eyes focused on the Kephi. She drew herself up tidily. 'It is a very clever idea too.'

'Are we to be told what this idea involves?' Thryssa asked.

Lula yawned and turned round and round on Lorak's lap. Lorak finally met Thryssa's hazel eyes.

'It involves fire d'you see?'

Thoughts raced through the High Speaker's mind but it was Pachela who spoke first.

'Jeela told us that Gremara said Zloy feared fire even though he hid behind it. That first night when Jeela came here in the rain.'

Thryssa nodded slowly while Orsim shifted in his chair.

'All of us can use fire to a modest extent. But even combined, I do not see how we could approach this creature close enough to use it.'

'Fenj said that he could.'

Thryssa and Orsim sat up, alert and hopeful at Lorak's words, but Lashek scowled.

'He would be at enormous risk,' he said.

Lorak nodded and shrugged. 'Old fellow said he knew what he were doing.'

Lashek saw both sorrow and fear gleam briefly in Lorak's eyes, then they were gone.

'We do not know where Prilla, or Zloy, actually are in Fira,' Kwanzi objected. 'We could trace her accurately of course, but only if we let our shields dissipate.'

'Can Fenj find her?' Thryssa asked. 'Does he know the mind signature which he would have to locate?'

Lorak squirmed in his chair. 'Old fellow knows what he's doing,' he repeated stubbornly.

Before any more questions could be pressed upon Lorak, Speaker Lashek got out of his chair.

'Come Lorak. Let me take you to the dining hall, and then I will show you the enclosed gardens which are a pride of the

276

Corvida.'

Lorak stood with alacrity, jamming his hat back onto his head and Lula under his arm, and departed with Lashek.

'Is Lorak a councillor of the Stronghold?' Pajar sounded puzzled.

Thryssa snorted. 'He is, or was, the Lady Emla's head gardener in Gaharn, until he met the old Dragon Fenj. I gather he spends more time concocting suspicious brews than he does gardening, but Fenj is devoted to him. The Dragon Lord also regards him highly,' Thryssa added thoughtfully. She looked at her husband. 'Something worries you already?'

'For Fenj to get close enough to this creature, would be to expose himself fully to its influence. I think, whether this Zloy is destroyed in the process or not, it is highly probable that the Dragon will pay with his own life.'

Thryssa's eyes widened. Her husband's words shocked her, and Pachela paled beside her.

'Explain,' Orsim demanded.

Kwanzi regarded his hands as he framed his reply.

'Fire may destroy this entity. It may not. But it would be the distraction that our mages need to invade Zloy's mind and take it apart. Zloy would necessarily focus all his attention on that distraction, albeit for only a few moments, which is when we would have to strike. But you have felt the strength of Zloy's anger against our shields. Could even the great Dragons withstand that? And could just one alone do so?'

'We cannot let him spend his life for us.' The words burst from Pachela. 'We cannot.'

Orsim shrugged. 'If he is willing to do this, we surely need some help.'

Pachela glared, regardless of the fact that she was but a student and Orsim the Speaker of Kedara.

'Would you do the same then?' she demanded, her fists clenched against her knees. 'Should the Dragons, or the people of Gaharn, or the Stronghold, be in peril, would you offer yourself for them?'

Orsim frowned at the girl but he moved uncomfortably in his chair.

'And don't you dare tell me that would be different. It would

277

be no different to what this Dragon is prepared to do for us.'

Pachela fled the study, unable to restrain either her tears or her anger.

'I believe Lashek will learn more from Lorak, in his own way, than we could hope to do by questioning him further here.' Thryssa spoke into the silence. She smiled at Orsim. 'And I do think Pachela has made a valid point. Fenj is old: older than any of the other great Dragons, from what I know. Perhaps he truly feels it is near his time to travel Beyond, and if he can help us, at the cost of his life, it would but speed his journey?'

Kwanzi sighed as he stood up. 'I must check the change of mages,' he said, opening the study door. He hesitated, looking back into the room. 'I fear that I side with Pachela in this matter. I would find it hard to live, knowing that the death of that Dragon was the reason I did so.'

Orsim too prepared to leave. 'It must be considered,' he insisted to Thryssa. 'Otherwise our people are condemned to this containment indefinitely. And I do not think that I could live with that.'

'Oh Pajar.' Thryssa closed her eyes for a moment. 'How do you counsel me then, my brand new, first councillor?'

'There is a case for both sides, obviously. The decision can only be yours High Speaker.' He fell silent and Thryssa recalled how instantly he had suggested the destruction of the three young Firans.

'I could not ask, or allow, the Dragon to die for me Lady Thryssa,' he finished softly.

'Then I fear that you must go, with all haste, and with Pachela, to Talvo. Regardless of what Lashek may dig out of that old gardener, we must refuse an offer entailing such risk for Fenj.' She smiled as Pajar's expression of relief was quickly replaced with doubt.

'I have never met any of the Dragons. Is it my place to go? As first councillor, I should surely be with you?'

'It is precisely because you are first councillor that you must go. You are second only to me, and thus Fenj must accept the importance and finality of our decision.'

The High Speaker tilted her head to one side and regarded the young man quizzically.

'Well? Have you more questions Pajar, or did you not understand your orders? I believe I said go to Talvo, and go with all haste.'

The door closed behind Pajar and Thryssa leaned her head wearily against her chair back.

'And may the stars ensure that you reach Talvo in time to stop him,' she murmured aloud.

Chapter Twenty-Seven

Tika had conceded to Farn's insistence that she stay out of that hole in the sand. He had become more than usually agitated and she suggested that they spend the day wandering along the shore, just the two of them. Farn had cheered up at once – he thought it a perfect idea. Storm came calling hopefully for Farn to join him.

'I am busy,' Farn told him. 'I will spend this day with my Tika.'

Storm clearly did not understand what Farn could mean, but flew off to the south anyway.

'That was not too polite,' Tika scolded, scrambling down over the great boulders strewn along the edge of the sea Dragons' cove.

Farn skimmed over her head, nudging a wing against her back and making her stumble. She stopped, hands on hips, and glared at him.

'If you are not going to behave, I am going back to help Ren.'

Farn settled on the wet sand, an incoming wave purling over his tail. His prismed eyes shone with innocence.

'But I always behave,' he said, and beat his wings furiously in the next wave.

Then he was in the air, flying ahead along the waterline, his laughter pealing in Tika's head. She looked down at herself: trousers and shirt were soaked through and her hair dripped into her eyes. She laughed, watching Farn swoop and turn. She wished Kija could see him – a young Dragon playing in the hot sun, carefree and inquisitive.

Tika caught up with him eventually to find him trying to dig something from the sand. Waves creamed against his back as he scrabbled and snuffled in the small hole he had dug.

'Should you leave your tail floating out like that?' she asked.

His head swung up level with hers, eyes bright with sudden concern and a neat heap of sand upon his nose. He whisked his tail in around him, shovelling water all over them both. Tika gasped and spluttered and bent quickly to scoop handfuls of water over Farn's head. Instantly, his tail flung yet more over her and she retreated up the beach coughing and giggling. Gleeful delight radiated from the silver blue Dragon and Tika suddenly realised how close her giggles were to tears: this was how Farn was meant to be. She sank onto the drier sand and pushed wet hair off her face.

'What were you looking for?' she asked, when he flopped beside her.

'It was a very odd thing. Many legs and horns. It just disappeared into the sand.'

'If you stop splashing me, I will help you look for it. You remember when Kemti made me try to feel through the ground when we left Hargon's lodge?' She ignored the surge of mixed feelings from her soul bond at mention of the Lord of Return and began poking with her bare toes in the place Farn had been searching. Tika was half aware, throughout that totally lazy, contented day, of Sket's watchful presence, but she was unaware of Mist and Salt's constant surveillance. Nor did she know that Khosa watched, from high on the cliffs above them.

Ren had taken several empty packs down into the passage which Riff had so inadvertently found. He hoped that he might find something tangible of the people who had lived here so long ago. They had tried to scratch or mark the exposed blocks on the surface to no avail. So Ren took down extra lengths of rope, which he tied to the one they used to get up and down. He also placed glow stones, about twelve paces apart, along the beginning of the passageway.

'It seems strange,' Olam remarked as they entered the passage after breakfast. 'If this is inside a building, as you seem to think, then surely there would be doors opening off such a long corridor?'

Ren came to an abrupt halt, turning to stare at Lord Seboth's brother. He shook his head.

'My brain is failing,' he said ruefully. 'We should check both sides from the entrance with our fingertips. If you would take this side Olam, and Navan that, we may find you a door.'

Riff had moved ahead to where the passage split into three and Gan was last, nearest the open door to the shaft. They worked unspeaking, the only sounds that of their breathing and the shuffle of feet on the smooth stone floor. It was Navan who called.

'Is this something, Offering Ren?'

Ren went to Navan's side, lifting the glow stone he carried high, to peer at the apparently flawless wall. He slid his hand beneath Navan's and felt the three tiny indentations. He turned his head, hearing steel leaving scabbards and saw all except Navan had drawn either daggers or swords. Muttering under his breath, he pressed firmly into the three dimples. The door swung silently away from him and he raised the glow stone he still held.

Olam and Gan stood close to Ren's shoulder while Navan and Riff held back a little, wary and watchful. Ren stepped into the room, asking for someone to fetch more glow stones. There was a strange feeling to the room, so long abandoned. At first glance, it appeared to be almost square, each wall about fifteen paces long. Shards of glass still lay below what had been floor to ceiling windows, but which now looked only onto rock. A boxlike desk stood between the windows and a half rounded chair tilted against it. As the five men advanced into the room, no one spoke. They all felt the weight of time pressing upon them in here.

'Look,' Olam whispered.

The wall in which the door was set had three large pictures to one side of the door, rows of bookshelves to the other. Ren and Olam held the stones aloft to see what the pictures revealed. They stared for a long time at the central one. It was a view from a high place, obviously in the heart of the city as buildings clustered close all around. Some were buildings of the type they all recognised, but others had domed roofs, or needle thin spires with what looked like bubbles spaced up the spires' height. Bridges linked some of the spires, delicate filigree work which looked too frail to be functional, but tiny figures could clearly be seen upon the bridges. As they stared, they all realised that the spires and their interlinking bridges formed a web like pattern across the sprawl of lower buildings.

In the left of this picture a market scene was depicted: stalls and barrows, heaped with fruit, vegetables, flowers, bolts of cloth.

The people were shown quite clearly and when Ren held his stone closer, everyone concentrated on those people. Many were fair haired, like the present day Sapphreans, but there were many others mingled with them – people with black or dark brown hair and dark honey skins.

'Look,' Olam breathed the word again, pointing to one figure at the edge of the market crowd.

It was a man, grey haired, his beard, in many braids, spread across his chest. And his eyes were unmistakably as silvered as were Ren's and Tika's. The picture was framed in a dark, carved wood, and Ren placed his forefinger against it. He jerked his hand back when the wood crumbled into powdery dust at his touch. He lifted the stone to examine the two pictures on either side of the city scene, but they were of lesser interest, showing as they did events of a rural life. The Offering stepped across to the shelves beyond the doorway. Books were tightly packed in each shelf, and some were wedged in any space available above others. His fingers itched to pluck one from its place but after seeing how fragile the picture frame was, Ren feared to be too hasty. He turned back to the desk and stared down at its cluttered surface. He bent closer. Scrolls lay loosely coiled but one was flat, held thus by means of two small stone jars on each end.

'I will need to copy this at once,' Ren muttered, and drew paper and writing stick from his ever present satchel. He put the paper carefully on a patch of empty desk and asked Gan to hold another glow stone above him. Gan stooped low over the desk, frowning at the lines of script.

'Can you read it Ren?' he asked. 'It is quite unfamiliar to me.'

Ren was concentrating, copying the tall spidery forms with complete accuracy onto his own paper.

'No,' he murmured. 'A few shapes seem to remind me of something, but no, I cannot read it at the moment.'

The room was surprisingly bare apart from the large desk: three other chairs stood along the right wall, one on its side, and an oval table against the opposite wall held three large bottles and a tray set with six goblets, only two of which remained upright. Riff and Olam left Ren copying and ventured further along the passage, their hands spread lightly across the stone.

'Here,' said Riff, just as Olam called that he had found more of the three little marks.

Riff turned in time to see another door swing open. Olam held a glow stone aloft and took a step or two inside. Riff hurried to join him when he heard a sharp intake of breath. A wooden settle with curved ends and a high back stood at an angle to the door and Riff saw nothing until he had moved around beside Olam. The armsman stared, as Olam was doing, at the tangled skeletons that lay upon the settle. Olam moved a little closer.

'All this dust.' He squatted down by the settle and pointed out what he meant. 'I would think that is from cushions and pillows.' He peered at the bones. 'It is the same beneath them. Look Riff, pieces of clothing I would guess and.' He stopped and swallowed as he straightened.

Riff looked to find what might have shaken Olam, and saw the husks of three shoes among the dust, one no bigger than the breadth of his own hand, the other two clearly adult sized.

'Four, no five, skulls Olam.' He glanced at the Armschief. 'Looks like one adult and four children.'

Olam nodded and lifted the glow stone to better see the rest of the room. It was roughly the same size as the first, but was all too evidently a family room. Metal dishes and jugs lay scattered on an oblong table and some had fallen to the floor. Again, glass lay sprinkled below windows now filled with rock. Various chests and dressers stood along the walls and child sized chairs lay overturned. A slab of stone was set by one of the windows, patterned in a circular design and a few black stones still rested on it.

'Oh my stars,' Olam whispered. 'Whatever could have befallen them so suddenly?'

While Hargon forced the pace of his men towards Tagria, Seboth was gathering his wounded from the way station. He had sent word to his people that any with a gift for healing should come forward to assist the injured armsmen brought back to the barracks. He stated openly that he saw no dangers in the old blood and he swore he would defend any of his people, unusually talented or not. The people had heard of Hargon's decree of course, that any suspected of such old talents be executed. For a day after Seboth's call for healers, none came forward.

Lady Lallia broke all traditions by appearing publicly to announce that both she herself and her Lord, bore the old blood and its concomitant powers. She announced her pride in both facts, and the people began to respond. Lallia was astonished by the number of those who presented themselves at the House, revealing their talents in many areas other than healing.

Seboth came back with the first line of wagons carrying wounded armsmen. He was taken aback by the results of Lallia's action when he saw one of the long barrack dormitories prepared as an infirmary and the crowd of waiting healers. He supervised the unloading of the injured and made the round of the dormitory, asking the names of all the townsfolk who had risked all in admitting to their ability with the power. When he eventually joined his wife in the sun tower apartments, he looked at her with renewed admiration.

'You are not angry Seboth?' she asked anxiously. 'I thought that if I admitted that we were both what Hargon would call tainted and accursed, our people would be more willing to risk themselves.'

Seboth hugged her. 'It was a brilliant thought.' He held her a little away from him, his head tilted to one side. 'Did Maressa suggest it to you?'

'Oh you.' She punched his ribs and moved to the fireside although she smiled. 'I thought of it all by myself, you fool. Tell me of the men – are our losses bad?'

Seboth stretched himself on the pillows opposite her.

'We have more dead than I would ever wish, but Hargon's losses…' He shook his head. 'I have never seen so many armsmen slaughtered. A few survivors were found and those who could speak, told a chilling tale.' He glanced at Lallia. 'Maressa said that Hargon did not have this illness she told us of?'

'She said that it was far worse than the affliction and that we must not go near him.' Lallia shrugged. 'She said no more than that.'

Seboth pulled his lower lip between his thumb and forefinger. 'Krov should be nearly to Maressa and Brin by now I hope. Would it be all right to try to mind speak them do you think?'

Lallia smiled. Seboth still found it very odd to mention such a thing as mind speaking as though it were the most natural thing in the world.

'Hargon is approaching Tagria is he not? I think it would be safe.'

'I sent three messenger birds ahead to warn Tagria, as well as two scouts. It would have been wonderful to use Merigs, but far too dangerous for them.'

Lallia let her hands lie loosely in her lap and breathed deeply to calm her thoughts, then sent her mind winging towards Maressa.

'What is it Lallia – please tell me no more trouble?'

Lallia felt Maressa's smile.

'No. We think Krov should soon be with you with the supplies you needed. Hargon is on his way to Tagria. There has been much fighting Maressa, many dead and injured.'

Maressa's sympathy flowed through the link.

Lallia explained that she had called on the people of Far to help if they knew the old magic ways, and had been overwhelmed by the response. Maressa's reply was reserved.

'You must protect those who have now exposed themselves Lallia. Should Hargon attack again, or put any future captives to the question, they would be at enormous risk.'

'I told our people that Seboth and I are as "guilty" as any of them.'

Maressa was silent, shaken by the courage of this long-secluded Sapphrean woman.

'Brin says that he can sense riders approaching. I will speak with you ere we depart.'

Maressa broke the link with Lallia and cast her mental vision in the direction Brin indicated. She found three men, dressed in the green uniforms of Far, riding koninas and leading three more. She drew her mind back to herself.

'It is Seboth's men,' she told Brin. 'They will be in sight soon if we go to the top of the ravine.'

Brin's eyes flashed. 'And then we can go back to the coast,' he said with satisfaction.

Maressa laughed. 'But you cannot hunt the fish in the great waters Brin, you have to fly quite a way to find food. Why do you like the coast so much?'

She climbed onto his back as she spoke and his huge crimson

wings lifted them effortlessly up the sheer wall of the ravine to settle on its topmost edge.

'I like the thought of flying out over the water,' he finally answered. 'Perhaps I will find land further off. I have seen such places – mostly rock, and only just large enough for me to rest upon. But I would like to fly on and on and on.'

His mind tone was dreamy such as Maressa had never heard it, but she decided not to question further now when she saw movement about two leagues to the east. Brin had also seen the distant koninas and was checking the area all around for any unexpected or unwelcome additions to Seboth's men. It took some time for the veteran Krov to reach the massive Dragon and Maressa. Maressa recalled that Krov was Seboth's greatly valued Master of Arms, responsible for turning new recruits into armsmen proficient with many weapons and skilled with at least one.

She also remembered that Krov was as aged as Pallin and guessed that this was a contributory factor for Seboth to send such a man away from Far at such a time. She approved of Seboth's discreet and tactful care for two old men and greeted Krov with a smile.

'I trust you met no trouble?' she asked when he had dismounted.

'There was a group of Hargon's men who came upon us. When we lost them, they travelled north.'

Krov ordered the two armsmen with him to begin unloading the koninas. He eyed the great Dragon reclining upon the rough grass assessingly.

'You tell my men how they should load that mighty one and they will do as you wish.'

He blinked as Brin began chatting in all their minds. Krov watched for a moment then turned back to Maressa.

'This group you saw, Lady – how many d'you reckon?'

'About thirty I think.' She hesitated. 'At least one of them was using power, whether knowing what he did or not. I suspect that he did know.'

Krov barked a laugh. 'Don't you worry Lady. I know more than I should. My father taught me a thing or two then he beat me hard enough that I never would be inclined to give myself away.'

Maressa looked puzzled. Krov laughed again and nodded at her cloak, rolled and slotted through her pack straps. It was Maressa's turn to blink as the cloak suddenly wriggled itself free, rose in the air and draped itself around her shoulders. She grinned at Krov.

'That was very good, Master of Arms!' She pushed the cloak out of her way and stooped for the pack.

'Look. I made this map for Lord Seboth. It shows two routes to the coast. There are places with sweet water marked.' She pointed to her map. 'This northern one is the way we first crossed the barren lands, and this one ends here, or a little further south anyway. It is about two and a half days to the first water, then two to the next. The longest gap is on the northern route, between the fourth and fifth watering places. It took us nearly four days between those.'

Krov took the map, his expression one of deep interest.

'We took fifteen days in all to reach the coast that way. Brin takes only four to fly the distance but I think this more southern route might be a day or even two less than the northern one.'

Krov rolled the map with care and tucked it inside his jacket. He gave her a shrewd look.

'Lord Hargon's going to come looking for you, you know. He is determined that he will kill all strangers and all the Dragons.'

'But from all I have heard, he does not know of the watering places through those lands. He could easily get caught too far out without water.'

Krov met her gaze. 'I have thought during this trip, and over the last ten day. I think that Hargon has his very own tame power user. Too unlikely that they found you so fast and so easy Lady. I suggest you keep sharp watch when you meet up with your friends again.'

Maressa nodded slowly, feeling somehow that veteran Krov could well be all too correct.

To the north east, Hargon had again divided his men: a hundred to keep Tagria nervous and uncertain, and a hundred to follow him to the west. Messengers had ridden to Return to order every available armsman to reinforce the band surrounding Tagria. To the men around him, Hargon seemed to be acting as if fevered. He ate little, drank water but sparingly, and apparently needed no sleep. Hargon was unaware of the exact location of the circle near Tagria and could spare neither the men nor the time to search for it now. He demanded that all the flasks from the armsmen staying behind be distributed among those travelling on with him.

M'Raz had observed all with interest, but was growing a little bored. The countryside did not impress him, seen through Hargon's eyes. He had yet to discover the significance of the patterned circle which appeared obsessively in Hargon's thoughts, and the methods of killing were tedious in the extreme. These simple creatures seemed quite unaware of the delicious delights of savouring a protracted means of destroying another creature. And it could be such fun. He had decided to allow Hargon only a short while longer to prove himself worthy of hosting M'Raz's spirit.

He would let him make this trip to the coast and then he would finally make up his mind. M'Raz was interested in the younger man, Trib. He had shown himself to be concerned only with himself, much more so than Hargon or any of the other men. M'Raz too was only concerned with himself and he appreciated finding a similarity at last in one of these beings. Yes. If he discarded Hargon, Trib would do very nicely as a replacement.

Chapter Twenty-Eight

The two children travelled down the Sy River, protected by the high bank, for most of that afternoon. When the sun began to sink below the trees ahead, Tyen grabbed at an overhanging branch and pulled them close into the side. He looked over his shoulder at Mena and his teeth showed white in the shadows when he gave her a quick grin.

'Look behind us girl.'

Mena twisted round and gasped. The huddled ruin of what had been the town of Syet lay about seven or eight leagues distant already, but towering high above the town was the mass of the Menedula. Its walls gleamed a dull black in the fading sun but as before, Mena thought the black stone sucked in the light rather than reflecting it as she believed it once had done. It seemed to stretch upwards forever, but Mena shivered. It was as if the great building was clawing at the very sky, trying to pull it down inside itself. Again, she had the sensation of having seen it before, when it raised itself joyfully skywards – she shook her head to clear the suddenly blurred image. How could she imagine a vast edifice such as the Menedula could laugh and be merry?

The strange little boat rocked when Tyen moved towards her.

'We have to leave the boat now. River gets narrower and goes under a bridge. Too dangerous for us.'

Mena pictured her map in her head. They needed to move away from the river with the setting sun well to their left. At the moment, it shone straight into her face. She recalled how the river squiggled away west and south on the map: yes, they needed to leave it now and make their way across the land.

Tyen tugged her arm and motioned her to follow. So far, the only hint of any threat had been the inhuman screams she had heard in the drain. Now there was the sound of the river murmuring and gurgling on its way, unfamiliar birdsong fluting from hidden places. But no sounds of human life. Tyen was indicating that she should continue to move as quietly as she could, informing Mena that they were far from being out of danger. A breeze sprang up from the east, rattling branches over their heads. Leaf buds showed on nearly all the bushes and trees around, although Mena noted that a few trees stood starkly bare still. Tyen led her just below the lip of the riverbank, then paused. Carefully, he crept to the top and peeped over. He beckoned urgently and Mena scrambled up beside him.

She saw a road in front of them, paved with great slabs of grey stone, wide enough for two or even three wagons to travel abreast. Tyen pointed straight across to where fir trees lined the edge of the road. He drew her to her feet, gripping her hand. Without warning, he was darting forward, dragging her with him. They plunged into the firs and kept running for more than a hundred paces. Tyen released her hand and leaned on a tree trunk, half bending to catch his breath. Mena too stooped, hands on her knees as she tried to slow her panting.

Tyen straightened, looking about him. Twilight by the river had become virtually full dark beneath the thick needles of the fir trees and no sky was visible above them. Looking back, Mena could just glimpse the blur of grey which was the road they had crossed, and knew they must keep it to their left whilst angling further away to the right. Glancing at Tyen, she pointed in the direction she felt they must go. He shrugged and nodded.

When it was too dark to walk without bumping into a tree trunk, Mena sank onto the thick needles at the bole of a tree. Tyen slid down beside her and she handed him two biscuits from her pack and a handful of fruits. They both froze as a wailing cacophony began to sob in the distance. Mena felt Tyen tense against her side and put her hand on his arm. The sound continued but grew no louder or closer, and slowly Tyen relaxed again. Mena was more worried right now about Cho Petak trying to find her mind.

Hazy memories of old Mayla instructing her on how to hide her thoughts drifted elusively in her head, mixed with things picked up from Kadi and the other Dragons. She yawned hugely and tried to concentrate her thoughts again. But her eyelids were too heavy and after another jaw cracking yawn, she slept. Tyen was already asleep, slumped against Mena's shoulder, so neither

291

child noticed the fragrance of mint which enveloped them like a blanket.

They spent two days getting deeper and deeper among the firs. At the end of the second day, they rested in a small clearing caused by the fall of a great tree which had brought down several others when it had crashed to the ground. A small clear stream ran noisily under the fallen trunk from which Mena refilled her flask. She and Tyen had spoken even less since leaving the Menedula than they had within the garden, and Mena noticed Tyen seemed far less sure of himself now.

'Have you been in these woods before?' Her voice felt rusty from so little use when she spoke that night.

Tyen hugged his knees to his chest. 'Only been from Syet to Paril – the next town down river, past the bridge I spoke of.'

She waited, but Tyen said nothing more and soon they were both asleep.

By midday of the third day, the trees were clearly thinning and when they stopped for a few of the remaining nuts and biscuits in Mena's pack, Mena unfolded her map and spread it on the ground. Tyen squatted next to her.

'Do you understand maps?' Mena asked.

'I only seen maps of Syet,' he said. 'Easy to work them out.' He jabbed a finger onto the paper. 'Reckon we must be somewhere here. And you want us to get there?' Another jab and a raised brow.

Mena nodded. 'Three days and we've done this much.'

She measured the space with her fingers between the Menedula and where they guessed they now were. Then she measured the same distance again, and again until she reached the Oblaka.

'About nine more days.'

She looked into Tyen's face. 'We will soon need to find food.'

He nodded. 'No berries about, too early.' He shrugged and stood up.

'Why did you need maps in the town Tyen?' Mena asked as they began walking again.

He walked in silence for some further paces then shot her a crooked smile.

'I had to learn everywhere in the town: roads, alleys, every footpath, the drains and the sewers. Then the ways over the rooftops.'

Mena frowned, trying to work out why Tyen would need to learn all that. He laughed.

'Don't matter now. Town's so burnt down, drains were the only safe places left.' He faced her defiantly. 'We was the best thieves in Syet, in all Drogoya I shouldn't wonder. Anything anyone wanted off someone else, we could do it.'

Mena grinned at him. 'I have never met a thief before. Not that I know of, anyway. I wondered why you should know your way through those drains so well.'

'One of the Kooshak told my father he should send me to the Menedula for a student, years ago. But my father got very angry, said he'd never allow such a thing.'

Mena glanced at him curiously. 'Would you not have liked to study?'

'Oh yes. Good in ordinary school I am. Was. Liked reading, specially tales of long ago days.'

As Mena drew breath to speak again, Tyen put his arm out barring her way.

'Hush now. See, the trees end soon. Light knows what may lie beyond.'

Mena dropped a little behind him when Tyen began to move from tree to tree until they had reached the edge of the woodland. They crouched together, staring over rough pasture land towards a sturdy stone building. No animals grazed there but Tyen pointed silently to where a few hens scratched alongside a broken fence. No smoke rose from either of two chimneys and nothing moved but the hens.

'Follow me exactly,' Tyen whispered. 'Maybe we'll find a couple of eggs at least.'

He led them through the tree line to the fence and they crept along the side furthest from the building. Mena's heart thudded so hard that she thought it would be heard paces away, but she stuck close to Tyen's heels. He gestured her to wait in the angle between a water barrel and the house wall, and he slipped around the corner out of sight. Mena crouched, ready to run, and kept watch in every direction. She jumped when a hen poked its head round the barrel and advanced to scratch the ground at Mena's feet. She heard the sound of someone being sick and was round the corner of the house in a flash. Tyen was doubled over, his face ashen. Mena glanced at the open door but Tyen grabbed her arm.

'Don't! They're all dead in there.'

Mena wiped his wet forehead with her hand. 'But there might be some food we could take,' she said gently, and turned to the door. 'Wait here – see if you can find some eggs.'

She did not hesitate, walking straight through the door into a stench worse than any she had smelt before. She kept her gaze up, only seeing jumbled shapes on the floor with her peripheral vision. The room was plainly the main living area of the house and Mena carefully crossed to a row of cupboards attached to the wall at the furthest end. Still not looking down, she dragged a chair with her towards the cupboards, biting her lip when something impeded the chair's movement.

Climbing up to the cupboards, she was surprised and thankful to discover food was still stored within them. She shrugged her satchel from her back and began to put in whatever she found. She breathed through her mouth in an attempt to mitigate the smell, but she knew she could not be too long in here for fear of copying Tyen's reaction.

She left the grains and dried vegetables: she doubted the wisdom of lighting any fires to do proper cooking, and her notions of cooking were fairly limited anyway. Behind the door of one cupboard hung a small canvas sack and she filled that as well as her satchel. She stepped off the chair and made for the door but she stopped when she reached it.

Tyen stood waiting for her a few paces away, his ragged shirt held bunched to hold the eggs he had found. Mena straightened her shoulders and lifted her chin. Slowly and deliberately, she turned around and took one step back inside the door. She looked down at the floor and saw the bodies which were sprawled there. Two men, a woman, three children all smaller than her. None of them had eyes, though whether that was due to whatever had killed them or to the hens, she couldn't guess. Their bodies were bloated and contorted. An arm lay several paces from a body. The two biggest children had their stomachs ripped and coils of intestines spooled around them.

Mena stared at the carnage, willing herself to remember this scene in every horrific detail. Cho Petak had allowed this, and Cho Petak would pay. Although quite how she could make him do so was yet unclear to her.

Sarryen realised that Arryol's diagnosis was correct. Finn Rah made no more fuss about keeping to her bed and taking whatever pills and potions Arryol presented to her. Occasionally Finn showed her impatience with her illness by a sudden irritation and a short tempered retort but mostly she was resigned. Soosha spent the evenings with the Offering giving Sarryen a chance to escape the sickroom.

Lyeto had led small groups of students onto the much widened viewing ledge where they attempted to approach the Menedula's immediate vicinity with their minds. They were all shown Mena's mind signature and told that was what they must trace. So far they had no success to report.

Melena frequently sat with the Kooshak in the common room and Sarryen had begun to see that the girl would become her pupil. Melena had a similarly broad spectrum of talents to Sarryen's own, and had been worried that she seemed to have no specific calling.

'Accept the many talents you have,' Sarryen told the girl one evening. 'Work on them all until one may begin to predominate. But accept your gifts first of all,' she repeated. 'Many students whom I have encountered are excellent in their one particular area, but they are often blinkered by that exclusivity. One such as you or I can see many parts that go to make up a whole, which those others cannot see.'

Melena nodded slowly. 'I had not considered that before,' she said and gave Sarryen a shy smile. 'I could not understand why my eyes silvered and yet I am unable to excel at any one thing.'

Sarryen studied the girl for a moment. 'If things were as before, I would ask you to travel with me, as my pupil Melena. But things are not so, no matter how we might wish them to be. You know that Finn Rah is very sick?'

Melena nodded.

'My time must be given to her for now but I will set aside

some time each day – when it is convenient for your other studies, and I will begin to instruct you in Kooshak generalities – if that is your wish.'

Sarryen grimaced as a group of students burst into noisy laughter across the common room. 'Amidst this noise, is not a good idea.'

'I am free of duties around mid morning most days. Would that suit you Kooshak?'

'That would be fine.' Sarryen frowned. 'It will be busy again in here at that time, so come to my room. I will make a note of some of the texts you will need to work on, which you can start should Finn Rah delay me.' She looked into the girl's grey silvered eyes. 'Yes,' she thought. 'I will enjoy teaching you.'

Making her way back to Chakar's sitting room, she tried to work out how long it was since she had chosen a pupil, one who was called to be Kooshak rather than continue the climb up the ranks within the Menedula. It must be nearly thirty years she realised with some surprise. That last one had been a boy, but wrack her brain though she might, she could not think of his name. Surely the longevity inducements could not be failing yet – she had not reached her first hundred years! Sarryen resolved that she would remember that boy's name before she allowed herself to sleep again and marched into Finn Rah with a scowl on her face.

'You look in just the mood to cheer an invalid,' Finn remarked brightly.

Sarryen's scowl gave way to a smile. 'I'm becoming forgetful Finn Rah. I have forgotten the name of someone thirty years in my past.'

'Happens to us all. I can't remember the names of half the people here – doesn't mean that I am falling apart,' Finn scoffed.

Soosha chuckled from his armchair. 'Finn called me "erm" for years.'

'I did not.' Finn was indignant, then held her breath for a moment as the hated cough threatened to erupt.

'Sit,' Finn ordered the Kooshak in a quieter voice. 'Soosha and I were wondering about the chance of finding the children by dream walking. It is far less strenuous than far seeking. That is probably why old Babach used that method so often.'

Sarryen took the other armchair. 'I have used dream walking occasionally, when I have needed advice from other Kooshak on cases I was dealing with.' She nodded. 'I had no difficulty with such a means of communication. But if we found the children through dream walking, would they comprehend its reality? They might simply think that they had experienced a rather odd but vivid dream?'

'No, I think not,' Finn replied after a pause. 'The girl would understand and act upon whatever advice we could offer.'

Sarryen said nothing although her face reflected her doubt. Finn glanced at Soosha as though asking him to defend her argument. He caught Sarryen's gaze and held it.

'Sarryen, this child is very special. Although totally untrained as far as I can guess, yet she could see Finn Rah fully when Finn sought her. You know that when minds meet when far seeking, they only appear as faint lights. If you choose to reveal yourself in an illusion to the recipient, you can do so – in whatever guise you wish. But the girl *saw* Finn Rah. It was almost as if she traced the mind link back here and saw Finn for herself.' The old Observer shrugged. 'How could that be done so fast, even as the child was speaking with Finn? No Sarryen. We have to accept that this child has strengths beyond anything we have known, aware of them or not. She would understand and act upon the advice of a dream walker.'

Finn's head jerked towards the door before an urgent knock sounded. Lyeto entered, ablaze with excitement.

'We found them,' he blurted at once. 'About twenty five leagues north west of the Menedula.'

'Any suspicion of Cho Petak or his minions near them?'

Lyeto shook his head. 'The Menedula felt, even at that distance, like a cauldron of heat – anger, hatred, perversion streaming from it to about five or six leagues round about.'

Finn looked worried. 'Cho Petak can reach here easily – as we know all too well. How is it that he has not tracked two children still so near the Menedula?'

'I keep telling you my dears, the child is strong and is also protected by someone, something, that we cannot fathom. It will not be easy but they will survive the journey here.'

'I wish I could be so positive,' Finn muttered.

Lyeto turned to each speaker in turn, following their words. He went to the table and dug a book from the pile, thumbing through its pages.

'This is where they are, as far as we could judge.'

He laid the book opened to a map of northern Drogoya on Finn's knees. He pointed to the forested region called Glair. Soosha and Sarryen joined him at Finn's bedside and stared down at the map.

'They have many leagues of hill country to cross, then the Gara Mountains and down into Valoon.' Finn's finger traced the line she was guessing the children would take. 'The cold is scarcely past, where will they find food?' Jade silvered eyes looked up at Soosha in real concern.

His eyebrows rose. 'They may get a little hungry, but Finn, they will reach us.'

Finn turned back to the map. 'It is mostly small farms scattered there as I recall. Probably safer than towns or villages.'

'We have found minds, few in number, which are no longer normal. No longer human,' Lyeto said quietly. 'I would guess that the great majority of people in this area are dead.'

'And no doubt throughout Drogoya.' Finn leaned back into her pillows. 'Light above, does Cho Petak desire this land emptied of all life?'

Lyeto bit his lip. 'We find no trace of animal minds Offering. A few birds, but no animals.'

'What is he doing? In fact, what is Cho Petak? And why oh why did we not act on our suspicions centuries ago?'

Soosha patted her hand and returned to his armchair. Sarryen began to make a pot of tea when, late as it was, another knock came on Finn's door. Lyeto opened it to find the beanpole cook outside. Finn lifted her hand.

'Come in Povar. The hour is late – surely you are not still busy in your kitchen?'

Povar went to Finn's bedside and handed her a folded, sealed paper.

'On a table by the common room door,' he said gruffly.

Finn turned the oblong paper over and saw her name written across it. Her thumb nail broke the seal and she spread the paper on top of the book still on her lap. She scanned the few lines and shook her head.

'Now will someone please tell me how Volk knew something that Lyeto has only just told us?'

Blank faces stared at her. She waved the paper. 'Volk feels that he should go back to Valoon, and further, to the other side of the Gara. He says that blizzards can still descend on the passes and children would never make it across alone.'

Lyeto frowned. 'Volk uses a cavern quite near the viewing ledge – could he have heard us speak of this among ourselves before I came to tell you?'

Soosha laughed. 'No, no my boy. Surely Volk would not have had time to prepare for such a trip and write his letter? Has he said anything to you of late Povar – of dreams perhaps?'

Povar looked astonished, as well he might Sarryen thought. She had rarely met two more taciturn men than Volk and his son in law Povar, and she could never imagine them sitting down to discuss something as bizarre as dreams.

'Well,' Povar began slowly. 'Two, three days past, he been grumbling about a smell contaminating his brews.'

'A smell?' Finn began to smile.

Povar nodded. 'Said the children must have hid some herbs in amongst his things.'

Finn's smile expanded. 'Thank you for bringing the letter Povar. I think Volk will be all right so do not be too concerned for his safety for a while.'

Povar looked surprised again. 'Ain't worried about that old fool. But who's to make the ale?'

Finn struggled to straighten her expression. 'Ask the students to help – I am sure they could manage something – not of Volk's standard of course, but good enough for now.'

Povar nodded moodily and took himself back to his kitchen. Soosha shook his head.

'Well, well. If it is truly Myata, she must enjoy playing these games with us all.'

Volk rode one horse and led two others as he moved round Oblaka town, his senses taut for any alarm. He had hoped that being outside would clear his nose and his head, but it did not seem to be having the desired effect. He swore under his breath.

299

If there was one herb he had no fondness for, it was that cursed mint and it seemed all about him during the last two days. He muffled another sneeze, swore again and picked his way in the starlight towards the high trail to Valoon.

Chapter Twenty-Nine

Mim was more affected by old Fenj's departure than anyone might have guessed. He longed to have flown south with him, to be free for a while of the darkness besetting the Stronghold. He was touched by Kija's obvious concern for him despite her own worries. Word had come from Gaharn that there had been inexplicable disturbances in the surrounding countryside. These disturbances sounded very much like the descriptions he had heard of the Vagrantian affliction: people waking, red eyed and mad, and soon dying. So far, none of the cases had reported any silver eyed survivors.

Emla's messages told of cases beginning in the plains and farming lands leagues to the west of Gaharn, then sweeping south and east. The latest incidents were approaching Gaharn itself and the Vagrantian air mage still in Lady Emla's House – Jilla – said that she sensed a being close by similar to the one Thryssa had encountered within the Asataria. Suppose it was this creature from the Void Thryssa had spoken of which brought about the eruptions of the affliction? Would it attack the Domain, work its way north to his Stronghold?

Fenj knew of many of Mim's worries and his solid presence had been a source of comfort to the Dragon Lord. He'd discovered, as had Tika, that his beloved soul bond, Ashta, despite her size, her strength, her inherited memories, was still only a baby. She offered him unconditional love and support, but she could not help his own understanding of what was happening in these lands. Tension rose once Fenj had flown away to Vagrantia: everyone felt it, down to the lowest of the Stronghold servants.

Chakar's owl, Sava, transferred his allegiance from Lorak to the Delver Bikram but was often to be heard hooting dolefully from under Bikram's jacket. The timid Kephi Rofu was in the Domain with Chakar and Kera, and Mim missed him more than he could have imagined.

Six days after Fenj's departure, Kija and Kadi left, carrying Elyssa and the Observer Babach. There were many tears at this departure – no one believed the Dragons would reach Drogoya safely or survive its dangers if they did. Jal gave them formal farewell in the name of the people of the Stronghold, but could barely restrain his own tears as first Kadi, then Kija lowered their long faces to press against his brow.

An atmosphere of empty gloom permeated the Stronghold, with an underlying thread of foreboding. The Snow Dragons were restless and Berri, the acting Wise One of the Delver people, came to consult with Mim. He and Dessi escorted her part way back into the Domain and the three of them paused at the egg cave. Mim explained what he was about to do, Dessi and Berri giving close attention to his words. After one last, lingering look at the cave, brilliantly lit with a light that almost seemed alive, he closed the entrance. Leading the two Delvers halfway back through the twisting passage, he stopped again. Another wall of rock appeared, closing off the way to the cave. He made both women reopen the rock until he was satisfied that they would remember the means of doing so.

'Why?' Dessi asked, just before she and Mim re-entered the Stronghold.

Mim lifted one shoulder in a half shrug. 'I feel it necessary to make them even more secure at the moment.'

'The creature in Gaharn?' She caught his arm to slow him. 'You think it will come here?' Her dark blue eyes were intent on the Dragon Lord.

'I hope it will not, but I think it well may.' His laugh fluted softly. 'Too many people know that there is such a hidden place Dessi, even if they know not its exact location.'

'And the treasures within must be guarded still?'

Mim's strange turquoise eyes with the vertical pupils rested on Dessi. 'Their time is soon – but not yet. They must be protected until the proper time, even if it means the deaths of us all.'

Dessi shivered at the intensity of both his words and his stare.

News arrived that evening of the first case of the affliction within the Domain. Amud was the southernmost settlement and as soon as the case was discovered, the Elder Falin caused all access tunnels leading north to be sealed, in a frantic hope that the affliction might thus be contained.

One case of a young boy's eyes silvering was reported in Amud, but eleven youngsters died, red eyed and insane. Throughout the whole Domain, Snow Dragons sang their songs of grieving and farewell, echoing the sorrow of the Delver population. Days passed without any more reports of the affliction. Then the first was found in the settlement of Arak and all knew that there was nothing that would stop it working its inexorable way north through the Domain, even to the Stronghold.

When word reached Mim of Arak's first two fatal cases, he took Ashta and flew high above the Stronghold. His fury urged her faster, higher, further north, than ever before in a futile attempt to lose his anger.

Why now, he raged aloud to the towering mountains and darkening sky. Why now, with the great Dragons departed when he needed their wisdom; Gremara gone too, stars knew where; disease creeping upon his people. And the pain. Oh the pain was becoming unbearable. Try as he might, he would not be able to hide it from his beloved Ashta much longer, soul linked as they were. Remorsefully aware at last of Ashta's weariness, he let her take them back to the Stronghold.

Observer Chakar returned hurriedly to the Stronghold with Daro and Chornay. They were informed that Mim had secluded himself in his high chamber, still blazing with fury, and had given orders that he was not to be disturbed. Chakar listened to Jal in silence, fully aware of his confusion. One armed he might now be, but Jal was prepared to fight any who had the temerity to attack this Stronghold and its Dragon Lord. But how did you fight an illness of this kind that could creep through the very rock of the mountains? There was no pattern to it – apparently neither contagion nor infection – utterly random in its choice of victim.

Chakar understood the Dragon Lord's anger, mirrored as it was in Jal and in most of the people of the Stronghold. How indeed could you combat such an adversary? But Babach had spoken to her before he left for Drogoya and Chakar knew the Dragon Lord had even more to worry him. She sat thinking for a brief while then looked up into Daro's calm face. He gave the

303

tiniest nod and she smiled.

'Daro and I will speak to the Dragon Lord now.'

Motass stiffened but Chakar forestalled his protest.

'If you and your brother will accompany us?' She glanced across the great hall to where Ashta slept between two Snow Dragons then got to her feet. 'I have an idea we may need to remain with him for some time Chornay. Please inform Kera and ask that we be not disturbed under any circumstance.'

She reached for the battered bag which held her herbs and salves and potions, and headed for the ramp. She paused outside the door of the smaller chamber to which Mim had been forced to move by the nesting Plavats. She looked at Daro.

'Dessi?' she asked.

Daro shook his head. 'We will call her if we need to, but it is better not as yet.'

Jal and Motass exchanged puzzled looks: they understood Daro to be but a young Vagrantian student yet the Observer Chakar sought his opinion. Chakar drew a deep breath and placed her right palm against the door.

'It's bolted,' she murmured.

A pale greenish light glowed around her hand, quickly deepening to an almost solid-seeming colour. There was the sound of metal sliding against metal and the light vanished. Chakar moved her hand from the door panel to the latch.

'Inside quickly,' she ordered softly as the door swung open.

Daro closed and bolted the door again behind them. They stood just inside the chamber, a lamp standing on a small table the only illumination.

The Dragon Lord was crouched in a corner to the left of the empty fireplace, his arms locked round his knees, hands clutching his shoulders. He raised his head and they saw the tears pouring down the scaled cheeks. His mouth opened and Motass tensed, expecting to be ordered from the room but all that emerged was a low moan of pain.

Jal could think only of the kindness this young Lord had shown him in his own time of agony and moved quickly to squat beside him, his left hand covering one of Mim's. Chakar too bent towards Mim but did not touch him.

'Babach told me, Mim. He was torn by his need to return to

Drogoya and with your impending need of his support. Let us help you now.' She reached for Mim's other hand, tugging gently to loose its grip on his shoulder. 'Come. It will be better I promise, but you cannot bear this alone.'

She nodded at Jal and between them they coaxed Mim slowly to his feet. Daro had pulled the top covers off the narrow pallet and removed the pillows.

'Motass we will need a fire and hot water,' Chakar requested as she and Jal helped the unsteady figure across the room.

Jal's eyes filled with tears as Daro eased the sleeveless jerkin from Mim's upper body with such tender care. Then his breath caught when Daro and Chakar helped Mim to lie face down upon the pallet. Chakar bit her lip, studying Mim's back while the fire crackled to life behind them. Jal stepped away, then felt his brother at his side, heard the hiss of his indrawn breath.

Blood streaked down each side of Mim's spine from parallel strips bare of scales. The strips were swollen hard nearest the top of his spine, slightly less so where the lines ran below the level of his shoulder blades. Wordlessly Motass fetched Chakar's bag from where she had left it at the door and put it beside her. She hooked a stool closer with her foot, sat and began sorting through the pouches of herbs.

Mim's body spasmed and fresh blood sprang from the top of the swollen ridges. His hands clenched and Daro leaned over, forcing Mim's hand open and putting a pillow between the bare palm and the taloned fingers. He moved round the pallet to attend to the other hand.

'Dear stars above, what's wrong with the lad? Is this the affliction we've heard tell of?' Motass whispered hoarsely.

Daro smiled at him, his silver hazel eyes full of compassion. 'Oh no, not the affliction. These are wing buds Motass – the Dragon Lord's wings are emerging.'

Chakar made poultices, muttering to herself while she combined different groups of herbs and fungi to pack between thin gauze before laying them on Mim's back. The night progressed and Mim was ever more tormented with pain, until finally Daro touched his forehead and Mim's tense body relaxed into unconsciousness.

'Why couldn't you have done that sooner?' growled Motass.

305

Daro spread his hands. 'Neither Observer Chakar nor I have any idea how this transformation is to be accomplished.'

'That's right,' Chakar agreed. 'We are still not sure if it will help or hinder to have him unaware. He may need to consciously assist his wings to emerge. We just don't know, Motass.'

Motass nodded in reluctant understanding. 'But how long will this take do you think, Lady? It is nearly dawn and I see no difference in his poor back.'

Chakar rose stiffly and went to swing the kettle over the fire again.

'Something else we have no idea of.' She glanced back at Daro. 'You should check on Ashta – maybe the Delver healers could help keep her calm.'

Daro smiled. 'The Snow Dragons are keeping her asleep for now, but I think we should talk with some of the healers perhaps. And it is time Dessi was informed. I will do so now.'

'I'll find us some breakfast, Lady. You need to keep your strength up to help young Mim.' Motass followed Daro from the chamber and Chakar smiled at Jal's expression.

'I know Motass meant no rudeness Jal. He is rightly concerned for this boy.'

Jal wedged a couple more logs on the fire then blurted: 'Why does that pendant not help him then? He wears one. So do you. Yet still he suffers so.'

Chakar sighed, rubbing her eyes. 'I don't know Jal. Sometimes these pendants become warm and they pulse as with a heart beat. That hasn't happened tonight.'

The door opened and Daro came in with Dessi. The timid Kephi Rofu squirmed out of Daro's arm and leaped on Chakar's knee. She put down her fresh made mug of tea to hold him. Distress vibrated through his tiny frame. His front feet kneaded against her arm then he leaped away to climb the pallet on which Mim lay. Dessi stared at Mim's still body then moved across to Chakar.

'I have been so deep in my own studies and concerns that I had no idea anything was wrong with Mim,' she said.

Chakar patted her hand. 'Only Babach knew, I think.' She frowned. 'Perhaps Fenj did too, but Babach told me only just before he and Elyssa left.'

She added some hot water to a bowl of herbs and covered them with a plate to steep. 'The poultices need renewing but I am having to reuse some of the ingredients – I've run out of supplies.'

Chakar bent over Mim and gently lifted the gauze-wrapped poultice from one side of his back. Bright blood welled instantly from the whole line of swollen flesh. Dessi pressed her hand to her mouth and Rofu whimpered, wiggling closer to lie along Mim's side. Chakar glanced up as the door opened again and Motass carried in a tray laden with food.

'The lad's gone for more medicines,' he offered.

'And I summoned Berri,' Dessi added belatedly. 'When Daro came and told me of this, I called her. We cannot hide what's happening Chakar.'

She was trying to staunch the blood while she spoke and Chakar hurried to fetch the new poultice.

'It isn't like this with other winged creatures,' she continued.

Chakar placed the fresher dressing on Mim's back when Dessi lifted away the blood-soaked cloth. They repeated the procedure on the other side of Mim's spine and stood looking down at him. Jal cleared his throat.

'I agree with my brother that you should eat, Observer.'

Chakar smiled at him and joined the two men at the table.

'I'm sure you're right Jal. There seems so little I can do – I can think of nothing at all that would help him.'

They ate in silence for a while, glancing often at the motionless body across the room.

'Will his, um, wings be like the Dragons', Observer?' Motass asked finally.

'Another thing to which I have no answer,' Chakar replied. 'I have studied birds for many years but all of them hatch from their eggs with their wings already formed outside their bodies.' She shook her head. 'I can only hope Berri or another Delver healer may have at least some ideas on this case.'

Chakar and Dessi had changed the poultices again before Daro returned carrying a large sack of herbs, and accompanied by Berri, the Wise One of the Delvers in Nolli's absence. Berri kissed both Dessi and Chakar and looked hopefully at the teapot. Motass handed her a steaming mug from which she sipped gratefully.

'I spoke with two Elders of the Snow Dragons on my way here,' she said without preamble. 'They told me that there are instances of a hatchling emerging with wings sealed against its body, but they had never heard tell of wings still within the body.' She looked from Chakar to Dessi and back again. 'They suggest that we – encourage – the wings to free themselves. If necessary to open his flesh.'

She looked at the four appalled faces staring at her and tried to smile. 'Daro suggested we try to massage or manipulate Mim's back before we resort to more drastic methods.'

Chakar chewed her lip, thinking furiously. 'Motass, we will need much more water here. Fetch another kettle too so we have plenty heating.' She began rolling her sleeves high up her arms as she got to her feet. 'He's bleeding constantly, not heavily but enough,' she explained to Berri. 'Any pressure is bound to increase it though. And Jal, we will need many more cloths to soak up the blood.'

As the brothers went quickly to do her bidding, Chakar lifted one of the poultices from Mim's back.

Berri paled. 'Dear stars!'

Daro placed his hand briefly on Chakar's shoulder and smiled into her eyes. 'You can do this, Chakar,' he told her softly. Then he moved out of her way, knelt beside the pallet and put his hands either side of Mim's head.

Briefly Chakar clasped the pendant hanging at her chest, took a deep breath and reached out to Mim. Pressing lightly at first at the highest part of the swollen ridge, Chakar slid her hands ever more firmly down towards Mim's narrow waist. Berri gasped. The skin split under the pressure and a dark line could be seen under the now spurting blood. Dessi grabbed a handful of cloths, passing some across to Berri. Rofu, against Mim's other side, watched in alarm, his whiskers quivering. Motass put a bowl of hot water within reach of the three women then moved the lamp closer to illuminate the ghastly scene more clearly.

'Motass, fetch pails of ice for me,' Chakar rapped. 'We will need to pack this whole area with ice for a time, once we get the wing free.'

Dessi moved closer to Chakar, putting her tiny hands on top of the Observer's who was immediately aware of power surging from the Delver girl. Again and again Chakar stroked her hands heavily down Mim's back. Again and again Berri swabbed away blood. The morning passed unnoticed as did Bikram's arrival in the small chamber. Without a word the Delver gardener took a place beside Berri and mopped at the streaming rivulets of blood.

'Look!' Chakar's hands stilled. 'Swab that top section.'

Bikram was nearest and did as Chakar bid. They all peered at the long slit, now gaping open about three fingers wide.

'I'm going to try to bring it out.'

Dessi moved her hands from Chakar's, placing them instead in the blood to either side of where Chakar indicated. The Observer's fingers dug down and a tremor ran through Mim's body. Chakar clenched her jaw and probed again. The watchers gasped as slowly a length of draggled matter emerged from Mim's back.

With the utmost care, Chakar took hold of the lower end and pulled gently. A wet, bloodied wing unfurled, as long as Mim was tall.

'Fetch a chair or stool to let it rest on. It will dry better outstretched.' Daro spoke softly as always. 'It needs cleaning too.'

He smiled at Jal and Motass who leaped into action. Chakar studied the exposed wing, wiping her hands and moving to the other side of the pallet.

'We need to put ice along that opening Berri, and herbs to speed closure. And his wings will not be like the Dragons', Motass – they are feathered!'

Bikram and Berri changed places with the Observer and Dessi, and Chakar began to work on the other wing ridge. Chakar was briefly conscious of her back aching from the hours she had spent bent awkwardly over Mim but she had no sooner become aware of the discomfort than it vanished. Her lips twitched. 'Thank you Daro.'

The day was ending again but the attention of all in Mim's chamber was focused only on the boy lying beneath Chakar's hands. When she finally eased the second wing free and extended it, there was a collective sigh of relief throughout the room.

Dessi leaned her shoulder against Chakar's side. 'We can do

the rest. Go wash yourself.'

Chakar opened her mouth to protest and exhaustion crashed through her whole body. She nodded. 'I think I will, but I will be straight back,' she warned.

Wiping her hands, she went round to where Motass and Jal had cleaned and dried Mim's right wing. She stared at it in astonished awe. Long golden feathers fanned out across a supporting chair, a deep buttery gold with their tips dipped in silver.

Imshish and Chornay were in Mim's chamber when Chakar returned. She felt refreshed by a hot bath and clean clothes, the shadows under her eyes the only sign that this was the second night since she had slept. The room was clean and comfortably warm, the harsh smell of blood banished by the tang of herbs. Chakar went straight to examine her patient and as she bent to lift a corner of the gauze dressing over Mim's spine she flinched at the sudden heat from the egg pendant she wore.

She hurriedly pulled it free of her shirt and realised it was pulsing as it had when she had worked on Kadi and assisted at Babach's healing. Why should it react now, when Mim was hopefully already healing, rather than last night when she so desperately needed extra help? She noted that the bleeding had stopped, the swelling was hardly perceptible and also that Daro had moved Mim's pendant so that it rested at the back of his neck where his head lay sideways on the pallet.

'Chakar!'

She turned towards the others and saw Dessi holding a mug towards her.

'There have been no more cases of madness in Arak,' the Delver told her. 'Three children with silvered eyes, the two who died five days ago, but no other cases!'

Chakar wrinkled her nose. 'Early days Dessi. Too soon to let your hopes rise too far.'

Dessi looked a little disappointed by Chakar's reaction but then smiled. 'That was a terrible thing you had to help Mim with, but stars! Look at the result!'

All in the room turned to look at the slender boy lying between two great sweeping fans of gold feathers. The feathers suddenly seemed to ripple and Rofu emerged from beneath the left wing by

Mim's leg. Imshish began to chuckle but then, as Rofu jumped to the floor, the feathers rippled again and Mim's feet twitched.

Chakar hurried back to his side and then stopped, startled. Song filled the chamber, apparently emanating from the very rock from which it was carved, and at the same time there came an almost overpowering scent of mint.

Chapter Thirty

Gremara flew northwest, passing to the south of the city of Gaharn. She flew high and fast, knowing time was crucial. As she approached the Spine Mountains, she became aware of an essence located deep within the rock. She hesitated, flying lower in a wide circle until she verified the essence as the being known as Rashpil. Twice more she circled, weighing her choices before lifting higher in the air and speeding on to the west.

Even the Silver One's physical strength was not endless and as the fourth dawn of her journey flung a pink arm across the sky behind her, she knew she would have to rest. Opening her mind, she searched ahead and found a great Dragon prepared to welcome her. The sun was nearing its apogee when Gremara slowed to spiral down in the heart of the Sun Mountains. A massive purple Dragon waited, larger even than black Fenj, rearing erect as Gremara drifted down to the rock.

'Seela, Eldest of the Sun Mountain Treasury, gives welcome to the Silver One.'

Gremara lay wearily a few paces from the huge Dragon. Seela lowered herself and paced closer, her lavender eyes sparkling.

'I sense that you have urgent need to travel on, dear one, but I also sense you need food and rest.'

Gremara sighed. 'Indeed Eldest. I would count it a boon could I sleep here until dark.'

Seela settled herself comfortably alongside the narrow silver body. 'Sleep then, and I shall bring fresh meat when the first stars show above us.'

A sliver of moon hung in the pale green sky of dusk when Seela woke Gremara. A freshly killed lumen lay within reach and Gremara fed gratefully but sparingly. While she ate, she told Seela of some of the events in Gaharn and in the circles far to the east to which Seela listened closely.

'What of the Dragon Lord in the north?' she asked finally.

Gremara shivered, her silver scales shimmering in the fading light. 'A great trial is upon him and I cannot help him, nor even be close by to lend what comfort I might.'

A wave of sorrow mingled with apprehension flooded into Seela's mind but she was at a loss to know how to respond.

'I would join you on your journey, if I could be of any aid to you,' she offered at last.

Gremara was about to refuse when she paused and studied the great Dragon more closely.

'Truly?' she asked.

Seela's eyes whirred indignantly. 'I do not make such an offer lightly, nor do I offer falsely. I am the Eldest of this Treasury.'

Gremara bowed her head. 'I am unused to company – so very many cycles alone – I meant no insult Seela. But the journey is long still and as you guessed, it is of great urgency.'

Seela drew up her neck and stared proudly down her long snout. 'You may fly faster than I, but I can endure as long as you might wish or have need of my presence.'

Again Gremara lowered her head. 'I would welcome your companionship then Seela, and I accept your offer. My name is Gremara and so you must call me.'

Gremara was surprised and pleased to find the great Dragon, once settled into a steady rhythm of flight, was in fact only a little slower than she was. While their wings powered them steadily through the night, Gremara told of the travellers from the hidden land they called Drogoya. She told of Kadi's wounding and of Kija leaving the Stronghold with Kadi to attempt the journey to that land of Drogoya. They rested at midday and drank from the icy waters of a lake high in the Ancient Mountains, and then Gremara told of the creatures from the Void released onto this world. Seela's eyes flashed indigo and violet as she absorbed Gremara's story.

They lifted into the sky once more and now Gremara slowed their pace. She showed Seela the mind signature of he whom she sought and the two Dragons flew on, half a league apart, scanning constantly for any trace of this creature. Three more days they flew westward, Gremara peripherally aware of pain rising from far below her. They were flying now over northern Sapphrea and the air was smeared and smudged with trails of smoke. Gremara insisted they fly high, well beyond the range of human eyes, but they still discerned no sign of the mind she sought.

It was the sixth day since Seela had joined Gremara and far ahead they saw the glittering line of the great sea flashing in the light of the setting sun. They spiralled down to a small pool whose water was brackish but drinkable. Settling for a brief rest, both Dragons felt it at the same moment. Before Seela could think a single thought, Gremara's mind blazed.

Seela flinched but tried to observe exactly what the Silver One was doing even as she lent strength to her. The very air sizzled although there was nothing burning. There was a parched, iron tasting smell and then a spherical shape was traced with snapping sparks of white light. The sphere seemed an empty outline as it jerked wildly between the two Dragons before coming to a halt in front of Gremara.

'You know me Grek Sen Karas. There is no escape. Why are you here?' Gremara's mind tone was hard and cold and Seela rattled her wings nervously.

'Doing the same as before, dear one.' The voice sounded resigned but also amused.

'Explain.'

There was silence for a few moments.

'Cho Petak is finally, indubitably insane,' said the voice Gremara had named Grek.

Gremara snorted. 'He has ever been so,' she retorted.

'Not so,' Grek disagreed mildly. 'When first he taught me and others of like mind, he was rational and convincingly sane.'

'He spoke always of his superiority, of destroying all lesser beings or twisting them to be his slaves.' Gremara's tone was flat. 'I see from your mind what he has done to the other land – a far worse destruction than he attempted here.'

There was another long pause then Grek gave a gusty sigh. 'I know. That is why I am here. I don't think Cho realises yet that I am not just trying to trace three others from the Void.'

'Rashpil is hidden inside the mountains far to the east. Zloy is causing havoc further east still. M'Raz is in this area. Why are you here in truth?' There was an edge to Gremara's tone harsh enough to cause Seela to shift her weight uneasily.

'I betrayed him before. I must do so again. And this time he must be destroyed.'

Grek ended with a strangled gasp and Seela saw that Gremara had laid Grek's mind completely open.

'Gremara, this time he must die, and I too if it is deemed necessary. I could not endure again punishment such as before.'

The sphere vanished and Seela blinked. She realised Gremara had released the creature called Grek but he was still present. She changed the focus of her prismed eyes to a slightly different spectrum and saw his vague shape apparently sitting on the ground beside Gremara.

'The child you inhabited?' Gremara asked.

'She is in the other land. Why should she interest you?' There was a hint of curiosity in his tone.

'No matter. Grek, the one you seek is far, far to the south. There are others, one in particular, who must go there also. Will you help them reach that place?'

'You would trust me, after I aided Cho's release again?'

'Grek,' Gremara's mildness sent shivers along Seela's great back. 'Understand that I have the power to unmake you. Or worse, far worse. And others will be given that information. Others in the group of people you will assist in reaching the Sanctuary.'

Gremara led them on towards the coast. Seela was aware of Grek's presence close to them but had no idea how he moved or how he existed. Gremara spoke in Seela's mind, showing her what could be done with Grek's essence to end his being or, as she had said, do worse. Seela's mind cringed at the thought of either unmaking a sentient being or twisting its threads into something torturously "other". But she stored the information carefully and flew on saying nothing in reply to the Silver One, nor attempting speech with this Grek.

Gremara left the purple Dragon to her own thoughts then, scanning southwards as they spiralled down to a rock strewn beach. Seela had visited the ocean shore in her far distant youth – young Dragons often wandered long distances from their Treasuries during their extended childhoods. Now she reclined along a slab of rock, tickled by occasional splashes from the surging water. Gremara slept further up the beach and Seela preferred not to seek the whereabouts of the Grek creature.

Yet another dawn was tinting the high clouds when Gremara woke to find three hoppers laid on a boulder beside her. Seela's eyes sparkled.

'Lean hunting here but not impossible.'

Gremara devoured the hoppers then stretched her wings to their full extent. When she spoke it was to both Seela and to the invisible Grek.

'The ones we seek are some distance down the coast.' Her rainbow eyes whirred. 'One of them is Brin – you know him I think Seela?'

Seela pushed herself up to a sitting position. 'A son of Fenj! Yes, I know him!'

'Another is Farn, also the child he is soul bonded to.'

'Tika!' Seela's delight was apparent. 'Whatever are they doing out here? Don't tell me Brin has lured them into mischief?'

'No, there is a more serious reason.' Gremara paused. 'There are several humans with them but none know as yet that they must go south. But go south they must, with all speed, to find those in the Sanctuary.'

Gremara glanced to one side where Seela presumed Grek must be, then at Seela.

'I will tell you more whilst we fly, but it is for you to know now, not for the child. You offered to travel with me Seela, but I must return to the east very soon. It is a tremendous imposition but I beg you to stay with these travellers and help protect them on their way. Their survival is of vital importance to this world.'

Thoughts raced through Seela's mind in less time than it took for her to extend her wings towards Gremara.

'I am proud to assist the Silver One in any way that I may.'

Gremara leaned up to touch her face against Seela's. 'One day I may be able to thank you sufficiently dear one.' She turned away. 'You heard my words Grek. These travellers must be protected, especially the female child. You will be judged by the way you act towards her and her friends when – *if* – you reach the Sanctuary. And always remember you are there as their protector, not their leader.'

A patch of sand flurried briefly and Seela rattled her wings. She was going to have to get used to Grek's presence but it wasn't going to be easy.

'I hardly dared hope a Sanctuary remained on this world – I have heard not a whisper of it in three generations of the family I embodied within. I will do whatever you ask of me Gremara.'

'Make sure that you do. There will be no escaping my wrath at the least, should you go over to Cho Petak again.'

With those words, Gremara lifted into the sky, Seela close behind, and began to follow the coast to the south.

Ren had been more quiet even than usual for two days. He seemed to lose some of his passion for what Farn called his "hole in the sand". Brin and Maressa had returned full of news and laden with supplies, and the company had talked far into the night gathered around the fire. When all slept, Khosa padded into the low cave in which Ren lay. Her thought touched him awake instantly and he stared up into her turquoise eyes a mere whisker above him.

'Salt awaits you on the beach.'

Pallin's snores rumbled from deeper in the cave and Ren pulled on his boots and followed the Kephi. Sket sat by the fire nursing a bowl of tea and he nodded as Ren passed him, heading for the gap in the cliff. On the sandy shore the Eldest, Salt, reclined, Khosa weaving back and forth round his forearm.

'I know this is hard for you, Offering Ren, but it is of great importance. I must take you to speak with Mist.'

Ren swallowed and darted a glance at the sheer cliff face to his left, gleaming in the moon and starlight, pocked with the dark holes of Sea Dragon caves.

'I can make you unaware for the few moments of flight,' Salt offered.

Ren swallowed again. Tika had not spoken of her talk with Mist, returning to the company clearly distressed but unwilling to speak of her encounter. Ren shook his head.

'I'm sure you think me very foolish, but I cannot help my dread of both heights and water. As you say, it will be but a moment for you to take me up to her.'

Salt scooped Khosa into the crook of his arm and Ren strode determinedly to the Dragon's side and scrambled onto his shoulders. He clamped his hands to the wing edges and closed his eyes. There was a hideous lurch in his stomach but before he could decide whether he was actually going to be sick he heard Salt's taloned feet scraping against stone and realised he was already at Mist's cave.

Khosa bumped against Ren's left foot. 'Step down here and keep your eyes closed,' she told him, and Ren noticed there was no sarcasm in her mind voice.

He followed her instructions and felt the draught of Salt's departure.

'Go further within my cave,' another voice spoke in his mind. 'I will lie across my ledge so you need not fear falling.'

One hand against the stone wall, Ren stumbled a few paces further until he felt Khosa batting at his leg again.

'You'll be all right now. Turn round and sit down.'

Ren turned and sat obediently before opening his eyes and Khosa climbed on his lap and began her soft soothing buzz. Ren blinked and saw the silhouette of a Dragon against a backdrop of stars. Mist shifted her body slightly so that she could face Ren directly and he gasped. The faint light was yet enough to reveal the disfigurement of the Sea Dragon's left side. But her right eye still reflected the stars. She tilted her head.

'I am touched that you feel such grief for me as did the child. But as I told her, I am well accustomed to my limitations now.'

Ren felt a flash of disgust for his own whimpering dislike of heights and the sea in the face of this Dragon's stoical acceptance of a dreadful fate. Mist angled her head to look up to the stars then back at the Offering.

'The Silver One has spoken to me,' she told him. 'She approaches as we speak. None of you have seen her I think?'

Ren shook his head. 'I only know what the others have told me of her. Maressa is the one who knows most I think.'

'Already she has vouchsafed information which amazes me. Fills me with apprehension, excitement and hope. She comes with another great Dragon and will tell you that you must all travel south.'

'But I am in the early stages of excavating an important site,' Ren objected.

'No,' Mist interrupted firmly. 'Hear what I am permitted to tell you and I believe you will begin to understand.'

It was close to dawn when a stunned Offering slid from Salt's back and made his way through the gap to the lower caves. Riff was keeping watch and made way for him beside the fire, reaching for the kettle.

'Sket said you'd gone for a walk,' Riff smiled easily. 'Can't see all that water so well in the dark.'

Ren forced himself to return the smile but made no other reply and Riff left him to his thoughts.

That evening Ren complained at the lack of artefacts they had so far uncovered and suggested they should think of moving further south to find a more promising site. Discussion raged back and forth over this suggestion.

Ren was silent most of the next day. Pallin suggested a dose of his never-known-to-fail purgative – it was plain that Ren was seriously out of sorts. Ren declined but without the acid comments they had all grown used to. On the third morning after Ren's interview with Mist, Khosa roused them all just before dawn. She fussed and chivvied until they were all on the beach. To their astonishment, most of the Sea Dragons were gathered there too, but for Mist and Ice still high on their ledges. All were facing northwards.

Tika and her companions stared just as hard. The Dragons were completely silent, no hint of communication among them. Brin and Farn watched with interest, obviously as ignorant of what might be happening as were the humans. Suddenly, Ice called from her ledge and two specks appeared in the sky. Slowly the specks resolved into two Dragons, one huge even at this distance, the other much smaller and flying with a different, almost swimming motion.

'It is Seela of Sun Mountain!' Brin exclaimed, but Maressa spoke at almost the same moment.

'It is Gremara, Silver One of Talvo!'

The Sea Dragons reared erect, screaming aloud their formal challenge and greeting. Human hands clamped over human ears as the unusual cacophony shrieked on. Then silence fell again when Dragons reared upright across the beach as the two arrivals spiralled down. Now the Dragons' mind voices rose in glorious song – a wild song befitting wild Sea Dragons.

Seela stretched to her full height when the song ended and announced her name and Treasury. But most eyes were fixed on the Silver One, Gremara. She lay on the sand, her wings furled along her slender body. Her rainbow prismed eyes swept over the crowd before her, lingering on Tika's small person then lifting to rest on Ice and Mist high on the cliff.

To her own surprise, Maressa caught hold of Tika's hand and took two steps forward. She bowed.

'I am Maressa, air mage of Vagrantia. I am glad to see you Gremara.'

Amusement rippled from the Silver One. 'And most relieved to know I am restored in mind no doubt.'

Maressa looked aghast. 'I meant no rudeness,' she stammered.

Outright laughter pealed from Gremara. 'I know, I know. I do but jest with you – forgive my foolishness.'

The Sea Dragons paced forward in order of seniority to touch brows with the Silver One but Tika stood to one side, finding herself with Ren, Gan and Sket.

'Is she as you thought?' asked Gan quietly.

'I don't know,' Tika replied thoughtfully. 'She looks like no other Dragon I've seen. I suppose, from all the rumours, I had imagined she would be as large as Fenj but silver. I hadn't thought she would be quite so – different. But she has vast powers, and she is shielding her mind.'

Frowns appeared on both Gan's face and Sket's.

'Why would she shield herself here? Among friends?'

Tika shrugged, smiling as she watched Farn formally greet both Gremara and Seela then wind his neck affectionately around the great purple Dragon. Gremara looked across the mass of Sea Dragons, catching first Ren's gaze then holding Tika's longer. Tika shivered and repeated: 'She has vast powers.'

'I will speak now with Ice and with Mist.' Gremara announced. 'Perhaps you could make Seela welcome – I think she may be hungry.'

Laughter rang across the shore and two young Dragons leaped seawards. Gremara rose above Seela's head and hovered for a moment, her eyes flashing as once more she located Tika and Ren. Her tail flicked and she undulated through the air up to the high ledges.

Attention turned to Seela who made her way through the Sea Dragons towards Tika. She bent her head to the girl, affection spilling warmly through Tika's mind. Farn proudly introduced her to all the company, including Khosa. The Kephi sat neatly on a rock, her orange tail curled tidily over her front paws, and surveyed the massive Seela. Something passed between them Tika realised, but it was a private linking and she wondered what it might mean.

On the high ledge Mist lay before Gremara. She had spoken briefly to Ice who had then left them alone. Gremara had not known of Mist's long endurance of pain and disablement and she crooned her sorrow even as she called to those Beyond.

The whole Flight moved behind the cliff as the day grew to its peak and tipped again to evening. Pallin and Riff baked some of the huge fish supplied by young Storm and his friends. Seela had little news to impart: she lived a solitary life in her mountains except for the Gatherings of her Treasury. She had to tell (several times over), of Gremara's arrival in the Sun Mountains and of their rapid flight here in search of Tika and her friends. Each time she reached this point in her story, Tika interrupted.

'But why does she seek me? If it is something so urgent, why has she not yet told me?'

And each time Seela pleaded ignorance of the Silver One's intent.

The sun was falling close to the rim of the sea when Gremara was suddenly in their midst. Storm shyly offered her one of the remaining uncooked fish and she ate a few mouthfuls with appreciation. She looked around at the many Dragon faces and the nine humans.

'I am here to warn you,' she said softly.

Her listeners became utterly still.

'Evil is abroad in the distant lands from whence Offering Ren has come. I cannot say if it can be halted, or slowed, or overcome. A similar fate may already be unfolding here.' She turned her brilliant rainbow eyes towards Tika.

'You and your friends must flee south. There is a Sanctuary there where together a solution may be discovered. Many leagues south is a desert land.'

Gremara noted Olam and Pallin nod confirmation.

'There live a wild people, but they have kept faith more closely than any other people in this world, and they will do what

321

they can to aid you. Salt, I must warn you to be prepared for dangers such as you cannot have ever imagined. When Mist awakens she will tell you more.

'I am proud to have met you no matter how briefly. I would speak alone with Tika and then I must leave. There is a great need of my presence in Vagrantia again and I find –' Gremara amazingly, seemed to falter for a moment then recovered herself. 'I face a great peril of my own. I must be in Talvo by that time which I fear is only days away. May the stars guide your paths and guard your hearts my dearest ones.'

She moved gracefully to the nearest Dragon and pressed her brow to his, working her way round the entire gathering. She repeated the action to an astonished Pallin, then Riff, Olam and Navan. Their expressions showed plainly that the Silver One communicated something privately to each. She studied Maressa carefully for a moment before lowering her head to the young woman, and moved on to Gan. Then she moved to Ren, whose face showed no emotion at all.

When it was Sket's turn, his face flushed scarlet but the watchers realised it was pride, not embarrassment as he straightened his back and pulled his shoulders square. The Silver One spoke with Brin and with Seela before turning to Farn. She rested her cheek against his and his eyes half closed. Gremara rose slowly above him, her body curving and twisting above his back. Tiny blue lights flickered around the silver blue Farn and he leaned more heavily against Brin. Gremara spun on her tail, locked eyes with Tika and flew over the gap to the beach.

It seemed only a few moments before Tika returned from her talk with Gremara but the sky was dusky with approaching night. She stared at Ren and he gave a tiny shrug and a rueful smile. Gremara appeared high above them, circled twice and shot away to the east.

Dragons and humans were staring at each other, unable to fully understand what had taken place among them when Salt's head whipped round towards the high caves. A Dragon drifted over the cliffs, landing a little apart. Hundreds of eyes stared at Mist. Her one eye whirred and glittered, and streamed with tears as she stretched out her wings and drew herself upright. Her two, whole, wings.

Chapter Thirty-One

It took Volk three days to reach Valoon. Dislike the smell of mint though he did, he decided it at least blocked the worst of the other stench. He'd kept well clear of the ruins of Oblaka town but, hidden up on an old hunting trail as he was, he still caught glimpses of the bodies in the fields. Some of them were twisted and charred, others were half chewed – he didn't like to think what or who had done that. There were several occasions when his horse sidestepped and snorted, baulking at something on the path ahead. Body parts mostly.

Volk was unbelievably bad-tempered by the time he overlooked Valoon. He dismounted and tied the three horses loosely at the edge of the trail. He had no wish to lose them, but he would rather they stood a chance of pulling free should anything threaten them. He sat half hidden by scrubby bushes and studied his town.

It was quiet as death. But he could see no bodies in the streets or in the few fields. Six or seven houses at the far end of the main street were burned out, but most of the rest seemed untouched. He watched the silent town for most of the afternoon and nothing moved at all. As it grew darker, Volk moved back to the horses and, staying on foot, led them on another two hundred paces. Again he tethered them, this time above the old track leading to the rarely used back gate of the stable yard behind his inn.

For a man of his bulk (although that was somewhat reduced since his stay in the Oblaka caves), Volk could move surprisingly lightly and stealthily. His hunting knife was held low in his right hand, his left eased up the latch on the concealed gate. He waited patiently, all senses alert for any untoward sound or movement, but nothing stirred. He squeezed through the gate and moved to the barn door. It was open, as it had been when he'd left. In fact, as far as he could see, nothing had changed – no sign of intruders or marauders. He looked into the barn and noticed that the smell of horses and hens had already faded. He sniffed hopefully. No, the smell of mint still seemed to be haunting him, but perhaps he was getting used to it.

Volk scurried across the open space, his heart hammering. He leaned against the door, fumbling for the large iron key in his coat pocket. The door opened silently on its well oiled hinges and Volk stepped inside. He strained to hear anything that might suggest any other presence but heard nothing at all. He checked the inn from the main cellar and its hidden addition, right up to the attics, and found all exactly as he'd left it. He grunted to himself. Just showed Valoon folk had a lot more sense than those southern dirt grubbers then. Hunters was always sharper than farmers – smelt trouble long before it arrived.

He hurried to fetch the horses in to the stable, pulled down hay for them and fetched water from the pump. He settled himself in the loft above the horses and waited for dawn. He'd been plagued not only by the smell of that dratted herb these past days, but also by a dream. He set no store by dreams – daft things, like fortune telling from tea leaves and such. But this one came back and back.

He scowled: just thinking about it made him fume. But here he was, out from the safety of the Oblaka with Light knew how many madmen dashing about the countryside, looking for two brats he'd seen in a dream! He'd just head back to the Oblaka in the morning and tell those Observers and Kooshak and whatnots that the land seemed safe enough to him.

'No you will not!'

Volk sat up so fast he hit his head, painfully, on the sloping roof beam. He swore viciously and a horse stamped in its stall below him. That's all he needed – hearing voices. Old fool. He froze as he clearly heard female laughter. Then the voice spoke again.

'You will collect those children Volk or I'll spoil every single brew you ever make in the future.'

It was as well that Volk was alone – he presented an unpre-possessing figure. Mouth agape, clothes stuck with hay, hair on end and wild eyed. He heard laughter again and pinched himself, hard, to see if perhaps he'd dozed off and was having another crazy dream. He rubbed his leg where he'd pinched it and reluctantly admitted to himself that he must be awake.

'Who are you?' he managed to croak.

'You know full well, old man. You must reach those children tomorrow. They are exhausted, terrified, hungry and one is hurt. They have walked from Syet.'

Volk closed his gaping mouth with a snap. 'Quite a walk,' he replied with masterly understatement.

'They have gone too far to the north and are nearer to the higher pass than the lower on the Gara. You must find them tomorrow.'

'Special are they?'

'All children are special.' The voice sounded chilly. 'But yes, one of these is very special.'

'Do they know that I'm coming? Surely they'll hide, or have you told them?'

There was such a long pause, Volk wondered again if he'd dreamt the conversation.

'I – cannot risk direct communication with the girl. Cho Petak can sense two powerful minds linking, but he would pay no attention to us speaking as we are now.'

There was another, shorter, pause before the voice spoke again.

'Their names are Tyen and Mena. If you think they are nearby, hiding from you, call their names. Tell them you come from Finn Rah and the Oblaka, and they will trust you.'

Volk sneezed as the smell of mint filled the hay loft. He cursed and sneezed alternately until he fell suddenly asleep.

High on the western shoulder of a spur of the Gara Mountains, Mena wriggled free of Tyen's still-sleeping body. A north wind poked icy fingers through the rags which were all that remained of her shirt and trousers. But at least she was slightly better off than Tyen. She had been better fed and clothed when they fled the Menedula and more used to living in the countryside than a town or a city.

Their journey was taking longer than she had hoped. Twice they'd had to hide when groups of creatures – she couldn't believe they could still be called humans – had blocked their direct route. Cries and shrieks ahead gave them time to hurry to the side of their chosen path and creep into rocky hidey holes.

The second encounter delayed them for a whole day when eleven such creatures settled themselves for a prolonged halt below where the two children lay hidden. The smell of meat cooking was torture to them, although Mena knew she wouldn't have been able to eat any of it – stars knew where such creatures obtained their meat. Tyen had buried his face in his arms and shivered and shook with both fear and hunger.

They had been two days without food by then and that had been three days past. There was plenty of water – a thousand tiny streamlets cascaded and muttered down from the retreating snowline, but Mena knew they must find food in the next few hours. And three days ago Tyen had slipped and fallen some way down a scree slope, wrenching his knee badly.

There was sufficient light now for Mena to see what she hoped was the pass shown on her map. They would have to climb perhaps five hundred paces or more through thin snow to reach it and she had no idea if the trail then dropped down to the other side or meandered on at that high level. She looked down at Tyen's thin face and tugged his arm.

'Come on. We've got to cross the pass as soon as we can now. Come on Tyen. We must be nearly there.'

Tyen moaned but struggled up to stand wobbling on his left foot. His right knee was swollen and bent to keep his foot clear of the ground. Mena pulled his arm across her shoulders and gripped his waist. Somehow she dredged up a smile.

'You can do it Tyen. We've got this far, we'll soon be safe.'

It took until midday for them to reach the entrance to the pass and as they moved onto the flatter ground a wind screamed through to batter against them. They were ankle deep in brittle snow and the wind hurled grains of the snow against them, scouring their unprotected skin. Tyen stared into Mena's eyes.

'Get us through as quick as you can. Drag me or leave me, but we can't last long in this.'

Tears had frozen his dark lashes into clumps around his eyes and Mena knew it was the pain from his leg as much as the vicious wind that caused his tears. They struggled forward, half bent against the force of the wind, and rounded a bend in the rock canyon. It was the sudden easing of the brutal gale that made them pause and look up. Another fifty paces and the ground seemed to fall away. Mena tightened her arm round Tyen.

'We're nearly through,' she began, when they both heard a noise.

They looked at each other, fear written on their faces.

'Is it a bird?' Mena whispered.

Tyen shook his head, concentrating on the sound. 'It's a song – everyone knows it.' He looked to Mena to explain this oddity.

Mena struggled to make her brain function.

'Whoever it is, they must be all right. Those other – things – just made noises, they never whistled songs.'

They stared at each other, then Tyen pushed her away slightly and leaned against the ice covered rock wall.

'You'll have to go and see. You can run back if it's something bad.'

Mena took two steps on, then both children froze again.

'Children! Can you hear me yet? Tyen and Mena! I'm Volk come to find you. Be not feared, I'll take you to Finn Rah!'

Mena glanced back at Tyen's trembling form and hurried on to the end of the pass. She peeped cautiously round the last high rocks and stared down. A man, so portly that she was amazed he could climb so high without just rolling off the mountain, was plodding up towards her. He halted, his breath puffing out in white clouds, and looked up. A huge smile split his face.

'There now,' he said in a tone of enormous satisfaction. 'Old Volk found you then, didn't he? Come little one, where's the lad?'

Cho Petak sat in his hidden room near the place where the Weights of Balance hung in their impossible suspension deep in the Menedula. He breathed with difficulty, his lungs bubbling with fluid. He was calm now though, after a brief and previously never-experienced bout of despair. Faced with the rapid failing of this body at last, Cho had panicked to think of actually having to unbody. He remembered Grek's acid remark that he, Cho, had been too long embodied. In his spasm of panic, he had flung out a command for Grek's immediate attendance but he had been unable to locate him. And the recent disappearance of the child from the Night Lands had enraged Cho, making his ancient heart trip in its failing rhythm.

He was now calm and thinking rationally. Used as he was to a human body, he would have little difficulty taking another. He gave a cough of amusement thinking of the contortions of those bodies possessed by his released servants. Such long years – centuries – they had been bodiless and had forgotten how restricted movement could be when one's essence was confined within such a cumbersome frame. No, he would have no problem taking another body for his use, but he was undecided whether it would be wiser to do so or not.

There might be difficulties now – so many humans in the immediate area at least had either been taken over or, more likely, destroyed. If he sought a body which was still fit further afield it would take time to make it walk back here, and he needed to be here for a while yet.

That female child must have perished. He had found no sign of her mind signature in or around the Menedula for a distance of twenty leagues, and she could never have travelled further than that. There was no indication that any of the maddened populace had found a way into the Menedula, therefore the child must have somehow slipped out. Again, he had searched the gardens with every means at his disposal but found no clue to where she had crept away. Once outside the Menedula's protection, she would be an easy catch for any hungry predator. An annoyance, but of little real importance to Cho's plans.

Rhaki, that fool with an overweening sense of his own brilliance, caused him increasing concern. Yesterday, Cho had not been able to block Rhaki and thus communicate solely with D'Lah. He reluctantly suspected that Grek had been correct: D'Lah was too long entwined with the other's essence and Rhaki was now apparently the stronger of the two. That would have to be dealt with before too much longer.

But now he must summon enough energy to move this wreckage that housed him and let it die somewhere else than in here. The Sacrifice levered himself to his feet and crept to the door. He tottered along the passageway, leaning frequently against the black walls to suck some air into his tortured lungs. The final door, and he sagged against the jamb. Unbodied, he would be unable to press fingertips to the secret trigger mechanism to reopen this door. He closed his eyes in exasperation then fumbled at his belt. The ritual knife hung as always from its silver chain, and his gnarled fingers seemed to take an age to pull it free.

At last he unhooked the knife from its chain and dropped it on the floor. He pushed it with his foot between the door and jamb and let the door close against it. He jiggled it briefly until the blade's tip was all that protruded. He nodded and murmured a soft string of words in a language of another world and the slightly misaligned door edge shimmered. Now anyone coming in here would see a smooth wall, even looking with power such as Offerings or Observers could command.

A final struggle to get to his official reception room and Cho let his body slump into a chair. He took a last gasp of air and freed himself from the flesh he had forcibly sustained for all these centuries. He was momentarily disorientated and had to concentrate on maintaining his position beside the corpse of that once strapping farmer's son. Seeing how he must have appeared to others caused him amusement. That body really had become disgusting. Already it appeared to be shrinking, deliquescing as he watched.

The disorientation became a flash of euphoria. He had forgotten how it felt to move wherever he wished, whenever he wished, without having to anticipate the pain such a movement inevitably brought. Abruptly he stilled from the wild whirl he'd allowed himself. He summoned Rhaki, and sent another command for Grek. There was work to be done and, at the most, Cho had calculated that there would be only two sidereal years in which to do it.

In the Oblaka cave system, Observer Soosha was sipping hot tea when he began to choke. He leaped to his feet, shaking his scalded hand in the air and trying to speak even as he spluttered. Finn Rah stared from her bed but before she could say anything, the door flew open and Lyeto burst in.

'He's got them! He is some way west of Valoon, but he has them!'

'Babach approaches!' Soosha finally gasped out.

Sarryen sank back onto the stool from which she had half risen and stared at both men then at the woman in the bed. Finn Rah's eyes glittered with sudden tears.

'Volk?' she asked Lyeto. 'Volk has really got them safe?'

Lyeto's usually serious face split into a huge smile. 'We found them just now. They sort of popped into view, as if they'd been shielding. Can the girl shield?'

Finn grunted. 'Light knows what she's capable of. She saw me remember, when I far sought her, and that's unheard of.'

She looked at Soosha who was still standing, eyes unfocused. She bit her lip, loathe to interrupt when he was clearly mind speaking someone. It was only a moment though before he blinked and nodded.

'Babach comes with a companion. And Dragons bring them.'

'Who comes with him – Voron? Chakar?' asked Sarryen.

Soosha shrugged. 'Neither. A female from the Night Lands. Babach would not speak for long. He is worried that the Dragons will be located if Cho Petak does another seeking.'

'The viewing ledge is wide enough for two Plavets,' Lyeto put in. 'It will not be difficult to enlarge it further – the back wall is part of the common room.'

Finn Rah opened her mouth then closed it without speaking. She could only pray that Dragons were better mannered than those ghastly birds. Soosha nodded approval of Lyeto's suggestion and the young man left, the door banging behind him.

Finn scowled. 'I feel so useless stuck in this bed,' she muttered.

'Well, it's where you're staying – at least until the dust has cleared from Lyeto's attack on the wall,' Sarryen replied tartly.

Finn remained silent and the Kooshak knew how hard she was struggling to adjust to the fact of how ill she now was.

'We'll take you there as soon as we know Babach is near,' she offered as some comfort.

Finn managed a smile. 'That would be good of you.'

Sarryen rose and crossed to the bedside. 'I will tell Melena to attend you Finn. I am going to meet Volk.'

Finn lifted her thin hands and let them drop again to the coverlet. 'I can't stop you, and truth to tell, I think one of us should go, and clearly I can't. Light knows, Volk might already be pouring one of his brews down their throats.'

Sarryen nodded and smiled, although her heart ached to see

330

the Offering brought so low. Impulsively, she leaned to kiss Finn's cheek, turning away immediately towards the door.

'Light send, I will be no more than three days.' She smiled over her shoulder at the Offering. 'And then you will see these mysterious children.'

Sarryen wasted no time, packing her travelling medicine sack while she instructed Melena closely on the care of Finn Rah. She was tying her cloak when she saw Melena's expression.

'Melena, you are more than capable of nursing Finn for a few days. If you are worried, call Arryol. She is much subdued, but should she get difficult, you just get difficult right back at her. Don't think of her as the Offering Finn Rah but as an ordinary, stubborn, and very sick old lady.' She grinned at Melena's dubious face. 'Just keep her supplied with books and any gossip you hear. The more scandalous you can think of – or invent – the better she likes it!'

The Kooshak laughed aloud now. 'Oh Melena! It's only for a few days. Now go along to her and think of something really rude to say about someone!'

And Sarryen was rushing down the passage calling to Lyeto. Melena turned the other way, towards Chakar's sitting room now occupied by Offering Finn Rah. Squaring her shoulders and taking a deep breath, she opened the door.

Lyeto sent a young student running to bring Sarryen one of the few horses hidden along the slopes of the hillside and by the time she had spoken briefly to Arryol, the horse was saddled for her. Lyeto had assured her that the way was clear, at least around the outskirts of Oblaka town, so she made good speed, trusting to Lyeto's word.

She reached the lowest slopes of the Gara that evening and, with clouds obscuring stars and moon, she dared not risk laming the horse by travelling on. She was on her way again before dawn, probing the area all around her as she rode. It was midday and she had stopped to let the horse drink from a stream when she heard hoof beats and the rumble of a familiar voice. Her pulse suddenly thundered in her throat and she felt a nervousness she had not experienced since her student days. And she was only meeting Volk and two children for Light's sake!

Sarryen had regained her usual composure when Volk's bulky

331

figure atop a horse came through the trees.

'Greetings Kooshak!' he called at once. 'Young Mena said someone was just ahead.'

Sarryen saw that Volk carried one child across his horse's withers but she only glanced at him. Her eyes were drawn to the small figure riding the second horse and leading the third animal. Hair so fair it was nearly white, a triangular face – broad across the brow and tapering to a small chin. But the large eyes held Sarryen transfixed: a blue so dark it was almost purple, and fully silvered. And yet she was clearly still a child, thin and small, maybe ten years old Sarryen guessed.

While she had been staring, Volk had drawn level with her. Sarryen dragged her gaze from the girl and looked up at Volk. He held out the blanket wrapped boy.

'Bad wrench to his knee. I just left it be, didn't want to do no extra hurt to it,' Volk explained.

Sarryen took the child, horrified at how little he weighed. She knelt, laying him on the ground and pulling the blanket away from his face. Black eyes under tangled black curls snapped up at her and the boy gave a hesitant smile.

'You a Kooshak then?'

'Yes I am,' Sarryen smiled back at him. 'My name's Sarryen – what's yours?'

'Tyen. And she's Mena.'

Tyen struggled to sit up and Sarryen realised the girl had dismounted and was kneeling at the boy's shoulder.

'Hello Mena,' Sarryen spoke as calmly as she could manage. She received an amazingly beautiful smile which lit up the girl's face.

'Hello. Can you fix Tyen's leg?'

'I can try. At least I can make the pain less for the rest of the way to the Oblaka anyway.'

It was late afternoon the next day when Volk led them up the meandering trail to the great boulder which marked the entrance to the caves. He dismounted as two students came out to take the horses. He reached up to take Tyen from Sarryen's arms and she too dismounted. She looked down as Mena tugged at her arm.

'I will stay with Tyen when you mend his leg, but first I have to see Finn Rah.'

Sarryen opened her mouth but Mena was already running into the caves. Students turned and stared as a small, unusual looking child raced unerringly through the labyrinthine passages to hurtle through Chakar's sitting room door. A strong smell of mint followed behind her.

Chapter Thirty-Two

Pachela fled from the High Speaker's study and hurried to the covered gardens in search of Speaker Lashek and the strange little man who apparently travelled with the great Dragon Fenj. She ran down paved paths, peering along side turnings until, with relief, she saw the two men bent over a small propagation area. She gripped an arm of each as she reached them.

'Fenj will surely die if he follows the plan he has made.'

Lashek frowned, his brain racing. Lorak stared down at his grubby hands.

'Old fellow misses that wife of his,' he said gruffly. 'Thinks it's time he went Beyond to be with her again. If he can be of help to your people –' He shrugged.

Pachela shook his arm, forcing Lorak to look at her. Her grey silvered eyes saw the grief Lorak could not hide. Lashek turned away, heading back to the building. Pachela followed, tugging Lorak with her while Lula flashed past on Lashek's heels.

'He said,' Lorak muttered, 'that his old life was little to pay for all the people in these Circles.'

'Never!' Pachela hissed. 'Each individual in the world, in the cosmos, is important and valued.'

'Well we won't get back to him in time to stop him. The waters were flooding across the paths outside the tunnel from Talvo already.' Lorak dragged Pachela to a halt and stood puffing for breath. 'And I can't move so fast no more.'

'Come,' Lashek called impatiently, beckoning them on.

'Lorak says the way may be too flooded,' Pachela told the Speaker as they caught up with him.

'Thryssa knows how to move us without the circles – she must do so at once.'

Pachela's face registered her astonishment at this piece of information. Lashek led them towards the stairs and found Thryssa and Kwanzi hurrying down. Obviously Lashek had ignored the ban on mind speech and had summoned Thryssa thus in the urgency of the moment. Lashek spoke softly but fast, explaining what he wanted her to do. She listened without interruption but Kwanzi could not keep silent.

'Lashek, all is disrupted about us. Mages work on the shield, we don't begin to understand the workings of the forces this Zloy is manipulating. You could all be lost.'

Thryssa touched her husband's lips with a gentle finger. 'My heart, we have little to lose at this point.' Briskly she called to a clerk struggling past with a great box of scrolls. 'Find First Councillor Pajar and send him to me in the visitors' sitting room with all speed.'

She led the way down a corridor, round several corners, finally opening a door on her right. Inside, she had the furniture moved back against the walls and closed the shutters at the windows overlooking the fruit gardens. Pajar arrived, breathless and with his flaming hair on end. Lashek was explaining their intent to him while Thryssa studied the room minutely, eyes half closed.

The floor was of chequered slabs of black and green stone and Thryssa moved to stand on the central black square.

'I intend to take us to a spot about two thirds of the way across Talvo.' She smiled at Pachela. 'You will know the place. Once there, I will immediately return Kwanzi and myself to this room.' Her voice became bleak. 'Events press so heavily – I must be here when Zloy communicates. You must not attempt to return this way Lashek – I have not the time to instruct you in this and a hasty lesson could spell disaster.'

Lorak scooped Lula into his arms and clutched her firmly to his chest. He readjusted his abominable hat. 'Ready when you are Lady.'

Thryssa moved to a green square at the edge of the room and began to tread steadily in a spiralling curve inwards, chanting softly as she walked. There was a faint popping sound, and the room was empty.

Five people and a small Kephi appeared in an open space in Talvo Circle and most of them breathed a surreptitious sigh of relief. Thryssa looked up at the sky.

'How wonderful not to be rained on again. But evening draws nigh. I must go back to the Corvida at once. Stars guide your

335

paths and guard your hearts my dears.'

She quickly kissed each of them and shooed them in the direction of Gremara's favourite ledge. They watched though, with some trepidation, as once more Thryssa paced out the circling spiral, Kwanzi behind her. A gulp of air, and they were gone.

Lula squirmed and hissed until Lorak put her on the ground and then she bolted in the direction Thryssa had indicated. Ignoring the others, Lorak stumped after her.

'I suspect Fenj planned to attack Zloy, or at least cause a serious distraction, once night has fallen,' Lashek remarked, hurrying after Lorak. 'We do not have long to dissuade him.'

A gout of water shot skywards to their left and as hot droplets landed on their faces, Lashek and Pajar stared in amazement.

'Fascinating!' Lashek murmured. 'I wonder if the Silver One will permit us to study this once our little problems are over?'

Pajar stared at the Speaker in disbelief. 'If, and when, they're over you mean,' he retorted, and hurried after Pachela. 'Come on Speaker, I think it safer to stay together.'

'I thought Jeela would know we were here by now.' Pachela sounded worried.

But even as she spoke the ivory Dragon skimmed over her head then twisted to circle above them.

'How did you get here?' she asked reproachfully. 'You didn't tell me you were coming, and I didn't see you – I was near the tunnel entrance, keeping watch on the water.'

'The High Speaker brought us. Is Fenj still here Jeela?'

'Of course he is. He's been looking at Lorak's plants all day long.' The small ivory Dragon twisted in mid air and flew in front of Lorak. 'Is something wrong Lorak? I thought you agreed to Fenj's plan?' Her mind tone was a touch peevish. 'He still won't tell me exactly what it is.'

'And we're here to tell him he'll have to change it,' Lorak replied. He stopped as he reached the eastern wall of Talvo's crater.

Fenj reclined against the rock only a few paces in front of them, Lula already buzzing happily from the crook of his arm. His eyes whirred the shadows on snow colour and he sighed. Jeela settled beside him, clearly puzzled. Pajar could only stare at the enormous black Dragon before him. This was his first meeting with one of the Dragon Kindred and he was stunned by Fenj's size and grace. Lashek nudged him sharply and he jumped.

'Oh yes.' He approached closer and bowed. 'I am Pajar, First Councillor to High Speaker Thryssa. She ordered me to come to you and to insist that you refrain from your plan. She bade me tell you that your death would be too great a burden of sorrow and guilt upon the Vagrantian people. And her words reflect the feelings of us all.'

Fenj pushed himself up to a sitting position and his prismed eyes blazed. 'You have not the strength to defeat this being alone. Unless his concentration is deflected, you will all be lost. My action will give you the time your mages need – quickly, before they are tired from holding against him too long.'

'No.' Pajar stood his ground, suddenly finding himself absolutely calm despite this huge Dragon's wrath. 'There will surely be another way.'

'It is fire this creature fears and I can provide fire. Several of your mages together could perhaps raise the illusion of fire which would take the thing but an instant to see through. I can provide real fire.'

'I'll help,' Jeela said eagerly.

'No!'

Fenj, Pachela and Lorak snapped the single word in unison.

Jeela drew herself up, her eyes sparking mutinously. 'I am Gremara's successor. In her absence I speak for Talvo. If I decide that I will use fire to help defeat this thing, I shall do so.'

'You will not, little one.' Fenj spoke gently. 'Because you are Gremara's successor, you must survive. You will keep well away from what must be done.'

Darkness had fallen whilst they spoke and Pachela sent her thoughts carefully back to the Corvida. She frowned and glanced at Lashek.

'What is it?' he asked.

'There is no communication as yet – all is calm. But it has become the norm for Zloy to speak to the High Council as soon as darkness falls. And he gave this night as his ultimatum, did he not?'

Lashek sent a cautious mind probe to Thryssa and then nodded. He glanced around their group. 'I wonder what might be delaying him, or is it just a trick?'

Lorak had set about making a small fire as soon as they'd reached Fenj and belatedly Pajar swung a pack off his shoulder.

'There isn't a lot, but I had little time to collect much food.'

He had a loaf, cheese, dried fruit and nuts and they shared the meagre meal among them.

'I suggest you all sleep,' Fenj said. 'You will thus be refreshed for whatever tomorrow might bring.'

Lashek chuckled. 'A good try Fenj, but do not think that I won't notice should you try to move one scale more than a handspan.'

A low rumble sounded from deep in Fenj's chest but Lorak, comfortably settled against the Dragon's shoulder, patted him soothingly. 'Drop of restorative old friend? Warm your bones.'

Fenj peered down benignly. 'Splendid fellow.'

Both Lashek and Pachela slept lightly, frequently checking back to Parima Circle, but although they both sensed tension in the people gathered in Thryssa's study, there was no hint of Zloy's presence there.

Dawn was edging over the high rim of Talvo Circle when Fenj got to his feet so fast that Lula tumbled onto Lorak's head. Jeela too had woken and was instantly spinning up into the sky, calling as she rose.

'What is it? What's happening?' Pajar was still groggy with sleep.

'Gremara,' Pachela breathed. 'Gremara returns.'

The sky over Talvo was a delicate blue, deepening as the sun crawled higher above the crater, when Fenj raised himself upright and his deep voice trumpeted in greeting. Lorak stood beside the old Dragon while the three Vagrantians stared as two Dragons spiralled down to the ground. As they landed, Gremara sank flat to the earth and even Lashek and Pajar recognised how exhausted she was. The silver scales were dulled, her eyes half closed.

'Gremara, are you hurt? Ill?' Fenj's tone revealed great concern and distress.

'No my dear. Just plain tired. I must sleep – I cannot talk to you now. Forgive me.'

The prismed eyes closed fully and Gremara slept.

The being known as Zloy, was not happy. He had taken the body of Prilla, First Councillor of Fira Circle and he disliked it intensely. He had rummaged briefly through Prilla's mind and destroyed it in disgust. Cho Petak had assured him that there were intelligent beings here. What nonsense! And what ridiculous bodies! If this was the highest life form then he preferred the company of the amoeba-like creatures he had once encountered on a far distant world. He was particularly appalled by all the hair. The females let their hair grow. Prilla's – now unfortunately his – reached to the back of his thighs. He kept getting mouthfuls of the stuff every time he turned round too quickly.

Speaker Kallema's mind was fractionally more intelligent than Prilla's but she had fought against the acquiescence he laid in her thoughts and so he had to destroy her. Zloy now sat in the Speaker's residence. A primitive hut in his opinion but it would serve. He was alone, and flames flickered in his eyes as he watched the clouds rest steadily above Parima and Segra Circles. Tonight he had planned to finally confront the Vagrantian High Speaker but he had been distracted.

He thought he'd heard a summoning from Cho Petak. It had been faint and distant, but he was sure he had heard it twice. It was unclear who Cho was summoning: Zloy knew Rashpil was on this side of the world while Cho Petak was on the other. Had Cho realised four of them at least had chosen to avoid an immediate reunion with him? Or guessed why? The thought of Cho's appearance here, or even a strong, direct mind contact gave Zloy pause.

He had spent many centuries in the Void and there had been little to do in all that time but think. He had never been as close to Cho Petak as, say, D'Lah or Grek. Since Cho had seen fit to let them and their multitude of fellow prisoners languish in the Void for so long, Zloy personally was in no hurry to rush to do Cho's bidding now. In fact, Zloy was quite taken with these craters.

He planned to remove the human animals from the other three craters and, probably, most from this one. Some would be kept to work on his experiments. Zloy had a great fondness for igneous rock and there could surely be no better place on this world than here in this clump of old volcanoes.

A knock on the door made him turn his head. Hair flew across his face and he clawed it out of the way as his eyes changed from red flame to Prilla's green. He opened the door to find a slim young man standing there, head bowed submissively.

'Well?' Zloy snapped.

'The water levels still rise Councillor. It is beginning to rise here, within Fira.'

'It will be dealt with.' Zloy closed the door on the young man and went to look out of the window again.

He should be frightening the lamentably feeble wits out of the High Council shortly, but he hesitated. He would need to use a considerable amount of energy to do so and such a large energy fluctuation would most surely attract the attention of Cho Petak. He swore in a strange, guttural language, then snapped his fingers angrily. Flames reappeared in his eyes as he focused on the clouds above the other Circles. He watched as the heavy rain eased in moments to a fine drizzle and then ceased altogether.

He turned away and sat at Kallema's desk, anger simmering through him. He leaned back and breathed deeply, forcing himself to a calmer frame of mind. Rashpil and M'Raz. He must try to find their exact location – he had no desire to have them encroach on what he already considered his territory. And Grek. Was Grek here too? Zloy thought Grek foolish in his old devotion to Cho. He knew that Grek and D'Lah had been on this world nearly as long as Cho himself. In their position, Zloy would have organised a comfortable niche in which to settle. It would take a very big enticement to tempt him to leave it and join with any bizarre plans Cho Petak might have.

Although Zloy had been here such a brief time, he felt possessive of these craters and welcomed no encroachment. He moved in the chair and swore again. This cursed hair tugged at his scalp. He leaned forward and pulled handfuls of the stuff from under him. His anger rising again, he caught the whole mass of blonde hair in one hand and reached for his knife. He winced, sawing through the hair at the nape of his neck until the great bundle he held came free. He stared at it with distaste and threw it from him. When he turned to glance out of the window again, he felt the coolness round his neck and smiled with satisfaction. How the females endured such torment was a mystery, but perhaps they were more stoical than he'd given them credit for.

It was annoying to delay his crushing of the so-called High Council, but he did not want to attract further attention from Cho Petak – if indeed he had been the target of the summoning. Today at least, he would quietly seek out those others – Rashpil, M'Raz, D'Lah and Grek. Once he could establish their whereabouts, he could continue his game with these Vagrantians. While the night darkened, Zloy lay back and sent his mind drifting to the north west.

In the high Speaker's study at the top of the Corvida, Kwanzi poured fresh tea.

'He's playing with us,' Orsim growled from his armchair.

'I'm not so sure.' Thryssa stretched her legs towards the fire.

'The rain has stopped,' Orsim argued. 'He is poised to strike.'

'Or perhaps he's busy elsewhere?' suggested Shema. 'Talvo?'

Thryssa looked momentarily alarmed then shook her head. 'No. Somehow we would know should he attack any Circle individually.'

'At least we know the great Dragon was prevented from attacking Fira,' one of the group of mages remarked.

Heads nodded in agreement. The senior mage Lori, raised a hand.

'I think we could risk contacting Pajar or Lashek if we do it through a shielded mind link. We have to know if the great Dragon continues to insist on carrying out an attack or if they have devised another plan.'

Kwanzi agreed at once. 'They must wonder what's happening here. Jeela at least will have been able to tell them that the rain has ceased.'

Orsim got to his feet. 'I have to ask you Thryssa, but how long have you known how to transfer without using the circles? And could you not have moved our people out of the danger here by that method?'

Thryssa smiled. 'I was told by my predecessor and had

341

practically forgotten it.' She stared hard at Speaker Orsim. 'Where would you suggest I move them to? I could manage maybe three or four such transferences, taking perhaps twenty at a time. Then I would need to rest at least for a full day, probably longer.' Her tone sharpened. 'Who would choose those to go, and in what order? We know nothing of what lies outside our walls – could we survive out there? Would Zloy sit back and allow small groups to be evacuated thus?'

'You could tell some of us how to work the transference,' Orsim insisted.

Thryssa's eyes narrowed. 'Could I really, Orsim? My first vows when I trained as successor to the High Speaker swore me to secrecy of many things – including this. I have broken that vow once and will not do so again. Orsim, one mistake and stars know where one could end up – in another realm of which we have no conception, or taken apart to our very atoms.'

'You broke your vows once you say.' Orsim refused to let the matter drop. 'To whom have you dared teach this supposedly secret art? We have a right to know this.'

Thryssa stood up, facing the Speaker of Kedara Circle. Her voice was icy.

'You have absolutely no right to know such things, Speaker. You have never been considered as a prospective High Speaker as you, and all here know. I designated a successor some time ago, but there is no compulsion upon me to name that person until I deem fit.'

Senior mages and Councillors nodded in confirmation of Thryssa's words, even Orsim's own First Councillor, Dashka, and in the face of such unanimous agreement Orsim shrugged, resuming his seat.

Shema repeated Lori's suggestion that they should try to reach Lashek or Pajar. 'It is nearly dawn, I do not believe Zloy will speak to us now.'

After a brief pause, Thryssa also sat back down and sighed. 'Very well. Shall we all link while I speak with them?'

Lashek was awake when Thryssa's mind touched him. She told him briefly of their uneventful night in Parima and then asked for his news.

'Gremara returned but moments ago. Stars know where she's

been but she is exhausted. She slept as soon as she touched the earth. I will mind speak you when we have spoken with her – I imagine that will be afternoon at the soonest.'

Thryssa bespoke Fenj then, asking gently if he understood the reasons behind her refusal of his intended plan. Affection poured through the mind link and also some puzzlement – he did not understand why she or her people should worry over the fate of an old Dragon. Thryssa laughed and broke the link, sending most of the mages to their beds to catch up on lost sleep.

Fenj brought a lumen to lay beside Gremara's sleeping form during the afternoon. He had brought one earlier for the humans to cook. Now he stirred, bending his head down towards the Silver One. A shudder rippled through the length of her frame and she whimpered softly.

'She may have need of some restorative dear Lorak,' Fenj murmured when Gremara's eyes flickered open.

But Gremara politely refused the medicinal drink and ate a small amount of the fresh kill Fenj had brought her. Jeela removed the carcass when Gremara had fed – Dragons disliked meat left to rot close to where they spent any length of time. Gremara studied the three Vagrantians and greeted them formally, her tone warming affectionately towards Pachela. She spoke no word of her travels but only of what they must do now.

She twined her sinuous silver neck against Fenj, then drew back a little. The onlookers did not hear her words to him, only saw the sudden blaze in the black Dragon's eyes. Gremara turned next to Lorak the gardener and spoke at length to his mind. When she spoke to Jeela, Lashek saw Lorak reach for Lula and hold her tight to his face. Finally Gremara spoke to all their minds.

'The creature in Fira is careless. He believes himself quite secure for the moment. His mind is seeking others of his kind, many leagues across this land. Lashek, you must call your Council now to ready their full strength. This being will return to Fira at great speed once his body is attacked and destroyed. He will probably try to take another body as his habitation but do not lose sight of the fact that he can easily exist without a solid form. As he returns, he must be unmade. Your mages will see the thread that links him with the body he uses now and they will have one chance to destroy him.'

The Silver One of Talvo Circle pressed her brow first to Pajar, then Lashek and Pachela. Her wings suddenly unfurled, enclosing Lorak before she twined necks with Jeela.

'Stars guard you,' she called and she and Fenj lifted together into the air.

Lorak sat down with a thump, watching the two Dragons race to the western rim of Talvo, rise up and then vanish down into Fira Circle. Lashek remained linked to the mages in the Corvida and gasped as fire seemed to engulf not just their minds but their bodies.

'It is illusion,' he muttered aloud. 'It is illusion. It is illusion.'

Pachela cried aloud as fire exploded against the rim of Talvo where Fenj and Gremara had lately vanished, and a great pall of all too real smoke rose slowly into the sky. Jeela paced. Back and forth, back and forth, her eyes glittering and whirring. Gremara had warned her that she must not fly until they returned.

The sun sank from sight as Jeela screamed. Two Dragons flew low from the high crater walls separating Fira from Talvo. One flew steadily. One wavered and faltered. Smoke streamed from that Dragon as slowly, so very slowly, she flew back to her favourite ledge.

Gremara flopped onto the ledge and Fenj stood below her. Her silver was gone. She was charred, encrusted with black burnt flesh. The rainbow eyes flickered towards Jeela and closed, steam rising from the length of her.

Lorak climbed up to the ledge where he dropped to his knees by Gremara's head and collapsed forward to lie against her poor body. Pachela ran forward but Jeela barred the way. Tears streamed down the ivory Dragon's beautiful face.

'You will not touch her. I will guard her and if any of you choose to remain, you may do so. But no one save Lorak shall touch my Lady.'

Chapter Thirty-Three

Search though they might through library and archives in the Asataria, no trace could be found of the tale Thryssa had related – of the world infiltrated by a maggot named Petak. Ryla, the most ancient Discipline Senior, had eventually been ordered to bed, although the battle to enforce that order had reduced everyone involved to nervous wrecks. Now only Nolli, Wise One of the Delvers, sat in Lady Emla's hall. All Seniors and Discipline Seniors with any talent for healing had been sent to check every reported case of the affliction.

At first there appeared to be many such cases throughout the farming plains to the south west of Gaharn. All cases were of a change in eye colour to red only, and all cases ended in death. So far, none of Emla's own people had been affected, only the indigenous humans. There had been no new cases near Gaharn for a full ten day although Nolli wailed aloud to hear of the first deaths in the settlement of Amud. They all feared that the illness would race through the Domain of Asat but after a dozen cases were reported in Arak – all resulting in death – no more had been reported in the settlements further north.

Kera had written from the Stronghold telling Emla of Babach's departure for Drogoya with Kija, Kadi and Elyssa, the young Vagrantian whose eyes had silvered. Kera reported concern over Mim. He was shut in his room with Chakar, Dessi and Daro. Motass seemed calm but puzzled whenever he emerged from Mim's room to collect food but was stubbornly uncommunicative when questioned. Ashta had been asleep for three days and Kera suspected the Delver healers were keeping her in that state with the assistance of the Snow Dragons.

Emla's mind reeled from all these reports. She was increasingly worried by having no news from either Sapphrea or from Vagrantia. Jilla, the Vagrantian air mage, was also concerned and had discussed with Emla the possibility of trying to far see either area. Emla could not decide whether to condone this action or to forbid it.

This morning she sat on a windowsill in her private study, gazing down into the grounds of her enormous House. Blossom frothed along the walks and circled the Pavilions. She watched Grib trundling a large barrow between tall hedges, Lilla, one of Hani's daughters, pacing beside him. Grib halted beside a freshly dug oval bed and Lilla settled to watch.

Emla sighed. If only life was so simple for all of them, but her own life seemed to grow ever more complicated by the day. She watched Grib unloading new plants under Lilla's interested eyes a moment longer then got to her feet. These few private moments were getting rarer in her life and she regretted the loss of them. She walked from her apartments to the winding staircase and ran lightly down to the ground floor. A maid was leaving Ryla's room as Lady Emla approached. The maid bobbed a curtsey when Emla asked how the patient was this morning.

'The healer, Senior Kollas, is with her now my Lady. She is very frail and weak but she is determined to be well.' The maid shook her head and lowered her voice further still. 'I truly can't see how she survives my Lady. She is so very tired in her poor body but her mind forces her on.'

Emla touched the girl's cheek, noting the tears on her lashes and was glad to know she had such caring helpers to nurse Ryla.

'She can't seem to eat,' the girl whispered. 'Pushes food away time and time again, even the thinnest broth. Cook's in despair.'

'I thank you for your concern for her. She has always been one of the most stubborn people I know. I think the time has come when we can only keep her comfortable.'

Emla opened the door and entered Discipline Senior Ryla's sick room. The tall figure of Senior Kollas was stooped over the bed by the window. Emla waited quietly until he straightened, his voice a low murmur as he spoke to Ryla. The maid Bara was folding towels onto a chest of drawers and she gave Lady Emla a sad smile. Senior Kollas leaned to touch Ryla's hands lightly then turned from the bed. Emla caught his eye as he passed her on his way out. He gave a fractional shake of his head and closed the door softly behind him.

Emla went to sit beside the bed, reaching in her turn to enfold

Ryla's hand. Ryla's head turned slowly towards her and a smile twitched at the corners of her mouth.

'Such a damnable nuisance, dear one.'

Emla bent closer to hear the words scarcely louder than a breath. Ryla had grown thinner during the last twenty cycles although none of their people tended much to fat, but now she was almost transparent.

'So much still to learn and to know. Just when everything becomes so fascinating again. And I hate to let you down Emla. Do you think Nolli could visit for a while? And Jilla?'

Emla's green eyes were magnified with unshed tears although she smiled.

'Of course my dear. I will have someone bring her right now.'

'I'm sorry Emla.'

'You have given us all a very great deal throughout the cycles dearest. You have nothing at all to be sorry for. Hush now, and I'll fetch Nolli.'

Emla glanced up as a shadow crossed the window. Ryla turned her head again with great effort and a real smile lit her face.

'Hani,' she breathed.

Emla opened the casement by the bed and the pale green Dragon's long face immediately poked in and lowered to touch Ryla's. The Kephi Bakra, identical to his mother Khosa, buzzed encouragement from his position under Ryla's right arm. By the time Emla returned, she was part of a small procession. The Vagrantian Bagri carried Nolli in his arms while her Delver maid Lanni trotted protectively beside him. Then Jilla and Shan walked with Soran behind Ryla's assistant Khalim. And the Kephi Resh danced through everyone's feet. The Discipline Senior Doochay hurried to catch them up. As a healer of renown and a long time verbal sparring partner of Ryla's, she had been in residence at Emla's House since Ryla had taken to her bed.

There was a small fuss when Bagri would have settled Nolli in a chair and he placed her instead on the bed beside Ryla. Emla's throat tightened when she saw three small blue Dragons and two green pressed close around Hani. In the short space of time since Emla had been with her, Ryla's dark eyes had clouded and were half closed. The healer Kollas stood behind Emla, his hand

347

resting lightly on her arm.

There was a stillness in the room despite the low murmurs as people spoke quietly to Ryla and then Hani began to sing aloud. Her song began softly and made her listeners think of the burgeoning growing season just beginning outside, of blooms and bees, of fragrances and fair breezes. Her song swelled, filling their minds as well as their ears, swelled to a peak and gradually subsided. There was an instant's silence and Hani withdrew her head from the room, rising erect beyond the window, the five young Dragons following suit. Then she began to sing again but this time it was the song of final farewell.

As tears began to flow down the faces of those in Ryla's room, Nolli admonished them.

'Why do you weep, when Ryla is free? Free of the body that caused her such pain for so long. Be happy for her. Talk of her. Remember her with gladness.'

Nolli twisted on the bed, placing her gnarled hands to either side of Ryla's face, then bent to kiss her lips. Bagri stepped forward, bowed, and picked up Nolli's tiny body and carried her from the room. Her Kephi Resh wound himself round his brother, buzzing and crying then settled to wash Bakra's face thoroughly – the Kephi way of giving comfort. His actions brought faint smiles from Doochay and Jilla, but Shan was blinded by tears.

Lady Emla finally drew the girl away from the bedside, holding her close.

'Hush Shan. You heard Nolli's words. She is right. We must not grieve.'

'But I was so cross with her,' Shan sobbed. 'I was cross about all those papers and boxes cluttering up your hall. I was cross all the time.'

'And do you not realise how Ryla loved to make you cross? I've seen her drop a pile of papers and peek at you to see what you'd say!'

Shan sniffed. 'I loved her truly, Lady. Both those old ladies mean a lot to me. I'd get cross when neither of them would rest, because I feared they'd make themselves ill. And that's just what Lady Ryla did.' She ended on a wail.

Emla gave her a little shake. 'Shan. Say your farewell to Ryla now and then join us in the hall.'

So saying, Emla first bent over Ryla herself and kissed the cooling forehead, whispering a private goodbye. She reached for Khalim's hand and tugged him gently with her out of the chamber.

Funerals were rare occurrences in Gaharn, at least among the long-lived Asatarian People, and crowds thronged the roads and market squares as the Discipline Senior Ryla's body was carried on an open litter back to the Asataria buildings. She was formally received by a full Gathering of Seniors, Juniors and students. Then she was taken to an open square in the centre of the complex called the Courtyard of the Future. All who had accompanied her now left her with the Discipline Seniors and Lady Emla. But those barred from the final Rites of Fire could hear the singing of the last chants rising over the rooftops as smoke rose, carrying Ryla's essence Beyond.

Once all the ceremonies were concluded, the outer gates of the Asataria were thrown open and all welcomed in for a great feast of celebration. Asatarians mingled with the humans of Gaharn and many high ranking Discipline Seniors were persuaded to perform small magics for the crowd's entertainment. The festivities would continue until dawn but Emla gathered her retainers and slipped away. She knew Nolli would be waiting to hear of all that had taken place to venerate Ryla this day. Jilla and Bagri, Shan, Captain Soran and the maids Lanni and Bara had all chosen to keep Nolli company on this occasion for which Emla was grateful. Despite Nolli's brave words at Ryla's deathbed, Emla knew how sorely the ancient Delver missed her friend.

Grib amazed everyone with a surprise for Nolli. He thoroughly irritated Shan by coming into the hall of the House and insisting on speaking to the Golden Lady in person. Emla, mystified, went down to speak with him but then found she had to go out to his workshop. Remembering Lorak's notorious workshop, Emla braced herself to refuse any sort of beverage Grib might offer her. But no. He suggested she sat on a stool some distance from the workshop while he produced "something he'd happened to think of."

Lilla and Shar emerged from some dense shrubbery and sat beside Emla, their eyes flashing with glee. The door of the workshop was flung open and Grib appeared, pushing an odd-looking barrow. Utterly confused, Emla nodded encouragingly as Grib approached. The barrow had two wooden wheels at the front, which was broader across than a usual barrow. And it had the usual two legs at the back to rest upon. But the body of the barrow was a chair, unmistakeably a chair. Grib came to a stop beside Emla and flourished a grimy hand in the air.

'I thought someone could fetch that little ole thing out for some good fresh air,' he explained earnestly. 'Do she more good to be out 'ere than stuck in that stuffy ole 'ouse all day. An' now 'er friend be gone like, nothin' like lookin' at bright new flowers for cheerin' a soul. My ole grandfer used to say that, and 'e be more right than many a cleverer person, I do say.'

Emla had raised a brow slightly at mention of her stuffy old House but let it pass in the delight she felt for Grib's invention. She got up from the stool and examined the chair-in-a-barrow. It was sturdily made with no pretensions to comfort or beauty, but a heap of pillows and quilts would solve both those difficulties. She beamed at Grib.

'Well! I think it is the most brilliant invention I've ever seen. I'm sure Lady Nolli will love it.'

Grib's face turned purple with embarrassed pride. 'They Dragons be tellin' I 'ow lonely she be these last days. Said they thought she needed a adventure like.'

'Oh absolutely!' Emla turned to hug first Lilla then Shar, their mind voices chiming together.

'Do you really think Nolli will like it?'

'We thought we might carry her, but someone would be bound to tell us off!'

'I really like it,' Emla assured them. 'A chair-in-a-barrow is a perfect solution for getting her outside.'

Grib scowled. Emla paused. 'Did I say something amiss?' she asked.

'T'aint no chair-in-a-barrow Lady. This be a chariot. Like in they ole stories.' He looked at the Golden Lady pityingly, doubting that she had ever heard any such old stories.

'A chariot!' Emla breathed in delight. 'Of course it is! Nolli's chariot!'

Nolli's chariot was a huge success. Piled with bright cushions and quilts, and propelled by an amiable Guardsman, Nolli took a vast delight in exploring the Golden Lady's extensive gardens. She blithely ignored the disapproval which greeted her instant affection for Grib. Emla noticed the lightening of the atmosphere from the moment Nolli made her first spectacular excursion. But watching Nolli's retinue of Jilla, Bagri, Shan, Lanni and six Dragons made her weep for lost Ryla again.

The weather remained clear, the sun warmer each day, and there was no keeping Nolli within doors. Thus Emla was working alone when a Guard brought a scroll tube just arrived through the Pavilion Circle. Emla saw from the seal that it came from Vagrantia and she opened it with some trepidation. She'd had no word from Thryssa since the High Speaker had returned home to face a similar problem to the one she had dealt with in the Asataria. Emla flattened the rolled paper with her long hands and began to read.

Thryssa wrote in considerable detail and Emla was horrified, imagining the terror caused by the steadily rising waters within the Circles of Vagrantia. She reread Thryssa's description of the being called Zloy, and the detailed account of how her mages had unmade him. She finished reading the first page and sat back, glancing once more into the gardens. Thank the stars that the Vagrantians were safe! Thryssa told of exhaustion but no deaths among her people.

Emla turned the large sheet of paper over and began to read again. Her relief turned rapidly to anguish as she learnt of Gremara's fate. A section on this page was written in a different hand and after a moment she recognised it as Pajar's script. She quickly realised that he had written this as an eye witness report from what he'd seen in Talvo Circle. He had returned to Parima, leaving Lashek, Pachela and Lorak with Fenj. Lorak had not stirred from his place beside Gremara. Neither Fenj nor Jeela would open their minds to Speaker Lashek or to Pachela.

Thryssa was now on her way to Talvo, greatly disturbed by Pachela's distressed state of mind. More than that Pajar could not tell the Golden Lady. The message ended with the usual formal courtesies and enquiries as to her health and the welfare of her

351

People. Emla read the whole paper again and then started to pace her study. It would soon be time for the midday meal when Nolli would come back to the House. Should she discuss this with Nolli first, or with the two Vagrantians? She had no idea how the news of Gremara's death would affect any of the three, but coming so soon after the loss of Ryla she feared it might hit them hard.

She did not understand what connection Gremara had with Mim, although she surmised it was of considerable importance. Which reminded her – what could be wrong with Mim? She shuffled through the papers on her desk and retrieved Kera's last communication. Then she checked the paper from Vagrantia. It looked likely that Mim had secluded himself at the same time as Gremara's hideous death took place. Had Mim known? Had they had a powerful enough link over such a great distance? Emla groaned.

She rerolled both messages and crossed to the window. Yes, Nolli and her entourage were heading back to the House. She stood undecided. Doochay was still staying here, working on new lectures in Emla's library. She would help Emla decide when to broach this new information and exactly to whom.

Acting on Doochay's advice, Emla waited until the evening when Nolli was settled beside the fire, the young Dragons were – hopefully – safely asleep in the guest Pavilion and the House was quietening for the night. Ryla's great chair had gone from beside Nolli's and Hani now reclined in its place. Doochay lay on one of the several couches arranged among the heaps of floor pillows upon which the others sat.

It was Nolli for whom Emla feared: the Delvers had some connection with the Dragons, so far unexplained fully. Now, Emla quietly told the company of Thryssa's news. When she described Gremara's final return to Talvo in Pajar's words, she watched for Nolli's reaction closely. There were murmurs of shocked disbelief from Jilla and Shan but Emla kept her gaze on the ancient Wise One.

Nolli's chin sank to her chest, her hands resting on Resh's back, but then she lifted her head, leaning back against her cushions. She smiled. There were tears on her cheeks but astonishingly, Nolli smiled. And Hani was utterly silent, no

352

change in the soft green flickering of her prismed eyes. Well, Emla thought privately, exactly what is going on? Was it the news of Mim that caused Nolli's tears, or Gremara's death – and why should either piece of information make her smile?

Jilla was immediately aware of Emla's gentle probe in her thoughts.

'I am relieved to know that my people have survived,' she told them all. She glanced at Emla and gave a rueful shrug. 'I did not know Gremara – only to be wary of her bouts of madness and the days of her screaming rages.'

Bagri nodded agreement. 'I do not know what may be wrong with the Dragon Lord,' he said. 'You know him and we do not, anymore than we knew Gremara.'

'What about Fenj and Jeela?' Shan asked.

'And old Lorak?' Soran added.

'I've told you all I know.' Emla produced the rolls of paper. 'Read for yourselves – perhaps you may find something I failed to grasp properly.'

'And what do you know, Nolli?' Doochay asked quietly.

Nolli sighed. 'I know now that there may be hope for this world after all.' She turned her head slightly to look into Hani's face, then looked back at Doochay and Emla. She waved a twisted hand at the papers being pored over by Soran and Jilla.

'Pajar reports no death song from Fenj or Jeela for Lorak, and Fenj would surely grieve most parlously for his beloved companion. So I think Lorak must live. Mim is keeping hidden but he is not alone. Kera says that Chakar, Dessi and Daro at least are with him. Thus I believe there is no cause to worry for Mim.'

Doochay listened attentively to Nolli's words and, like Emla, knew at once that Nolli had spoken with care, concealing more than she had revealed. But they had to accept the small comfort Nolli seemed to offer – were they to interrogate the old lady, press her for more information? Of course not.

When the company parted for the night, Doochay and Emla went up to the Golden Lady's study.

'I suggest you send to Kera,' Doochay said, leaning against Emla's desk. 'The boy can surely not be kept hidden indefinitely.' A thought occurred to her. 'Could he have the

353

affliction do you think?'

Emla shook her head slowly. 'The affliction seems never to last more than two days – Kera says it is now over three days since Mim has been seen. And if, stars forfend, he had died, there would no reason to keep the fact secret.'

'The young Dragon – Hani's daughter?'

'Ashta.' Emla supplied the name.

'Yes, Ashta. Kera says she has slept all this time. Would this mean the boy also sleeps?'

'Doochay, I have no idea. Perhaps they both sleep, but I have a strong feeling Ashta is being deliberately kept unconscious. They would do that to spare her any suffering. If for instance Mim was hurt and in pain, she, as his linked soul bond, would share every twinge.' Emla shuddered, remembering Tika's agonised battle with herself as she healed Farn.

'And did Kera say what happened immediately prior to Mim's seclusion?'

Emla frowned. 'You read the message too – I think she said only that Mim and Ashta had been gone from the Stronghold for nearly a whole day, and Ashta was close to total exhaustion on their return.'

Doochay pushed herself away from the edge of the desk and headed for the door.

'Should one of us go through the circles do you think? But to which troubled place should we go?'

'I think it unwise for me to leave here at present.' Emla rubbed her forehead wearily. 'But if you would truly travel the circles, I would suggest you go north. Thryssa should be in Talvo Circle by now, but you are the eldest Discipline Senior since Ryla passed on. You could insist on knowing what's happening – your rank is far higher than Kera's.'

Doochay grinned, looking centuries younger. 'I'll leave in the morning then. It's been far too long since I did any real fieldwork.'

Emla sat at her desk and drew a sheet of paper towards her. She would write to Kera before she slept, but dear stars, she was so tired.

Many leagues to the east, a million stars glittered above the

Vagrantian Circles. Thryssa and Kwanzi had arrived as the moon set and now Thryssa sat by Pachela's sleeping form. Kwanzi was worried by the disruption apparent in the web of power in Pachela's brain and felt a deep sleep might restore a balance to her mind.

Fenj and Jeela had both pressed their brows to Thryssa's but made no reply to her greeting. Now the black Dragon lay watchful beneath Gremara's ledge while ivory Jeela slept close by, Lula curled on her back. Lashek and Kwanzi were in low-voiced discussion a little apart from where Thryssa sat with Pachela's head in her lap. On the ledge the black, knobbled husk that had been the Silver One had hardened, solidified, and Lorak lay just as stiff and still against that husk.

A breeze riffled through the crater and Fenj's eyes whirred, reflecting the starlight. Deep within Lorak's mind a voice whispered.

'You have done well little brother. We glorify your name.'

Chapter Thirty-Four

The Sea Dragons stared at Mist, frozen where they stood. Tika broke their silent stillness, throwing herself across the sand to reach her arms round Mist's neck. Mist lowered her face to Tika's shoulder as the girl stretched her hands to the left wing. She stared at it, feeling the bones, the sinew and muscles, the pulse of blood through leathery hide. She turned her head to look at Mist's face, the sparkling brilliant right eye, the puckered empty left socket. Mist pressed her wet cheek against Tika.

'She mended my wing,' Mist's voice whispered in Tika's mind. 'She wept because she could not restore my eye, but what is an eye when I can ride the wind once more? I did not ask for such a healing, and I know what strength it must have called for. Tika, the Silver One has flown into great danger and yet she gave so much in healing my wing that I fear she may have weakened herself too far.'

Tika felt an icy prickling down her spine. 'Did she speak to you of Mim – the Dragon Lord? I asked her but she didn't answer.'

'Then I can say nothing small one. She was insistent that you travel south with all speed, to the desert of Biting Sands.'

This interchange took place in less than ten heartbeats and Mist's Flight now approached with cries of delight and amazement. Tika squeezed between the mass of Dragons and found her human friends and Seela had gone through the cliff path to their camp. Farn still slept against Brin's side and Tika paused, gently probing his mind. But he was deeply asleep. She caught only flickers of dreams from her soul bond.

'The Silver One strengthened him,' Brin told her. 'She was too drained from her work on Mist to do more than a little, but he will be stronger now.' Brin's eyes glowed in the starlight. 'We must go south Tika. At once.'

Tika sighed. 'I know. She seems to have impressed that idea

on everyone.'

Sket handed her some hot tea when she joined her friends around the replenished fire. Ren broke the silence.

'Did she tell you of Grek?' he asked her.

Tika frowned. 'Yes she did and I don't know if we should trust such a creature.'

Seela rattled her wings. 'He is here now. I have been told how to deal with him should he show sign of causing us trouble. I will teach you to unmake him also.'

'If Gremara gives me her partial trust at least, surely you could do no less?' The voice in all their minds was mild, the voice of a youngish male.

Ren cleared his throat. 'We will trust you within limits Grek. Now answer me truly: why must we go to the south?'

There was a considerable pause before Grek replied and then it was apparent that he was choosing his words with care.

'South is where solutions may lie. Although I have been here for many human generations, I did not know Survivors remained hidden anywhere on this world. Never have I been to the desert lands, but Gremara told me that within that region lies help for you to travel yet further – even to the Survivors themselves.'

'Who are these Survivors?' Gan asked.

After another long pause Grek replied, his tone sounding wistful. 'I may not tell you that. Not yet at least.'

'Gremara said you flee from the evil one in Ren's land. Why have you run from him and why should we trust you at all?' Maressa surprisingly spoke aloud.

Khosa jumped from Navan's knees and went to sit a few paces from the fire, staring steadily at empty air.

'Cho Petak is finally mad. Gremara says he has always been so, but I do not think I believe that. He spoke long ago of building such a wonderful world, and I followed his ideas. I believed others corrupted his teachings for which he suffered the blame.' Grek sounded thoughtful now. 'Perhaps Gremara has the right of it though and I was just a foolish boy, blinded by clever words and high philosophies. That does not excuse me of course, in fact it drives me to seek a way of reparation. I do not expect forgiveness, but I can try to make some amends.'

The company sat pondering Grek's words until finally Pallin

357

got to his feet.

'If we're to travel tomorrow we should all be in our blankets by now.'

Everyone obediently began to move towards the awnings and to arrange their sleeping places. As Tika took her blanket to curl up on the beach with Farn and Brin, Ren caught her arm. He nodded towards the dark stretch of sweet grass. 'I wish we'd found that mint plant – it smells so strong yet I cannot find a trace of it. And I also wish I could stay and search those rooms we found.'

Tika managed a smile. 'Surely we'll do both on our way back.'

Two pairs of silver eyes met and held for a long moment until Ren nodded.

'You're right. Of course we'll be back. Goodnight Tika.'

Next morning the party divided as before, most climbing onto koninas although Seela offered to take riders. The awnings were neatly packed and loaded on the spare animals and the party made their way through the gap in the cliff to the beach. Farn was excited at the prospect of more adventuring but Tika noticed an underlying calmness about him.

The Sea Dragons had gathered to bid them farewell and Salt announced that Storm would travel with them – he could at least keep them supplied with fresh fish. Tika noted Storm's eyes whirring with an excitement that matched Farn's and sincerely hoped they wouldn't cause too much mischief between them. Khosa wound herself round Salt's great chest and he bent his head to the orange Kephi Queen. She ran to Mist to give a similar show of affection before returning to Tika to be stowed in her carry sack.

Grek's voice rang in their minds. 'Beware of men from inland,' he warned. 'There is one such as I among them – one who has always been truly wicked. These men in his company would kill Dragons.'

A furious hissing arose from the Dragons and several lifted into the air, darting over the cliffs to watch for any such men.

'Mist and Ice know how to destroy such a one,' Seela said firmly.

'They will not be able to do so should they be taken by

surprise,' Grek retorted.

With no more ado, the company parted from the Sea Dragons. Olam led the way on his konina along the firmer sand at the sea's edge. Seela, Brin and Farn lifted into the air, followed by Storm and then, to Tika's delight, Mist rose effortlessly from the beach. She flew with them for a league then swerved out to sea trumpeting her last farewells before turning northwards.

They made good travelling for several days, the Dragons flying ahead to locate any tiny pools or streamlets of fresh water. For two days the koninas trotted between high cliffs and the great sea. Then the cliffs dropped away and seemingly endless sand dunes took their place. Heartily sick of the sand, Pallin was not the only one to welcome the sight of cliffs beginning to rise again on the sixth day out.

Several times Tika flew on Seela's back so that Farn could dive through the sky, tumbling after Storm. Maressa, aloft on Brin, cast her mage's sight further south at the end of each day's travelling. They usually found a suitable place to make camp by late afternoon. Materials for fire making grew more and more scarce, and on three nights now Brin or Seela had heated piles of pebbles with their own fire to enable the travellers to at least heat the fish Storm brought them.

'We are out of reach of Far by now I suppose?' Olam asked one evening.

Maressa thought for a moment. 'Yes I'm afraid so. I have been unable to reach Mist for two days as I told you.'

Khosa chirruped and the sand flurried briefly beside her. The company had grown somewhat used to this method the Kephi and Grek had devised to warn them of his presence, and that he was about to join their conversation. But they still found it unnerving to know an invisible being was among them.

'I could go wherever you wish – it takes me but moments to move unbodied between locations. Show me a mind picture of where you wish me to look and I will do so,' Grek offered.

Olam shifted uncomfortably, looking to Tika and Ren for their opinion. Tika let her mind touch Grek's more closely than she had yet dared. To her surprise, his mind seemed open, enough for her to see no dark, hidden areas.

'Very well,' she said. 'This is the place we would know of,

and these two people.' She pictured Lallia and Seboth. She hesitated then formed an image of Hargon. 'This one also – we would know of his whereabouts.'

'No,' Grek's reply was instant. 'I know him, but he now harbours another such as I – the one I warned the Dragons about. He would sense my nearness at once, and for now I don't think he is aware that I am in this land. Let's leave him in ignorance as long as possible.'

Khosa did one of her front-end-down, tail-end-up stretches and yawned mightily.

'Grek will not be long,' she announced, scrambling onto Seela's broad purple back and settling herself comfortably.

In truth, the moon had scarcely moved a finger's width before Grek spoke again.

'They were together and both were aware of me at once.' He sounded surprised. 'I told them you were well and they hoped you would remain so. There has been fighting. The towns of Tagria and Andla have been put to the torch and many farming communities also. They last heard that the other one you named – Hargon – is reported moving towards the coast. It seems he is tracking your company.'

Olam sprang to his feet and paced round the fire. 'I should have stayed to help fight Hargon! Dear stars, what of the Lords Raben and Zalom – do they yet live?'

'Seboth said he has reliable reports that they do survive and are regrouping their forces to join with Seboth's own.'

'I should be there,' Olam fretted.

'No sir.' Pallin's gruff voice rang with years of authority. 'You are here. For whatever reason, you are here, and this is your fate as it is all of ours.'

The following day they could not travel. They took what shelter they could behind the cliffs and waited while a storm blew in from the sea. Raging winds and torrential squalls of rain continued unabated until late in the day. Only Maressa enjoyed the experience and let her mind swirl with the twisting clouds. A wonderful exhilaration, she explained in the face of unanimous disbelief from her companions. But even she conceded that soaking clothes were none too enjoyable. Huddled round the heated stones that evening, Maressa told them she thought they were quite close to the desert.

'I let my mind go so high in that storm that I saw further than I would usually be able to. I could see right back to where your Sapphrean plains lie, just beyond these unwelcoming lands.' She paused. 'The desert looks worse I'm afraid. I could see no end to it, south or east.'

Sket grunted. 'No matter. 'Tis where we must go. We'll manage.'

Tika grinned at him. 'We can go anywhere – as long as there is tea, isn't that so Sket?'

Her personal Guard grinned back. 'Quite right,' he agreed.

They settled to sleep, all trying not to anticipate a land worse than they'd already crossed. Khosa toured the little camp as the companions slept then curled against Gan's chest. A voice brushed her mind like a caress.

'Beloved little daughter.'

The cliffs continued for a few more days then disappeared again to be replaced by sand dunes. A tough grass grew in places but it had not much goodness in it for the koninas. Pallin and Maressa had been careful with their supplies, relying so far on the fish Storm brought them. They argued the necessity of keeping their dried foodstuffs for if or when they had to turn inland. It didn't make the rest of the company complain less about the continuous fish diet.

Storm had been disturbed that they met no other Flights of Sea Dragons along the coast. He'd expected to find at least one, but the caves and ledges on that section of cliff were all empty. Then Storm flew ahead early one morning and returned in some excitement.

'There are two legs down the coast. Three of them and they have creatures the same as the ones you ride. They are just sitting there.'

Gan checked his sword and shared a look with Olam and Navan. Khosa hissed at them from Seela's back.

'It doesn't occur to you that they may be there to help you, does it?'

'Very few seem inclined to help us,' Olam retorted. 'These three are our friends are they – are you sure about that?'

Khosa stared down her short nose without deigning to reply.

'Well? Any ideas?' Gan asked the company generally.

'It might be best if two of the Dragons went first to meet them – they would surely attract their attention at least,' suggested Navan.

Gan smiled. 'And you could come along the beach unexpectedly, just in case?'

'Exactly.'

'And the other two of us?' Seela sounded as disgusted as had Khosa.

'Perhaps two of you could fly more inland to approach from behind while these strangers are busily watching the others approach from the sea?'

In spite of her concern, Tika smiled at Gan with admiration: he'd put just the right amount of humility in his tone. Oh yes, Gan was finally learning just how susceptible the great Dragons were to flattery.

'That could be quite effective,' Brin agreed thoughtfully. 'But which of us goes where?'

'Brin and Farn,' said Tika without hesitation. 'You will take myself, Sket, Ren and Gan.' She waited for Ren's protests. She stared at him when none came. He shrugged in some embarrassment.

'Gremara said I would not suffer as I used. I suppose now is as good a time as any to see if she's right.'

'Maressa should go with Seela – she can far see and also far speak best of us all. And Navan should go with her. Storm will fly without a rider. Olam should lead the riders along the beach but you must keep your mind open for either me or Maressa to warn you of any danger.'

With the exception of Maressa and Ren who were unarmed, the company checked their weapons ensuring swords slid unhindered from scabbards, that bows were strung and arrows to hand. Maressa had sat on the sand staring blankly at the now familiar sea. They waited, knowing she was seeking the three strangers. She stood up.

'I feel only a calm patience. I think they really are only waiting for us. There was no tension in them as there would be should they be anticipating action of a violent nature.' She frowned. 'Grek, did you think they were shielding?'

Sand flurried beside Riff's foot and the Guardsman prudently edged away.

'They were not shielding, but their minds were awakened.' The invisible being sounded slightly surprised. 'I had believed all this time since the fall of the Valshebans that the vast majority of human minds slept – that they could not touch the source of power within them. It would seem far more can do so than I would ever have guessed.'

'The plan remains the same.'

Tika climbed onto Farn's back, Khosa in her carry sack against her back and Sket behind her. Gan sat behind Ren on Brin. Maressa and Navan took their places on Seela and the three other men mounted their koninas. The remaining animals were already on two leading lines attached to Riff's saddle. They all looked to the south where the land curved gently, forming yet another wide bay.

'Once at the point there, the strangers will see us,' said Tika. 'You ride on Olam, and we will head out over the sea so that we fly landwards just as you get there.'

Olam nodded his understanding and heeled his konina forward. Tika stared hard at Storm whose eyes whirred and flashed with his great excitement.

'You will do exactly what Seela says,' she told him sternly. 'Is that quite clear?'

'Of course!' Storm's reply in such a tone of offended indignation sounded too like Farn for comfort.

Tika linked minds with her soul bond. 'And you will do whatever I tell you, won't you Farn?'

He twisted his long neck to look at her, sapphire eyes innocent and reproachful.

'Of course, my Tika!'

Tika smiled but catching sight of the scar running down Farn's neck made those dreadful memories stab her heart again.

'It's time, Lady Tika,' said Sket, pointing to the konina riders.

Brin and Farn lifted from the sand together, arrowing out low over the waves. As the two Dragons turned and began to rise, Tika glanced across at Offering Ren and Gan. Ren's eyes were wide open and his face wore an expression of bemused wonder.

Tika could see the six shapes now, ahead on the shore – three men and three koninas. The men were holding the plunging animals, trying to calm them even as they watched the fast approaching Dragons. Crimson Brin screamed his challenge as he manoeuvred above them, curving his massive body through the air to land four square and facing them. Silver blue Farn repeated Brin's call, his voice higher and lighter. He landed beside Brin, Tika and Sket at once sliding from his back to stand in front of his chest while he reared erect, wings extended and eyes blazing. Gan and Ren were already beside Tika when Olam's small group rode up.

The three strangers wore tunics belted over loose trousers and were bare footed. Short, curved swords hung from their belts. The koninas had calmed a little and the three men went to their knees, bowing over until their foreheads touched the sand. Seela and Storm chose that moment to arrive, causing the men to jump to their feet again as their koninas shrieked and reared in renewed panic. Maressa walked forward, Navan close at her shoulder. She sent pulses of calmness to the wild eyed animals and they steadied, although their sweat-streaked bodies trembled still.

Olam and Pallin were also on foot now and Tika's company stood in a half circle round the strangers. One of them handed his reins to another and stepped forward, bowing deeply to Tika. Gan wondered why or how this man had so instantly picked Tika out as their leader. Ren and Maressa were both taller, older and both had an air of authority.

Tika was no bigger than when Gan had first met her, her hair snarled in black tangles and her skin burnt darkly tan by wind and sun. Her eyes were startling chips of green surrounded by silver, but Ren's eyes were as strange. Then he realised that all three men were staring at Tika's sword and at the pendant which hung outside her shirt for once. Khosa yowled and Sket released her from where she hung at Tika's back. She stalked round to sit firmly upright a pace before Tika. Gan noted looks of surprise and then pleasure cross the three men's faces.

The first man spoke, but the words were a jumbled liquid trill. Maressa frowned as did Ren. Tika shrugged, one hand resting lightly on the hilt of her sword.

'We do not understand your speech – do you speak our

Common Tongue?'

The first man bowed again. 'We do indeed great Lady. Forgive my stupidity in using my people's speech which, of course, is unknown to any outside our Desert.'

'Were you expecting us in particular to come here?' she asked. 'And who exactly do you think we are?'

'We know not your names great Lady. But we were told to greet travellers here and you were described to us as were these magnificent Dragons.'

They all noted he showed only admiration for the huge creatures, no fear at all.

'My name is Tika. I am bonded to Farn of the Broken Mountain Treasury.'

A third time the man bowed low. 'Lady Tika, it is the greatest honour of my life that I should be the one to welcome you to our Desert. My name is Kirat. These are my brothers, Hadjay and Sirak. May we offer you refreshment while we speak together?'

Tika's mind touched Ren's and Maressa's and found they only reflected her own bewilderment.

'Very well,' she agreed. 'But we have few supplies to share with you – unless you would like some fish?'

Storm quivered in anticipation and Tika was unexpectedly touched, seeing Kirat's quickly hidden smile. He bowed to the young Sea Dragon.

'Fresh fish would be a boon greatly appreciated.'

Storm was gone before Kirat straightened.

Pallin and Riff tied the koninas to boulders whilst the others sat cautiously round the strangers' fire. But Tika, Gan and Sket all heard Kirat's soft words to Khosa.

'You are so very welcome, little sister.'

One of Kirat's brothers, Tika thought it was Hadjay, declined Maressa's offer to share their meagre supplies. He smiled, producing a fatly packed sack from the shade of a large boulder.

'We have fruit and cheese, travel bread and herbs for tea,' he explained.

Storm hurtled back to drop a large fish on the sand and rocketed out over the water again.

The brother named Sirak smiled too, catching Tika's eye.

'I think he is very young yes? As your bonded one is young?'

Tika relaxed. Whatever was happening here it felt right. These men might not be quite what they seemed but she was sure her friends need have no fear of them.

'Yes,' she replied. 'They are both less than one cycle old yet.'

Riff and Pallin quickly cleaned the first fish and put it to bake. Storm was disappointed when he brought the second fish to be told two were sufficient.

'Two will be ample sky brother,' Kirat told him gently. 'And these two are magnificent fish.'

Storm was mollified further when Seela suggested he bring fish for Brin, Farn and herself. Her eyes whirred soft lavender as Storm rushed off once more. The three Desert men all looked at Seela as she spoke, obviously hearing her mind speech. Tika made no comment then, introducing her company. She gave a very edited account of their travels since leaving the Sapphrean town of Far. Then she sat back against Farn's shoulder, sipping a bowl of tea that tasted of a slightly tart, tangy fruit.

'Tell us who you are, where you come from, and who sent you to find us,' she suggested.

Kirat set aside his bowl of tea and folded his hands in his lap. 'We are of the Qwah people. We have always lived within the bounds of our great Desert. The elders of our council have known you would come here for many long ages. We are sent by the Council of the Dome. That is our sacred place, the place where most of the Qwah people live. It is in the Valley of the Star Spiral, eight days travel from this place.'

'How have you kept yourselves so secret from the other people who share this land?' Tika waved a hand to the north. 'Herdsmen say no one who enters the Desert is seen again.'

Kirat laughed. 'The Desert is our friend – a living thing as we are. Dust and sand storms conceal us from all prying eyes.'

'You did not say who sent you in search of us,' said Ren mildly.

Kirat laughed again. 'The Survivors sent us. They have need of you.'

Chapter Thirty-Five

Finn Rah was in one of those light dozes common to the very sick, and Observer Soosha was swinging the kettle over the fire, when the door burst open. He looked over his shoulder and slowly straightened, smiling at the child who stood there. The girl's gaze left the still small shape on the bed to stare at the old man.

'She sleeps?' she whispered.

Soosha nodded. 'She does child. She is very ill.'

'I know. I felt it.' She bit her lip then remembered her manners. 'My name is Mena, Sir,'

'And I am Observer Soosha. I am so glad you reached us safely. We have been very worried for you and your friend.'

'Tyen hurt his leg.' Mena looked again at Finn Rah. 'I should go and be with him while Sarryen fixes his leg for him.'

Soosha held out his hand. 'Finn would want you to wake her – just to say hello.'

'Really?'

A brilliant smile lit the oddly triangular face and small warm fingers caught his. Soosha led her to the bed, touching Finn's shoulder lightly. Her eyes opened at once and she stared up into Soosha's face. Her brows drew together when she saw tears glistening on his cheeks. Then she felt another hand twine its fingers round hers where it rested on the coverlet. She looked down from Soosha's face, staring in disbelief at the radiance beaming at her. Finn found her mouth stretching into an enormous smile in return, even as tears gathered.

'Thank the light you are safe!' she managed, holding out her other hand.

Mena pressed past Soosha to hug Finn close, part of her mind registering in terror how frail was the woman in the bed. She stood back.

'I have to go to Tyen, but I'll come back as soon as he's

mended.'

'Oh do child, please do.' Finn whispered.

Mena turned to the door. She paused, looking back at the Offering and Observer with a puzzled air.

'There should be a –' She held her hands cupped. 'Shaped like an egg. Is it here? – I'm sure it should be.'

Finn Rah's face paled. 'An Observer took it to the Night Lands – the lands I believe you came from. Oh child, she has it. Is it important?'

Mena gave a smile which was all too plainly forced. 'I don't expect it was. Never mind. I'll come back when I've seen that Tyen is comfortable.'

Soosha found his knees were suddenly unreliable and had to sit down heavily on Finn's bed.

'The pendant, Soosha. Clearly the child meant Myata's pendant. Chakar took it with her and she is not returning with Babach. Just how important can it be?'

Soosha stared at his hands. 'Of great importance I fear. Perhaps Babach or his companion could travel back and fetch it do you think?'

Offering and Observer sank into a gloomy silence until the kettle's hissing stirred Soosha to make some tea.

'Lyeto has made no mention of any students contacting Babach since that first time – four days ago – five?' Finn sounded fretful.

Soosha carried a mug of tea to the bed. 'It is just over three days Finn – the same day Volk found the children. Calm down or your temperature will go up again.' He patted Finn's hand. 'I know you have never been renowned for your patience, but do try Finn dear.'

Finn glared and struggled to push herself higher in her bed. Soosha put the tea on the bedside cupboard and easily lifted Finn to the position she wanted. He held her steady while he plumped up the pillows behind her.

'What's wrong with the boy?' Finn asked, leaning back with a sigh.

'Mena said Tyen's leg is hurt. Sarryen was healing him.'

'Where is Melena? Or Lyeto?' Finn's eyes blazed with frustration. 'Oh surely I could be taken to the common room for a while – I feel so isolated here Soosha.'

Soosha studied the Offering, with his eyes and with his power of deeper sensing, then smiled.

'I see no reason why not. The viewing ledge has been enlarged and the dust has gone.' He folded back Finn's top covers.

'Wait! I need a shirt at least, you old fool!' Finn laughed, pointing to the cupboard behind the door.

'Oh. Yes. Of course.'

Finn wore only a sleeveless shift in bed and Soosha considered the folded shirts and trousers on a shelf in some confusion.

'Soosha, just grab the first one – it is only to keep me warm.'

They met Melena in the passage, Soosha carrying Finn cocooned in bright quilts.

'I was on my way to you, but Arryol asked for my help,' she apologised.

'No matter. Is the boy all right?'

'His knee was badly dislocated but Arryol realigned it. Tyen will have to rest a few days but will recover quickly we're sure.'

They had reached the common room and a gust of chill air whisked across from the expanded viewing ledge. Soosha hunched protectively over Finn Rah and hurried to take her to a sheltered spot beside the hearth. Volk waved a large mug of beer in their direction.

'Old Volk found them,' he said smugly.

Several students were gathered here and they gave Finn shy smiles and nods. Then Sarryen appeared with Arryol who regarded Finn impassively.

'I can't stay hidden away when so much seems to be happening,' Finn defended herself before Arryol could comment.

His mouth twitched in a smile. 'Who said you had to?' he retorted. 'It will do you good perhaps, but –'

'There is always a but,' Finn groaned, eyeing him with suspicion.

'But – you must rest when you need to and no heroic denials when you do get tired.'

Before Finn could argue, Mena arrived, leaning against Finn's knee as though she had known her since birth. The child tilted her head.

'Tyen's fixed,' she said, then smiled at Volk. 'That lady makes the most wonderful bread.'

Volk glanced at Teal where she sat talking with two students. 'She does that, and with those poor hands too.'

Mena frowned. 'What's wrong with her hands? I haven't seen them.'

'They were burned when she was a small child,' Arryol explained. 'That's when she lost her sight. I can do nothing for her eyes and only have pain easing salves for her hands. She should have had healing too long ago.'

Finn touched a finger to Mena's cheek and the girl turned back to her with another smile.

'Babach is on his way here from your land. He is an Observer, like Soosha. He brings one of your people – Elyssa.'

Mena shook her head. 'I do not know that name.'

'They come with Dragons.'

Mena gasped, colour draining from her face, her eyes enormous. She spun away, staring out into the chasm of air beyond the viewing ledge. Finn exchanged concerned glances with the two Kooshak and Soosha.

'Mena, is there something wrong with that?'

The child's shoulders slumped and she turned back to Finn, head bowed and face hidden.

'I hurt a Dragon,' she whispered. 'I think I killed her.'

'What?' Finn struggled to free herself of her enfolding quilts. 'A child such as you could kill a Dragon? I do not believe it!'

'Unless she used power,' murmured Soosha.

Mena raised her chin. 'I do not remember it all, not clearly, but I made Kadi bring me here to the Menedula. At least, I think I did.'

'Tell it all child,' Finn commanded. 'We will get to the bottom of this but I tell you now, I do not believe you could kill a Dragon.'

Mena began to speak, slowly and softly at first, telling how something within her had gained ascendancy over her very thoughts. She faltered when she spoke of her brother Bannor and his "accidental" death. She told of her admiration for someone named Tika, of a young silver blue Dragon who was somehow linked to this Tika. Her listeners asked no questions, did not press her when she fell silent. But when she spoke of dominating the Dragon Kadi's mind and forcing her to fly to the limits of her endurance, tears streamed down her face. Without speaking, Volk reached for her, lifting her to his lap until she had calmed enough to continue her story.

She was unaware that all in the room had drawn close, all listening to Mena's incredible tale. She reached the part where Cho Petak released her from whatever power had held her in thrall, and took a shuddering breath.

'Enough for now little one.' Volk glared at Finn Rah, daring her to contradict him. 'Parched you must be, and still hungry I'll swear.'

Mena managed a watery smile and Volk's beanpole son-in-law Povar lifted trays of buns and tiny tarts onto the serving counter. People moved then, released from the spell of the child's voice, and students handed round the tea and food, talking quietly again. Silence fell once more after this brief period of chatter and Mena began to talk again.

Now she spoke of finding the neglected garden, and how the plants gave her solace. She had believed she was doomed to stay prisoned there forever until she had found Tyen hiding in the little hut where tools were kept. Mena's voice was growing husky when she stopped in mid sentence, her body stiff within Volk's arm. She slid from his knees and took a step towards the exposed viewing ledge.

Arryol's apprentice appeared, carrying the boy Tyen who stared wide eyed at the people in the common room. He wriggled and the student lowered him carefully to the floor. He hopped towards Mena and caught her hand, his arm going round her waist. Their two small figures stood like statues as a melodious call came from outside and above.

A great shadow swept across the opening, a flurry of wings and a massive shape landed on the ledge. Huge wings furled back to lie close to the body and the Dragon paced forward. Gold scales glittered and sparkled, while another huge beast was landing behind. A short sturdy figure slid from the first Dragon's back and most in the common room recognised Observer Babach. He spotted Finn Rah and held his hands out towards her.

'Finn,' he cried. 'Finn Rah! I would introduce Kija of the

371

Broken Mountain Treasury.'

The gold Dragon's faceted eyes whirred and flashed, her voice ringing in their minds.

'I cannot greet you formally, your caves are too low, but greet you I do, and may the stars guide your paths.'

She moved to a side wall and lowered herself to recline gracefully there allowing her companion to pace forward. A slim girl with hair as gold as Kija's scales and bright blue silvered eyes slid from the second Dragon and joined Babach.

The second Dragon was blue as a midnight sky, her eyes flashing sapphires. And Finn gasped, seeing the oval pendant that shone high under her jaw. A great stillness filled the room, the blue Dragon lowering herself nearly flat to her belly, her eyes unwaveringly on Mena.

Offering, Observers, students and ordinary folk saw great tears rolling down the long beautiful face. She stretched her neck until her brow touched Mena's.

'Child you are safe.' Her voice rang with joy in their minds, but Mena cried aloud, her hands outstretched to the Dragon.

'Oh Kadi, can you ever find it in your heart to forgive me?'

Cho Petak summoned Rhaki to his presence. It would have been a simple matter for him to locate Rhaki's mind and transfer his own essence to that point. Cho preferred to summon Rhaki here to gauge his reaction to finding the Sacrifice unbodied. Cho positioned himself beside the long bookcases and waited. He sensed Rhaki approaching. He realised he'd forgotten that when unbodied himself, he could "see" an outline of another unbodied being. The air shivered by the door and Cho saw a tall blurred figure take shape within the room. His face was clear enough for Cho to see the shock as Rhaki looked at the unpleasant corpse sprawled in the chair. Rhaki's gaze passed over Cho on his first sweep of the room: he discovered him after a second, slower, search.

Cho filed the fact that, newly unbodied as he was, his essence must be thinner, less defined, than one unbodied so much longer. Cho moved to a spot closer to the table and saw Rhaki's long arrogant face shiver, briefly changing to the broader, intellectual features of D'Lah. He wished suddenly that Grek was present.

He could trust Grek, devoted boy that he'd always been. If he was here, he would support Cho's attempt to separate D'Lah and Rhaki.

'I did not know you were to shed your body,' Rhaki remarked.

'It had become a troublesome nuisance. I shall replace it sometime but there is no urgency to the matter.'

Rhaki drifted to the window. 'I will be honest with you Cho Petak. I am growing more bored by the day. I understood a life of some excitement and interest awaited me here, and the truth is very different. I will return to my own lands – I can be of great effect there.'

Cho's thoughts raced. He came to a decision.

'Do you realise, my dear, that you have hosted one of my – friends – since your birth?' he asked calmly.

Air currents swirled and Rhaki's faint shape distorted and reformed.

'You lie! I would know if there was any attempt to infiltrate my mind!'

'He joined with you in your mother's belly.' Cho gathered his resources to focus on Rhaki. He was sure Rhaki could not overcome him but he could prove difficult enough to deplete large amounts of his energy. Now was the best time to strike, to force the two apart, while Rhaki was confused and searching his own mind patterns.

A flare of dark light, like a pointed finger, shot from Cho towards Rhaki. Shrieks of pain rebounded from the shielding Cho kept around himself. Ah, but it was difficult to differentiate between the two minds! They had been together far too long, as Grek had warned him. Rhaki's mind writhed and struggled, aware for the first time of the alien mind entwined with his own, and desperate to free himself of it.

D'Lah's mind screamed in terror: he wanted only to cling to the long familiar existence that he knew within Rhaki. Cho relaxed, knowing Rhaki would do the work of separation for him. He watched carefully though, on guard for any whiplash attack on himself. Colours flashed in the energised air as two minds fought, Cho concerned suddenly at D'Lah's apparent weakness. He had underestimated Rhaki's strength and power.

The colours flashed faster until air particles splintered apart with a deafening roar. Cho flinched, forming the heaviest shielding he could devise. He waited before cautiously probing outwards to where Rhaki and D'Lah had fought. D'Lah remained. Cho quickly assessed his state and found him much damaged, much reduced, whimpering with shock. Cho sent comfort pulsing softly to the wreck of his old associate and once again regretted the absence of Grek. It would take time to calm D'Lah and only then would he know how much could be restored and how much was irretrievably lost. He cast briefly for Rhaki's mind signature but could find no trace. Rhaki had fled.

When Rhaki felt the alien mind's hold weakening, he had loosed all his power, forcing free and hurtling up through the lava rock of the Menedula and into the higher atmosphere. Parts of his mind hurt, stung as though bleeding. He was disorientated, confused and yes, afraid. He hurried to the east, instinctively wanting to put distance between himself and Cho Petak.

Weaving through the air, Rhaki realised he was too weakened to travel as far as he'd like. He saw snowfields to the north and descended, sliding through the snow and on through the rock. He rested, he knew not how long, but eventually he was restored enough to test his mind for the effects of that – thing. Had he a body, he would have shuddered and retched: the idea of another creature inside his mind was utterly abhorrent.

Slowly, patiently, methodically Rhaki tested his mind. He sealed off sections that hurt, the places where the thing had dug too deeply. Above him, days and nights passed unnoticed while Rhaki healed what he could. Finally he felt nearly whole again and began to consider his position. During the healing he'd worked on himself, he had uncovered many memories that had apparently slipped from his conscious mind. Or been concealed by that creature.

He remembered experiments of a foulness that sickened him, faces filled with terror, and names. One name hurt him immensely – Bark. Bark had truly been his friend, and now he remembered how he had ruined him. Knowing, as he now did, that most if not all of these actions had been implemented by the other creature within him, gave him no comfort. Had his great pride in his abilities been encouraged by that thing as well?

Rhaki's torment began all over again. Who was he? How

374

much was he still Rhaki of the Asatarian People, and how much tainted by Cho Petak's machinations? Iska! Her memory suddenly confronted him and he groaned aloud, the rock vibrating with his agony.

He had no idea what Cho's plans were for this world but, judging by the rapid ruination of Drogoya lands, Rhaki had little hope that his own lands would long be spared Cho's attention. If he was to return to Gaharn, would anyone trust him, listen to his warnings? Surely not. And yet they should be warned – they must be warned. Rhaki shivered in the interstices of the rock, summoning the courage to travel back to Gaharn. A faint sound seemed to filter down to him, or was it from the very rocks themselves? It sounded like a distant singing.

Another of Cho's missing lieutenants was in the far west of Sapphrea on the other side of the world from Cho. He was bored. He found the humans very slow-witted and unambitious. They had no great pleasure in inflicting pain on others, no idea of the exquisite delight that could be found in the delicacy of torture.

M'Raz was amused that the human he now possessed still struggled against him. Admittedly, he was proving stronger than M'Raz had expected, but then, it was so delightfully simple to play on his prejudices and beliefs. Lord Hargon of Return hated and feared any hint of abnormal mental abilities. Such abilities had nearly destroyed these lands once, and must never be allowed to regain so much as a toehold in society again.

The fact that the catastrophe Hargon dwelt on happened millennia past was irrelevant: it must never be repeated. M'Raz merely prodded those thoughts in Hargon's little brain and the man was ready to destroy anything in sight. It had been amusing at first but was becoming deeply boring now. M'Raz had felt Cho's summoning and buried himself within Hargon's mind.

Cho Petak was crazy. M'Raz had concluded as much centuries before and planned to extricate himself from involvement in Cho's conspiracies. But he'd left it just too late: he'd found himself wrenched from his body, trapped in the Void, and hurled into space. He had been furious. He'd witnessed Cho's freeing of D'Lah and Grek and fumed further for more centuries. When Cho's call came at last, he had made sure that his loyalty and adoration were shining beacons to Cho's searching mind and thus secured his release.

He had no intention of going anywhere near Cho Petak ever again, but the summoning he'd heard bothered him. Had Cho grown so powerful he could span a world? M'Raz looked out of Lord Hargon's eyes, ignoring the way the closest armsmen flinched and averted their faces. He saw endless, barren land, undulating in all directions. He had no real understanding of why this man wanted to travel in such an inhospitable region. The animals they rode were suffering – already several had collapsed and been slaughtered where they fell. At least their blood provided liquid and their flesh, food.

No, M'Raz was uncomfortable. Twice he'd felt Cho's summoning and once, he was sure, he had sensed either Grek or Cho himself actually within the immediate vicinity. He did not want to confront either of them trapped in this human. On the instant, he pulled free from Lord Hargon's body and without a pause headed south east.

Men pulled their koninas out of the way as Hargon fell from his saddle. Trib cautiously bent to peer at his Lord. Hargon groaned, his eyes fluttering open. Trib stepped back, then stared again. Lord Hargon's eyes were blue, as they had not been since the retreat from Far. Trib glanced quickly at the armsmen nearest him and saw they too were staring at their Lord's eyes. Warily Trib knelt, lifting Hargon's shoulders from the ground. He hesitated, then unclipped the water flask from his belt and let a few drops trickle onto Hargon's lips.

Hargon stared at Trib then at the surrounding armsmen. He struggled to his feet, leaning on both Trib and his konina. He looked over the konina's back and gave an audible gasp. He looked at his men again.

'Where are we? What are we doing in these lands?'

'Erm, you led us here Sir Lord,' Trib replied carefully. 'Do you not remember? After we fired Andla, you led us here.'

Hargon stared at Trib in horrified disbelief. 'Fired Andla?' he repeated.

'Yes Sir Lord.' Trib felt it prudent to keep to the briefest of comments.

'Dear stars, what has happened? Have I been ill, fevered?'

Hargon's expression was of utter bewilderment. 'No. Tell me later. First, where exactly are we?'

'Fifteen days into the Bitter Lands, Sir Lord. You, erm, said we would reach the great sea before nightfall.'

'I did?' Hargon looked at each of the twenty-seven armsmen gathered round him and shook his head. He hauled himself back into his saddle. 'Lead on then Trib, and where is Captain Navan?'

'Erm, you were leading us Sir Lord. None of us has any idea where we are. And you ordered Captain Navan executed'

Chapter Thirty-Six

Nine days had passed since the Dragon Lord had been seen. Ashta slept for the first four of those days and then was roused by Snow Dragons and Delver healers led by Berri, acting Wise One in Nolli's absence. Kera and Nesh watched closely but Ashta seemed calm and untroubled. She flew from the great gateway to hunt and, apparently, just for fun as well. She encountered Baryet on one of her returns and the hissing and squawking that ensued worried everyone. None of the Dragons appeared much interested in the two Plavats and this sudden spat of animosity was cause for concern.

Kera wrote a note which she gave Motass on one of his excursions for food. She had to wait nearly a full day for a reply and then she was only told that Chakar was "occupied" with Mim and not able to say when she would be "unoccupied". Kera swore in a fashion that shocked Voron but made Nesh grin and comment that perhaps the Discipline Senior was spending too much time in proximity to the Guards.

During this time they had learned with great sadness of Ryla's death in Gaharn. Kera and Nesh, the only Asatarians at the Stronghold, spent an evening remembering the ancient Lady and wishing her well on her journey Beyond. During the time of Mim's seclusion, it became apparent that the affliction had come no further into the Domain than the settlement of Arak, despite their fears.

Scrolls came through the circle from Vagrantia once more, causing great excitement mixed with sorrow when they heard not only of the destruction of the strange entity but also Gremara's appalling end. From the description of Lorak's unmoving state, it seemed he too had passed Beyond, but neither Jeela nor Fenj would allow anyone near him or Gremara.

On the tenth morning since Mim had been seen, Kera sat after breakfast with Bikram, the Delver gardener, and Nesh. Kera had read a letter just received from Emla in Gaharn, giving her suggestions regarding Mim's disappearance from general view and Gremara's death.

'If the two events are linked, surely we should be concerned for Mim – his mental state at least?'

Nesh was reading Emla's letter again as Kera spoke. 'I think Lady Emla has made a likely connection, but I cannot see a reason or what any outcome might be.' He shook his head. 'If Chakar won't tell us, we'll just have to wait.'

'Surely she would tell us if there was something badly wrong?'

Nesh passed the letter back across the table. 'I have tried to mind speak Dessi,' he smiled at Kera. 'I'm sure you've tried too.'

Kera grunted. 'The whole area around that section of the upper level is shielded.' She grinned reluctantly back at Nesh. 'Yes, I've tried – several times – all to no avail.'

Nesh shrugged. 'So we wait.' He got to his feet. 'I must check the herb beds in the first level while I remember, Kera, but I'll be back by midday.'

Kera glanced at Bikram as Nesh's tall figure vanished through the tunnel opening. The owl Sava poked his head out from under Bikram's jacket, clicked his beak and hooted dolefully. Bikram stroked the feathers along Sava's wing. 'I don't believe old Lorak would have died, Lady Kera. He'd so many plans for the gardens here, and for things he and that great Fenj were going to do. He'd be most put out if he'd died, Lady.'

Before Kera could think of an answer to that, Jal's third Guard Officer marched smartly down the ramp from the upper levels, escorting a tall thin figure. Kera gaped, leaping to her feet.

'Doochay! How marvellous to see you. Is all well in Gaharn? We were distressed at the news of Ryla but –'

'Oh do stop, Kera. I would appreciate a drink, tea if you must, but preferably something a little more fortifying.'

Bikram produced a leather flask from a pocket and Sava peered out briefly to survey the stranger.

'This is Bikram. He is an excellent gardener and a friend of Lorak's.' Kera clamped her lips shut before she could burble any more nonsense.

Doochay took a considerable gulp from the proffered flask. Her eyes watered and she was a trifle breathless but her tone was respectful as she returned the flask. 'Amazing. Most amazing. Sorry about my sharpness Kera, but I did not enjoy the experience of being hurtled through those circles.' She looked thoughtful. 'I wonder if anyone's ever worked out exactly how they function.'

Doochay stared around the immense hall, empty at this time of day, then looked at Sava who stared unblinkingly back.

'What a handsome owl. Did you raise him yourself Bikram?'

'Oh no Lady. He belongs to Observer Chakar but he doesn't like the Plavats so he moved in with Lorak and now he's with me.'

As though on cue, there was a screech from outside the gateway which sent Sava burrowing inside Bikram's jacket. Doochay stared in appalled fascination as the giant Plavat stilted into the hall. Cocking his head from side to side and raising and lowering his neck feathers, he eventually concluded Chakar was absent.

'I have not seen Chakar for many days.' His mind tone was definitely peevish.

'May I give her a message, Baryet?' asked Kera politely.

'I suppose so.' His chest swelled. 'Syecha has ten eggs,' he announced.

'Oh dear. I mean, how perfectly marvellous for you both. I'll surely tell Chakar your news.'

A yellow rimmed eye glared at her over the lethal black bill and the Plavat stilted from the hall.

'Thank the stars there was no one else here – ten eggs!' Kera sounded quite faint.

'That was a Plavat?' asked Doochay.

'Mmm. Very little intelligence, over-blessed with conceit, and unbelievably ghastly,' Kera explained.

'They came here with Observer Chakar, who has been closeted with the Dragon Lord for nine days?'

'Is that why you've come here?'

'Partly.' Doochay grinned. 'As I am now the eldest Discipline Senior, Emla and I thought I outrank anyone – anyone – here.'

Kera snorted disrespectfully. 'That won't work with Chakar.'

'We'll see.'

Doochay seemed in no hurry to confront Chakar so Kera gave her a brief tour of the Stronghold's growing areas – copied from the Delver system in the Domain. Doochay was most impressed with their ingenious methods. She met workers tending a long bed of medicinal herbs in one section of the lower caves. They became involved in complicated botanical discussion and it was nearing midday as they joined labourers and Guards heading back to the hall for a meal.

Voron had returned from the Domain and was delighted to meet Senior Doochay. Kera was listening in amazement while Doochay related the most scurrilous gossip to a highly amused Nesh, when she realised the chatter in the hall was gradually quieting. She noticed Ashta and three Snow Dragons had come into the hall, reclining in Fenj's favoured spot. Their eyes were all whirring rapidly and they were focused on the ramp.

Chakar and Jal appeared first, Jal serious as befitted a Captain of Guards, Chakar with a beaming smile. When they reached the bottom of the ramp they stood to one side, looking back. And there stood Mim. Kera heard Doochay's intake of breath as she had her first sight of the Nagum boy.

Gold scales glittered on his chest, arms and face. He wore trousers and soft boots. A long knife hung from his belt. On a gold chain hung an egg shaped pendant, backed in red gold and its amber front pulsing with light. He stepped forward, looking down at all in the hall. Kera squinted. What did he have on his back – an old fashioned shield of some kind? Two more steps forward and Ashta called aloud, rearing erect, as did the Snow Dragons.

And then Mim gave his sweet smile, holding himself straight and proud while the huge gold feathered wings unfurled, newborn from his back. Effortlessly, he lifted from the rock floor and with three beats of his magnificent wings, he landed before his soul bond. Truly, a Dragon Lord.

Thryssa and Kwanzi remained in Talvo with Lashek and Pachela. The young student with the silvered eyes woke much calmer the day following Thryssa's arrival. She adamantly insisted that she must stay in Talvo and Thryssa felt she should remain with her.

381

Only small amounts of rain had fallen here despite Zloy's manipulation of the weather systems, but it had been enough for the plants to grow even more luxuriantly. Lashek had occupied himself with Lorak's nursery bed – weeding and tidying diligently. Thryssa managed to persuade Pachela to join her in looking for more of the tiny flowering plants beloved by Lorak, but the girl became anxious if they were out of sight of Gremara's ledge for too long.

Pajar mind spoke the High Speaker at dawn and dusk, relaying information to her. He reported that guards had accompanied representatives of Segra, Parima and Kedara Circles into Fira, where they found a chaotic situation indeed. They had been shocked at the numbers of dead within Fira – and by the fact that the corpses had been left to lie where they fell. Pajar estimated that the population of Fira was reduced from two and a half thousand to less than seven hundred. And many of those seven hundred were too shocked to know where to start putting their lives back in order. He asked for volunteers to help clear the bodies and try to restore some normality.

He felt proud, he told Thryssa, that so many had instantly answered his request for volunteers. People from all the other Circles had not hesitated or shown reluctance to help. Water levels were down, still overly high in places but no longer presenting any danger. Pajar had also informed them of Discipline Senior Ryla's death in Gaharn which grieved Thryssa enormously. In the evening of that day the three who had known the ancient lady spoke of her to Pachela, remembering her to help her journey Beyond.

Even Kwanzi had given up trying to reach the minds of the two Dragons. One of them always lay beneath Gremara's ledge. Around them and around the bodies of Gremara and Lorak was a form of shielding none of them had ever encountered. Lula still slept on Fenj's head, or against his massive chest. She still pounced on his feet or his tail when he moved. And she did speak with the Vagrantians. But she told them absolutely nothing more than they could observe for themselves.

On the ninth evening since Zloy's destruction, the four sat round their small fire. Fenj had gone to hunt and Jeela lay watchful against the rock face.

'How long can this go on I wonder?' Thryssa mused, a question asked repeatedly by one or other of them every evening.

Kwanzi poked at the fire with a stick. 'I have no idea what is happening, but the fact that Fenj and Jeela are so calm makes me think it is not a final thing. Even Lula.' He smiled at the tiny Kephi who sprawled, fast asleep, across Lashek's ample lap.

'How can it not be final? You've seen how burnt Gremara was. Perhaps Lorak is in some kind of coma – it happens in some cases of illness, particularly in older people,' objected Pachela.

'There just isn't a sense of finality here. More than that I cannot explain.'

They woke the next morning simultaneously and sat yawning.

'Just look at that sunrise,' Lashek murmured.

They watched as a flare of pink quivered along Talvo's rim, the sky above slowly flushing a darker pink smudged with a buttery gold. Fenj suddenly rattled his wings against his body and the four Vagrantians turned to look at him. He was standing, staring up at the ledge, his black scales gleaming in the early light.

'Dear stars,' breathed Lashek.

Something moved on the ledge, stilled, then moved again. Thryssa got to her feet, Pachela clinging to her. Kwanzi moved forward, stopping at once when Fenj's wing stretched warningly to bar him from coming closer. The light grew in the eastern sky and they saw Lorak struggling to push himself to his hands and knees.

Several times he nearly succeeded only to slump forward again.

'For the love of the stars, and the love I know you hold for Lorak, let one of us help him,' Kwanzi pleaded.

Lula, sitting between Fenj and Jeela looked over her shoulder, blue eyes shining. 'He must do this alone.'

They could only watch therefore as the pink glow faded from the early sky and the blue deepened above Talvo, and Lorak struggled on. The sun was overhead when he made it to his knees, sitting upright on his heels. His head was bowed with weariness and he remained thus for some moments. Then he stirred again, fumbling in his old coat and they saw him withdraw his pruning knife.

Shuffling round on his knees, his back to the watchers, he raised his hand. Light flashed off the blade as it plunged down into the husk that had been Gremara. The four Vagrantians gasped. Lorak somehow hauled himself to his feet, standing astride the blackened figure of the Silver One. He bent, working his knife down, shuffling backwards until her reached the end of her body. His breath came in gasps and he seemed to be muttering. He staggered back to what had been Gremara's head and fell to his knees again.

Now he put his knife tip in the slit he'd made, working it back and forth. Pachela and Kwanzi both flinched when the black shell split with a sharp crack. It gaped open now about a handspan and Lorak rested. He straightened his shoulders and began wrenching the two halves apart, working up and down the whole length until the gap was perhaps eight handspans wide. Only then did Lorak turn to look down from the ledge.

His face was tired, more lined than before if that was possible, but he gave the familiar gap toothed smile, above which his now silver eyes glittered. 'Well then Lady Thryssa,' he croaked. 'Welcome the Lady Gremara.'

He reached down and another hand reached up out of the black casing to grip his. He tugged gently and a silver scaled arm and shoulder came clear. Fenj and Jeela reared erect trumpeting greeting when, with Lorak's assistance a naked silver scaled, silver eyed girl stepped clear of her cocoon.

A tight cap of silver hair curled close round her face. She swayed, clinging to Lorak's arm, her talons clear against his dark coat. Still holding on to him she looked at Fenj, Jeela and the four Vagrantians. Smiling, she moved away from Lorak and a great fan of feathered wings flared around her – silver wings tipped with gold. And Gremara glided from the ledge to land before Thryssa.

A man sat on a broad window sill, enjoying the warmth of the sun on his face. The breeze blowing in carried a multitude of scents from the walled garden below, the orchards beyond, all underlined by the sharp tang of the sea. The man was of average height and build, looking fit and healthy although his white hair suggested considerable age. One hand rested on the white stone framing the window, the other held two small pebbles. His fingers caressed the pebbles, turning them constantly in his palm while he gazed over the ocean which stretched leagues to the horizon.

He tilted his head suddenly, as if he'd heard someone call him. He got to his feet, hurrying from the room, down a spiral stair of white stone. Several doors stood open in the lower hall and he went through one to his right, coming out on a plateau of short rough grass. Out of sight of the house, a narrow path wound round the cliffside. He climbed upwards, until he was far above his house. The breeze was stronger here and he paused, again appearing to listen. Sea birds were screaming high overhead when the man reached a niche worn in the cliff. He sat, his back fitting snugly against the rock, his bare feet stretched in front of him.

Bright blue eyes framed in silver stared out again at the water, but he no longer saw that view. His senses sank into the rock, expanded into the air, became the breeze. He felt the grains of soil grating against each other where a worm burrowed through; he was the leaves of a forest a thousand leagues away. Namolos felt the touch of the other minds and smiled. He moved on, sweeping across the great land mass where his plans were creeping to their fruition.

He was constantly aware of the darkness growing on the other side of the world, of the pain of the burning trees and grasses, the horror of the people hiding wherever they could find a secret place. He was also conscious of a pale beacon of light glowing steadily in a remote northern corner of Drogoya. He dared not approach closer yet for fear of alerting Cho Petak too soon. It had been torment for Namolos to bide his time. So many failed attempts to manipulate events in this land, presently called Sapphrea, had come to nothing; but now, finally, his protégées had proved strong enough.

He found he had reached the city built by the newcomers, the Asatarians. He tightened his focus and saw a tiny ancient woman nestled among quilts and pillows, a young Kephi curled snoring on her lap. Namolos's mind brushed the gnarled and swollen hands which rested on the Kephi's back and slipped into the old woman's dream.

'Such a people we asked to be Caretakers!' he whispered. 'Verily, we chose well my sweet one.'

He dared not linger, remembering his body growing chill on a high cliff leagues away. He had told no one of his travelling and though it was unlikely anyone on that path would dare try to rouse him, he had taken a risk. He allowed himself no more dawdling but raced north where the brilliance of the transformed Nagum boy drew him like a magnet.

The Stronghold slept as Namolos's thought spun through its rock. He found the boy in his room, asleep on his narrow bed. One wing was furled tidily against his back, the other half extended, trailing to the floor.

'So much still to ask of you precious child, but how well you have so far succeeded!'

Namolos grew more sharply aware of the dangerous cold his body was experiencing and moved his mind instantly to the five conjoined craters in the south east. He had watched that place so often through the millennia, his heart bleeding for the growing insanity of the Silver One. When he was notified of her successful battle to recover her mind, he had wept, then caused a great feast of rejoicing to be celebrated throughout the string of islands he had made his home.

She was waiting for him, had somehow known he would visit her. She stood on the very rim of Talvo Circle, her wings slightly extended, helping her balance against a gusting wind.

'Beloved! We are so proud of you – I am so proud!'

'I remember,' Gremara replied to his mind. 'I remember it all and I am ready for whatever comes next.'

He made a last effort to increase his focus and saw her beautiful smile. She felt the faintest impress of his lips against her forehead and heard his words.

'Soon we will be reunited at last, most precious daughter.' And he was gone.

Namolos sat, his back against the cliffs, his body shuddering with both cold and exhilarated joy. He closed his eyes against the queasiness brought on by a too extended, and unprepared for, travelling, and breathed deeply. He would tell the others when they gathered for supper at dusk, but first he would go to Star Dancer. She would know already of course, but she would appreciate a visit from him. He stood up and shook dust and pieces of grass from the long robe he wore – the usual clothing of most islanders.

He retraced his steps to the house and made his way first to his own quarters. He stripped off his robe and showered quickly in the tiny bathroom, the needles of hot water removing the last of the chill that had permeated to his very bones. He towelled himself dry and went to the tall cupboard opposite his bed. He hesitated, then pulled out a dark blue shirt and matching trousers. He looked at the boots, wriggled his bare toes and decided against footwear. The shirt bore an insignia on the left breast: a circle of stars around a stylised flower.

He padded back down to the lower hall and opened the only closed door in that place. At every second turn of the spiral, Namolos touched a glow stone which burgeoned to life. Eighteen stones were lit behind him when he reached the lowest level. The muffled sound of the sea came from ahead of him. At times of great storms, sea water had breached this area. Stepping from the last stair, the cavern flooded with a soft light.

His ship lay there in front of him, repaired as far as they'd been able to do so, but still scarred and battered. Her main door slid open as Namolos approached. A soft feminine voice spoke.

'Greetings Captain.'

'Greetings Dancer.' Namolos entered the ship, turning left to get to the navigation unit at the upper front level. He sat in his captain's chair and laid the palm of his hand flat against the skin of the ship wall. The ship thrummed with pleasure.

'I know your news Captain, but I'm glad you see fit to visit me.'

'Events may be going our way at last.'

'I saw Gremara through my siblings' minds. She is beautiful once more Captain.'

'Dancer, we still aren't sure we can restore all your functions.'

'You never promised us we would fly again Captain. We knew there would be doubts about that from our arrival here. We also know in which particular ways each of us is damaged. We have repaired many synapses, many circuits. When you name the time, we will know our chances.'

Namolos bent forward, leaning his head against the ship wall

387

next to his hand.

'You have always inspired my hope, Star Dancer.'

The ship laughed. 'And flattery cannot make me do more than I can Namolos. Just remember: we are Survivors.'

The story continues in 'Survivors' …

Books in the "Circles of Light" series

Soul Bonds

Vagrants

Drogoya

Survivors

Dark Realm

Perilous Shadows

Mage Foretold

Echoes of Dreams

Printed in Great Britain
by Amazon